continued . . .

The Mark of the Vampire Queen

"Superb . . .This is erotica at its best with lots of sizzle and a love that is truly sacrificial. Joey W. Hill continues to grow as a stunning storyteller."
—*A Romance Review*

"Packs a powerful punch . . . As the twists and turns unfold, you will be as surprised as I was at the ending of this creative story."
—*TwoLips Reviews*

"Dark and richly romantic. There are scenes that will make you laugh and cry, and those that will be a feast for your libido and your most lascivious fantasies. The ending will surprise and leave you clamoring for more."
—*Romantic Times*

"Fans of erotic romantic fantasy will relish *The Mark of the Vampire Queen*."
—*The Best Reviews*

The Vampire Queen's Servant

"This book should come with a warning: intensely sexy, sensual story that will hold you hostage until the final word is read. The story line is fresh and unique, complete with a twist."
—*Romantic Times*

"Hot, kinky, sweating, hard-pounding, oh-my-god-is-it-hot-in-here-or-is-it-just-me sex . . . so compelling it just grabs you deep inside. If you can keep an open mind, you will be treated to a love story that will tug at your heart strings."
—*TwoLips Reviews*

MORE PRAISE FOR THE NOVELS OF JOEY W. HILL

"Sweet yet erotic . . . will linger in your heart long after the story is over."
—*Sensual Romance Reviews*

"One of the finest, most erotic love stories I've ever read. Reading this book was a physical experience because it pushes through every other plane until you feel it in your marrow."
—Shelby Reed, coauthor of *Love a Younger Man*

"The perfect blend of suspense and romance."   —*The Road to Romance*

"Wonderful . . . the sex is hot, very HOT, [and] more than a little kinky . . . erotic romance that touches the heart and mind as well as the libido."
—*Scribes World*

"A beautifully told story of true love, magic and strength . . . a wondrous tale . . . A must-read."
—*Romance Junkies*

"A passionate, poignant tale . . . the sex was emotional and charged with meaning . . . yet another must-read story from the ever-talented Joey Hill."
—*Just Erotic Romance Reviews*

"This is not only a keeper but one you will want to run out and tell your friends about."
—*Fallen Angel Reviews*

"Not for the closed-minded. And it's definitely not for those who like their erotica soft."
—*A Romance Review*

VAMPIRE MISTRESS

Joey W. Hill

HEAT
New York

THE BERKLEY PUBLISHING GROUP
Published by the Penguin Group
Penguin Group (USA) Inc.
375 Hudson Street, New York, New York 10014, USA
Penguin Group (Canada), 90 Eglinton Avenue East, Suite 700, Toronto, Ontario M4P 2Y3, Canada
(a division of Pearson Penguin Canada Inc.)
Penguin Books Ltd., 80 Strand, London WC2R 0RL, England
Penguin Group Ireland, 25 St. Stephen's Green, Dublin 2, Ireland (a division of Penguin Books Ltd.)
Penguin Group (Australia), 250 Camberwell Road, Camberwell, Victoria 3124, Australia
(a division of Pearson Australia Group Pty. Ltd.)
Penguin Books India Pvt. Ltd., 11 Community Centre, Panchsheel Park, New Delhi—110 017, India
Penguin Group (NZ), 67 Apollo Drive, Rosedale, North Shore 0632, New Zealand
(a division of Pearson New Zealand Ltd.)
Penguin Books (South Africa) (Pty.) Ltd., 24 Sturdee Avenue, Rosebank, Johannesburg 2196,
South Africa

Penguin Books Ltd., Registered Offices: 80 Strand, London WC2R 0RL, England

This book is an original publication of The Berkley Publishing Group.

PRINTING HISTORY
Heat trade paperback edition / May 2010

Library of Congress Cataloging-in-Publication Data

Hill, Joey W.
    Vampire mistress / Joey W. Hill. — Heat trade paperback ed.
        p. cm.
    ISBN 978-0-425-23418-1
1. Vampires—Fiction.   I. Title.
    PS3608.I4343V35 2010
    813'.6—dc22
                        2009053454

PRINTED IN THE UNITED STATES OF AMERICA

10   9   8   7   6   5   4   3   2   1

VAMPIRE MISTRESS

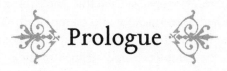# Prologue

Morena Wilson had looked like Laura. Not the same color eyes or hair, but the gentle expression, the sweet, open smile. It had been a vivid, punch-in-the-gut reminder of what was starting to blur at the edges in his memory, no matter how he fought against it. He'd been right to kill Morena's murderer. It didn't matter why the vampire had taken Morena's life; she hadn't deserved death. By taking her life, the vampire had forfeited the right to his own. That was justice. A justice he'd never been able to give Laura.

Gideon stared down at the shower floor, no energy to turn on the water yet. He stood motionless on the cold, dull white tile, the yellowed and cracked caulk rough beneath his callused feet. He'd stripped off his clothes in the stall, the blood-soaked fabric falling with a wet splat, the excess oozing out, creating red-brown puddles that collected around his toes. His hair and face were covered in it, like some Stephen King nightmare. No one would know he was the hero.

But he wasn't, was he? Because it didn't matter how many of them he killed; he never got to them soon enough. Morena was still dead, just like Laura. So there were no heroes. There was just the cleanup crew. He was a goddamned janitor.

Pushing his forehead into the wall, he twisted on the cold water full blast, gritting his teeth. Jacob would say he was punishing himself like an Inquisition priest trying to wash away his sins. Gideon bared his teeth. Sometimes he hated his brother as much as he loved him. Like everything in his life, it tore his soul—what was left of it—into two rough pieces that cut his insides like jagged glass.

But then, that was what had started this whole thing tonight, hadn't it? For months, he'd been tracking and taking down vampires whose names Jacob sent him. Through whatever mysterious contacts he had, Jacob identified the vampires who'd stepped outside of the Vampire Council's rules, who were more brutal than most. However, the plain and simple fact was all vampires killed humans. Morena Wilson's death was a forcible reminder of that. Twenty-four years old, a nurse with a fiancé whose helpless rage and grief Gideon understood too well.

He shouldn't be cherry-picking these monsters, merely because his brother had become one of them. He should be going after every single one of them. Every single one.

Squeezing his eyes shut, he slammed his fists against the wall. He hadn't expected to feel better when he'd gone off the grid to take out Trey Beauchamp. He never expected that. But he'd expected to feel . . . restored to a purpose. Instead, he kept seeing the vampire's face in those final few moments.

Trey was a hundred-and-fifty-year-old vamp who taught at a community college in the downtown area, conveniently deserted this time of night except for the type of people who kept their heads down or looked for trouble. Of all the freaking things, he taught a night class in advanced geometry, for adult students seeking engineering and architecture degrees, shit like that.

Gideon had stalked him alone. He was hunting on his own far more often these days, something he knew would piss Jacob off, but he didn't really give a damn. He was more effective this way, and it had the added bonus that he didn't have to talk to anyone else. Or worry about them getting killed.

No human could beat a vampire toe-to-toe. It was hard enough with advance planning, but time, experience and way more near misses than he deserved had taught Gideon they could be tricked, same as anyone else. Particularly if you put in the time to study their habits and schedules, and especially if they'd handicapped themselves by trying to pass as mortals. Or maybe he'd gotten that damn good at this.

Tonight he'd baited the trap with a junkie whore, about thirteen years old. All she had to do for the twenty dollars Gideon had promised her was to hit Trey up for money. When he did what Gideon expected a teacher to do—question her, try to offer her more help than the drug money she wanted—she scuttled back into her alley. That wasn't scripted, because it didn't need to be. She was jumpy as an alley cat. Trey followed her. After all, he was a vamp. He wasn't worried about her pimp getting the jump on him, because he was far stronger and faster than an oblivious mortal.

Behind him, Gideon had risen up out of a pile of boxes, where he'd posed as a sleeping wino, the scent of booze all over him. Trey whirled around, sensing the strike, so the cut of the axe had taken only half his head. He'd had his hands around Gideon's throat, his fangs bared, eyes red, when the rest came off and sprayed Gideon with blood. The junkie whimpered, but she knew that screaming attracted attention. She wanted cash for her fix more than she wanted saving. She cowered in the corner by the Dumpster, gnawing on her fist, while Gideon cleaned his blade and tossed the body in the Dumpster, dousing it with accelerant and lighting it up.

When a vamp burned, there was nothing left. If there was, the brief passage of morning sunlight between the buildings would finish it. No one would even know a body had been there. No police would be called for a trash burn in an alley. Regardless, he'd still gotten the girl on her feet, taking her away from the scene before he tucked the money into her thin hand. He'd brushed off her offer to give him a blow job for another ten.

It probably would have been a mercy to take her head at the same time, end her suffering. He'd lived among the street people long enough to know who was too far gone to be helped. It was easy to recognize them, particularly when he was one himself.

Morena Wilson hadn't been one of Trey's students. She'd been his annual kill. The careful ones, they scoped out their annual kill months in advance, just as Gideon had studied Trey to set him up. All predators used similar skills, no matter the face they wore. He suspected that was why inner city cops sometimes felt more at ease with criminals than they did with their own families. They understood the codes that governed their lives, kept them separate from the worlds they protected or preyed upon, respectively. Another fact of life Gideon accepted, as well as the understanding that such lines could easily get blurred as a result, so that a man had no idea what he was anymore.

In order to remain physically and mentally at their peak, all vampires had to take at least one human life every year. An annual kill couldn't be scum of the earth, or someone terminally ill. It had to be a healthy person, a decent human being, in order not to contaminate the vamp's blood with weakness or evil. But the Vampire Council allowed a vamp to take as many as twelve lives a year, including their annual kill, to keep the higher bloodlust craving in some of them managed. Real sporting of them. Gideon's lip curled. Rules for murder.

He wondered who Jacob's annual kill had been. It had been more than a year since Jacob had become one of them, thanks to Lady Lyssa. He couldn't think of Jacob, who'd never raise a hand to an innocent, definitely not a woman or child, who . . . Hell, he couldn't take it further than that.

Gideon dug his fingers into the shower wall. Maybe that was what he needed to do. Take his brother out. End his own life at the same time, like one of those crazy domestic violence cases, news at eleven. But Jacob was a father now. Gideon had a nephew. If Gideon was going to take out the father, he'd have to take out the child. Kane, with the kittenish fangs and still, watchful eyes, but a sweet laughing mouth. Jacob's smile. Their mother's smile.

He'd have to take out the boy's mother as well, the enigmatic, jade-eyed Lady Lyssa. One unforgettable night, she'd shared her body with Gideon and his brother both, to give his heart a night of peace. Subsequently damning him to this quagmire of indecision, a new and even more challenging level of his own personal hell.

Yeah, as if he could kill them. He had no illusion about the differences between Trey Beauchamp, mild-mannered vamp teacher, and his brother, a former vampire hunter himself and a natural-born warrior, and Lady Elyssa Amaterasu Yamato Wentworth, Queen of the Far East Clan.

Gideon slid down the side of the shower, planting his bare ass on his sopping clothes, and folded his arms over his head, letting the frigid water pound down on him. As he shivered, he told himself it was the cold. Not the tearing sobs he wouldn't permit past his raw throat.

If only he hadn't met Morena Wilson before she died. She'd been on shift in the ER the night he'd come in with a ripped forearm that needed twenty stitches. She'd been careful around him, as women often were, sensing he wasn't entirely sane or safe. But her touch had been gentle and firm, her eyes kind. She'd already been marked for death, and Gideon hadn't known a damn thing about it.

They'd used her nursing school graduation picture in the obits, and for that moment, it had been Laura's face there, smiling at him. She'd loved him so much. So fragile, so in need of his protection, and he'd failed her.

He took that obit as a sign. He'd lost his way, and it was time to get back on track. Since he had no idea where the road was anymore, he'd decided to kill the one most likely to take him back to it. Trey, someone who hadn't done a damn thing to offend the Vampire Council's sensibilities. Underscoring that Gideon was enforcing human laws, not goddamn vampire ones.

Damn it. When he snarled, the echo surrounded him, as if he were a caged animal. He'd go to Club Atlantis tonight. Maybe he'd find some relief there, if only for his aggression. They probably wouldn't let him in. Though he'd been in this town only long enough to go three times, he'd gotten the distinct impression he was wearing out his welcome. He didn't blame them. While he'd been to other BDSM clubs on his travels, they'd been less reputable, more willing to overlook his uncertain temperament in favor of his money.

Money was never a problem. Like the witch hunters of old, he took it from the homes and bank accounts of his quarry when he could swing it, poured it into more weapons, more hunts, more training. That was another reason Jacob made the damn Inquisition comparison, though Gideon didn't care for it. He was hunting creatures that were killers, and he wasn't living like Donald Trump. Hell, that temporary club membership was the only significant cost he'd had unrelated to his hunting. He always had plenty left to hide in his cheap room, because what else did he care to do with it?

He didn't like establishing routines, because he was hardly unknown to the vampire world. But he'd been here just over a month, longer than he'd been in most places, and the mystery of Atlantis kept him coming back. It was as if something was hiding there, a faint song in the forest, leading him to the enchanted castle. He went each time, expecting to find it, but had only ended up frustrated.

Hell, he shouldn't be going there at all. He knew the terrible, secret reason he went to those places, even if he wouldn't admit it to himself. He was seeking to re-create that one moment of peace. A moment created by a Dominant female vampire, his brother's Mistress, and given to him as a gift.

He didn't deserve any more gifts. He didn't deserve anything. But in some twisted way, he knew he went there seeking punishment. To give or take it, he didn't know, but he had a feeling tonight might be the night he finally found out. It wouldn't be a good thing for anyone crazy enough to mess with him.

I don't even know who you are anymore, Gideon . . . This is beating you down . . .

Jacob's words from that night. It had been a long time ago, but they haunted him. The way a million other fucking things did. He was a haunted house, unable to burn himself down, no matter how often he struck the match.

1

ANWYN stood in the security room, her eyes trained on the surveillance screen for the Queen's Chamber. With the high canopy bed, lush draperies and polished restraint systems, it was one of her favorite rooms. The stainless steel and gleaming wood instruments of pleasure and torture had been rendered by quality craftspeople. She'd spent a lot of time designing it, her own private fantasy room in a club dedicated to fantasy. In some ways, she considered it hers, though she took very few sessions herself anymore.

Running any business consumed a great deal of time, and Club Atlantis more than most. An exclusive BDSM club, Atlantis dared to cater to the most extreme players, the ones who wanted to step boldly over the lines and fully immerse themselves in a world few understood, even those who played at less strenuous levels. Knowing diversity was key to business success, Anwyn had an upper level for those softer-lifestyle people, as well as the dabblers and thrill seekers. This was the underground level, its geography enhancing the psychological impact of what it was about. The deep core zone.

Though everything that occurred in Atlantis was legal in the ways that mattered, they had the same philosophy as an illegal business. The people who came here paid a high price for the painful pleasures they sought, and therefore they weren't interested in lawyers and liability suits. It made it easier to meet those needs.

Down here, people were fully dedicated to hard-core Domination and submission. They understood that *consensual* was a term used by the politically correct. While soul-deep consent was the unspoken treasure that made their Dominance or submission possible, they wanted to lose themselves in their craving to dominate or be dominated. For those purposes, choice was often a disruption to the fantasy . . . or the need. Because that was a line that required careful straddling to make sure everyone stayed safe, her largest cost was well-trained security outside each playroom door, and video surveillance of what was happening inside. The eyes she paid to watch those screens never wavered, her staff making a play-by-play judgment as to where the line was. A private ambulance and an on-staff medical team were ready to help those who needed it.

At this level, it was about a desired, if temporary, reality, and she was committed to giving it to her clients. However, since many personalities were incapable of handling what they thought they wanted, the vetting process for this level was strict. She herself personally approved or rejected all applications after viewing videotape of the entry interviews. Which was why she was sure none of her staff understood why she'd approved Jon Smith. He had every warning flag that resulted in a rejected application.

He was aggressive. Passive, active and every spot on the spectrum in between. He was a tiger trapped in a small cage, almost mad with confinement, though only he could see the bars. In his interview, he couldn't define what he wanted, but he had an obvious, burning need for what they were offering. He'd given the name "Jon Smith" with an insolent sneer, daring them to challenge it, even producing a driver's license that backed it up, but that didn't mean she believed his lying ass for a minute.

He was 120 percent trouble. She'd known it the first time he'd darkened the club's doors in a battered leather jacket, scuffed boots and faded jeans, those midnight blue eyes vibrant with a breathtaking energy and passion. Because she knew only one other with eyes that piercing, she'd taken a second look to be sure their new guest was a mortal. He was, through and through. The badly cut dark hair that fell to his shoulders tempted touch, enhancing the fact he was all wild animal, fierce and beautiful and scarred. Most people dressed up for their sessions in some way. He'd come as he was; she was sure of that. Probably his only adjustment was leaving behind whatever weapons he'd been packing, because that was one rule the club never bent. There were weapons here, for controlled use, but that was it. Only the highest level of her security team, most of whom were ex-military, ever carried.

He was so overwhelmingly alpha she'd wondered—and still did—if he might need a Master's hand in addition to a Mistress's. But during the entrance interview, he'd reacted to that as if the interviewer had threatened his testicles with pruning shears.

"No, I do not want to be ass-fucked by a man." He'd surged out of the chair and loomed over Madelyn, who was fortunately one of her more unflappable Mistresses. "Do I look like a faggot to you?"

It was a knee-jerk hetero reaction, and one Anwyn quickly dismissed. People in the vanilla world were so caught up in their categories and labels. What people needed inside these walls had little to do with their sexual orientation, politics or gender. They needed to be stripped down to their souls, in order to find the lost treasure of themselves again. That was why she'd named her club Atlantis. That, and because it had lingered in her own childhood memories, a young girl who read the legends of the enlightened city, trying to find her own answers.

Of course, his violent reaction was another reason his ass should have been booted out of here. She'd watched his taped interview, read his terse, uncommunicative responses. James Watts, the head of her security team, said flatly he was a risk, that he wouldn't recommend Jon Smith's admission. Instead, following her intuition, Anwyn approved his temporary pass and met with her more experienced Mistresses, several of whom agreed to take the plunge.

In his first session, he wouldn't be bound, but he was okay with pain. He kept goading Madelyn, his assigned Mistress, asking for higher and higher levels, and as he did, he'd get more worked up. He never moved to hurt Madelyn, but when his frustration level got too high, he destroyed furniture, equipment, got verbally abusive. Then, contemptuously, as if paying a whore, he'd thrown down a wad of cash for the repairs and stormed out.

But he came back. He'd seemed a little surprised that he'd been let back in, and Anwyn had felt her staff's speculative glances when she made the decision. During that visit, she'd ordered a camera trained on him, so that later that night she could watch it. Alone. From beginning to end.

He'd sat at the bar, watched the public play, but hadn't tried for another private session that time. There'd been a female slave bound for a flogging, and the few times his eyes strayed toward her, his gaze would just as quickly slide away. Anwyn had a trained ear for the begging note in a cry of pain, a clue to building desire and pleasure, so she knew the woman was receiving what she wanted. Though he apparently recognized it enough not to interfere, his shoulders had hunched, as if he found it difficult to bear the woman's cries.

In contrast, he'd watch the play involving a Mistress without flinching. When a scourge landed on a bare male back or buttock, leaving red welts, his fingers would tighten on his glass. Even through the screen, Anwyn felt his yearning, a gas fire that threatened to consume. It was too similar to what she knew and remembered, and she felt oddly stripped as she looked into his face and saw how lost he truly was, this feral creature who'd come to her door, not sure if he wanted to beg for a bowl of scraps or break in and take whatever he wanted.

His next private session had gone no better than the first. Tara was strong, tall, an almost masculine woman. He'd hated her, with a viciousness that had almost come to blows when she'd tried to force him to his knees. Tara's MO was that she got physical with her clients, and she was trained for it, a former MP and karate black belt. Madelyn had tried pain, Tara brute force, and he'd responded to neither.

So tonight, Anwyn had sent in her best psychological Mistress, Chantal. She'd tried clever manipulation and head games to break him down, and now Anwyn was looking at a destroyed dresser, a shattered mirror. The rich hangings on the bed had been ripped down, shredded. Their problem child sat on the bed, his head in his hands. He hadn't moved since Chantal had gone to the door, dropped her persona and told him in an even tone that the club didn't have what he was seeking. She'd made the private signal to the camera that she was done with the session, no intention of returning after he had a cooling-off period.

"He's a loss, Anwyn." James had come in behind her and now leaned against the wall, his well-developed arms crossed and brow furrowed, the intent gray eyes as focused as she'd expect from a man who'd spent twenty years working with the DEA. "You've got the best instincts I've seen, but I think you're off on this one. He's not a psychopath, but he's too close to it. Too damaged. Completely unpredictable. We need to cut him loose. He's going to hurt someone."

"I agree with your assessment. But I want to try one more thing." Leaning over, she pressed the button to reach the security guard posted outside the Queen's Chamber.

"Yes, ma'am?"

"Engage the locks on the door, Alan. I want Mr. *Smith* to know he's not free to leave."

She straightened, glanced at James. "I'm going to take over this session."

His jaw tightened. "I could send in three men to secure him. Maybe that's what he wants. You know we've had clients before who want the forced binding."

"Yes, but not him. If we go that route, I think we *will* push him over that dangerous edge you're concerned about." She studied Smith's broad shoulders, the scarred hands clenched at his neck. "He's all beast, James. A male will be a threat to him, only make things worse. He's seeking a woman's touch, but he's looking for a specific woman. One he knows he shouldn't have, shouldn't want, but with every wrong woman we've sent him, his need has only gotten sharper, his self-damnation deeper. The goal is surrender, James."

"To what? Or whom?"

"The only opponent he's been fighting all along. Himself. I'm going to clear the ring so he can go hand-to-hand with his soul. Then maybe he'll let go."

James gave her an arch look. "I have absolutely no idea what that means."

"I know." She shrugged. "It's a lot like watching *Dog Whisperer*.

Cesar can't always explain what he's doing. He just knows, because he feels what the dog feels. That's something most people don't get." Though she kept the smile on her face, she knew James was sharp enough to see there was no humor behind it. "In order to understand a creature's pain, you have to step inside him, see through his eyes. And be strong enough not to feel sorry for him, in order to teach him how to be a dog again. Live in the moment, because this moment is all there is."

"I didn't realize Cesar was Zen," James muttered.

"All good trainers are, James." She laughed. "Feed that link to my private changing area, please. I want to watch him while I get ready."

"Speaking of animals, you've had another alley cat show up. She looks pregnant. I think they're spreading the word that you're handing scraps out the kitchen door on the graveyard shift."

"You can stop sounding so disapproving. I know you do it, too." She gave him an absent smile. "We'll have to catch her, get her spayed. Maybe she'll be more tameable than the others so far."

"If anyone can do it, it would be you. Just be careful," he advised, nodding toward the screen, telling her he was referencing Jon Smith, not her assortment of alley cats. "I know who will have my ass if someone hurts you. As scary as this son of a bitch is"—he dropped his voice so only she could hear him—"I'd rather deal with ten of him than a tenth of Daegan."

James, you don't know the half of it. "I run this club," she said crisply, snapping his spine straight at the reminder of who paid his check. "If I get hurt, he will take that up with me."

The security chief held his tongue until she'd left the room, but then he grimaced, attracting a curious look from the two nearest security techs monitoring the screens. "Yeah, right," he muttered. If something happened to the remarkable Mistress Anwyn Inara Naime, Daegan Rei would make everyone within these walls responsible. There'd be hell to pay.

James returned his attention to the Queen's Chamber. *You hurt her, buddy, your personal demons will look like Disneyland characters next to what will come after you. You better hope she's right.*

2

OKAY, so maybe this time he'd really pissed someone off. They probably wanted him to stew until some stuffy club owner in a suit gave him a strong talking-to about his bad behavior. Delivered the official word that they didn't want him here again or they'd call the cops. Or hell, maybe they'd actually called the cops. Somehow he doubted this place handled its problems with official law enforcement, though. Most of their security team looked like ex-military.

He wasn't particularly concerned by a locked door, but the fact he wanted to leave and it was locked irritated him. That irritation continued to grow. He knew he was under video surveillance, so he'd prowled about some, kicked a prissy-looking vanity stool across the floor so that it made a satisfying dent in the velvet wallpaper. Queen's Chamber. He hadn't seen a queen grace it with her presence yet. Maybe some ladies-in-waiting. Pretentious bullshit, but he'd liked the room. That was why he'd destroyed it.

"All right," he snapped. "I get it. You want me to leave and not come back. I don't need your lectures. You know I have the money to cover it. Just let me the hell out of here and I'll go. Throw a bottle of Jack on the tab."

Another long, ten-minute silence. Fuck it. He was going to take down the door. He'd had enough.

Just as he was determining which of his picks he was going to use, or if it might be just as satisfying to rip it off its fucking hinges, the locks snicked back, and the doorknob turned. When the door swung inward, he curled a lip, ready to leap and snarl at whatever inferior being came through it.

Instead, he went still.

Though he'd scoffed at their efforts, he'd recognized that the three Mistresses they'd sent had been formidable in certain ways. The first, the one who'd conducted his application interview, had been older, stout and more experienced, with a superior rack. Beautiful, full tits just begging for a man's adoration. Then there'd been the Amazon with the martial arts moves, kind of a tall and better-cut Lara Croft. Today's contender had had that slim, upright look of a spinster schoolteacher.

This one . . . she wasn't formidable at all. Not physically, but what she did bring into the room preceded her by about ten feet, and packed a punch.

Maybe about five-six. A little on the slim side, but a body that wouldn't quit, C curves and an ass that would fill out a pair of jeans in a way that would make even a non-vampire crave to bite. Instead of such casual attire, she wore painted-on latex black pants and stiletto heels she worked like a pro. He'd expected some equally intimidating corset, so that she was tight and armored from neck to toe. Instead, she wore a lace camisole, one that gathered on her hips and gave the outfit a casual, sexy look. Her slim throat displayed an onyx choker with an earth goddess pendant on it, and her hair, a sable brown, was loose on her shoulders, shining waves that coaxed a man's fingertips.

It was an unsettling mix of Mistress and sub, vanilla next-door girl and experienced woman. Hard to pin down. He'd never seen her before, because he was sure as hell certain he'd have remembered her. Maybe even asked for her, when he'd asked for nothing else. He'd basically said, *Figure out what I want or go fuck yourselves.* He'd been kind of surprised they'd accepted his membership, and suddenly he realized they'd never stopped auditioning him. This was who'd been evaluating him, the guy who couldn't tell them what he wanted because he didn't know himself.

When her gaze came to him, he was pinned by killer blue-green eyes that should have belonged to a mermaid. They were framed by brown lashes, and underscored by a soft, small mouth that was an unbelievable tender pink, frosted with a light gloss.

Though he was unbalanced, he wasn't fooled by such fragility. This woman ran the show.

"Your real first name, Mr. Smith. Your given name. I don't care about your last name."

He'd heard of women who purred, or who had a touch of velvet in their tones, a practiced art. But he realized he was wrong when he thought the way she walked in the stilettos and wore the latex was professional, learned. Her sexuality was innate. There was a rasp to the voice, a husky pleasure just in the speaking, that touched him as if she'd run fingertips up his bare spine while he was strapped to a whipping post, unable to do more than strain toward her.

Holy hell, where had that thought come from?

She moved into the room, sliding a shard of wood gracefully out of her way with her foot. The stilettos were boots, laced with scarlet ribbon, crisscrossed on metal hooks that stopped just above her ankle. Tiny charms clinked together at the ends of the laces as she moved. "Please pick up the broken dresser and set it against the wall. Then I would like you there."

She nodded toward a prayer bench in the corner, set before a tranquil fountain and stained glass depiction of a male angel. Backlights drew the eye to the blue of the angel's robes, the silver of his sword and wings, the darkness of his hair.

"I'm still waiting on your name, Mr. Smith."

"Why should I do anything you ask? What makes you so different from the others?"

Of course he knew, but he wanted her to prove it. Was afraid she would.

She considered him. He knew body language. If she was daunted at all, if there was any tension to her, it was faint, and it wasn't anxiety. It was the irresistible drug of female arousal. He knew the really good ones were into what they did, even in a place where you paid for it, but some part of them stayed detached, that invisible line between client and proprietor, strangers.

She wasn't detached at all. That beast that had been raging in him, that he'd carelessly unleashed toward the others, made him fear for her now. Because the beast wanted her. It hadn't wanted the others. That soft hair alone was taunting him closer.

As if she knew his thoughts, she tossed it over her shoulder in a smooth, elegant move, a faint smile coming to her lips as his eyes followed it. "You should do it because I did not *ask* you to do anything. And because you're not a coward."

Unlike the last Mistress, she wasn't trying to goad him. Her voice remained smooth, thoughtful, not derisive. "You're here for what I have to offer. So let's proceed. Tell me your name, and go to the bench, please."

"Trey," he said.

Her expression didn't change, the eyes didn't even flicker, but he swore he felt the ocean of blue-green color close over his head, the slither of a feathery tail as the mermaid swam past, leaving him behind.

Turning, she moved back toward the door. "Stop at the accounts office to pay for the damages. I wish you a good night."

She didn't hesitate, didn't slow down. If it was a game, she was damn good at it, and usually so was he. When she reached the door, he didn't even have the extra moment her turning the latch would afford him, because the same security guard who'd opened the door for her did it from the outside now, confirming not only the interior surveillance, but the fact this was a woman who didn't have to touch doorknobs. Not if there was a breathing male within fifty feet.

"Gideon," he snarled.

She didn't stop. In a blink, she was gone, the door closing on well-oiled hinges behind her. Gideon stared at the door, his hands closing into useless fists at his sides. Hell, he shouldn't be here, shouldn't be doing this. She'd been right to leave. Vaguely, he knew he'd paid them for the right to be here, that he should be pissed, but he understood this place better than he would have at one time. This underground level wasn't about memberships and having your ass kissed.

Then he realized something. The door was closed. They left it open after a session's completion. At this point, the security guard would have put his carefully blank face back in and told him how many minutes he had before his ass was expected to be out of there. Instead, he heard the locks snick in place again.

Something loosened in his chest and tightened even lower.

∽

He cleaned up, and not just the dresser. He didn't know how to rehang those tapestry things, but he laid them on the bed, so they weren't on the floor. He picked up the candlesticks he'd snapped when he'd ripped a candelabrum from the wall, righted the vanity stool and put it back in front of its table and mirror. For the broken glass, wax shavings and splinters, he used his hands as broom and dustpan, scraped it all together, ignoring the cuts that bloomed. He used a bowl that looked like an old-fashioned washbasin to hold the pieces. Gathering cut, limp flowers, he stuffed them back into the vases he hadn't broken.

What started as grudging compliance to her wish to move one piece of furniture became a tense, almost obsessed need to change what he'd done, even though he couldn't undo or erase it. But as he continued to be alone, he knew he was avoiding doing the one thing that might bring her back.

He turned toward the prayer bench. It was innocuous looking, polished wood with spaced depressions on the inclined floor piece, intended for placement of the shins. Adjustable wooden pieces were at the end, providing a place to brace the foot, so the kneeler wouldn't slide back during his devotions. The riser in front of the bench, and the upper rail, would prevent the knees or body from sliding forward, no matter what force they were experiencing from behind.

She hadn't said to undress, though he had a curious desire to be stripped bare. Still, it was hard enough to walk to that bench, and force himself to his knees, fitting his shins in the places provided and adjusting the brace pieces for his longer legs. It wasn't too uncomfortable, but he expected that, after a while, the knees would start to ache. There was no padding, after all. Two hand-sized holes in the upper riser led through to wrought-iron handles, obviously intended for gripping. None of it seemed to be mechanized, nothing that would suddenly engage and hold him fast, but again, he knew this room wasn't about that. In here, bondage was a state of mind, either embraced or rejected. He'd rejected it three times. But this fourth time . . . He remembered his analogy of the enchanted castle, and thought of sirens and sorceresses, of men turned to pigs.

He clenched his jaw. "Fuck it." Threading his hands through those two holes, he took a good grip on the iron handles. He stared at that stained glass angel, who stared back at him with an unreadable yet mesmerizing expression. He couldn't determine what lay in the winged warrior's face. Compassion, detachment, anger . . . It was like Mona Lisa, every expression and none able to be read there.

"I'm here, damn you. Come back now." He swallowed. "Please."

Anwyn had returned to her private office, calling up the Queen's Chamber on her monitor in there. "Let's see what you've got, angry man," she murmured. When he at last began to clean up her room, not just the dresser, her chest tightened, the constriction increasing as he tried to fold the tapestries, push the flowers back in the vases. As he got down and scraped glass and wax into his hands, her own fingers closed, feeling the pain of the small cuts. He looked so incongruous doing such tasks, and yet she knew this was harder for him than fighting a physical enemy. The most frightening monsters were the ones that lived in your head. The aroma of a red rose, sensory memory, could be as painful an assault as a bullet in the chest.

"You are a strange and unsettling woman, *cher*. One who plays with a vampire hunter."

She didn't take her eyes from the screen. Anwyn always knew when Daegan Rei was near her. It bemused him, she knew, because in his world, such cognizance was usually accompanied only by a marking. Perhaps because vampires had a physical way to inflict immediate mind, heart and soul intimacy upon humans, they didn't realize that a human foolishly, deeply in love could acquire the same awareness, without a blood-link. His scent wrapped around her like a longing for what could never be. It made the craving even sharper, bittersweet.

"That intrigues you. It's why you like me playing with him." She stood behind her office chair, which she'd positioned in front of the monitor screen as if it were a barrier between her and what she was watching. Much like the barrier she'd always held between her and Daegan. It was an unexpected discovery, that she felt some of the same wariness about Gideon's impact upon her senses as she did Daegan's.

However, when the vampire slid his hands with possessive familiarity over her latex-clad hips and caressed the bare skin beneath the camisole, she leaned back into him, unable to deny her desire for his touch.

"Play, yes. But if you get hurt, his end will not be pretty. Take care that your toy doesn't get out of hand. You've never wanted to put your hands on him before."

"On the contrary, I wanted to put my hands on him the very first time he walked through the door. My mouth, every sweet, slick part of my body that you have touched." She turned her head so she could catch his ear in her teeth. He gave her an indulgent growl, though his muscles hardened, a predatory response that the Mistress in her liked to goad. "You taught me the sweet pleasures of anticipation," she whispered. "Denying me until I beg, until I would die to have the barest brush of your mouth at my throat. Even if you only intended to tear into it, take my life."

His fingers dug deep into her hair, tugging so her throat was exposed to him in truth. She shivered as the tip of one of those sharp fangs drew a line unerringly down her thudding pulse. "It would be an unforgivable insult to abuse such a beautiful thing. I would make the smallest possible punctures"—he pressed a sharp tip into her—"and sip until you drifted away, a gift to Heaven."

She closed her eyes. When she detected a dangerous tension sweep through him, she raised her lashes to see his nostrils flare, his lip curling in a feral warning. "I can smell the blood of his latest kill on you. Have you allowed him to touch you already?"

"No. I've been in the room with him. A few minutes ago."

Daegan's senses were so sharp, on every level. Though guarding her true feelings for him could be agony at times, the challenge of giving so much of herself to him, and so little at once, of being slave and Mistress both, was irresistible to one with her talents. The reason she took so few sessions now was that every interaction with Daegan was as fulfilling and exhausting as any session she'd ever experienced.

Gideon had called to her in a way she recognized as complementary to both what she had and what she lacked with Daegan. Even for a Mistress, she knew her needs and hungers were more complex and unusual than most, and this was untapped territory. It gave her a shiver of fear and anticipatory pleasure at once. Daegan, she was sure, registered both reactions. His hands cruised up to her breasts, cradled them with deceptive gentleness.

"Gideon Green," he said, voice laden with irony. "The best vampire hunter in the world. Hard to find, hard to kill. Should I worry over your obsession?"

Using her response to his touch, she gave him a breathless laugh. "I would never destroy Nature's perfection by allowing him to cut off your gorgeous head. I might ask him to snare you, though. Restrain your body so I could stroke it with the tip of the stake, then slowly, slowly, ease it into your flesh, the way your cock eases into me, my body welcoming and destroyed by it at once. A gift to the flames of Hell."

He muffled a sudden chuckle against her shoulder, and Anwyn relaxed into his arms, giving herself that brief pleasure as he caressed her throat. "You are such fiery torment, *cher*, Hell would seem like a vacation. Do you know how many vampires would like to capture him, take days to teach him the error of his career choice?"

Where their macabre teasing gave her erotic shivers, that didn't. A cold ball formed in her stomach as she turned her gaze to the screen again. She studied the tilt of his head, the way his uncombed hair fell in unruly disarray over his creased forehead. *He's mine. I won't let any harm come to him.*

She masked the unexpectedly vehement reaction with a light shrug. "Good thing you care nothing for such temptations."

When he gazed down into her face, she held his dark stare. In the beginning, his sensual punishments had been most severe for her refusal to turn her gaze downward, something vampires expected of their servants. But she bore no mark of Daegan Rei's. She was not his servant. As a result, she had no real idea what she was to him, the strange path of their relationship, while she was all too aware of what he was to her.

He'd described the effect of the different marks. It took more than a vampire bite. The vampire had to release each of the three separate, special serums from his fangs. One mark was merely a geographical locater, allowing the vampire to find the human he had marked. The second mark allowed the vampire access to the human's thoughts. They knew everything the human was thinking, and they could speak in the human's mind. Daegan had said the third mark deepened that mind-to-mind link, took it down to the heart and soul. Practically, a second- or third-marked servant could lend strength to the vampire if he was injured, but if the vampire was killed, a third-marked human would die within moments. If that human was killed, depending on how long they'd been together, it could be a powerful emotional blow to the vampire, but he would survive it.

He'd told her that words were not sufficient to describe the third mark, to understand why it differed so much from the second, but she could read between the lines. It was a complete surrender, a giving to the vampire of all that particular human was. But in the vampire world, humans were viewed as an inferior species, the property of their Master or Mistress, slaves in truth. A human servant gave her vampire everything, while in turn accepting whatever part of himself he chose to give to her.

"I don't want you playing with him while I'm gone, and yet you know I must leave tonight. If I forbid you . . ."

"I would disobey."

"Perhaps my discipline wouldn't be to your liking."

"There's no discipline you have that isn't to my liking." She made sure her eyes warmed as she looked up at him. "You know that."

Even without the marks, that edge was between them, whenever they came together. Vampires were powerful predators, so domination was an instinct, even when dealing with their own kind. Her instincts as a Domme were natural, and had been honed by experience, but he had centuries of blood behind his. In the still, sacred privacy of her own mind, she'd realized a long time ago that if she was a cat, then he was a lion, and though he might be more powerful, their aggressive tendencies were similar. She wouldn't fully surrender herself without complete trust.

He'd always been brutally honest with her, and that meant she trusted him more than she'd ever trusted anyone. Yet he'd made it clear that with the third mark, he would have a limitless ability to scour to the bottom of her mind, know her fears and sorrows, her insecurities and most elemental needs, things she had difficulty facing in herself.

At one time, early on in their five-year relationship, he'd pursued his desire to make her his servant with a single-mindedness that had resulted in volatile, agonizing arguments. He could be terrifying when he was determined, and he'd come so close to winning so many times, knowing just how to undermine her female defenses. He knew so much about who and what she was already.

She'd withstood the assault until the storm passed, but he'd left, disappearing from her life for six months. It was then she'd recognized how much he'd become a part of her. Even moving and breathing were difficult, pretending she was still Anwyn when he'd apparently torn her soul out of his body and taken it with him. In her despairing moments, she'd told herself if he ever came back, she'd give him what he wanted. She would walk into the cage he offered, and somehow learn to trust him enough that she no longer saw the bars.

But when at last he returned, he'd told her he would not ask her again, nor would he permit her to agree to it. Perversely, she'd felt a sense of loss, that he'd turned his back on the bond that his species viewed as the closest possible link with another living being. Ironic, considering that link was possible only with a species they considered inferior.

His fingers stilled against her. Pulling out of her thoughts, she caught her breath as Gideon knelt at the prayer bench. The man's obvious struggle with himself made Anwyn's own body clench. He was rigid with tension, from the breadth of his shoulders in his thin T-shirt, down to the braced thighs and taut ass in the worn jeans.

"He keeps a toe blade in those boots." Daegan's attention sharpened on the screen.

"I'll be fine, Daegan. He won't hurt me. I know it."

Gideon's hair fell farther forward across his brow in his penitent position. It only enhanced the fierce resistance in the brilliant blue eyes that flashed through the unruly strands. When she heard his words—*I'm here, damn you. Come back to me*—an insolent demand, her heart soaked up his pain, her pulse accelerating against Daegan's palm.

He kissed her there, letting his lips linger. His hands had returned to her breasts, and now they were drifting, stroking, plucking so that her body was shifting restlessly, a rhythm to his erotic motions. "I suppose you intend to keep him waiting," he murmured.

"It's part of what he needs. Do you have time . . . for me to need you?"

Gideon had touched her own healed wounds with his rabid suffering. It made her willing to let her guard down. Though deep in her heart, she knew she could trust Daegan with far more of herself. It was herself she didn't trust.

He'd stilled at her soft request, but now his lips increased their pressure against her throat, becoming more insistent. "You so rarely ask me for anything, *cher*. You know I would deny you nothing."

"I want to keep watching him."

"I know. You will taunt him with that, too, that another took your body while he knelt in loneliness."

"Serving me with his obedience. A gift I'll reward. But with him, I need to hold back. That's the key."

"You're afraid you'll want to give too much of yourself to him, too soon."

She couldn't deny it. It was in the quiver of her body, the way her nipples continued to harden beneath Daegan's touch, elongating under his skilled fingers. The aching pleasure became more uncomfortable as he pinched them again. She bucked against him, throwing her head back onto his shoulder, the violence taking her by surprise. Sometimes she came to life like the slowest boiling water, tiny bubbles of response barely quivering below the surface, and other times it was like this, as if the time Daegan had spent away from her had turned her blood to lava, such that she would erupt at his merest touch.

He was ready for her, though. Sliding the side zipper of the latex over the curve of her hip, his hand teasing bare flesh, he peeled the pants down but didn't push the tight garment past her thighs. "Bend over; clasp the chair in front of you, *cher*. I want to take you tight, where you cannot spread as wide for me as you wish."

"I want to come."

"That is for me to decide."

"Daegan."

He wrapped his hand in her hair and in one smooth motion, he'd pushed her forward, lifting her around the waist so her breasts were shelved on the top of her office chair and her toes barely reached the floor. Her heels stabbed at the denim of his jeans.

"You will go to him wanting more, wet with my cock, vibrating with the memory of it thrusting hard into your pussy, but you will not release. To be denied will make you cruel, needy. He needs you cruel and needy."

Anwyn closed her eyes, her breath short. Always he knew her so well. It hurt so much. He was right—to be denied could make one cruel, as well as needy to the point of silent, suffering anguish. If she knew she had all of Daegan Rei's heart, she would give him anything he wished, without reservation, rather than playing such games.

"For you both, then," she breathed. "The one who will take me, and the one I will take for myself."

He opened his jeans with one hand and then brought her back to him with that hand in her hair, the rolling chair providing an anchor point under her breasts as she arched back like a crescent moon. When he drove his cock into her, the thick, turgid length of it, he earned her cry, pleasure in how he filled her. Reaching back, she curled her hands into the open fabric of his jeans and held on, as he leaned forward and enveloped her in the folds of the duster he hadn't bothered to remove.

She was a Mistress, but he alone compelled her to surrender like this. While he had stopped demanding her agreement to be his servant, she knew the surrender she gave him fell short of how much he truly wanted from her.

Though he'd never said why he stopped asking, she thought she knew why, and it made the pain a little sharper, a blade she willingly drove into herself every time she clasped him to her.

In the vampire world, there was no greater crime than to fall in love with a human.

3

G IDEON didn't wear a watch, because digital ones beeped and wind-ups ticked, and both could be heard by vampire ears. He'd gotten pretty adept at knowing the passage of time without one, and though he knew it had been only fifteen minutes since he took the position on the prayer bench, it felt like twice that. The door didn't open, and with the soundproofing, the only noises in the silent room were his breath and heartbeat. Which increased his tension to the point he was grip-ping those iron handles as if they were a lifeline.

A strange thing had happened to him, kneeling here. The decision to obey had been spontaneous, a reckless "oh fuck it." But the more time passed, the more it was as if she was compelling him to stay there. Challenging him. Somehow he knew her eyes hadn't left him. She was watching him, not one of her staff. He was going to stay here, in this position, until Hell froze over. Because that door hadn't opened and no one had told him to go home.

The longer he'd remained in this position, the harder he'd gotten, until his cock was a fucking steel bar, aching. It was at an uncomfortable angle beneath his fly, but once he'd grabbed hold of those iron bars, he'd pilloried himself. He wouldn't let go.

Jesus, he'd fucking lost his mind.

Despairing, he dropped his head so his brow rested on the padded rail. Cushioned velvet, an interesting choice since everything else about the bench was penitential hard wood. He was in that position when the door opened, and he heard her step back in.

He stiffened, but didn't move, keeping his head where it was, too messed up to make a decision about whether or not he should lift it. He held on to the sound of her coming across the floor, the sharp shot of stilettos, briefly muffled by a throw rug, then back to the wood again. The wet slide of the latex, the whisper of the camisole as her body moved beneath the clothes.

Then her scent and heat were close. He didn't know about flowers and perfumes. He just knew she smelled totally Female, capital *F*. He wanted to bury his face in her hair, that sable sea of comfort and torment.

"Keep your head down."

Her hand touched his hair then, stroked along his temple, his skull. He stared at the velvet cushioning, the rich red color filling his vision like blood, the iron handles hot under his sweaty grip. Pain, such as what the other Mistresses had given him, would have galvanized his normal instinct to rebel, but he had no strategy to fight this kind of attack. Lyssa had done it, too, that night long ago. Simply stroked his head, teaching him that a cruel goddess could turn mercy and compassion into a weapon. A treasure a man would sell his soul to experience.

Her touch was gentle, but there was a firmness there, too. She dug into his scalp, massaged. Her thumb had a sculpted nail, painted silver white, that he caught out of the corner of his eye when she shifted it forward, passing over his cheek. It drifted behind his ear, along his jaw. She caressed the scar where a vamp had tried to rip open his throat. He'd nearly succeeded before Gideon's small crossbow had sent a bolt straight under his rib cage and into his heart.

"You've been very ugly to my ladies, Gideon. Been rude and surly as well. I expect better of you."

"Better lower your expectations. This is as good as it gets."

As she shifted her hand, he saw a flash of metal. He should have ducked away, swept her legs, knocked her to the ground and pinned her. It was how he reacted to the appearance of a blade, but for some reason this time he merely went still. It was a razor blade, cut and fitted to the underside of that long nail. When it followed his jawline again, the fiery sting, concentrated and precise, told him she'd drawn up a thin line of his blood. What would happen if she bent, licked it away? He clenched his fists against the metal handles, fighting to banish such sick thoughts.

"Maybe you should have gotten your ass in here and done the job right the first time." He tossed it out, a desperate Hail Mary. "Though I guess you make more money being wrong."

She tightened her fingers in his hair, making him grunt as she put her knee in his lower back. The only thing that kept her stiletto from staking his calf to the floor was the protection of his jeans as she leaned in. Her lips, her blessed lips, were so close to his ear he scented the gloss. A dark fruit of some kind, juicy, sweet and rich, but with a bite. As she held his head down to the rail with brutal efficiency, her breath caressed his jaw and cheek as if she'd rubbed her pussy there, moist and heated.

"Many men resist when they come here. It's part of what they need, so even if their resistance is violent, we can subdue them, because that's what they expect. They want to be here, want to be dominated. You, on the other hand, feel compelled to be here, forced by something in yourself you despise. That's why the other three only fed into your anger."

"Sounds like you're into dogfighting, sweetheart." He wished she'd use the razor again, take his mind off what was happening at a lower altitude, the twisting in his gut, the unabating throb of his cock. Jesus, nothing but her voice and the pain of that jabbing spike heel made his organ convulse, dampen thin cotton. "You threw a couple cats and a golden retriever in the ring to get my blood raging. You're the prize bitch, here for the real fight."

"Hmm." Trailing her fingers down the back of his neck, she teased the small, fine hairs so an unexpected shiver ran down his spine. She kept going, down the back of the T-shirt, the pads of her fingers caressing the tense range of muscles layered on either side of that center column, the branches of ribs. Only when she got to his waistband did he realize the purpose of taking her thumb down that center line. He muttered a curse as she used her knuckles to nudge aside the sliced fabric, but he couldn't prevent another, different type of quiver as her nails scraped his bare skin.

"That's one of two shirts I own."

"I'm sure Goodwill has plenty more where this one came from." Letting the fabric fall away from his tense flesh, she moved around the rail, between him and the stained glass alcove with its peaceful fountain. She eased a hip onto the cushioned rail, the long thigh encased in latex no more than an inch or two from his nose. The folds of the silky camisole gathered just above it, making it hard to swallow. The fabric was nearly sheer, giving him the hint of bare flesh so close.

He had a death grip on the handles, knowing her ass had to be hanging just over his knuckles on the right. Lifting one of her booted feet in an astonishingly flexible movement designed to reduce a man's mind to a puddle of lust, she threaded it between his forearms so she was straddling the rail. One boot was planted on the prayer bench between his knees; the other remained on the outside of his body. His head was now essentially between her legs. If he turned his face, his mouth would be mere inches from the slick black juncture of her thighs, shadowed by the folds of lace.

Despite that temptation, he lifted his head, following the fall of her hair up to her implacable face, those blue-green eyes that studied him with powerful intent. "I'm not going to try to force you to do anything, Gideon," she said, her voice a ruthless, feminine murmur. "I'm not going to manipulate you. You don't need that. It's a shield. I'm taking away your shields so you can face what you really need."

"What's that?"

"I also won't give you answers you already have." She leaned in, and the camisole slid away from her body, so that he was staring at two perfect breasts, the tips just beyond the range of his vision. Her hair brushed his face as she whispered in his ear. "There will be no money between us, Gideon. You will pay for your drinks, you will pay for any damage you do, but there will be no paid sessions. I am not your employee, nor your whore. When we are in this room, you are here to serve me, and you serve as I choose or you get out."

"What am I, then? *Your* employee? Your boy toy?"

She straightened, tipped up his chin. When she did, he stilled, real-

izing she'd brought that blade right under his throat, was casually stroking it back and forth over his windpipe. He swallowed against the
pressure of the razor edge.

She could kill him. All this time spent fighting vampires, and this
night, weary and hungering for something only she could provide, he
could be ended with barely a flick of her thumb.

For a moment, he wished she would do it. Almost wanted to beg her
for it. She'd taken him right into a dark part of his soul he tried to ignore, but always knew was there. Growing larger every day. There was
a flicker in her gaze, a tightening of her mouth, as he saw her recognize
it. But her voice was terrifyingly mild.

"There's a segment of society that serves, but is not paid. That's what
you are to me. In this room, you are my slave." The edge of the blade
dug in, but he found himself more agitated about the fact her words
had accelerated his pulse than any physical harm she could do.

"I know you're big, brave and strong." Her voice changed, hardened.
"Come in here with your hidden knife, with your predator's eyes and
clenched fists. Would you use them on me? Turn all those weapons
against me?"

"No," he muttered, wondering how she knew about the toe blade.
When her hand dropped, he shuddered as her fingers stroked his fly,
caressing the aroused beast beneath. She hadn't even looked, had
known exactly how and where to touch. As she teased the ridge of his
head underneath the strained denim, his breath got ragged.

"You think this is a weapon, too, don't you? But I could make you
come like a boy in your pants."

"Talk is cheap—"

She slapped him. She did it quickly enough it caught him off guard,
and it was no girl slap, either. His ear was ringing. If his hand had been
over the rail, he would have caught her wrist in reaction, but he'd kept
that death grip on the iron handles. So he just stared at her, his nerves
singing along his jaw and cheek, his blood boiling.

"That's enough, Gideon. Do you understand me?" Her voice remained cool, but her eyes could laser skin. It wasn't uncontrolled anger.
In fact she felt perfectly, frighteningly, in control. "Say, 'Yes, ma'am', if
you understand. You will call me nothing other than *ma'am* or *Mistress*.

I hear anything else, or you push me once more, I get up and leave. This time I won't come back."

He held her gaze a full minute, his jaw tight. "Yes, ma'am."

He was going to get up. Demand her name. Leave. Break more furniture. He didn't have to take this shit. He wished she'd stroke his head some more. He wanted to throw her down on the ground and fuck her, feel her body struggle beneath his, because he knew he was stronger. But as he looked up the slope of her abdomen, the rise of her breasts and slim column of throat, all delicate, feminine features, he couldn't make himself move. Instead, he lowered his head, pressed his lips to the inside of her thigh, turning so his temple rested on the opposite one, his forehead pushed into the curve of her stomach.

She lowered her hand to his head again, a slow, slow stroke now, one that followed his hair from his brow all the way to the ends at his shoulders. The movement brushed the lower curve of her breasts against his head, and he was fine with that, as well as with the flex of the muscles beneath his cheek. "I'm going to have three ladies come in now. They're going to strip and restrain you, at my direction."

He tensed, but her fingers kept up their soothing and implacable motion. "If I sent in three men, you'd fight them, bloody their faces. Your choice now is to submit to what I want, or disprove my theory about your chivalrous nature."

"You can do anything you want to me without restraints."

"Yes, I can. But the restraints aren't for me. They're for you."

"I can't." The rawness of his own voice disturbed him, but he couldn't move as long as she was touching him this way, the comfort of her thighs against his face, the reassuring, intimate female scent of her so close. Arousal. She'd been aroused when she came in here, and that scent was still there, as well as the hint of a different musk, one that seemed familiar but he couldn't quite place. He wanted to lift his head, use his mouth to find out if her nipples were hard, stiff little points that would welcome the wet, demanding heat of his tongue, the bite of his teeth, the pressure of a suckling squeeze with his lips.

"I know you think you can't. But you will, anyway. Because you are my slave, and that is what I demand. In here, you fail no one if you submit, if you give in to what you want. I accept everything you are. There is no dark room inside you that I won't open."

"I want to fuck you. I want that to happen."

He knew that never happened with a hired Dominatrix. But she'd said there'd be no money between them, hadn't she?

"That's up to me. We'll see how well you obey, and if you deserve something that special." Her fingers tightened, a warning. "In this room, you are not in control, Gideon. You are not God here. I am. I am the only one allowed to pass judgment on you. Your Mistress."

A Mistress. An owner of his soul. *Guardian of his soul.* The insidious whisper came from that sly part of his mind that knew what buttons to push. Seductive, misleading. *You are not in control.* She'd called him her slave. But she would walk into those dark, secret rooms inside of him and find other names. *Murderer. Coward.*

With a painful growl, Gideon let go of the handles. The loss of her mesmerizing touch was his punishment, a deprivation he deserved, but which filled him with rage. At her, at himself. As he surged up, he shoved against the railing, splintering it on its base.

~

She didn't fall. Anwyn had time only for that brief impression as the beast she'd thought she'd lulled into a temporary peace came to savage life again. As he did, he tore the railing right out of the floor. Lithe as she was, she should have fallen ignominiously on her backside, because she'd spun her own enchantment. Having this dangerously powerful man on his knees, his head in her lap, had made her wish she could stay like this for the whole session, just soothe the rabid monster in his soul that called to her. That was her weakness as well as her strength. A lion tamer, Daegan had called her, on more than one occasion.

The most terrifying part is you have no fear of the lion, cher. *He fascinates you. No matter how close you come to his fangs and claws.*

Well, she was pretty damn close right now. Gideon caught her upper arms before she could topple, cleared the debris he'd created and slammed her up against the wall in the recessed stained glass alcove. The small fountain toppled, splashing water across their feet. Glass shattered behind her, the stained glass as well as the backlight bulb, sparks popping.

Despite that cacophony, he'd done it all in one superbly graceful movement that told her exactly what this man did for a living. He killed. It was a calling, not a profession. His deadly grace came from more than practice and experience; it was natural instinct, a terrible gift of the gods. Even if her courage didn't falter, her body had the sense to tremble.

He shifted her into the corner, away from that jagged bulb, and kissed her, hard, fierce, his fingers biting into her arms. He wasn't seeking pleasure, but brutal domination. Her feet weren't on the floor. His thigh pushed between her legs, holding her up, riding her on flexing muscle; his cock ground into her hip. His split shirt slid off his broad shoulders, exposing part of his chest, the hard cords of muscle in his throat.

His lips were drawn back, teeth clashing with hers. During those few harrowing moments, she forced herself to calm docility, despite the desperate thumping of her heart against her rib cage and the unexpected spike of arousal the grip of his hands and press of his body incited. She didn't reject his kiss, merely waited him out, waited for him to realize she was neither resisting nor accepting. She hoped that James and the security guards were obeying her orders, which were to leave them be unless she gave the prearranged signal for assistance.

Mostly, though, she thanked Goddess that Daegan had already left. That was all she needed, a testosterone match between a pissed-off vampire and an enraged vampire hunter.

Gideon drew back, his breath coming fast, his eyes cold and hard. His mouth was a rigid slash, wet with hers. During the kiss, he'd shifted one hand to the base of her throat. Gazing at him, she knew he was feeling her rapid pulse beneath that grip. "Gideon," she said softly. "Put me down. You are hurting me, and you are hurting yourself. I won't tolerate either one of those things in here."

His lip curled in a half snarl, but it was silent. A quiver ran through his limbs, and she saw the muscles in his neck work, his shoulders bunch. The hands clenched on her, enough that she wondered if she would have to use that signal after all. Then he moved.

Not to obey her, not exactly. He shifted his grip, so he was beneath her legs and back, and lifted her out of the broken glass. Fortunately, his hard biceps pressed below where her shoulder had hit the stained glass. He carried her away from it, putting her on her feet next to the wing-backed chair. Then he stood there for a moment, staring at her. He was a tall man, more than six feet, but with her heels, the height difference was reduced. His hands crept up from her waist, his fingers tangling in her hair, almost like a child playing in his mother's curls, only the movement of his fingers inspired entirely nonmaternal feelings. He slid along the surface of the camisole, the heat of his touch burning the skin beneath the thin barrier of cloth.

This man was not a submissive. There was nothing innate about it to him. She'd sensed that from the beginning. But what had fascinated and drawn her was what she felt now, in full, raging demand. He was seeking a form of submission, of surrender, that didn't have to do with whips and chains and kissing the sole of her shoe. It had to do with service and loyalty, with something so absolute the soul, not the mind, was the one pleading to be called into service.

She'd said she had a theory about his sense of chivalry, the type of man he was. Even in his rage against Tara, he'd confined his violence to the objects around her, and defensive maneuvers only. By opening him up, Anwyn had pushed him closer to direct violence than he'd probably ever committed against a woman. She could tell, because it was in the damning self-condemnation in his eyes, the tremor in those large, dangerous hands that held her.

The world outside Atlantis was one of intellectual, self-righteous cynicism, which mocked acts of nobility. It scorned the notion that there was a definitive right and wrong, a structure of morality and code of honor. In such a world, the soul of Gideon Green was quite lost.

"I'm sorry," he said at last, his voice rough, a wounded lion's growl. "I'm going now. I'll come back and pay later, but I won't bother you again."

When he stepped back, she reached out, hooked her hand in the waistband of his jeans. Her knuckles brushed his abdomen, her sharp-edged rings scraping his flesh under the cotton shirt. Holding his gaze, the color of midnight skies that never felt a hint of sunlight, she closed her other hand on the shirt collar where it hung low and tugged. The split back made it easy to take it off his long arms, over the lean muscles that rippled like strong river currents. Since she hadn't cut the shirt all the way down the back, it got caught at his hips, but she stepped closer, worked it free of the waistband and let it fall to his feet, around his boots.

Broad chest, gleaming shoulders, a lightly furred abdomen that couldn't hide the striations of hard, tough strength there, either. Maybe he'd used a gym to get to a certain point, but she was looking at a warrior. Her lips pressed together at the scars. She knew what she was seeing. After all, in a former life, she'd been an emergency room nurse, having a front-row view of man's violence toward man, and toward himself.

Gideon Green bore scars from bullets, knives and punctures. There were burns, faint tracks along his rib cage that she knew would originate in the back, because they came from a brutal flogging, not meant for anyone's pleasure but a true sadist. Without the scars, he would have had a beautiful body. It was still a work of art, though, the cost interwoven with the potential.

"Stay completely still. Don't move. I'm going to show you the right way to get a kiss from your Mistress."

He looked puzzled, but then she closed those several inches and brought her lips to his, staring into his eyes. His body constricted under her touch, her fingers resting on his chest and at his waist, all that lovely bare male skin. He kept his eyes open, gazing into hers, and she breathed into his mouth, brushed her lips over his, tasted them with a delicate tracing of her tongue, until she started to feel him sway toward her, the tortured pain in his gaze flickering with something else.

She stepped back as his hands were lifting to close over her body. He could have stopped her, but his fingers merely slid along her waist and hip as she backed away.

"I require two things," she said. "That you tell me the truth, consciously. I will, on occasion, forgive the unconscious lie, the one you believe yourself, but I will dig it out, force you to face it. Outside this room, you can be a liar. Most of us are, to be what we need to be. But here, I only accept the truth that comes directly from your soul."

"That's not what I want."

Wrong, angry man. She arched a brow. "It's what I want that matters, Gideon. Remember? I'm in control of that."

"What will you do to me, if I let those women tie me up?" His pulse was up again, she noted, and the fingers were clenching, but from the very question, she knew his mind was circling around the temptation of it, his need to surrender. It made it harder to keep her voice steady.

"Whatever I want. Your choice is to trust me, even if you've never trusted anyone in your life."

"Why should I do that?"

The truth was there, but she almost hated to say it. The look in his eyes would break a Goddess's heart, let alone a mortal woman who found him too irresistible to be safe.

"Because you have nothing left to lose."

4

GIDEON stood there. As his eyes shuttered, looking inside himself, she gave a signal to the cameras. Otherwise, she held her position, knowing if she moved, it could break the moment in several different ways.

Ten minutes later, he was still standing there, but his gaze had focused back on her, disturbing in its intensity. She didn't flinch, though. He didn't break the link when the door opened, either, though it cost him, his shoulders twitching.

"An Amazon brigade?" he asked, that defensive flash back in his eyes.

"No. Something different for you."

Gideon turned then to discover the three women she'd summoned were not Dommes, but three club slaves. Natural submissives employed by Atlantis to help wherever they were needed on the underground floor. All three were completely naked except for collars, their three different body types all tempting to the male eye.

Janet was a Renaissance beauty, with full hips and belly, heavy breasts and wavy golden hair long enough to belong to a fairy. It was twisted into a tail, the barrette fastened to a ring at the back of her silver club collar, while the rest of the locks tumbled down her back, brushing her pale buttocks. Charlene was slender, small breasted with just a hint of hips, a willowy beauty with pale green eyes and elfin features. Ella was the classic hourglass, the kind that would cause every man on a beach to get hard, watching her sway and jiggle her way down the sand in a scanty bikini. Her red hair was caught up on her neck, whereas Charlene had close-cropped hair that only enhanced the elf impression.

The one thing they all had in common was a vulnerability that was entirely nonthreatening. They would do her bidding without hesitation, while a man who was any gentleman would hesitate to do anything to thwart them.

She nodded to Janet. "Take him into the bath chamber. I want all his clothes removed. Chain him there and oil his body. I'll handle any other preparations."

From the wry resignation laced with a tad of desperation in his face, she saw he understood how well she'd outplayed him. So she spoke in a quiet, almost gentle tone. "They'll obey me without question, Gideon, so don't resist. I'm trusting you not to harm them. Is my trust misplaced?"

He shook his head, a sigh lifting and dropping his wide shoulders. She nodded. "Then I'll join you shortly."

When Janet took one of his hands, Ella the other, he stared down at their fingers, holding his scarred, strong ones. The women, irresistible nymphs, smiled at him. Janet emitted a sudden, playful trill of laughter, a girl's giggle, and then they were tugging him along, headed for the bath.

When he was out of view, Anwyn's own shoulders drew back at last, trying to relieve her discomfort. Pressing another button, she moved stiffly through the narrow staff exit and into an antechamber that paid staff could use to give themselves a break, while allowing them to still view the room, unseen. Madelyn was already there with the first aid kit.

"Well, that was exciting," she said dryly. "You've lost your mind, haven't you?"

Anwyn grimaced, pulled her long hair forward and presented her back to the other Domme so she could examine the glass shard lodged in the tender flesh inside her shoulder blade. "Damn, I loved that angel," she grumbled. "It was an original, too. Don't fuss, Maddie. It hasn't hit anything vital. Just pull it out straight, clean the wound, put some adhesive over it and I'm good to go. I'll change tops so it won't distract him. I'm lucky he was too worked up to notice it. He has a protective streak."

"Yeah, I noticed how he carried you over to the chair like you were a porcelain doll. After he nearly impaled you." Maddie shook her head, withdrew the shard with a firm but constant pressure that gave her the minimum amount of pain, though Anwyn still sucked in a breath. "You amaze me, how you figure out the tough ones like that. Be careful, though. You're nowhere near home free with that monster. You wouldn't have caught me giving him free sessions. I'd charge him double."

"Sometimes it's about more than that."

Being a Mistress had long ago become an art form to her, but as the club's owner, she picked up the brush only if she felt the canvas was specifically for her, too intriguing to pass up. This underground level was as much an extension of her nature as it was to cater to the hardcore needs of others. It was successful because she understood the need to reach that savage cutting edge, where civility and rules didn't apply.

When she was in this kind of mind zone, her staff knew she didn't have patience for explaining what she was doing or why, so Maddie had subsided. While she worked, Anwyn tilted her head to watch the monitor, which showed the fully tiled bath chamber. Eye bolts for chains or ropes were embedded in a variety of positions, some on tracks that could be locked or adjusted. Jets activated from all angles, and there were multiple detachable showerheads. Next to it was a deep hot tub that could be used as a dunking area, if sensory deprivation was preferred.

Ella had guided him to sit on the wall of the tub so Janet could remove his boots. She straddled his legs one at a time, her ample rear within touching distance, the pink, glistening folds of an aroused and lubricated pussy visible, an additional aesthetic pleasure as her buttocks tightened to remove the boot. When she shifted to remove the other, Gideon's fingers brushed her backside. Anwyn suppressed a smile as he snatched his fingers back. She knew better than to assume he'd realized he hadn't been given permission to touch. Instead, like a stubborn child, he refused to let her see he was getting unwilling pleasure out of his surroundings. Of course, a man's cock didn't know how to lie.

Janet chose that moment to pull a little harder, so that the boot came off fast. She tumbled back. When he caught her on his lap, she smiled impishly into his bemused face before she slipped off, giving him a provocative little wiggle. It almost made him smile back, an automatic reaction, though he was too worked up to relax that much.

The hint of that smile disappeared when Charlene had him stand. She had a silver manacle and chain, which made Gideon stiffen when he saw it.

All three women were trained to handle a client who became violent, knowing when to back off, how to protect themselves for the key few seconds before security could enter. It had always been sufficient, because she did vet the applicants so thoroughly. When a client was stripped down to raw emotions, most would still hold on to impulse control, even if it was by their fingernails.

But Anwyn was keenly aware of Madelyn's attention, her doubts, and she cursed herself for letting them infect her. When she'd asked, "Is my trust misplaced?" and Gideon had shaken his head, she'd known for certain that they would be fine. No, she hadn't expected the reaction that had put glass in her shoulder, but this was different. There was nothing threatening to him about these three women. He wouldn't hurt them.

Though his body was abruptly as tense as if a vampire had sprung up in front of him, he let Charlene raise his wrist, fit the manacle around it. What probably helped was that the chains appeared thin. He'd believe he could break them, if needed. But the chains were titanium. The bolts to which they would be attached were embedded into a concrete and steel rebar block behind the tile. Even Daegan might need a few moments to get loose. For a mortal, it wasn't going to happen. She held her breath as Charlene ducked under his arm to lift his wrist and cuff the other arm. She did her job well, brushing intimately against him on one side as Ella moved in front of him to unfasten his jeans. As her fingers played over the button, slipped it free, Charlene turned the control so the chains tightened and his arms were drawn out to his sides and up, muscles stretched out in his upper body, a mouth-watering display of male flesh.

However, the show was far from over. When Ella brought the zipper down carefully, they discovered the pleasing fact that he wore no underwear.

Madelyn's hands slowed in their ministrations on Anwyn's back. Whatever else she thought, she and Anwyn were in perfect agreement right then, watching the girl push the snug denim down his hips, revealing the long, thick cock that practically breathed a sigh of relief as it stretched out, hard and erect.

The tip was glistening, and Anwyn could see where the inside of his jeans had gotten damp from his arousal. As Janet took over, taking the pants down his long legs, she let her full breasts drag over them. He drew in a breath, his hands tightening in the cuffs. Ella moved behind him, taking a pitcher from Charlene. Gideon shifted his attention to her, and then his cock jumped, his chest expanding as she poured the warm oil over his shoulders, letting it run forward and back.

"He's beautiful," Madelyn said. "In a hard, painful way."

Anwyn nodded. He needed to eat more. The man had no body fat she could see, and while he was all striped muscle, food and less physical deprivation would give those muscles a smooth, sexy appeal, rather than the dangerous, lean appearance they had now. However, his eyes were his sucker punch. The burning gaze promised he could fuck a woman to death and leave her moaning for more, even if it was her last breath.

As Anwyn's thighs strummed in response to a surge of moisture between her own legs, Madelyn put pressure over the wound, taping it down. Anwyn kept her eyes on the screen as three sets of female hands began to rub the oil over him. Shoulders, arms, back and then chest, down to his cock. Janet got that pleasure, her hands slick as she ran them up the impressive stalk, back down over his balls. While he tried to stay still, he of course couldn't, twitching under her hands, letting out a groan as Charlene rubbed herself against his back, spreading the oil with her body as well as her hands. Ella knelt to do his legs. As she reached his ankles, she efficiently locked a manacle around each of them. Though that discomfited him, Char snapped his attention up when she pressed the switch to drop the chain with its collar cuff from the ceiling. Leaning against his back, letting him feel the press of her small tits, her pubic mound against his ass, she caressed his throat, then locked the collar around it. His quivering increased, such that even from her distant position, Anwyn could feel the effort it was taking him not to resist. He would keep his promise to her, but it was costing him. The overwhelming need to resist, that unreasoning rage, was building. She needed to get back in there.

Next time she wouldn't deny herself the pleasure of putting on his restraints. It was one of the most arousing parts of breaking in a new slave. Being close enough to see and feel the body's tremors as the male mind fought to obey the Mistress, capitulate to being rendered absolutely helpless. Next time, she decided she'd also have Janet remove the hair in his pubic region with a straight razor, something that never failed to simultaneously arouse and terrify a male.

As she'd foreseen, he was getting way more agitated now, his fingers flexing in his bonds, his body twitching as Janet locked the stainless steel three-ring harness over his cock. Her fingers stroked his turgid length before she gave him a naughty kiss on the end of the broad head, her tongue flicking out to take away the salty moisture. Then she attached another chain embedded into the floor to the ring underneath that harness, significantly inhibiting his movements.

"Wait," he said, but Ella was already going up on her toes to kiss his mouth. It distracted him enough that she used that moment to take the ball gag from behind her back. In a deft movement, she slid it in, replacing her tongue. He thrashed, but it was already buckled around his head. Charlene, behind him, cinched it tight so it dug into the corners of his mouth, a relentless bit for a headstrong stallion.

"Taking care of that troublesome mouth of yours, Gideon," Anwyn murmured.

"Didn't seem to bother you much earlier," Madelyn commented.

Anwyn had an amiable retort for that, but she saved it, because he'd reached the red zone. He hadn't expected this degree of restraint, and now he knew just how caught he was. He snarled and jerked, flinched as he forgot his cock and balls were fastened to a ring in the floor. When Ella put the blindfold over his eyes, taking away sight as well as voice, his low-level growling turned into a desperate roar around the gag.

"He's all yours," Madelyn said. "Don't know if you're lucky or a fool, but watch your step either way. There's such a thing as pushing a man too far."

"Mmm." They both turned as another staff member slipped in, bringing Anwyn the long-sleeved, formfitting stretch top Madelyn had requested over her headset as she administered the first aid. As Anwyn donned it, she knew Madelyn was right. She also knew the most delicious point of pleasure clung to the edge of going too far, that hovering line where pain and pleasure balanced, and the mind surrendered. She was better at finding it than anyone, maybe because she'd had to find it to save her own soul.

She wondered if she could help Gideon save his.

∽

That bitch. Conniving, manipulative, let-me-the-fuck-go-now bitch.

His breathing was like a hurricane in his ears, blindfolded and gagged as he was. Everything told him to go postal, to rip the chains from the walls. The three rings on his cock were snug, disturbing and arousing at once, as if someone had metal fingers wrapped tight around it. But the collar, feeling that restraint as he tried to move his head, was the most disturbing thing of all. What the hell had he been thinking? He knew he couldn't handle being trapped like this.

He'd been caught twice by vampires, and in both instances had had the good fortune—or misfortune—of them trying to torment him instead of killing him outright. So he'd had to learn to keep his wits about him when restrained, boxed in. But he was in a different mind-set tonight. This wasn't about vampires. She'd raked those sharp, razor-laden nails over his defenses, shredded them so he wasn't sure what to do or be in this situation.

Normally, he was fine with the fury that could erupt from him. It was a deadly tool he could use against his enemies. But Mistress Queen Bitch was a mortal woman, and he could hurt her. He reminded himself of that, but it was lost in the red haze. The restraints had become the suffocating walls of a coffin, his lack of ability to see or speak increasing the sense of claustrophobia. He'd shaken off the soft, female bodies pressing against him, snarling and spitting at them, letting them know he was no longer playing along, and they'd retreated. Were they still here? He needed to calm down, listen, try to get a grip, rather than turn into a berserker who would do something irreparably stupid.

"You aren't in control right now." Her voice, only a few feet away, had him stiffening. He hadn't even heard her. Was she still wearing the heels? "You need to accept that. I have all the control. All the decisions to be made are mine."

Yeah, she was still in the heels. That hollow *tap, tap* came across the tile, a rhythm that easily brought to mind how her hips swung with the help of those fuck-me-blind shoes. She was sauntering, the bitch. He couldn't talk. He needed to talk.

When her palm slid over his slick shoulder, he jerked, but it was that same soothing stroke, as if she understood how close he was to losing it. Her knuckles drifted over his chest, drawing little circles in the oil over his nipples, teasing them, then up to his jaw, painting that same slickness over his lips, stretched over the ball gag. The caress sent electricity straight down to his groin. The oil had a tart lemon flavor.

"Easy," she crooned. She moved her fingers along his nape as she shifted behind him, following the curve of his spine, down the oily line of one ass cheek. His cock bucked hard in its restraints; then he tensed up like a virgin as her fingers probed. "Nice and tight."

He made a helpless growl, a denial, as her fingers eased in, then . . . oh, holy Christ. The blunt end of a dildo. "No, no!" He shouted it against the gag, yanking against his restraints. The rings tightened against his cock, biting hard enough that the pain rocketed up his body. *Fuck*. He groaned.

The dildo continued to fondle his rim. She wasn't trying to push in, just caressing, stimulating, making his cock ache in a decidedly disturbing way. "I see scars on your back here . . . and here . . . and here. Everywhere. Terrible things, terrible moments. Yet you fear this? Though you've obviously never had anything in your ass, you know this little cock won't hurt you as badly as these things did." Her other hand settled on a jagged knife scar, eased down to press on two shiny bullet marks. "What you fear is what it might do to you. What you might reveal to me about your desires. Your needs."

"Fuck you." The gag interfered, saliva sprayed, but he was pretty sure she got the drift. Her laugh was soft, mocking.

"That has to be earned." Both hands went up under his hair, gripped and pulled back so the collar put pressure on his throat. "Behave, angry man."

The fact the dildo was still at the lower level told him she was wearing it as a strap-on. *Fuck.* He didn't realize how hard he was clenched until she gave his buttock a playful pinch, setting him off balance. "You know," she said, "if a child holds his breath, all you have to do is wait for the body's survival instinct to kick in and force him to breathe again. Sometimes you have to wait until he passes out for that to happen, but I don't think that will be necessary."

It was as if they were holding a casual conversation in a park, rather than her circling his completely restrained naked body in a room that echoed every purring word. "Easy, Gideon. You're going to want how this makes you feel."

Subjugated. Dominated. Nothing. Used. And yet, under her touch, those words seemed different, more provocative than condemning. Even so, he couldn't get himself to relax. Every muscle remained rigid, his buttocks clenched tight. He made another furious, strangled noise of protest.

Her palms pressed on his buttocks like wings, her thumbs teasing the seam before they moved up his back again, slow, firm, a thorough massage that traveled up to his shoulders. Leaning into his body, despite the oil, she pressed hers against the planes and valleys of his torso and ass. The phallus slid innocuously between his legs, stroking his testicles. Her thigh pressed to the inside of his, making his balls draw up at the friction.

"Do you understand what you're looking for here, Gideon? We have men who seek pain and restraint for one reason. To give themselves permission to be helpless, to cry for what they've lost, what they can't control. But you'd rather die than be that vulnerable, right?"

He was swaying into her touch, that erotic kneading. It was as if she was individually assessing every muscle in his shoulders, his back, then along his nape, pulling his head back onto his shoulders again, tugging at his scalp, reminding him of the collar around his neck and stimulating nerves there as well. As she shifted, her breasts rubbed beneath his shoulder blades, her nipples a distinct, tantalizing pressure beneath a thin, stretched fabric. He realized she'd changed shirts, a fabric that didn't seem to have any trouble sliding over the slick surface of his skin. But he wanted the intimacy of her flesh.

"If it was only sex you wanted, you'd jerk off in whatever dive you burrow during the daylight hours. From your clothes, your body, I can tell you don't give yourself much. But for some reason, you've given yourself this. Which means it's a very, very powerful need. You hate that, believe that it's weakness that brought you here, searching for something you don't understand."

Her fingers dropped, closed around his cock, and he made that strangled, involuntary sound again, even as he grew more solid in her hand, every nerve ending straining toward the touch of slim, firm fingers. "You sought the darker levels of my club, like you seek the darker levels of yourself. Down here, sex is merely the gateway to what the soul wants."

She didn't need implements of torture. Her tongue was sufficient, and with his pressed down by that ball gag, he was helpless to stop her. Letting him go, she moved around to his front. Her fingers glided wherever they wished, in no pattern he could anticipate, another torture. Up, caressing his throat beneath the collar. Down to a nipple, skirting it to explore his rib cage. Then a serpentine, lazy path across his abdomen. Her thigh brushed his again, the hard rubber of the dildo a vague threat. His cock leaked more fluid, and a drop splashed against his foot.

A soft, moist tongue licked it away, making him start as it teased the sensitive crevice between two of his toes.

"Janet is still here," his Mistress said in a conversational tone. "I could tell you particularly liked her. Men may look at supermodels, but that's not what they want beneath them. When it comes to fucking, males want the full, big tits, the soft belly and generous, ripe ass."

Gideon sucked in a breath as Janet's mouth closed over his cock with a blissfully flexible tongue. She teased the base ring, sucked on the length of his shaft, a slow, easy rhythm that made him groan with the friction of the metal against straining flesh.

Was she going to watch him totally lose control, be blown off?

His Mistress laid her head on his shoulder now, her arm sliding under his to stroke his back in broad, drifting sweeps. From the shift of her body he thought she might have passed an affectionate hand over Janet's hair as well. The strap-on was pressed to his belly, where his own cock would be, hard and tall, if it weren't chained down.

"You're looking for more than that generous ass, though." She moved again, another circle of touches, the occasional treasure of her mouth, sipping here and there on his neck, his shoulder, the tender skin between his shoulders. Which tensed as his Mistress leaned in behind him again. Meanwhile, Janet sucked away at his cock, so that his legs were trembling. She was too damned good. He was going to explode, and he didn't want to do that. Couldn't do this.

His tormentor rubbed her face between his shoulder blades, wound her arms around his chest. It was a gesture of comfort, reassurance, that lasted one breath before she scraped across his nipple with that razor blade.

He arched up with a hiss, the fiery pain wrapping itself up with the thrust into Janet's mouth. When he felt that dildo again, pressed against his buttock, he tensed immediately, but his Mistress remained leaning against his body, holding him in a light clasp of her arms. Idly, she played with his nipples, then followed the line of hair that arrowed down his abdomen toward the busy Janet. The submissive was making hungry little humming noises in the back of her throat, such that he couldn't help but imagine her before him on her knees, head moving and gorgeous ass quivering and tits wobbling as she worked him. If he was free, he'd be tempted to pull back her head and spill his seed over them, or work his cock in that slippery valley between.

He wondered what it would be like to have this cool Mistress on her knees before him and almost came then and there. Would have, if she hadn't scored the other nipple with that sharp edge, as if she was anticipating the edge of control he was riding.

"You won't come until I tell you that you can. You won't be weak. You'll hold out for me, won't you?"

He gave a muffled curse, and her smile pressed against his shoulder. "That's what I thought. You want to know what else I think? Sometime, not so long ago, there was a night where you finally got those terrible voices in your head to be quiet. On that one blissful night, it wasn't about how you'd failed, or what you had to do. Things got so intense and simple at once, it was all about feeling, but not the bad kind of feeling. You moved past conscious thought to what your heart and soul wanted, needed, so desperately. They could breathe for a little while."

She lifted on her toes, her voice dropping to a whisper, as if she spoke to him through a closed door, telling him that she had the key to free him, that his shields were an illusion she could swing out of her way at any time. "A woman held the reins that night. Your heart and soul keep bringing you back to my door, because you know Atlantis has what you're seeking."

Not Atlantis. Her. But she was still talking, her voice stripping him more effectively than the removal of his clothes. "Your problem is your mind came here looking for what you want, rather than what you need. Your soul is the battleground between those two forces."

A helpless, angry groan escaped him as her words, her caressing touch and Janet's mouth distracted him enough that the well-oiled dildo slid past the opening of his ass, sinking inside a couple inches. A wealth of nerve endings awoke, obviously responding well to her pioneering efforts. He bucked against the stimulation, though, and the cock harness bit into his turgid flesh.

"There you go. There's my boy," she crooned, and used his movements to slide in farther. Christ. It burned and yet it felt good, too good. His cock was pulsing in an alarming way.

"A sweet, fine, virgin ass. Stop resisting, Gideon. Just be my slave. Let me use you until you're mindless. This is actually very slim, a beginner's size. Slim enough that you can't keep it out, but a nice flared head to give you the proper friction and pressure."

"Stop it," he mumbled around the gag, and saliva escaped onto his chin, embarrassing him. Janet's mouth withdrew, and a handkerchief touched his mouth, as if the submissive were a nurse, ready to mop up the blood or wipe away the result of his Mistress's surgical incisions into his soul.

Now past the clenched muscles that could provide any resistance to her, she sank in to the hilt. He shuddered, his cock spasming. No, he couldn't, he wouldn't, let go. As if she knew how close he was, both women went still as he fought the release. It was a near thing, his heart thundering in his ears, his face tight with concentration, her breath on his neck, waiting.

"You are powerless, and yet you are also invincible, Gideon. Nothing is so dichotomous as human beings. You're a warrior, a killer . . . yet you're helpless against this need in you. You need to serve a woman's desires, her demands."

He shook his head, kept shaking it. In answer she moved again, a thrust and rock that took her right against his prostate, pushing with the right amount of pressure. And again, and again, until his cock was pulsing. He yanked against the restraints, yanked hard, and got nothing. Damn. It incensed him, but she increased her thrusts, starting to fuck him in earnest. He groaned as Janet's mouth closed over his cock again, taking him to the root, tongue flicking in a way that took the rest of his brain cells. The women worked in tandem. As he jerked forward, he plunged into Janet's mouth. When he jerked back, he impaled himself.

She'd said not to come, but he couldn't stop it. He was going to fail her. Fail himself. But then she gave him Heaven from inside Hell's grip.

"Come for me now, Gideon. I command it."

He roared against the gag as his seed came boiling forth. Despite that, he fought his own body and the stimulation like a battle in truth. No matter what she said, this wasn't what he wanted, needed. But she didn't care. She worked him deeper, harder, drawing the climax out longer than he expected, so that his roar became a bellow, a snarl of frustration. Particularly when Janet pulled off him, leaving him hot and hard, hanging in the wind, jetting out onto the tile floor.

Even without that wet heat closed around him, it was one of the most intense orgasms he'd ever experienced, the combination of stimulation and deprivation together, his hot, relentless pump into the air, the contraction of his balls as his cock flooded with one last, hard expulsion of semen. He rocked against the chains, swayed, the world spinning. Without the chains' support, his knees would have buckled.

As it was, when he was done, he was breathing hard, a winded animal. She was still moving in and out of his tender ass, making it clear this was about what she wanted, not him. He was a slave, just as she'd said. No responsibility but doing what she said.

"Beautiful," his Mistress purred softly, her voice entirely too calm. "You think I'm cruel, but trust me, I can be much worse. One of my favorite things is watching a powerful, naked man on his hands and knees, scrubbing his come off my floors. I typically make him do it on his elbows, so his ass is high in the air, knees held open with a bar spreader. It makes him shuffle along beautifully. All those lovely muscles bunched up, eyes flashing fire at being so degraded, while his cock and balls swing free between his legs.

"You'd put your back into it, though. Just like you did cleaning up my Queen's Chamber. Or maybe," she mused, "I'd make you use your mouth, tell you to imagine it's my cunt you're cleaning. You'd be angry at first, but then, as your tongue slid across the slick tile, tasted the musk of spent sex, you'd start imagining it, seeing it, smelling it. That's the key, Gideon." Her voice dropped to a whisper as she withdrew, then thrust back in, deep, inexorable, strangling another guttural noise out of him. "We can always be made helpless, but in our helplessness we find that enduring core of strength, the part of ourselves that reminds us to live, to lust and hunger. To never despair."

She *had* seen that suicidal moment, when her nail had been at his throat earlier. The hard edge entering her voice said she wouldn't be forgetting it anytime soon. That she would punish him for throwing away what belonged to her. Bloody hell, where were these crazy thoughts coming from?

She curled her fingers in his hair, drew his head back, and bit his neck below the collar, suckling it. A sound of pleasurable arousal hummed in her throat, making him pathetically glad to be given that small gift, to know that she wasn't as detached as she seemed. Her nails moved over his chest. He anticipated it now, maybe even welcomed it,

God help him. He opened himself up for it as she began leaving small cuts on him, drawing his nerve endings up, keeping his lethargic body in twitching response. Then . . . holy Christ, a mouth was back, working his cock again. A different mouth.

"This is Charlene, the tall, thin girl. I'm going to let each one of them suck you to climax, Gideon, no matter how long it takes. Because they need the practice, and I have you for the night. Would you like it if I had some of my boys come and suck you off as well? They've much stronger mouths. Many of our male clients like them."

"Not . . . your . . . client," he managed against the gag. She'd said so, hadn't she? That was the way he wanted it, too.

From the way she stilled, but her fingers still twitching on him with the hint of pain and blood, he knew she'd understood.

"No . . . men." He shook his head again, more emphatically. Now her hand tightened on the juncture of throat and neck, a sharp muscle pain that kept him where he was.

"Still haven't learned, have you? Charlene, tell Terence to come in next. He has such a pretty, pretty mouth. Gideon won't be able to tell the difference between his mouth and a girl's, except that I'll tell him. Keep saying no, angry man." She was the voice of a devil in his ear. "Every no means yes to me. You'll be sucked off and fucked within an inch of your life tonight until you learn to let go. To give me everything I demand and thank me for it."

His ass was burning and sore, his mind floundering between arousal and rage, weariness and disorientation. But he was still shaking his head, would keep shaking it. He couldn't do any of it. He couldn't bear it. He would break. He *was* breaking.

With that powerful climax, something had cracked inside of him. She was right. It was worse than any of the physical wounds he'd suffered. He couldn't fight this, but he needed to be released from the chains. He had to go to his knees, had to curl around that pain in order to bear it. To survive it.

"Let me go . . . let go . . ." He was saying it, but he wasn't struggling against her touch. He was just standing there, limp and exhausted, held at her pleasure and will, a woman's mouth working his decently interested cock.

He decided he was too damn tired to care about pride. "Please." All of his words sounded garbled with that gag, like a stroke victim. God, he wanted to know her name.

Was it mercy, or did she realize he really couldn't bear anything else? Because of the haze of unwelcome emotion, it took him a few moments to realize that Charlene's mouth was no longer there, and his Mistress had withdrawn from him. When firm but gentle hands released the tether from his cock, he knew it was her, because only those hands could coax his cock past semilife again. She caressed him; then Charlene's touch took the manacles from his ankles. His legs trembled, and when the one hand was released, he reached out, trying to stop his fall, but he was too late. He was on one knee, one wrist still chained and the collar still on, its tether and the one on his arm thankfully slack enough to allow him to reach the floor. Those same hands unbuckled his gag, guided the embarrassingly wet thing from him, soothed the corners of his abraded mouth.

When she went for the blindfold, he covered it with one hand. "Don't," he said in a husky whisper. "Just don't."

Instead, she brushed his hands aside, and took the blindfold off. He kept his eyes closed for a minute, but her fingertips were teasing his lashes. Though he felt only the soft pads, he kept his head still, mindful of the razor tips he now knew she wore on several of them, not just the thumb.

Then he forgot care, lost all his attempts to pull himself together, when her mouth pressed against the corner of his.

5

Coaxing his lips open, she startled him with the deep, soft embrace of her kiss, her hand coming behind his head to hold him there. He opened his eyes to find her face close, stark tenderness and deeper shadows in her blue-green gaze. Charlene was gone, and it was just the two of them.

Closing his free hand on her forearm, he coaxed her down to the tile with him, her knee resting between his spread thighs as he slid his arm around her back, brought her closer, and then that kiss renewed itself in earnest.

She hadn't seemed to mind that he was covered in oil, that it had smudged her pretty, sexy clothes. He wanted to take those off, rub oil on her so they would slide against each other. Intertwine fingers.

Comfort. He needed the comfort of her body. There was no thought or role to play; it simply was. When he began to ease her down, himself above her, he hoped that the chains around his throat and one wrist were long enough. At the flicker in her gaze, he swallowed, pain gripping him at the tension that rippled through her, having him over her like this. "I won't hurt you," he said. "I just . . . I need."

She nodded, those blue-green eyes filled with understanding, and something else. Though this moment was unexpected, an unusual tactic for what he knew of Dommes, he knew she was like nothing he'd ever known. She'd known he wouldn't scrub tiles, or suffer having a man's mouth on his cock. But she'd convinced him that she was entirely in control, capable of doing it to him. For that brief treasure of time, the voices had stilled, caught in the same paralysis as his body. Whatever, whoever she was, it couldn't be described. As she said, it simply was.

He moved down her body to the boots. Swallowing, fighting with a new idea, that the relative position of their bodies had nothing to do with who was in control here, he lifted his gaze. "May I remove your boots, Mistress?"

"You may, Gideon." Her voice was soft, her mouth a wet promise, still glistening with their kiss.

He undid the intricate laces and buckles, and then, on impulse, he slid a hand beneath her slim calf, lifted it so he could kiss her instep. Electric current ran up her leg, the way she shuddered. His cock was starting to rise to full performance again, which he'd consider nothing short of miraculous if it wasn't for the stimulation in front of him. Slowly, watching her, he adjusted her leg a few inches to the right so he could move between them, up to the side fastener of the latex pants. Watching her face, he slid the zipper down. She was the only thing under them, and his fingers trailed over that slim strip of bare skin, a precious indulgence, before he worked them off her smooth, long legs.

She was shaved of course, the pale lips of her pussy as delicate as rose petals around the darkly flushed clitoris. Another time, he would want to taste that, drink his fill, nuzzle the silken labia, bury his nose in her musk. But now he was swamped by the power of a Mistress, letting him lie down upon her, sink deep into her. Like a Goddess allowing man to return to Her earth, be buried in Her comfort and promise forever.

This was a woman, but something more than either one of them was commanding this moment. It was in the vulnerable set of her mouth, the quiver of her body. A connection, a delicate house of cards that he didn't want to shatter, so he kept his mind out of the equation. Even if this wasn't what a Mistress would normally do, it was all right. He didn't have to analyze it. No thinking.

He was barely able to reach her, the collar keeping his chest a few inches above her uptilted breasts, a temptation even still encased behind tight fabric. It was as if he were a beast, kept chained while a lady took her pleasure of him, the restraint intended to keep his teeth away from her. He could accept that. He wanted to keep her safe, especially from himself.

She'd held such iron control, but here, holding her, she was all female. More delicate than himself, smaller, less physically strong, with bones that could be broken. He placed a hand on her knee, then slid it up her thigh, seeing his tanned, weather-roughened skin, the size of his hand against the milky expanse of slender leg.

She could deny him. He wasn't sure why she wasn't, because he knew that intimacy didn't happen here that often. It was more about the head games and physical release. But when she'd walked in, she'd been the answer to the question of this place, the one that had nagged at him, made him ache, and kept him coming back. She was the one he'd sensed here from the first.

He and Jacob had shared that, an intuition that some would say bordered on psychic, anticipating something that they often couldn't define. He'd used it in times past to stay alive. Maybe this was the same, because some vital element of survival certainly lay in this room.

"Will you take off your shirt? Be completely naked with me?"

As she removed it, she arched up, the way she would if he'd entered her and she'd lifted herself toward him, an unconscious offering. Her breasts brushed his chest, a brief contact. His heart hammering up behind his ears, he helped, closing his hands on the delicate fabric and setting it to the side. Her breasts were round and firm, a perfect size for her torso and hips. He wanted to devour. He wanted to worship. He wanted to find what felt so close, what he hadn't had in so long, that she seemed to hold in those blue-green eyes.

As he shifted forward, bracing himself on one arm, she rested on her elbows, lifting a hand to his face. "Take your cock and guide it into me, Gideon. I want to watch."

"Do I . . . I'm not wearing . . ." He didn't want to say it, because he had a powerful need to feel her without any barriers, but he struggled to remember that there was a reality that couldn't be ignored. As always.

She held the depressing thought at bay, sliding that razored thumb-nail along his jaw, a gently lethal motion. "I can't get pregnant, and I'm not worried. You've always shielded yourself, until now. Haven't you?"

Not in a million years would he have ever fucked a woman without a condom on. Not the kind of women he'd sought for release and comfort. But the fact she knew it, as well as accepted how much he needed to do the opposite now, was enough to strangle him with the need to be inside her.

He nodded, unable to speak, and she pressed her thumb against his lip, making a tiny cut. "Then obey me, Gideon. Guide your cock into me."

Gripping himself, he took his eager member to those soft lips, rubbed the head there. As much as he wanted inside, he wasn't a complete dick when it came to being a lover. He wanted to be sure she was ready for him, but there was no worry of that. She was so slick he slid halfway in without intending it. When she contracted on him, he growled at the bliss of it. Her gaze lifted to his face, her lips parting.

It was Heaven and Hell. He'd never teetered so close to both at once. Then her legs widened, ready to take him all the way into the cradle of her body, rock them both to completion.

Instead of continuing that slide into Nirvana, his mind froze.

High on the inside of her thigh, there were two puncture scars. The kind that remained when a vampire fed from such an intimate spot. Not just once or twice, but on a regular basis.

There was no mistaking it for anything else.

∽

He jerked back on his knees as if he'd seen a rat trap waiting to snap down on his cock. "Let me loose."

Because she was obviously adept at reading people, he wasn't surprised to see her body language change as swiftly as his. Her expression went blank, her body tensing. But as her muscles flexed, telling him she was about to slide out of range, he shot a hand out, clamped down on her arm. "Unlock the rest of these fucking chains," he said.

She looked down at his bruising grip on her arm, and then her gaze came back to him. Her eyes were hard to read, but her tight mouth said she didn't care for being manhandled. "Or what? You'll break my arm? Hit me? Threaten me? We have twelve cameras on us right now, Gideon."

"Which you signaled your staff to shut down when you decided to go this route with me. I saw the hand motion, the red lights blink off, cut the audio. You didn't want them to see or hear their unflappable Mistress spreading herself like an eager bitch in heat."

The flicker in her gaze told him he was right, but it didn't hold fear, as he'd expected. It was ice. He told himself he didn't care that he might be hurting her, that he'd destroyed this moment. It was a house of cards, right? He should have known. It was another trick, another dead end or dark alley holding nothing but more of what he always knew. He shouldn't have looked for more. This was as much a lie as that night with Jacob and Lyssa had always been. He should have accepted that a long time ago. His cock was just fucking with his head.

Regardless, he must have felt he owed her one shot, because he didn't block her when those lethal nails raked across his chest. One swipe of an angry cat's claws, laying him open with a burning flesh wound. Then he caught the arm. He was tempted to twist it, but he didn't. She didn't struggle against him, though. She glared at him as if she were fully armored in her clothes, not wrestling naked with him on cool tile. Her hair slid over his arm, a reminder of how he'd wanted to bury his face in it earlier.

"If you let go of my arm," she said coolly, "I will release your chains and you can collect your things and go."

"Are you willingly his?" He knew the truth would hurt, because this woman didn't unwillingly give anything of herself. He was certain of it, which made what she'd been about to do that much more excruciating. *Ah hell.* As if his mind wanted to torture him further, he realized now what the unidentifiable musk mixed with her arousal was. Another man's seed. It was the scent of his own, staining the tile beside them, that helped him make the connection. It could be some other man's, but he'd lay good money it was the vampire's. She didn't seem the type to spread her affections casually, which only made this hurt worse.

"I'm not a servant, Gideon. No vampire owns me."

"So you're just his drinking buddy." Gideon's gaze flicked down to her thigh. Since she was up on her knees now, not delectably on her back, he couldn't see the dual puncture scar. "Unlock my chains and I'll let go of your arm."

"To do that, I have to go there." She nodded to a panel in the wall, beyond the range of his bindings. "You will have to trust me, Gideon. Just as you did a few moments ago." Her brow rose. Her armor was a foot thick, no evidence left of the vulnerable woman who was about to give in to something they'd both wanted. "If this was some elaborate trick to kill you, I expect we could have done that earlier, or on any of your other visits here."

"Vamps like to play with their food," he said flatly.

"In which case, the security outside the door will kill you, no matter what you do to me."

"I've gotten out of tougher spots."

"Let go of me, and you will walk out the same way you walked in. You are in no danger here, which you would see if you weren't obsessed with your hatred of an entire species because of the life of one girl."

Gideon's expression froze. In that blind second he was gripped with the damning desire to do her real harm, just as he had in that crazy moment when he'd ripped up the prayer bench. Seeing it, she threw up her chin, dared him, her eyes flashing.

"You don't know shit about that," he gritted out. But she did, didn't she? *Warrior, killer.* She'd called him that. Lost in a haze of lust, he'd thought she was role-playing, rather than exposing her knowledge of who and what he was.

"Why do you think you're not dead, Gideon? One man dedicates himself to a personal war against the vampires, and there's no Council decree to hunt him down? No territory that decides to pull together a posse, of sorts, and take you down?"

This bitch had known all about him the first time he'd walked in the door. Probably because of whoever was sucking her blood on a regular basis. He'd been unbelievably stupid. He hated her.

"Because vampires are very clannish," he retorted. "If you don't take out one of their own, they don't give a shit. They also see it as a sign of weakness when the vamp loses to someone like me."

"Yes, there is that. But for many vampires, it is a regrettable part of their life that they have to take an annual kill. They don't hold your grief against you."

"How fucking noble of them. Let me go." He snarled it, his patience at an end. "Whatever game you're playing with me, it's over. Unlock the chains from here." He seized her beneath the chin, his grip tight enough to pull her head up, strain tendons. "Or I break your pretty neck."

"I can't."

Gideon tightened his fingers, so her air became constrained. "I'm not playing."

"Neither am I." Her breath rattled over his grasp. "Are you ready to cross the line and become the monster, Gideon? Or are you already there, so you don't care?" Her eyes were hard stone, the color brilliant. "You do whatever you're going to do, but I'm not going to play *your* game. You have been treated fairly here. What happened here happened as you experienced it. There is no trick. Everything is not about you."

When he sneered at that, her voice remained even, despite her obvious disadvantage. "The fact that one of my associates is a vampire is irrelevant, as it is to any patron of Atlantis. This is my club. My decisions, my choices."

He could do it, break her neck in less than a heartbeat. She wasn't even lifting her hands to defend herself, simply hanging in his grip, but her lack of fear was a defense strategy all its own. She was so pissed off, it penetrated his suspicions. "Let me go," she repeated. "Right now."

He held her gaze another long minute; then, with an oath, he dropped her, drawing back as if he'd touched poison. She rocked back on her hips, but recovered her grace quickly. Rising, that mask in place, she didn't even bother to pick up her oil-stained clothes, no attempt to shield or protect herself superficially. As she turned away from him, walked toward the wall panel, his gaze latched onto the taped square of gauze on her back. There was a bloodstain in the center where the wound had been aggravated. Now he knew why she'd changed shirts. He remembered them hitting that alcove together, her shoulder leading the way.

Fuck, he hadn't even thought about it. He'd hurt her, and she'd . . . He gritted his teeth. She was a vampire's bitch, probably took worse from him. It didn't mean shit. It shouldn't bother him, but since he couldn't avoid the truth that he hadn't known about her association with vampires then, it meant he'd carelessly hurt a woman in his need. Something he would never, *ever* do.

Reaching the panel, she flipped a switch. The camera lights flickered back on. When she pressed another button, he heard the latches releasing the collar and remaining cuff. The sound was loud in the silence. Gideon pulled them away from his body and stood, facing her.

"You're free to use the locker facilities to wash off the oil and get dressed," she said. "There will be a cleaning crew coming to prepare the chamber for our next guest, so please don't linger. When you're dressed, stop at the accounting office to pay your bill for the room damages."

The frost in her voice, the cold detachment in her gaze, penetrated his own anger, made him want to howl. Ask questions. "Why are you with him?"

"I'm not with anyone, Gideon. I think you've demonstrated why I'm not. I saw something in you that convinced me to cross the line. It was a mistake, as it always is." When she drew in a breath, her nostrils flaring, he saw her consider him, an inch at a time, from head to toe. Where her gaze had been appraising earlier, as if she were caressing him with every movement of her thick lashes, now it was clear she was doing a far different type of evaluation. "Chantal was right. You don't belong in a place like Atlantis. This is for people who have the courage to reach for something more than what they know."

She turned as Madelyn entered from the staff door. The woman looked neither left nor right, holding out a robe. The Mistress slid her arms into it, regal as a queen. Madelyn placed another robe on a hook, apparently for him so he wouldn't have to stride naked through the hallways to the locker area, or put his street clothes over his oily skin. He didn't give a rat's ass. The shirt was ruined anyway.

Madelyn drew the sable hair out of the robe's collar, let it fall. Despite himself, Gideon couldn't help a twinge of lingering hunger.

Now that he was free, his mind was considering the possibilities. He was the one who had come here initially. He hadn't been lured. It was possible that she might be telling the truth, that who she spent her time with had nothing to do with his presence here. It didn't make him any less wary, because she obviously knew who and what he was. A vampire knew of his comings and goings here, but for whatever reason, the vamp hadn't taken advantage of it.

Nevertheless, probably proving how stupid he was, he couldn't stop the ache in his lower belly at what he'd just denied himself. He'd get over it. It didn't really matter, because it would have been an illusion. Right?

"What's your name?" he demanded.

"You don't have the right to ask me any questions. 'Mistress' was more than sufficient, and more than you deserved." Her gaze could freeze tree trunks, let alone his shriveled libido. "Good-bye, Gideon. Don't come back here. Since you are determined not to accept what you need, I hope that you at least get what you want."

"What the hell do you think that is?"

He hadn't meant to ask the sudden, desperate question. He expected the same smart-ass retort she'd given him earlier, about him already knowing the answer. Of course, the way he'd asked, he might also get another fuck-you look and nothing else, but she surprised him. As she glanced back over her shoulder, her face remained carefully expressionless.

"Death. While fighting the fight you have allowed to consume your soul."

6

IT was surreal. What had happened in the past few minutes, and what he was doing now. Maybe he was slipping, because in a similar situation he would have scooped up his things and beat it out of there, his surroundings no longer known or trusted, infected by a vampire presence. Instead, he went to the damn showers. He was covered in oil like a greased pig, and he didn't have many clothes to his name, as he'd told her. He had to travel light, after all.

When he reached the shower area, which he was relieved to find was vacant except for himself, an Atlantis staff T-shirt had been left for him. Black and in his size, with a vellum card perched atop it with his assumed name. *Compliments of Atlantis, for Mr. Jon Smith.* Picking it up, he brought it to his nose. New T-shirt, straight-from-the-factory smell. Disgusted with himself, he balled it in his fist. Of course it wouldn't smell like her. One of her lackeys had brought it, and why should he want her scent, anyway? She was a damn vampire groupie.

He'd run into a few of them, but they were always marked. Vampires were a secretive lot, and they usually didn't permit anyone in their inner circle who wasn't blood-linked to them. Despite what she said about not belonging to anyone, she was likely carrying one or two marks from the bastard.

He stepped into the shower, let the spray rain down on him. Second shower of the night. First to wash off blood, now to wash off . . . Hell, he didn't know what to call it. Another form of damnation, maybe. His cock was pissed as hell at him, so close to the golden gate before his mind had fucked it all up. But he couldn't stomach the idea of sliding into her, having his balls or any other part of his anatomy brushing against that mark, where *he'd* suckled her. Or fucked her. Of course, if he hadn't smelled the evidence of male seed, he'd say it could be a female vamp. She was hard-core, and she had issues with men. That flicker in her eyes when he'd been above her had told him. She didn't trust a male easily, if at all.

But in those few suspended moments, it was as if they both shed everything they'd built around themselves, and offered something different to each other. The people they wished they could have been, or who they'd been before everything else in their lives had happened. When he'd put his arm around her waist, and she'd brushed her lips against his, it had been just the two of them.

And an unseen vampire. With a snarl, he ducked his head under the water and resolved to get the hell out of there. It was all bullshit.

∽

Anwyn poured herself the brandy and sat back to look at it. The swirl of amber liquid glittered in the candlelight of her retiring room. It was an old-fashioned concept, the retiring room, but she liked it. A place for a lady to go collect her thoughts, be by herself, unmolested. She lifted her gaze to the empty chair across from her as if it belonged to an unseen guest. Only in this case, the brandy was the only guest, an unwelcome one. But occasionally she needed this lesson, this reminder. She really needed it tonight.

Picking up the glass in a decisive movement, she brought it to her lips, tipped it. The liquid burned, but she swallowed hard and fast, taking in the smell, the memory. She was gagging by the last swallow, but she managed it, slamming the heavy crystal down and coughing.

You did not consume me. I consumed you, turned you into one of my strengths. I consumed my enemy, consumed his power.

She'd resisted the desire to have the shower footage sent to her room so she could watch him bathe, see his angry movements, the frustration that fueled every inch of his enticing, powerful body, the furious blue eyes. What had happened between them, in the Queen's Chamber bathing area, had been unexpected. But when he'd surrendered to her, to whatever she would do to him, something in her heart had bled. She'd surrendered as well. It had been too long since she'd allowed herself that.

When he wouldn't open his eyes after she removed the blindfold, just reached out for her, touched her with trembling hands capable of such deadly force, she'd heard the click of connection. A bond had formed, too unmistakable to deny.

The empty part of her she wanted Daegan to fill, but knew he could not, had been drawn to Gideon Green, as if she were poised on the fulcrum of a scale. Somehow she'd believed the secret to Gideon held that balance. As if confirming her intuition, Gideon hadn't known what he wanted, and then, in that split second, he had. He'd wanted her, what she could offer, not just inside these walls, but more. That need had curled around her, drawn her close into his almost-tender but demanding embrace, making her do what she never did: kiss a client with stunning intimacy and such emotion she was still shaking inside.

But in the end, it didn't matter what his soul had whispered to her. He'd seen Daegan's marks, and that fragile reality had been destroyed by a much more brutal one. No matter what it was about Gideon that had called to her, apparently the Powers That Be had allowed her only one moment of it.

She was a disciplined woman. Though her soul was wounded from the near miss, she wasn't going to get mired down in it. She'd been wrong. She'd file Gideon Green in the place in her mind she kept all pleasurable puzzles. Would Daegan be glad her obsession was over? He'd been odd about this one, seemingly almost as fascinated with Gideon as she was. It was a mystery, but then, so much about Daegan was.

"Anwyn?" Her earpiece beeped and she heard Leona, the front desk hostess. "Sorry to bother you, but there's a group of gentlemen asking to see someone named Daegan Rei. I told them there's no one on staff by that name, and we don't release client names, but they've asked to talk to the owner. They're being very insistent."

Alarm bells went off in her head. Only she and James knew Daegan's name, and what he was. It was another reason she was glad she'd blocked audio and visual on Gideon before he began to talk about vampires. Occasionally others might see Daegan coming and going, but they were told he was a particular friend of Anwyn's, and no further questions were to be asked. In the type of establishment she ran, such discretion was a job requirement.

"Is Jon Smith still in the showers?"

"Yes."

"Has he made any calls?"

"No."

Of course not. How would he know Daegan by name, anyhow? Her stomach tightened. "Is James up front already?"

"Yes."

"Advise him of our visitors and tell him I'll be there shortly to deal with them."

The only one looking for Daegan would be another vampire. Taking a deep breath, she shoved the glass away from her and opened her office closet. She couldn't go up front in a robe. She wished she had time for a full shower, but in truth, she found herself reluctant to wash Gideon's scent from her skin just yet.

～

When she returned to the front area, she had her hair twisted up, and wore black slacks and a satin red and gold dragon-patterned tunic, a sexy but austere look she hoped would serve its purpose.

There were three of them. Even before she reached the private foyer where the front hostess had brought them to sit and wait, she knew they were trouble. The one in charge put her radar into red-alert mode. Short-cropped copper hair, dark brown eyes and a drawn, skeletal look to his face reminded her of a handsome rock star living way too hard. His two companions could have been his drummer and guitarist, for they bore the same gaunt look and burning eyes, their passions an un-healthy hunger for them or whomever they met. They looked barely legal to be in here, but with vampires, she knew the apparent age didn't mean anything.

James stood at the door, his posture seemingly casual, but she knew he'd already sensed they might have a problem. The three sat in the provided chairs, facing one another. When she was still ten feet from the doorway, their heads came up, eerily in sync, and swiveled toward her. Anwyn's gut knotted, but she forced herself to calm. Like all predators, vampires and men smelled fear on a woman as quickly as they scented arousal. When she reached the door, her security head glanced at her, his mouth grim.

"Thank you, James," she said. "You may go now."

His look of surprise was quickly replaced by something else. "I should stay, Miss Naime."

"No, you shouldn't. I don't require any assistance with this." *James, please, please listen to me.* She needed her head of security alive. "I'll call you if I need you." She tapped her earpiece, gave him another nod.

He glanced at their three "guests," then back at her, a muscle twitching in his jaw. "All right, then. I'll be close." His expression said he'd want to talk about a few things that had happened this evening. While he was her employee, he'd been with her long enough to earn the right to worry and fuss if she took risks. But right now, she needed his obedience. Fortunately, as he took his leave, it helped her own nerves. Now it was just her and them, no innocent bystanders.

Fixing on a smile, she turned and faced the copper-haired one. "Mr. Barnabus? You were seeking a guest here?" She didn't extend a hand as she might to most guests. She wasn't intending for them to get a grip on her in any way, and vampires could be like wild dogs if meat was dangled in front of them. Easily distracted from their objective.

"Daegan Rei owns this place." His sibilant lisp ran a chill up her spine.

"I'm afraid you've been misinformed. I own this place. And there are no previous owners. I created Atlantis."

Barnabus gave her a once-over, and his nostrils flared. "You got vamp smell on you. You're his. Where is he?"

"Excuse me?" She raised a brow. "Mr. Barnabus, you may not be aware of what kind of club this is. I'm not sure what you mean by 'vamp,' but if you're implying I'm some kind of prostitute, we run a legal BDSM club here. I'm one of the practicing Dommes. If you . . . smell someone . . . perhaps it was one of the clients I tended tonight? While I'm not at liberty to provide member information, I can tell you I don't recognize that name. Aliases are often used."

He stared at her. That empty expression chilled her further. When he took a step forward, she stood her ground, forced everything trembling inside to stay inside. The brandy helped, a fiery source of courage. "He's not here," Barnabus repeated.

"No." She held his gaze. "No one by that name is here."

"Pity," he said at last. "I guess I'll figure out another way to get a message to him."

Before she could blink, he was touching her face, his finger sliding along her cheekbone, others coiling in her hair. Not his fingers; his friends'. They'd closed around her left and right sides faster than she could follow, and their hunger was a repulsive, overpowering heat.

"Gentlemen," she said, knowing her pulse rate was increasing in a perilous way. It took enormous effort to keep her voice steady. She had to slow her words down to accomplish it, and she still cracked over a few syllables, mentally cursing her lack of composure. "As I said, I am not a prostitute. If you are interested in the club's services, you may return to the front desk and we will take your membership application. Review takes several days, however, while we run a background check."

During which time, she would do everything possible to keep them from coming back into her club. Making her movements firm, decisive, a dismissal not a retreat, she stepped backward. She backed into another solid male.

Glancing up, she saw Gideon stood behind her, his gaze fixed on the three vamps. He had the look of a warrior focused on one single objective. His hands settled on her hips, steadying her. Vaguely, she noted his hair was still damp, unruly because he'd carelessly slicked it back with his fingers, and he wore the staff T-shirt she'd provided.

Notwithstanding the abrupt and disappointing end to their session together, pride and anger couldn't suppress the knee-weakening relief. Or the foolish spike of response ricocheting through her woman's body at the sight of him here, championing her, all tough leather and denim and sharp blue eyes. Of course, fear almost instantly laced the reaction, because she didn't want him to come to harm, either. Daegan had told her not many vampires actually knew Gideon Green's face, only his reputation, but it might be a matter of minutes before he changed that.

"Mr. Smith." With additional effort, she kept her tone pleasant, professional. "I'm so glad you stopped in before you left. There's some paperwork I need you to look over. Mr. Barnabus, if we're finished . . ." She raised a brow, and looked back at the vampire, hoping her expression was suitably neutral and unassuming.

His lip curled, revealing a flash of prominent fang. "Not finished, Miss Naime. But done for now." She had the disturbing feeling he was laughing at her, in the nasty way a cat laughed at a mouse for thinking it had escaped, when the cat knew exactly where the mouse's nest was and would be waiting there later. "If you happen to meet 'someone' named Daegan Rei, you tell him that he takes one of mine, I'll make one of his. He'll understand."

Fortunately, there were two openings to the room. The vampires took the other one back toward the lobby, so they didn't have to come anywhere near Gideon, though the other two vampires kept their gazes locked with the vampire hunter's until they turned and followed Barnabus. Gideon, however, didn't take his eyes off of them until they disappeared around the corner.

"Thank you for not interfering." Anwyn spoke after a still moment, realizing they'd both remained silent, waiting until they heard Jack, the doorman, obliviously bid the vampires good night. She touched the earpiece. "We're clear, James. They're gone. I'm with a client now, but will come to the security office shortly."

Gideon's hand moved from her hip to her arm, turning her toward him. Anwyn drew in a breath at the feel of his heated palm. "I didn't give you permission to touch me, Gideon."

"I thought we pretty much agreed playtime was over," he returned, his gaze shuttered. "Who is Daegan Rei, Anwyn? I've never heard of him."

"You found out my name."

"I listen. That's how I found out you might be in a tight spot. Heard your security chief telling a couple of your guys to be ready if Anwyn needed help dealing with a Code Seven. Which I assume means unruly guests, rather than specifically vampires. Answer my question."

Her chin came up. "I believe we already covered that. You haven't earned the right to question me. I'm also sure you heard me say there's no guest here by that name."

"I saw the marks. You've got a vamp claim on you, whatever you want to call it."

"Keep your voice down."

He stepped closer, so the heat between the two of them caressed her face, made her press her lips together in irritating need for what they'd left unfinished. She could have helped him to surrender, given him so much of what he needed. But sometimes a toy was too broken to be fixed, right?

"Do you really know what you're doing, Anwyn?" The true concern in his gaze leaned on her already thin defenses. He was used to protecting, took it seriously. Seriously enough that it may have destroyed his potential to give any part of his heart to another, as she'd clearly seen tonight. "You can't be friends with one of them. Their whole world comes with them. Trash like what just left. Does your vampire understand that?"

"You don't have the right—"

"Don't play Mistress with me. This is your life—"

"Nothing about what I do here is play," she shot back, low. "Now, get out. I may not have the manpower to throw those three out bodily, but I think James and his crew can handle you. And remember"—she tossed her hair back—"I'm merely some vampire's bitch in heat."

His jaw tightened. "I shouldn't have said that. I'm sorry."

"No, you're not." Her nerves, stretched thin by that near miss, by the personal truths his observations had touched, snapped. "You couldn't have been more repulsed if you'd seen open weeping sores on my leg. So don't pretend like you care. This is about you wanting the whole world to see things your way. Black and white. Vampires are evil, and should all be dead. Well, I can tell you something. I've seen evil up close, and it didn't have a whiff of vampire to it when it took what it wanted. It's not the physical form that makes something evil."

"And one more thing." She forged on when he opened his mouth.

"Nothing outside of you destroys who you are, what you want to be. If you're strong enough, you can put it back together, no matter who or what shatters you. From everything I've seen, you're strong as hell. So when you look in a mirror, stop blaming vampires for the wreck you've made of yourself. There was no vampire in that room tonight. Whatever did or didn't happen there was your fault, and your fault only."

She stopped herself, appalled at her outburst. She prided herself on her calm, her reserve, and here she was, snarling at him with almost as little control as he'd demonstrated earlier. His expression was nearly bloodless.

"Anwyn—"

"No. We're done here, Gideon. For the last time, get out." When he lifted a hand, she stepped back. "Don't try to touch me."

If he did, she was afraid the many things roiling through her now would detonate. She should have had two brandies. What she hated most of all was that she wished Daegan were here. She wished there were someone in the world she could rely upon and trust, no matter what. It was an old longing, and a dangerous one. She shoved it aside.

"Anwyn." Ignoring her demand, he settled his hands on her shoulders, those long arms easily reaching over the distance she'd put between them. His hands were strong and sure. Reassuring. Gideon's gaze was steady, not seeking anything from her, but offering something of himself.

"I'll go, I promise. But are you sure you're okay?"

Damn it, damn it. Goddess save her from alpha males, and their irritating habit of switching from emotionally closed, dysfunctional pains in the ass to knights in shining armor in a heartbeat, sweeping a woman's legs right out from under her.

She drew a deep breath. With deliberate intent, she closed one hand over his wrist, knowing that while she was doing it to appear composed, she was using the contact to actually reclaim some composure. "Thank you, Gideon. Yes, I am. I shouldn't have spoken to you that way."

His lip curved at the corner, a wry self-deprecation that surprised her. "You weren't all wrong. Doesn't mean I enjoy hearing it."

She shook her head. "I meant saying you don't care. I know right

and wrong matter to you. Protecting those who can't protect themselves. But I can protect myself. You don't need to worry about me."

He brushed a hand across her cheek. "Too late." Then he hooked his
thumbs in his jeans pockets, as if irritated with himself. "I won't come
back here. Not to the club. But . . . if you find you'd like a cup of coffee
or something tomorrow . . . You do have a life outside here, right?"

"As much as you have a life outside of what you do. It doesn't often
go well when I try."

"Well, we've already established I'm a train wreck, so what do you
have to lose from visiting the crash site and having a latte at the same
time?" He sighed, his hands curling as if he needed the restraint to keep
from touching her. "I'm rough, and I fuck up everything, Anwyn. But
I don't dress things up, and I don't play games. When I figure something
out, I say it pretty plain. I shouldn't want anything more to do with you.
You're right about the way I felt, when I saw that mark. The way I feel
about them." He shook his head, a quick jerk, when she stiffened. "But
the other things that happened between us . . . I'm no good for any
woman, and I fully expect you to tell me to fuck off, but I'll only be here
a little longer. No matter how stupid it sounds, how little sense it makes
to either one of us, I want the chance to see you again."

The residual heat of their battle became a different kind of warmth
as he stumbled over the words. But then, she'd known it was a smoke
screen all along. "That is a terrible apology," she observed after a long
silence. "Probably the worst I've ever heard. You're not really sorry
about the way you acted, but you want to see me again."

"Well, me and Don Juan, we don't hang out as much as we
used to."

Reaching out, she touched his face. A long time ago, she'd learned
to live in the moment, just as she'd told James. Just because they'd had
a pretty bad moment, it didn't mean this moment couldn't be better.
She had to proceed cautiously, though. It had been a far too interesting
night, and while she believed in seizing opportunities, she was careful
about her grip. And he was correct. Just because he couldn't shake the
inexplicable connection he felt to her, nothing had changed in his opinion of vampires or those who associated with them. Wanting to be with
someone who represented what a man despised usually led to more

self-hatred. Gideon was already carrying around a world's worth of that, enough to bring down everyone in his proximity if his rage and frustration with it got out of hand.

The problem was, she couldn't shake that lingering sense of connection, either.

Gideon's hand closed over her wrist, a gentle but firm touch, his thumb sliding up her pulse as he turned his head, pressed a kiss into her palm. He held that position as she stroked her other hand through his damp hair, down to rest on the juncture of his throat and shoulder. "All right," she said quietly. "Let me think about it. Check back at the desk tomorrow night. If I decide to meet you, I'll leave a message there. But I'll set the time and place, and you may want to work a little harder on that apology in the interim."

"I can't apologize for my beliefs, Anwyn." His jaw set, lips pressing together. "I won't lie about that just to see you again. I can't be any less than what I am."

"Can you be more?" Before he could respond to that, she added, "You should never lie to me at all. But I can tell you, Gideon, as repulsed as you are by what I may or may not be, there's a part of you burning to understand it. Maybe that's as much why you want to see me again as anything else."

"No," he said, locking with her gaze. "It's something far different from that. Otherwise, I'd be leaving town tonight."

He stepped back then, but he held on to her hand a second longer before he let go. Anwyn didn't say anything further, but then, neither did he. His eyes and expression spoke eloquently for him, though the myriad emotions were hard to untangle. Giving her a nod, he turned on his heel and walked away.

After he disappeared and she heard Jack bid him a good night, Anwyn folded her fingers over the heat of his touch. Closing her eyes, she imagined him stepping out into the darkness, swallowed by the shadows. While he was so close to being consumed by them, he'd been possessed of a deadly confidence and lethal calm with Barnabus. Sometimes, in the struggle to strip a man bare, she forgot how formidable and competent he could be with his armor in place.

Because, as she well knew, those shields weren't an illusion. People needed them for the daily battle. The problem was, if Gideon had lost the person beneath them, he'd lost the war.

Good grief, enough of the Obi-Wan internal narrative.

She shook her head at herself, shook herself out of this moment. It was time to deal with James and any other pressing matters, take a long, soaking bath and catch up on paperwork. Feed her troop of feral cats. No matter her difficulties taming feral men, she was determined to gentle a feline enough that it would come live in her quarters, curl up in her bed at night. A dependably regular warm body, for Goddess's sake.

Daegan had teased her about it. He'd pointed out that, while she could easily adopt a kitten from a shelter, she'd apparently be satisfied only with a fierce tom she'd tamed herself.

The thought gave her a bit of a smile. Time to turn it all off for a little while. Like Daegan, her day was her night, and she'd sleep most of tomorrow away, in preparation for Saturday night. It was even busier than Friday. Still, she might make time for a late afternoon coffee break. Particularly if it meant the chance to tame another fierce tom.

Nursing that smile, holding on to it, she strode back into her world.

*H*ᴇ *takes one of mine, I'll make one of his.*

Gideon woke, his heart thumping hard against his chest. Glancing at the clock, he saw it was three thirty a.m. Of course. The mystics all said that evil had a special hold on the three a.m. hour, and that was why so many woke near it, as if something had crawled over their graves. Only his intuition was sharp enough to narrow it down further than that.

Sitting up on the abysmal piece of plywood that passed for a mattress at his cheap motel, he rubbed his face, listening. His body was tense and loose at once, as it often was right before he entered a fight. But there was something else here. A bitter taste in his mouth, a tightness in his gut. Anxiety. He didn't feel anxiety, not when he was fighting a vamp. Not for some time now. Only if the vampire had a victim . . . someone's life at stake.

I'll figure out another way to get a message to him.

"Son of a bitch." He was out of the bed, pulling on his shirt and jeans fast. What had he been thinking? He should have freaking stood watch outside her place. Hell, followed them out of the club, started to track them. Unlike his conflicted feelings about killing Trey, there was no question in his mind about *those* three making a positive contribution to their human community. Stupid, fucking idiot.

The battered gray Nova had a dragon's heart. It roared to life as he squealed onto the road from the hotel parking lot, headed back toward the city's west side, where the lights of Atlantis were still on. He hoped it was a good sign, that the Mistress of Atlantis was shining just as bright.

~

He practically barreled through the door, mowing down a couple patrons. James was handling the closing shift at the desk. His gaze snapped up, then cooled at the sight of Gideon. "I believe Mistress Naime—"

"Is she here?"

"That's none—"

Gideon snarled, brought his fist slamming down on the desk. "I don't need to see her. Is she here? Have you seen her tonight? Verified she's okay? He said he was going to leave another kind of message. You did hear that, right?" While most of her staff wouldn't know a vampire from a pasty actor with fake fangs and a trendy hairstyle, it had been clear James was in the loop. Gideon wasn't in the mood to play games.

The man's eyes narrowed, but he reached for the radio on the desk. "Tom, I need a location check on Mistress Naime. When was the last time you saw her?"

"About two hours ago. She said she was heading to bed after she checked with the kitchen staff. Aka, after she fed those cats we're not supposed to know she feeds."

James's lips twitched, but Gideon leaned into his personal space, earning another warning look. His hand was already below Gideon's line of sight, and while he was sure the man had a baton or Taser under there to calmly use if needed, he didn't give a shit. "Has anyone checked on her?"

"Her private rooms are on an underground level," James said flatly. "There are no windows or other access points that wouldn't go past me."

"I mean, did anyone see her coming back from feeding the cats?"

"That's the alley outside the kitchen. The staff would have noticed if she didn't come back in."

"This was your Friday night crowd. You've had what, a billion people come through here? Would the staff really be paying attention to whether or not she came back in?" Gideon clenched his jaw hard enough to break. "Check on her. Get a visual. Where's that alleyway?"

James proved he was worth the money Anwyn paid him by not getting his dick in a twist at Gideon's attempt to order him around. In fact, Gideon could see him considering his words seriously, though his gaze remained steel. "If it gets you out of my face, it's on the east side, in the back, behind the Dumpsters. We'll go check her rooms. But I can tell you, you aren't going to get anywhere with the stalker routine. She'll eat you for lunch. She doesn't intimidate."

"That's what's worrying me," Gideon said curtly. "I'll be back here, waiting for you."

He strode back out the front doors, checked the gun in the small of his back and wrist gauntlets loaded with wooden arrows as he cut past the corner and into the darkness on the east side. No matter what demons had rattled him earlier, this he knew. He fell into hunter mode, moving with the shadows. He knew where his weapons were, was ready to use them in a blink. Faster than a blink even, his intuition on full alert and sharp as a blade.

Despite that, he hoped he was wrong, that he was crazy paranoid and she was fine. She was going to be in her bed, as James said. Maybe she'd don some satiny, flowing robe that showed off all those curves, march up to the lobby and tell him he was a fucking menace who needed to be committed. And that would be just fine.

As he slid deeper into the alley, his heart rate increased. Laura had been killed in an alley. Her pale yellow dress had been soaked with blood, the gold chain with his senior high school ring wrapped tight on her throat to keep it out of the way of the vampire who'd torn into her carotid. The ring idea had been old-fashioned, yeah, but she'd been like that. So had he. She'd even liked wearing his varsity jacket. Guess the two of them would have made more sense in the fifties. When what scared people were Communists, not vampires. Not facing a lonely, empty existence because you threw away what you loved, didn't protect her when she needed protecting.

Fuck it. Focus.

He saw the line of Dumpsters, the service door to the kitchen. He

remained motionless in the darkness, his gaze coursing over every object, identifying it, searching for movement or any still spot that felt
wrong. There was no wind in the alley to carry his scent, but if they'd
heard him coming, they could have melted back. He knew he wasn't
alone. He felt it, crawling up his neck. But it wasn't someone ahead. It
was behind. It was—

He twisted, the gauntlet already in position to fire. The arrow sliced
through the air high, his arm knocked upward. His body was spun
around and slammed face forward into the brick. A relentless hand
clamped on the back of his neck, another pinning the arm.

"I am not here as your enemy, vampire hunter."

The voice was how a ghost's might sound. A whisper in the night
that sent chills up the spine and made the gut tighten. Then the grip
was gone. When he shoved away from the wall, whirled around, nothing was there. Except the voice, now coming from above.

"She is here." With those words, the whisper became a hiss and the
shadow sprang from the fire escape above him. It landed on the Dumpster and then made the jump into the debris behind it, practically faster
than he could follow, and in total, eerie silence.

Gideon's feet were in motion, his heart in his throat. When he skid-
ded around the Dumpster, past and present meshed, and he reeled,
disoriented. *No.*

So much blood. She was wearing . . . God, what *was* she wearing?

After seeing her earlier in the latex and sexy silk, the simple cotton
nightgown embroidered with blue flowers at the modest vee neckline
was a bit startling. A blood-soaked ribbon caught in her hair suggested
she'd had it tied back, maybe her face washed, ready for bed. She'd been
wearing ridiculous, cliché bunny slippers. One was still half on her foot.
The other was upside down, a few feet away, the pale pink now marble-
ized brown with dried blood.

He focused on the clothes, because he couldn't yet handle seeing the
remains of the woman beneath them. He shifted his gaze to the male
crouched over her.

The ghost who'd spoken in his ear tilted his head up in a quick jerk,
an animal's movement. Gideon had an impression of a pale face, glittering dark eyes and close-cropped dark hair. Fangs glistening as the

vampire bared them in a snarl. In a coil of unleashed power, he leaped.

Gideon cursed and activated his other gauntlet, but the vampire had already cleared him, the rush of air startling for its force. It whipped him around, let him see the vampire land on what he'd flushed from the shadows. Another vamp, young, maybe just a fledgling. He had a trickle of blood at the corner of his mouth. Not high enough in the pecking order to be in on the entertainment, but left behind as a scavenger to enjoy the dregs, because what Gideon saw on the ground had been a group effort.

When one vampire took a human life for an annual kill, the amount of visible blood was very little, of course. Anwyn had been attacked by a vicious pack that wanted only to play. The purpose here hadn't been nourishment.

I'll figure out another way to get a message to him.

Perhaps the fledgling tried to run, for his muscles tensed with the futile effort. However, like a baby gazelle flushed by a cheetah, the predator was on him before he could manage more than a frightened hiss. One strangled protest, and then Gideon's ghostlike vampire had taken his head with a blade he hadn't even seen. A simple, economical slice, made with enough force that the decapitated portion spun off and hit the pavement, rolling across the alley. The body sank to its knees in a parody of how it would have moved with a brain to direct it, then collapsed, alone. His executioner was already gone.

No, not gone. The tall, swift vamp was back in a half kneel next to the body. Gideon didn't want to face it, didn't want to know they were too late, but he forced his feet to move. As he did, he kept a watchful eye on the shadows in the alley, covering their backs instinctively, even though it was obvious the vampire was more likely to sense a lingering threat than he was.

As Gideon approached, he saw that her chest and neck had been torn open, exposing glistening muscle. The bodice of the gown had been ripped down to her navel. Blood gathered in the crease beneath one breast. He saw puncture marks in the nipple, around it.

He remembered the soft press of her lips, the sharp intelligence in her eyes, the foolishly brave way she'd held her ground against

the three vampires. How she'd seemed to know him from the inside out . . .

The nightgown was hiked up. They had bitten her everywhere, everywhere they could find tender, sensitive flesh. The vampire was doing
the same assessment Gideon was doing, such that they reached the
juncture of her splayed thighs at the same time. There was torn and
bleeding flesh there as well, unmistakable bruising.

The vampire's hand passed over her upper thigh, his thumb wiping
away the blood that had obscured the bite scar to which Gideon had
reacted so strongly earlier in the evening. A scar he was now certain
this vampire had made. This had to be the elusive Daegan Rei.

Those dark, glittering eyes rose, and though the vampire's face remained unreadable, Gideon sensed the monster beneath the opaque surface. Barely leashed violence emanated from the tensile body. Since he
wasn't bothering to fight a similar fury rising inside of him, it was an
unexpected moment to feel a click of solidarity, a shared purpose, with
the creature that was his enemy. Then Daegean's head turned, and he
was leaning back over Anwyn.

Gideon couldn't bring himself to look, couldn't bear to see the
empty, staring eyes. But the vampire touched her forehead, and suddenly Gideon's heart jump-started, so abruptly it was almost painful.
She moved, her lips parting to let out a soft moan of pain.

Though the vampire cut him a measuring glance, Gideon lunged
forward, dropping to one knee on her other side.

"What, *cher*?" Even with his exceptional hearing, the vampire had
to fold his large frame down farther to bring his ear to her mouth. He
closed his eyes at her whisper, one large hand cradling her face with
undeniable tenderness. "It's all right," he murmured.

"What is it?" Gideon demanded in a low voice. "What does she
need?"

The vampire shook his head. "She is saying, 'Stop.' Over and over.
She is in shock."

Gideon closed his own hand over her other one. It was sticky with
blood, the fingers twitching. He was afraid to hold it too tightly, for fear
it would distress her further. Instead, his heart broke when she clasped
his hand like a lifeline, her dilated pupils going to him. They began to

swing back and forth between him and Daegan Rei in an eerie rhythm, like one of those old cat clocks. Though it was unsettling to watch, the rock of it seemed to soothe her.

She had some abrasions around her mouth, the corners of her lips torn. Bruises where she'd been struck in the face. She would have fought; he was sure of it. They'd had to knock her down. While her hair was disheveled, he could tell it had in fact been braided, held with that ribbon still snarled in the thick strands. He wanted to fix it for her, comb it out and braid it again, as if by doing that he could fix what had happened.

What the hell are you doing? She was in pain. She needed help.

Laura had died when he went for help, though. She'd died alone. He hadn't even done that right. He couldn't let go of Anwyn's hand, not when she was clasping it so weakly. He wouldn't.

"Do you have a cell phone?" he asked. Dimly, he realized his voice sounded hoarse, stricken. "We need to call an ambulance."

"No. They cannot help her."

Gideon jerked his attention to the vampire. "What the fuck are you talking about?"

Daegan Rei turned an expressionless face toward him. "They turned her. They raped her, drank from her and turned her. She's begun the transition. Without his blood to help her through it, she will go completely mad." He spat to the side, well clear of Anwyn's quivering body.

"His?"

"Three vampires did this to her, but only one turned her. Lift her up, gently."

Daegan stripped off his black duster. Gideon slid his arms under Anwyn so the vampire could get the coat beneath her, wrap her up. An unconscious person, or partly conscious, was usually deadweight, but she seemed light to him, as if she was so much air that might pass through his fingers if he dared to hold her as tightly as he wished. But when he detected her unique scent, that fading fragrance, hidden deep beneath the stink of blood and pain, it was an effort not to crush her to his chest. Hold her in the shelter of his body and say, *I'm sorry*, over and over, like her plea to stop. It didn't change anything, but it was always an involuntary compulsion, the childlike hope that such mantras might be heard, and the clock would turn back and all would be right again.

He helped Daegan get the coat securely around her, bringing warmth to her shivering, battered body. Her eyes continued to watch them both, refusing to close. Perhaps she was afraid they might disappear.

"Be easy," Gideon murmured. "We've got you, and we're not going anywhere. I swear it." He thought she tightened her hand, a small victory. Her lashes drooped.

As one, the males began to lift her together. When they straightened, Gideon didn't let go, but neither did the vampire. They stood close together in the alley, squared off like combatants, except for the cant and angles that allowed them to cradle Anwyn between them like a bird's egg.

Daegan gave Gideon a hard stare. "You have known her one night, Gideon Green. She has been mine for five years."

"If she was yours, she never would have been in this alley alone," Gideon retorted. "You would have been in her head and known—"

Anwyn made a quiet sound of distress, a shudder going through her abused body. She shifted, turning more into Daegan's hold. But she had a grip on Gideon's shirt and didn't let go.

"Fuck it, fine." *Jesus.* Sliding his arm out from beneath her, he made sure Daegan had her. Carefully disengaging her hand, he folded it against her abdomen with a squeeze. The vamp adjusted his hold, bringing her closer to the shelter of his body. Leaving Gideon out in the cold, it had him clenching his hands at the loss.

What the hell was the matter with him? She needed him. He was acting like a kid being robbed of a favorite toy by the school bully.

"I'll get the doors and clear a path," he said shortly. "Most important thing is getting her to a bed."

"No," Daegan said, his grim tone foreboding. "It's not. But we will tend to her first and then handle the most important thing."

~

Daegan did have a cell phone, and he used it to call James. The man let them in through an isolated maintenance entrance, not the kitchens.

After the man's initial cursing, taking his share of the guilt they were all feeling, then his shock when Daegan let him into why they weren't calling an ambulance, they headed for Anwyn's private quarters, which were at the lowest level of Atlantis.

Gideon had learned on his first visit that the underground portion of Atlantis had been a parking garage. There'd apparently been two levels. While the upper one had been converted into the extreme playground he'd experienced, the bottom level was Anwyn's home.

From the outside, he knew there was a private top living area for Atlantis, too, a rectangle of smoked glass that could be seen from the streets. Because it was smaller than the floor below it, and trees could be seen at the right angle, he suspected there was an outdoor area up there for sunning, perhaps a roof garden or even a pool. Maybe she'd spent time there when she wasn't entertaining a vampire. But Anwyn would never experience it during daylight again. She hadn't even had a chance to say good-bye to the sun.

The dimly lit tunnel through which they were passing had an array of equipment and maintenance storage for the BDSM club that offered everything to its clients. Beyond the extra chairs and booths, there were cases of chemical cleaners for sterilizing the toys and equipment, a couple open boxes of discarded whips, probably waiting for oiling. Restraints hung on pegs on the wall and there was the occasional whipping bench or St. Andrew's cross in need of repair.

James gave the military signal to halt and wait in silence, and left them to scout the room they were about to cross. Daegan had made it clear no one could see her like this. Questions would certainly be tricky at this point, but Gideon wondered if it was more than that.

During their session, he'd been angry at her, threatened her once or twice, but he would have cut off his own hands before he crossed the line and done anything to break . . . whatever it was that had drawn him so strongly to her. It seemed Daegan, too, didn't want anyone to see her in this state, as less than what she truly was.

"It's clear," James said, returning to hold the door open for them. "We should be able to cross through here, and take the accounting office corridor to her elevator. No one will be there this early in the morning."

Gideon glanced back to see Daegan incline his head in acknowledgment. He and James held open the double doors so the vampire could pass through. Anwyn's hair drifted across Gideon's forearm, her face pressed to Daegan's chest. He hoped she'd passed out, wasn't worrying about anything right now. Her hands were curved over her breasts, like a baby trying to sleep in the womb, but she was still trembling.

"So you know what he is," Gideon commented, as they fell in behind Daegan.

"Yes. I'm the only one, other than Miss Naime." James's face was hard and closed, not encouraging conversation. Gideon knew the security chief wouldn't have been the one who leaked Daegan's presence at the club to Barnabus. Though the staff might have no knowledge of what Daegan was, they were familiar with seeing him. Was that how Barnabus had tracked him here? And what business between them had led to this?

Living on the fringes of their existence, Gideon knew that vampire society was brutal. Hell, the main reason the Vampire Council had been formed was to impose rules that would keep bloodshed, both their own and human, to acceptable limits—by vampire standards. Even the goal of those rules was not more peaceful, crunchy-granola vampires, but to hide the truth of their existence from human scrutiny.

It pissed him off anew. Daegan had brought her into contact with his world, and hadn't even imposed the protection of his marks upon her? She'd clearly stated no vampire had a claim on her. So what the hell *was* their relationship?

The business office area was deserted, as James had said, and they reached the elevator in a matter of a few strides. It appeared like a simple service elevator, but there was a security keypad. When James stepped aside so Daegan could shift his precious burden and enter the code, Gideon realized Anwyn allowed no one, even her security chief, access to her rooms. Only Daegan.

Daegan's gaze swept over them, but before he could do what Gideon anticipated, he stepped into the elevator ahead of the vampire, held the door open and gave him a pointed look. *Not getting rid of me that easy, bastard.* He had no problem taking advantage of the fact that Daegan wouldn't want to prolong their time at this level with an argument, in case another staff member appeared.

Daegan glanced at James and tilted his head, and the security chief stepped on with them, pressing the proper button. They all stared forward, and Gideon thanked whatever gods might listen that there was no elevator music. It would have been unbearable.

However, as short a trip as it was, he realized he wouldn't have minded something that would cushion the sound of Anwyn's ragged breath, evidence of her pain and distress. Her fingers were curled into Daegan's shirt, white-knuckled and tight. She kept her face hidden against his chest. The smell of blood and vomit, the dregs of human suffering, quickly became apparent.

When the doors opened, they revealed a spacious sitting room with shelves of books and a gas log fireplace. Wide hallways leading from it showed snatches of a bedroom, a study with desk and computer, and a small TV and reading room. There was a kitchen over to the right, with a wide pass-through and bar area. No obvious alternative exits, but Gideon assumed she had to have a fire stairwell somewhere, probably with the same passkey protection.

Daegan was speaking to the security chief. "Transition times can vary. Start with a couple weeks. Come up with the proper explanations to cover her absence for that time period, and I'll keep you informed about her progress. Hopefully, in a few days, she'll be able to do so herself."

Gideon's attention sharpened. He'd assisted his brother's transition with the help of Lord Mason, a vampire almost as old as Lyssa. Mason had said that transitions were pretty much all the same. There were several months of learning to control bloodlust, which was the vampire equivalent of raging hormones in a teen on Viagra, but with the sire's blood, it was manageable. In a normal transition, she would likely be able to check on her staff and appear relatively normal for monitored excursions—very brief ones—within a short time period.

But this hadn't been normal, had it? And they still didn't have the sire's blood. Jacob had needed a drop of Lyssa's blood each day, but that was because of her age and strength. If this vamp was young, she'd need more than that. Fast.

"If I have need of you, I will call," Daegan continued. He shifted his gaze to Gideon. "You can show Mr. Green to the door on your way up."

"Not unless he's dragging my dead body there."

Gideon met the vampire stare for stare, making sure his own was as badass. Of course, without the element of surprise, he was outmatched in speed and strength, so he added logic to his defense. "You're going to need help. You said the sire's blood is needed. I can help you with that. I can help you watch over her, because you're going to have to sleep during daylight hours, and James is going to have to keep things running up there."

"She is becoming what you kill, vampire hunter. Forgive me if I will take my chances."

"She didn't ask for this. She's a victim," Gideon retorted. "I'm not going to stake her for something she couldn't help."

"Not right away, at least." The caustic tone and Daegan's forbidding countenance were a clear fuck-off, a threat he was obviously prepared to back up, but a ragged whisper intervened. "Both."

Daegan shifted his attention to the woman in his arms. Giving Gideon a warning look, he brought her to the couch. When he took a knee beside her, retaining one of her hands, Gideon slid behind the couch to flank her other side. The flicker of Daegan's lashes told him he was tracking his movements, but the vampire kept his dark eyes on her face. James had moved in a couple steps as well, his attention also trained on Gideon, reinforcing Daegan's flank.

"What, *cher*?"

Her free hand lifted, but instead of moving toward Daegan, it floundered upward, toward the back of the couch. Catching it, Gideon leaned over so she could see him.

Her eyes were glazed with pain, but Gideon saw cognizance. Of course, with orientation would come the stabbing pain of memory. He never wanted her to relive what had happened to her tonight. With a gut-punch feeling, he recalled the brief shadow of fear, an unwelcome memory intruding into her blue-green eyes when he'd loomed over her in the Queen's Chamber bathing area. Tonight was not the first night she'd been treated like this.

God, he was so sick of this fucking awful world.

"I want you both. Daegan . . . let him stay."

Daegan's attention slid over their clasped hands, rose to Gideon's face. "Then he stays."

Just like that. It startled Gideon, that the vampire didn't try to talk her out of it or seem put out by her plea. In fact, his tone made it clear that, since it was what Anwyn wanted, it was no longer Gideon's choice. Just like a vamp. Of course, not too long ago, he would have said a vampire had no feelings for a human, beyond the enthusiasm a kid might display at having an always-accessible Happy Meal. But that was before Lady Lyssa sacrificed almost everything to save his brother's life. It hadn't changed Gideon's feelings toward vampires as a whole—what had been done to Anwyn was more often the rule—but it did make him warily willing to acknowledge this vampire might have some strong feelings when it came to Anwyn's well-being and wishes.

It also didn't change the fact that he was still a bloodsucking monster, and somebody with whom Anwyn never should have gotten mixed up. Obviously.

Her point made, Anwyn drew her hands away from them both, shifting to burrow against the couch back. Her body curled into a ball, her eyes closing.

Daegan's dark gaze lifted back to Gideon and hardened. With a quick jerk of the head, he rose and drew Gideon and James to the corner of the room. "You stay at my discretion," the vampire said low. "Do not piss me off."

Gideon decided now was not the time to mention he had a pretty much unbroken record for doing just that, with everyone whose path he crossed. "I helped my brother through his transition," he said instead. "Jacob Green, Lady Lyssa's servant." At Daegan's lack of response, Gideon snorted. "But you already knew that, didn't you?"

"I know many things about you, vampire hunter. Which is why I have my doubts about having you near her."

Before Gideon could retort to that, Daegan continued. "However, whatever happened between the two of you tonight made an impression. On her, at least. I expect you will be begging to leave within twenty-four hours."

"Don't count on it," Gideon said flatly.

He meant it. He knew he'd stick. Still, as Daegan sent James on his way with further instructions, Gideon knew there were also going to be plenty of times in the next few hours he was going to *wish* he could leave. Enduring his own pain was one thing. Enduring hers was going to be hell.

8

AFTER James left, Daegan returned to Anwyn's side, brushed her cheek with his fingers. She didn't open her eyes, staying curled into the sofa, but Gideon could tell as well as the vampire that she was conscious. "Let's go into the bathroom, *cher*," Daegan said. "Get you a bath and into some fresh clothes."

"Is there a woman who might...one of the other Dommes?" Gideon suggested quietly.

Daegan shook his head. "As he told you, only James knows about the existence of vampires. It is safer for it to stay that way. I will take care of her."

Too little, too late, Gideon thought nastily, but quelled it. Not the time, and he was just venting his own frustrated guilt. "If the transition is happening, why isn't she healing faster?" He nodded at the bruises on her face, the torn flesh on her upper body. It was no longer bleeding, but the flesh was still ragged, ugly. Jacob had sustained a couple wounds right after his transition, but they'd healed within minutes.

"If a transition is...particularly traumatic, sometimes it slows a fledgling's healing energy. She needs her sire's blood." Daegan's jaw flexed.

The brief flicker of his glance brought that hint of hellfire again, as if within his body was the doorway to the eternal flames. Gideon had faced some scary vampires, but the cauldron of violence that flared in this guy's face with those mere five words would send them scurrying back to their teeter-totters and monkey bars.

He knew it was nearly dawn, which might hamper Daegan, but Gideon had no problem heading out to get the bastards now. He could pick up the trail from the alley. The vampire anticipated him with a short negative movement of his head, another sharp warning. "Her first," he mouthed.

Anwyn turned her head away from the couch cushions then. She squinted, as if the light hurt. Gideon had been through a couple traumas in his life, and knew how things could seem too bright, too focused. How the body instinctively wanted to draw into darkness and hide. When she tried to speak above a whisper, her voice was hoarse. He noticed she winced as her abraded and cracked lips stretched to form the words. "Yes. I want a bath. Alone."

Daegan shook his head. "You're too weak, *cher*. You will need my help."

"I want to brush my teeth."

When he reached out to touch her mouth, she recoiled from him like a snake, revulsion on her face. "*Not* until I brush. Okay?" Her voice broke.

The significance of the abrasions, the cracks at the corners of her lips, came to Gideon then. It made him want to burn something down. Apparently, there was enough in that cauldron to go around. Suppressing it in favor of something else, he moved toward the foot of the couch.

∼

Her violent reaction had startled Daegan, she could tell. Anwyn hated seeing the knowledge that passed through his gaze as both he and Gideon fixated on her mouth. She wanted them near, but she didn't want them to look at her. She'd surveyed herself only once while Daegan was carrying her and nearly retched, terrified by the wreck her attackers had made of her, marks that she didn't think she could bear to carry all her life. Then she'd heard Daegan's soft murmur and remembered she wouldn't have to. She already knew she'd been turned. Barnabus had told her right before he did it.

You'll need my blood to keep from going mad, sweetmeat. He'd purred it, his breath hot on her throat. *You'll come and beg me for it.*

In reply, she'd spit on him, told him she'd stake herself first. He'd laughed, but it was mean, angry. He'd speared her flesh like a vicious panther, making it hurt as much as possible as they held her legs open and did other things to her. Her blood had rushed away and the serum rushed in, disorienting her in a way she'd never experienced. She'd been determined not to show any of her fear or terror, but she'd broken then. She hated that moment worst of all.

She thought about burrowing back into the couch, but then someone touched her feet. She looked down.

She had small feet, a size five and a half shoe. They looked even smaller as Gideon placed his callused hand on the one remaining slipper, the one that had valiantly held on to her painted toes. She'd had a French pedicure this week. The white tips were matched by a delicate, tiny white flower painted on the big toes. Chantal worked in a nail and hair salon during the days, and she had done them for Anwyn.

The floppy soft bunny ears slipped through his rough fingers as Gideon withdrew the slipper. His head was down, his profile intent as his hand came back to rest on her bare instep.

When her eyes had opened earlier, she'd seen a mirror image of Gideon's feelings in Daegan's face, bottled under such high pressure. Male rage, so helpless in a situation like this, a desperate need to give her back what had been destroyed. It had been too overwhelming. She'd turned into the couch because she didn't want to see it, couldn't see it.

Men were physical when those they protected were attacked. Their solution involved action. Fixing or punishing. Justice.

Bloody vengeance was the last thing she needed right now, her body still shaking from its encounter with such violence. What she needed was a cocoon of generous, passive emotion to rock in, like a quiet ocean. In that quiet, maybe she could coax her hiding soul from the dark shadows into which it had fled. Once she did that, she would begin to fix herself. While she might use a man's hand to steady her own as she assembled the pieces, glued the cracks, she would do it.

But she needed a rock on which to stand while she did it. A rock that wouldn't go away no matter what storm blew over it, what waves hit it. A rock that wouldn't demand more if she needed it merely as a place to rest, absorbing such solitude. The rock saying nothing, offering everything, silent and constant.

She'd heard Gideon ask about a woman. If Anwyn had a close female friend, a family member, she was sure Daegan would have called her in an instant. But she didn't. Anwyn had him. And Gideon.

When he moved down to her feet, gently took off the slipper, her fractured soul felt a glimmer of cautious relief. They would figure it out. Something in her had known it had to be both of them. She didn't know why; she just knew it. Now she had to hope she was right, because she didn't have the strength to follow any other path. The agony of the bites and larger wounds were subsiding to a dull throbbing, but shock was a bone-deep ache that made it difficult to move her limbs.

Putting the slipper on the floor, Gideon came back to the top side of the couch. He locked gazes with her as he leaned over it, moving slowly, letting her see his intent. He guided her arm up to his shoulder and slid his own under her legs and back.

"I'll hold her if you want to get the nightgown off," he directed Daegan.

"I'm not taking that thing over your head." Daegan gave her the quiet warning, but before he could reach for the knife she knew he inevitably carried, Gideon had slipped his arm from beneath her legs and produced one, the blade flipping out in smooth silence. Daegan took it, efficiently cut the front seam of the soft gown.

She was sorry to lose it. It had been one of her favorite "off time" nightgowns. She had a range of lingerie that could make a man lose his mind permanently in his cock, and she loved shopping for it, wearing it. But there was a time each day she was just Anwyn. When she wore jeans and a T-shirt. Or a simple gown like this. In those moments, she was as close to being unguarded, her true self, as she ever was. Thinking about that, she almost drew into herself again. She would have preferred if they'd attacked her while she wore thigh-high boots and corset, rather than when she had no shields raised, nothing to defend her inner self as they'd destroyed everything else.

She was naked now, since her attackers had torn off and taken her panties. She shut her mind to that quickly, because it brought up images she didn't want to face. There were too many shadows flitting through her mind right now as it was, like the shadows that ran across a child's wall when there was a storm outside, because of the trees reaching their clawed arms to the sky. She couldn't dispel them, their sly whispers.

"Anwyn." Daegan rarely used her name, except in command or anger, and so it drew her attention now. He'd left the duster wrapped around her and was fastening it in front so she wasn't so exposed. As she watched his long fingers do that, she looked up into his dark eyes. His firm mouth was taut with care for her. His voice, while gruff, had a tender and unexpected patience to it. "Let's focus on this. We'll figure out the rest later."

∼

Gideon slid the knife back into his front jeans pocket after retracting the blade, continuing to hold her as Daegan slid the gown free, then buttoned the duster. Gideon helped straighten the fabric to make it easier, the two of them working together, hands and forearms brushing. Anwyn pressed her head into Gideon's shoulder, her quivering thigh pressed against Daegan's hip where he now sat on the couch next to her.

Daegan allowed Gideon to carry her this time, leading the way to the bathing area. Typical for a female with the resources to meet her desires, it was almost as big as the seedy hotel room in which Gideon had been staying. There was a separate sink and vanity area, a large Jacuzzi tub capable of holding three or four people, and a separate shower area.

"I'll run the bath. I know what temperature she likes," Daegan said. They'd both kept their voices low and soothing throughout, which seemed to let Anwyn phase in and out of the conversation as she wished. Glancing down, Gideon saw she was staring into space. "Mouthwash and toothbrush are on the counter, as well as her water glass," the vampire added.

Gideon nodded, taking her there. Behind him, the water turned on in the tub with a rushing noise. Not wanting to let her go, and because he was certain she was too weak to stand, he shifted her and dragged the vanity chair over to the sink to sit down on it, keeping her in his lap. She was cold where her face and hands were touching him. He thought that was residual shock, not part of the vampire transition. However, the heat of the steam was already curling against his back, so he knew they could take care of that part soon. Leaning forward, he pulled the mouth-wash, toothpaste and brush closer.

At the sight of them, she came to abrupt life. Bolting upright in his lap with an awkward stiffness, she seized the mouthwash. When her fingers shook too hard to manage the top, he put his hands over hers, helped her do it. Then she wrenched it away from him, tipped her head back and took it straight from the bottle. He steadied her, as well as the edge of the bottle as it quivered, his brow creasing as she swallowed the large draught, rather than spitting it out. He didn't think it could make her sick, but . . .

Catching the counter's edge, she levered herself up off him. He noticed the gash in her shoulder from the stained glass window, felt an additional stab of guilt. Bending over the sink, she put her finger down her throat.

"Anwyn—" But either she was well practiced, or she was already nauseated, because the mint liquid shot back up, along with the contents of the rest of her stomach. Most of what came up was thick bile mixed with the mint green liquid. His own gut turned, knowing what she was trying to sear from her throat and stomach lining.

She tipped the bottle again. A button of the duster had slipped so that it gapped open, showing him torn flesh and a handful of those many bites. At her throat was the one that had turned her. He knew it not only because it was the deepest, the most pronounced, but because he could still see traces of the silver serum that turned a human.

She bent to force herself to vomit again. In this position, she awkwardly straddled his knee, half sitting on it as she curved over the sink. Her loosened hair was swinging into her face, but it didn't stop her. He caught a glimpse of her eyes, wild and filled with tears from the strain. Muttering an oath, he corralled her hair, bringing it back over her shoulders to hold as she retched twice more. She did it until the small bottle of mouthwash was gone.

He expected her to sink back down in exhaustion, her frenetic fit of energy draining her, but instead she twisted around to catch his face in trembling fingers. Her mouth descended on his like a desperate invasion, her tongue plunging in, her insistence such that her new fangs scraped his lips. The grip on his shoulders tightened, a strength in her hands that hadn't been there a blink before.

Instinctive resistance stiffened him, but Daegan's hands overlapped hers, his thumbs resting on Gideon's collarbone. "Easy, vampire hunter." His voice was barely a murmur, such that he wasn't even sure Anwyn heard it. "She's all right. She's just using the power she knows, to command a man's body."

While he wasn't thrilled to be touched by the vamp, the quick, neutral tap of those thumbs reminded him they were dealing with a hurt, frightened woman trying to come to grips with things in her own unique way, not an attacking vampire. He didn't relax, but he did stop struggling, trying to focus on something else other than those fangs so close to his throat.

When a turning first happened, there was a short, intense adrenaline surge, which he expected had been spent by the stress of what Barnabus had done to her. That first surge was followed by weakness, which she'd been demonstrating up until now, but then bloodlust and fits of vampire strength would begin to occur in unpredictable staccato bursts that would get longer and longer, until the savage bloodlust took over entirely. Without the blood of the sire, as Daegan had said, it would descend into permanent madness.

He'd gone through the worst of those cycles with Jacob during the first week or so, though of course his brother hadn't felt the need to mouth-fuck him. Which was a good thing, because Gideon would have staked him, blood relations or not.

A wave of trembling took her. Strength drained away, the fit passing and weakness returning.

"Feels wrong," she gasped as her hands slipped off his shoulders. Gideon caught her waist again as she swayed. "Sick, Daegan. I feel so sick."

"Let's get her in the tub," Daegan advised, threading his hand through her hair and massaging her skull as she leaned into the touch, closing her eyes. "She's not going to throw up yet. It's just the body's conversion—"

"Not physical," she snapped, her head jerking up. "It's like bees, and boiling . . ." With a howl, she clapped her hands to her head, her nails digging in.

Christ, the nails. Gideon remembered a second too late. Fortunately Daegan, while not remembering any sooner, had vampire reflexes. He snatched her hands away from her face a mere second after she sliced herself with the razor blades fitted beneath the tips, leaving a shallow cut across her cheek that had come perilously close to the eyes.

"Those need to come off," Daegan said shortly. "Give me your knife again."

"No." She tried to yank back from him, but Gideon had her body and Daegan her wrists. *"Don't touch me."*

Though it came out as a vicious scream, the irrational anger fortunately wasn't backed by another round of that burgeoning new strength. As Gideon held her, Daegan did it, so quick he saw only brief flashes as he skinned the nails as smoothly as a pear's skin. The lethal tips hit the floor with tiny plinks.

"Anwyn." Daegan caught her shoulders.

The vampire's command resonated through the bathroom, and possibly the entire lower level. Gideon knew generals—not to mention high school teachers—who would give a left nut to freeze motion and rivet attention as Daegan did with two syllables. Who the hell *was* this guy?

"That's enough, *cher*. We are trying to help, not hurt you."

Anwyn was breathing hard. "I know, I know." When she sagged back into Gideon, he closed his arms around her, his throat tight at her distress. "I can't bear this. Oh God, Daegan, I can't control it."

"You don't need to." Kneeling before her, he cradled her face. With his knee pressed to the outside of Gideon's, the vampire was close enough for Gideon to see the strain around his mouth. "You're here, with us. I've never known your intuition to be wrong, *cher*, and you have asked the two of us to be with you. Which means you know you can trust us to care for you, no matter how bad it gets. All right?"

She lowered her head, pressing her face deeper into his hands, even as her fingers increased their clasp on Gideon's forearms. Giving in to natural impulse, Gideon brushed a kiss along the crown of her head, let his lips linger there.

"You don't trust each other, though." She murmured it into Daegan's flesh, her face too pale and gray.

"One is not required for the other," Daegan responded, giving her jaw a light, reproving squeeze. "Don't ask for miracles, *cher*. One is enough for today. Do you still want your bath?"

She nodded, her gaze moving to Gideon. "I want you two with me. Please. I'm sorry."

He wasn't sure why she was apologizing, because neither of them would willingly leave her side right now, but he nodded to reassure her. As she grasped the counter and began to lever herself out of his lap, he restrained his desire to carry her to the tub. If it was him, he knew he'd want to prove he could do something on his own, even if it was only the ability to walk. Once she was upright, though, she had to lean back against his body and rest.

Daegan watched her, his eyes gentle where a blink before they'd been stern, though the authority in his voice remained steady as he echoed Gideon's thoughts. "You will not apologize to us again, *cher*. There is nothing for you to be sorry about."

She nodded, her chin tightening. She took three steps toward the tub before she staggered. Or she would have, but Gideon and Daegan were already there, each man placing a steadying hand under an elbow.

Daegan nudged her toward the shower, though. "Let's rinse the blood off first," he suggested.

Gideon remembered earlier in the evening, when he'd washed Trey's blood off his clothes and body, watching it swirl crimson and pink into the drain. Thinking of Anwyn having that blood with her in a bathtub, where she'd be sitting in it, he grudgingly appreciated Daegan's foresight.

When they reached the shower, Daegan removed the duster as Gideon steadied her from behind. As he pushed it free of her shoulders, it dropped to the floor, puddling on Gideon's boots. Whatever was in her expression made something kindle in Daegan's dark eyes, something that reminded Gideon of how quickly she'd turned to him at the counter and kissed him, seeking to abolish the memory of other tastes in her mouth.

That had been a moment of desperation, and he'd been convenient. Though she'd said she wanted them both here, feeling the energy of that obviously long-standing link between them start to fill the room like the bathtub's steam, he realized he didn't belong here. It was a cold and unpleasant feeling, but this was about her, not him.

"I'll wait outside while you two . . ."

Anwyn turned immediately. "No. I want you both in the tub with me."

Daegan locked gazes with him, and Gideon recognized the look well enough. He damn well better not make her beg. She couldn't take that right now. Of course, looking at her raw eyes and shattered expression, Gideon didn't think he could, either. He nodded.

The vamp guided Anwyn into the shower. He turned on the sprayer, keeping it away from her until the water warmed; then he took the nozzle out of its holder and began to gently run it over her head and shoulders. He stepped in with her, heedless of his own clothes, let her hold on to his waist and arm as needed as he washed away the surface blood.

The lacerations on her upper body had closed a little more. They were still ugly gashes, but where the skin had been torn back, it had now realigned itself. She was still moving stiffly, but didn't seem to be in high levels of pain anymore. That was an encouraging sign, but Gideon knew she would scar if they couldn't get the sire's blood. He wished again that Anwyn had some close female confidante who could handle all these things at which he sucked so badly, the nurturing and caring. He wanted to run that bastard down. How could Daegan remain so calm, so unhurried?

Yet Gideon couldn't accuse him of not giving a damn. The very control that Daegan was exercising had a simmering power to it, a reserve that was building into something. He wondered if Anwyn even picked up on it, because it seemed to vibrate on a very male frequency that thrummed between him and Gideon whenever their eyes met.

Taking her out of the shower, Daegan brought Anwyn back to the tub, easing her down on its porcelain edge. Making sure she was steady, he turned away, carelessly unbuttoning his wet black shirt and straightening the cuffs to unfasten them. The garment fit his shoulders perfectly, as only custom-tailored clothing did. It wasn't the first time Gideon had sourly wondered why *GQ* style always seemed to come along with the great looks of the vampire species. Even Jacob, who'd always had bohemian taste in clothing, wore his T-shirts and jeans with an entirely different air, as if the clothes melded to his body better since he'd become a vamp.

Fuck it. Since it was obvious they might need to help her wash, he could take off everything but his jeans, so she didn't feel so vulnerable, sitting there fully naked, the curves of her body so female and exposed it made it hard for him to speak. When he slid the tongue of his worn belt free, she leaned against the tile wall, her eyes drifting to him. "Stay facing me, Gideon," she said softly. "I like to watch a man undress."

It was damned unexpected, hearing the shadow of the tone he'd heard only a few hours before. But each time he'd had a narrow escape, he'd felt an almost immediate, burning urge to find another vamp and stake him with a vicious triumph, reinforcing that he still lived. That Gideon Green the vampire hunter still existed. Because that was the core of his identity, who he was.

Anwyn Naime was a Domme. He'd known it, felt it down to his soul when she first walked into the Queen's Chamber. Just like him, she was already moving to reclaim that, reassuring herself that they hadn't destroyed what made her who she was.

It was so good to see her reaching for it, he obliged without complaint. Propping a shoulder against the wall, he tugged off one boot, then the other. Hell, it was just skin, and he wasn't that modest, anyway. He was still pretty clean from his earlier shower, except for the blood that he'd gotten on his shirt from carrying her. Before his fitful few hours of sleep, he'd refused the relief of his hand, knowing he'd only imagine it was her slick cunt, what he'd denied himself.

He bit back a curse, realizing that was entirely the wrong thought to have, because his brainless cock started filling with blood. She noticed, of course, her blue-green gaze sliding to the sudden strain of denim accommodating his greater size. When she straightened, her hair fell across the right breast, the strands so long they tickled the seam of her thighs, drawing his gaze to the point of her sex.

"I'm sorry," he said gruffly, and would have turned away, but her hand fluttered up, stopping him. She wasn't close enough to touch him, but her expression said she might want to. As a result, it continued to harden, oblivious to his irritation with it.

"I like seeing your desire, Gideon. They won't take that from me, will they?"

It was as if she'd read his mind. Meeting her gaze, he shook his head, but said nothing else. For one thing, he wasn't sure any other response was needed, and he was way too conscious that they weren't alone. However, a quick glance to the right showed that Daegan was hanging his shirt on a hook, his back to them.

It was automatic instinct to assess his potential enemies. Gideon noted the shoulder span was comparable to his own. While that wasn't really relevant for vampires, since a skinny geek could still rip open the side of a cargo ship, it told him things about Daegan's combat training. This vampire was as fit for that as he was himself. Muscle was whipcord lean, both speed and power apparently important to Daegan Rei. Whatever he did kept his body prepared for both. Again, Gideon wondered what purpose Daegan Rei served. He had the bearing and authority of a Region Master or overlord, but with his predilection for staying under the radar, he was obviously neither.

With the lack of modesty that so many of the creatures had, Daegan dropped his slacks in a smooth movement and shoved snug boxers off his legs, revealing a tight ass and long thighs. Gideon's gaze snapped back to Anwyn before the vampire turned around, suddenly getting the significance of her earlier words. *I want you both in the tub with me.*

No way. He could stay close, even sit on the tub edge, but there were certain things he couldn't do. He definitely had rules about bathing with naked male vampires he didn't know. Hell, with naked men he didn't know. And he sure as shit wasn't leaving his weapons out of easy reach to have group bathtime.

Noting her shiver, he stepped forward. "Here, let me get you into the water. You're starting to get goose bumps." She willingly closed her hands on his arm as he steadied her with the other. Placing her feet into the water, he slid her off the edge, controlling her descent. When his arm touched the surface, he gritted his teeth.

"Holy crap. Do you always like it that hot?"

"Actually, she prefers it hotter, but I prefer not to boil like a lobster."

Anwyn laid her head on the tub wall, her wet hair drifting around her in the water, the silken waves closer to her face hiding her expression. Yet she put a hand on both of them, one gripping the denim of Gideon's jeans at the knee, her other caressing Daegan's bare thigh as he stepped closer.

At this proximity, there was no choice but to get an eyeful of the vampire's other attributes. Of course the guy was well hung. Most vampires didn't suffer in that department, either. Since they didn't have any body hair from the neck down, it just made it even more obvious, the sleek, pale cock and smooth balls looking like alabaster sculpture. Unlike Gideon, he didn't seem the least concerned he was semiaroused. Which made Gideon all the more alarmed. Had watching Anwyn's exchange with him gotten him hard, or was it something else?

Vampires were notoriously sexual and very nondiscriminating about what they fucked—male, female, or anything in between. Except for the stiffening cock, everything he'd seen of this one so far suggested his focus was on Anwyn. While it pissed Gideon off that his mind couldn't stay as aligned, forking off in suspicious directions, he couldn't help being damn uncomfortable.

Anwyn's shoulders gave a little jerk, and his attention snapped to her. From her tighter grip on his jeans and the way her head bowed lower, Gideon realized that tears were slipping down her face. They made soft drips as they rained into the water.

"Anwyn, sweetheart. It's okay. You're going to be all right." Manfully ignoring the fact that Daegan was so close Gideon was almost pressing against his leg like a faithful hound, Gideon dropped to one knee. Sliding his arm around her slim back, he let her grip shift, dig into his forearm, as she pressed her face to it, silently crying. "Just let it out."

"Here, *cher*." Daegan stepped into the large tub, and sank down behind her. In agreement on this at least, Gideon guided her back so that

Daegan could draw her into his sheltering embrace, let her lie against his chest. He directed a nod to the corner of the tub and Gideon handed him the large cup with a handle there. While plastic, it looked like a frosted glass, with an etching of a graceful lily on it. Like everything in this bathroom, it was as lovely and precise as the woman who owned it.

Daegan used the cup to wet her hair anew, pouring it slowly over the brown locks and following it with the stroke of his fingers. There was still some blood, because the water did get a faint pink tinge around her. For now, her eyes were closed, but Gideon didn't want her to notice that when they opened. He rose, dimming the lights. Noting a bevy of white candles on a silver tray on the counter, he found the lighter next to them and further shadowed the details of the room in flickering candlelight.

While he didn't appreciate such ambience, he knew women did, using it to calm themselves. He'd recognized the candles' scent as the one that lingered in the room from her last bath. Maybe it was ridiculous to think such simple things could mute the horror of the violence done to her, but sometimes reclaiming the normal helped, fooled a victim into thinking she could make it no more than an unpleasant memory, give it no more claim on the present than anything else. *Went to work, fed the cats, got beaten, raped and turned into a vampire, took a bath, watched CSI and went to bed. Jesus.*

"Gideon." Anwyn's blue-green eyes were riveted on him. "Will you deny me?"

He clenched the lighter in a death grip. While he couldn't respond to her, he couldn't make himself move to undress either, which he guessed was the answer to her question. When she closed her eyes, turning her face back into Daegan's shoulder, he felt as though she'd kicked him in the balls. Daegan gave him another of those inscrutable looks, as condemning as an angel's.

Damn it, damn it, damn it. He barely knew her. He didn't have to do this. She didn't have the right to ask it of him. As for Daegan, he could just fuck off, because Gideon didn't owe him anything.

Deliberately, he put the lighter down, and stepped out of the bathroom. Once out of their sight, he stood for several moments, staring blankly at the wall. Then he shrugged out of his jacket and unstrapped the two wrist rigs, as well as the nine-millimeter in its shoulder holster. Removing the T-shirt Anwyn had loaned him, he stripped out of the daggers he wore on his upper body. He shucked off his jeans to get rid of his clutch piece and a couple more wooden blades he wore there. With a deep breath, he removed boxers and socks.

With or without his clothes, in or out of the tub, if the vampire wanted to attack him, he would have already had him. His boots were in the bathroom, and he could detach the toe blade fast if he needed it, but it was false comfort. Without the element of surprise, he'd have as much chance as an infant. Particularly against a vamp that fast and obviously trained for battle.

He had to believe that wasn't part of the equation here. The one thing he knew for sure was Anwyn wanted them both in the tub. Needed them as close as she could get them. Her reaction to his refusal, as inexplicably painful to him as a lashing with a metal-tipped cat-o'-nine, was what tipped the scales in her favor, despite every strenuous objection his mind was roaring. He'd endured being tortured with a cat-o'-nine; he couldn't bear the disappointment and need in her blue-green eyes.

Anwyn's soft voice cinched it. "Where did he go, Daegan? You didn't make him leave, did you?"

"No, sweet *cher*. He's divesting himself of his arsenal. He'll be right back, fifty pounds lighter, I'm sure. He's coming back to you."

Gideon stepped back in. He'd intended to give Daegan a scowl, but the vampire was involved in washing her hair, massaging the lather slow and easy on her skull. Bubbles were spreading out over the water like foam across a tide line, further masking anything being washed off of her. Anwyn had her eyes closed again. Gideon thought tears were still running down her face, and then he was sure as he saw her chest hitching in silent sobs.

Damn it, he couldn't do this. It was like red-hot shrapnel in his chest, seeing her distress and not being able to do anything but be here. God, he wanted to kill something. He really should go, start tracking, let Daegan do this . . .

Instead, he crossed the room, braced his hands on the tub wall.

Doing his best to ignore the vampire, he leaned in and brushed his mouth over hers, an easy, tender caress, undemanding, a silent apology. Her eyes opened, seeking him, and he stayed there, letting her stare into his soul, see the things he didn't understand himself.

He didn't doubt that getting into the tub with her and a vampire was insane. But the instant relief in her face told him he was going to do it. Then her gaze coursed over him, settling on his cock. It had lost some of its waywardness, but at her attention, it began to rise again, heedless of her tears. God, he was a beast. Before he could apologize for it again, her lips had curved, a tear caught on that tremulous but brave upward turn. He had a sudden urge to place his lips there again, gently suck it off, tease her mouth to opening, let her lose herself in the sensuality that was so much a part of her, banish the horror with it, even though everything he'd ever known about rape victims told him she wouldn't want that. But her response to that kiss suggested a different path, at least for her.

"Come be with us, Gideon," she said.

9

It was a large Jacuzzi tub, but he and Daegan were large men. However, as if anticipating a need to make some room, Daegan had his knees bent, also forming a convenient cradle for Anwyn to lean against. Gideon lowered himself into the water, sucking in a breath. As the hot water closed over his balls, he sent an apology to the sperm being incinerated.

Well, it wasn't as though he was expecting to produce heirs. Last thing he'd ever do was bring a child into this kind of world.

"I can help with the washing," he said gruffly. "If you want me to."

"You know what soap is? I'm stunned."

Gideon's eyes narrowed, but Daegan's remark brought a cautious flicker of amusement to Anwyn's gaze that made the barb worth it. She gave him a slight nod of permission.

Daegan angled his chin toward a bottle of creamy soap in the corner. When Gideon picked it up, along with a clean washcloth, he found it had a fresh scent to it that matched the smell he'd experienced on Anwyn's skin earlier. For all that they'd done in the Queen's Chamber bathing area, somehow doing this was far more intimate and personal, something that worked its way below the physical and made him feel a little more exposed. But nothing could feel more exposed than she was, with her wounded throat and chest, the recollection of the bruises and blood. He was about to kick his own ass if he didn't get past his own hang-ups.

It's because she matters to you, you prick. Pretend like she's any other victim you've pulled away from a vamp, and you'll be fine. There hadn't been many of those. Only four scant times in his bloody career had he arrived in time to save a vampire's victim. He'd soothed them, cleaned them up if they needed it, gotten them to hospitals, and it hadn't rattled him like this.

He worked the soap in the cloth as Anwyn curled up on her side against Daegan, her arms folded over her breasts. Her head rested on the firm curve of his biceps as he rinsed her hair with the cup again, fingers stroking through the strands. When he was done, she watched Gideon approach with those intent mermaid eyes, enhanced by the silken trail of wet hair outlining her temple, cheek and throat. Even so, he touched her knee, warning her before he began to smooth the soap down her back.

He wasn't sure what she would be comfortable with him doing, but guidance came from an unexpected source. "Wash it all off, Gideon," Daegan said quietly. "Don't leave any part of them on her soft skin." He nodded to a basket. "If you put some of those soap petals in, then the water will have soap in it and you can take the washcloth below the waterline and rub her with it."

"Sounds like you've done this before."

"No. Not this."

A particularly harsh sob caught her then. Daegan tightened his arm around her, his hand pressing against the side of her head. He propped his arm on his knee, shielding her face from them both.

Gideon understood that this was best, to let her cry herself out without their interference, as often as she needed to do it. She didn't need their words right now. But he couldn't help moving in closer, even if it meant he had to slide his feet over Daegan's shins, though he took pains to clear them without touching. Those silent sobs were wrenching his heart out of his chest. Daegan put his head down on hers.

This was just Part One of the evening's agenda. Somebody was going to live to regret Part Two, big-time. If Daegan thought he was leaving Gideon behind for that, he'd better think again.

For now, though, Gideon began to rub the washcloth over her skin in slow circles. A plaintive sound escaped her lips. He could tell she welcomed the cleaning, but perhaps the touch reminded her of other hands that had been on her tonight. He knew it reminded him. Even if they got the sire's blood and all these wounds disappeared, she'd still have to deal with them on the inside. The worst scars never showed on the outside. Moving beneath the waterline after depositing the petals as Daegan suggested, he ran the cloth slowly down her side, across her stomach. Though the vampire had said to wash it all off, he avoided her breasts, or too high on her thighs, anything that might cause her to flinch.

Even so, she turned in Daegan's arms. Putting her hand over Gideon's wrist, she held his movement, her fingers trembling.

"I'm sorry, sweetheart. I'm trying not—"

She shook her head. Despite the fact her eyes were still glistening, dangerous fire bloomed behind them. "I want you both inside me. Please. Get rid of it. I can't . . . The bathing is . . . It's good, but what I want is for them to be gone."

Her hands had clenched, and though savagery was heavy in her tone, this wasn't the burgeoning vampire. It was the woman, though her lips had curled back from those new fangs. Female fangs were so much smaller than the males', even elongated in bloodlust. Almost dainty in their deadliness.

"I don't want to hurt you." Though her legs were folded together now, Gideon remembered the raw, torn skin between them. The wounds on her chest and abdomen were fused now, and he assumed that something similar had happened down below, but still . . . Daegan was silent behind her, his gaze lowered to the crown of her head so Gideon couldn't tell his reaction.

"I'm commanding you. Please." Her eyes filled with those tears again. Her face held a rictus of controlled determination, a combination he couldn't refuse. Her psyche was as stretched as a rubber band but fragile as a thread. One more refusal from him might snap it.

"Hurry," she said thickly. She shifted her grip to his forearms, clawing, trying to pull him to her. "Now. I can't bear the feel of them anymore. Please. Don't take any time. Just come into me."

Jesus, his cock was ready for it, wanting it, too. And he admitted it wasn't entirely mindless. *He* wanted to sear those cock-sucking assholes away from her flesh, and God help him, he wanted to do it in the most primal way a male could do it, removing their touch from the flesh of the woman he considered his . . . or rather, under his protection. Maybe both. The feeling was shocking, made all the more so because when Daegan's gaze lifted, locking with Gideon's, he saw the same thing there, only Daegan's sense of possession of this woman was far more clearly stamped, no matter her feelings on the matter. *No vampire has a claim on me*, she'd declared, only hours before.

I'd think twice about that one, Mistress, Gideon thought, seeing the vampire's eyes flicker with fire. He should have felt out in the cold again, but she was calling on them both. Her urgency wove around them, drawing the three of them irrevocably together.

"I will take her from this side, vampire hunter," Daegan said. "You take her from there."

Lifting himself up to prop on the edge of the tub, Daegan reached for a bottle of cobalt blue glass, nestled in the same basket that held the soap petals. As he poured some of the lubricant in his hand, preparing to work it over his cock, it was already high and hard, reacting with the same primitive eagerness as Gideon's.

Gideon wasn't into staring at guys on even his horniest days, but for some reason his heartbeat increased, watching Daegan take himself in hand to make his thick organ slick for Anwyn's rear entry, minimizing her discomfort.

However, before he could get started on that, she'd turned toward the vampire with a slippery sound of skin squeaking over the bottom of the tub, like a vehicle spinning its wheels when the gas pedal was slammed down. She closed her mouth over Daegan, took him deep.

Gideon knew he'd have to be dead not to be stirred and admiring of the way she went down on the vampire to the hilt. He was a substantial guy, so she had to take part of him down her throat. She didn't gag a bit. When her hands pressed into Daegan's thighs, the vamp closed his eyes, a muscle flexing in his jaw as he gripped her hair, holding her as she sucked hard on him. She scored him a couple times with her newborn fangs, if his stoic flinch meant anything.

Then her mouth slid back up, the soft lips pausing over the head, coaxing viscous fluid from the tip and swiping it away with her tongue. She would have gone down again, but Daegan caught her hair, held her off of him, gave her a warning look. With a defiant expression, she turned in the water, creating a rolling current that lapped across Gideon's belly as she left Daegan to prepare himself. Her gaze fell on Gideon's cock now, just as turgid. She leaned forward, braced on her knees as she slid her hands down his chest, her nails digging in to his flesh, drawing red lines. He drew in a breath as she snagged a nipple painfully, but then she bent forward and her mouth closed over him as well.

Gideon surged up into her mouth, an involuntary reaction that summoned a clear growl of approval from her throat. He held himself above the waterline for her, but she didn't look up at him, sliding down his length as expertly as she had for Daegan, tasting and sucking, drawing his flavor into her mouth fully to get rid of the one she didn't want. Her tongue had the flexibility of a snake, coiling and teasing, stroking and lashing so that his cock pulsed in crazed, confused need, warring with the horror and guilt still boiling in his mind.

As if that wasn't enough stimulation, Daegan generously lubricating his cock, growing even harder and thicker, made Gideon imagine in detail how it would bury into that other tight entry point.

"Just this moment." She came up for enough air to mutter the ambiguous comment, but then she was down on him again. Her knees adjusted, spreading, her heart-shaped buttocks positioned in the air, her need clear. He'd never seen a woman go into a subservient position and yet be so clearly in control.

Daegan set aside the lubricant, his hand still working himself. That glistening tumescent organ slid through his clenched long fingers like a living beast. Gideon's cock pulsed, making Anwyn growl again. When she swallowed, he knew he'd leaked pre-come into her mouth.

Then Daegan slid back into the tub. Meeting Gideon's gaze again, he maneuvered one foot under Gideon's splayed knee, so that as he went down to a sitting position, he was threading one long leg beneath Gideon's, then the other, so the two of them were forming a diamond eye, with her in the center. Setting his hands to her hips, then her waist,

Daegan drew her off of Gideon's cock with effortless strength, straightening her as she reached down to hold on to his thighs.

"Spread your legs, *cher*." Daegan uttered the husky demand. Gideon could tell he'd found her snug anal opening from the way she caught her lip in her teeth, her body shuddering in preparation. "Put them around Gideon so that he may do as you desire."

Her legs unfolded. As she looked into Gideon's face, he had no idea which expression would bring her the most comfort, so he let his attention move over the uptilted breasts, seeing past the wounds, and then down to her waist where Daegan's fingers pressed into her pale flesh. Then farther, to the delicate petals of her sex, now open for his gaze as her small feet slid over the hair-roughened terrain of his thighs. Putting his hands on her ankles, he helped guide her. Daegan slid them both closer so that her legs could curve around Gideon's back, brace against the tub's slick walls.

"Aaahh . . ." Her cry was desolation and desire at once as Daegan pushed her down on his lubricated cock, easing deep into her ass. Her face suffused with a reaction so torn between relief and pain, Gideon couldn't bear it. He really didn't think he could do this. But his cock leaped in her hand when Anwyn grasped it, her fingers sliding over the engorged head beneath the water, liquid and firm heat together. "Inside me," she whispered. As her head fell back onto Daegan's shoulder, the vampire slid his hands up her abdomen to cup her breasts, his fingers capturing the nipples.

Gideon had always been a breast man, and hers were superbly shaped, high and firm. With Daegan holding them up like that, Gideon felt the damning saliva gather in his mouth. "Come closer," Daegan said. "Suckle her sweet nipples. Give her comfort, Gideon."

His mind shut down and his body moved. He'd felt helpless with the four victims' pain, but there were certain things he could do for them. Medical help, assurance that they were safe, even the occasional embrace as they shook through the shock portion of their experience, until a family member or medical person took over and he could melt into the shadows once again. He knew how to bring violent justice. But this . . . He'd never experienced a victim needing what Anwyn was *demanding*. He wondered if it was the vampire carnality that had led her to this craving, or if it was the nature of the woman herself. Or if that part of her was already so close to a vampire's the answer was irrelevant.

Sliding closer meant his thighs slid over Daegan's, but the vampire's head was bent, his lips on her neck as she made quiet whimpers in the back of her throat. Gideon's cock brushed her pubic bone, close to her clit. Anwyn jerked up, making the water slosh, her hands digging into Gideon's shoulders again. Gideon positioned himself, but then Daegan's knuckles brushed the center of his chest, snapping his gaze up.

"Make sure she's ready," Daegan said.

Of course. This was about need and purging, not a slow, sensual build of pleasure. She might not be able to produce enough of her natural lubrication, and he could have hurt her worse, the last thing he wanted to do.

Though Gideon flushed hot, he knew it wasn't the time to nurse a hurt ego. He squelched the desire to snap at the vampire, tell him he knew how to give a woman pleasure. The harsh reality was he probably needed the reminder. For the past couple years, up until Anwyn's decree that there would be no money between them, he'd paid for sex. It was easier that way, so he could ram into a woman's heat and release, relying on the woman's professionalism to handle her part of things.

It wasn't about a give-and-take, a sharing or melding, like this. This was far more than physical. While she desperately needed the physical scourging, it was an emotional one, too, driving back her attackers' brutality and indifference to her pain with the opposite. Two men who cared unconditionally about her needs, about what happened to her, at least in this moment.

He didn't understand why she'd known he could offer her that, when he hadn't even known it himself. Yet he hadn't questioned it when she said he needed to be here. He *felt* he did, and for more reasons than misplaced guilt.

Putting his hand to her face, he drew her gaze to him. "Tell me if I do anything you don't want," he said roughly. When she didn't respond, gazing upon him with that hungry yearning, he put his other hand below the water, keeping the emotional connection with their held gazes. He stroked the opening of her pussy as he'd stroke a kitten, his knuckle teasing the lips, over the clit, sensual circles that had her hips lifting infinitesimally, a sweet whimper emitting from her lips that had Daegan's eyes flashing in approval. He could use the lubricant, but he wanted to try it this way first. He was relieved to discover that the flesh was no longer torn, the injuries in that area obviously less severe, at least physically.

Still caressing her below the water, Gideon leaned forward to close his mouth, warm and wet, over her left nipple. Daegan's hand still held the breast, and his grip tightened, rounding the generous curve farther, letting Gideon take the peak even deeper. As he did, Daegan's knuckles inadvertently pressed into his throat. Gideon chose to ignore the fact he was completely defenseless, that the male could rip his head off. In all fairness, Anwyn had held a razor blade over his jugular earlier in the evening and he hadn't flinched then. *Yeah, double standard for sure.*

His knuckle slipped into her opening, and was rewarded by that slippery substance that tasted so tempting on a man's tongue. He straightened the finger, went a bit deeper, stoked the heat so the fluid increased, the passage preparing to take him. Her hands were back on his shoulders, biting in once more as she arched back against Daegan, gasping at Gideon's skill at her breast, augmented by Daegan's clever kneading to give it even more friction. When the wetness increased noticeably, Gideon slowly drew his finger out. Lifting his head, he took his cock in his hand and seated it at the opening to her pussy.

"Yes," she whispered, her eyes glazed with a delirious need for escape. "Gideon, come into me. Now."

As he slid in, the channel was tight, pressure caused by the male vampire already so deep in her ass, their two organs separated by that thin wall of tissue, blood, muscle and all the other miraculous and yet far too fragile systems of a woman's body. Unintended, his gaze met Daegan's. The vampire's fangs bared, his eyes firing, and Gideon felt an answering pulse in his own blood as they both filled the woman they cradled between them. Then male priorities brought both their gazes to her face, to see her reaction to their mutual possession.

"No . . . hands. No hands." Her lip was curled back in a feral expression, a red glint in her eyes again. The blue-green still held sway, telling Gideon she was balanced on a precarious edge between what she was and what she was becoming, but the desire suffusing her face held his alarm at bay. Putting her hands over Daegan's, she drew them away from her body, brought them out into the air on either side of her, just above her shoulders.

Squeezing hard, she left them suspended there for a brief second as she grasped Gideon's hands where they were on her hips, taking them out as well to meet Daegan's.

Incidental limb contact was bearable in this situation, but the intimacy of clasping hands had Gideon suffering a moment of rebellion. He tensed, but at her insistent pressure, the urgency in her face, he knew he'd do almost anything she needed. So when she brought his hand to Daegan's left, pushing their fingers together in a knotted clasp, and then did the same with the right, he held the contact, forming a tense male circle of muscle. He eschewed eye contact with Daegan this time, though, making her the center of his aroused attention.

It was quite a focal point, her body arched, nipples tight and flushed with blood, the muscles of her upper body quivering with pleasure. At their joining point, he could see his cock moving in and out, stretching her labia, the hint of her ass cheeks compressing against the pressure of Daegan's pelvis each time he thrust into her.

Gideon worked to follow her rhythm, timing his withdrawals with Daegan's. Because of the precarious angles, they had to keep it slow, torturous. He couldn't help but be aware of the slide of the male's thigh beneath his, the brush of heavy testicles against his own as they began to come together, thrusting at once into her trembling body. They used the pressure of their palms, the grip of fingers, to withdraw, surge forward.

Her gaze clung to Gideon's face as she reached back, curled her fingers in Daegan's scalp. She scraped his neck when he put his fangs to her throat in reaction, lips peeling back in a way that had Gideon's heart accelerating dangerously, seeing it this close.

She contracted on them both, distracting him, and her voice was hoarse, guttural. "Bite me, Daegan. Take my blood where he took it. Make it deep. I want it to look like your mark, not his."

Gideon had a glimpse of Daegan's powerful fangs lengthening. Right before they sunk in, he had to look away. He couldn't handle seeing that shit, no matter how much some sadistic part of him wanted to look. Daegan's fingers tightened on his in reaction to the blood that filled his mouth. Anwyn's hands flailed out, seeking an anchor, and landed on each set of theirs, curling over them. Of one mind, both men loosened their grasp, let hers in between them. Now their hands emulated the state of their bodies, a protective circle around her, tangled together in the three-way give-and-take of tumultuous emotion, a need to release.

A drop of blood rolled down her throat. Gideon felt a terrible, inexplicable desire to lick it off her collarbone. He lost the battle. He didn't want it to get into the water, after all, and he wasn't going to let go of their hands. So he leaned forward, brought his lips to it, suckled the skin. Following it back from the high curve of her breast, up and up until he reached her throat, his brow brushed Daegan's.

The vampire's head lifted. Before Gideon could withdraw, the vampire made a quick pass over Gideon's mouth, swiping that taste of blood off his lips. It left a feeling of wet male heat lingering there as the vampire leaned back, renewing his hard thrusts into Anwyn's body, responding to her own violently spiraling arousal. It was over in a second, but shook Gideon to the core. Though he recovered quickly enough to catch up, restore the rhythm between their thrust and withdrawal into her, he almost pulled back from the male's touch on his hands. Anwyn's slim fingers were a touch of Heaven in between, though, caressing both their palms, the spaces separating their fingers. She trembled, on the cusp of climax and held in stasis, pinned between their two bodies.

In contrast, the water heaved with their motion, steam and fragrant soap and musky sex smell rising from the agitation. Her growl became an outright snarl. Her gaze locked on Gideon and she bared her fangs.

Fledgling or not, he never saw her move. One moment her face was a couple feet away. The next, her heated breath was feathering his bare shoulder, and he was staring into her fully red eyes where she'd come to a stop, inches from reaching his throat.

He would have been out of the tub in a heartbeat, if not for the fact Daegan moved faster than even that. He yanked her back against his chest, locking a hand around her throat as she struggled, yowled. Admirably, the vampire continued to stroke inside her, letting Gideon feel the contracting friction in her cunt that encouraged him to keep moving inside her.

"He's mine," she snarled. Though she tried to twist her head around and snap at her captor, Daegan held her fast.

"No. Not unless he consents." Daegan's gaze met Gideon's. "Stay inside her. Bring her to completion. Help her."

It was the last that summoned him back into the moment. Looking past her distress, he saw the maelstrom of need and desire fighting with the vampire blood inside of her. At Daegan's barked command, Gideon understood. He began to pump into her again, being less careful now, meeting her need for animal lust. Putting his now-free hand down below the waterline, he teased her clit again, transforming the bloodlust in her gaze to something different, a sensual focus. She writhed and squirmed, but Daegan held her fast.

"Let us give you pleasure, *cher*, just as you demanded. We are following your desires. Just let us give this to you . . ."

Gideon's own control was flagging, and from the rough note in Daegan's voice, he thought the same was true for the vampire. Whether base male instinct or not, having her pinioned in between them, so desperately craving what they could give her, brought renewed lust surging forth.

"Wear her out," Daegan growled. "Make her come hard, Gideon. Take her far past this."

Gideon thrust, working his fingers over her swollen clit, using everything he knew about a woman's body, her pleasure. He was rewarded, watching that vampire ferocity turn back into a woman's passion, a needy woman who cried out at every stroke, whose eyes glazed and hand at last gripped Daegan's forearm, her other flailing until Gideon caught it, held it against his thundering heartbeat. Her fingers curled, vulnerable and needy, into his chest hair, and then he felt victory at the telltale ripples along his length.

Daegan chose that moment to skillfully renew the energy of his thrusts. Her cry of release became a scream. Her fluids flooded over Gideon like a hot spring he could feel, despite the heat of the surrounding water. But then such rational thoughts were lost in his own release, his cock pumping hard jets into her, bathing her cervix as Daegan filled her with his seed from behind. The vampire's face was pressed into the side of hers, his grip locked hard and fast on her delicate neck.

It wasn't until Gideon finished and found his brain, minutes later, that he realized something else. Sometime during their climactic finale, their three sets of hands had come back together, fingers tangling anew. Glimpsing it through his post-climactic haze, he sensed those clasped hands had forged more than a temporal bond. They had the disturbing weight of a life-altering oath.

10

HER surge of vampire transition energy ebbed again, dying away with the aftershocks, until she was lying limp between them. Now she was tracing Daegan's knuckles with her slim fingers, her face turned into his neck. Her other hand slid in a drifting rhythm up and down Gideon's biceps. Gideon could still feel the thump of the blood where they were all joined, and though he was loath to end that bond, he could tell they needed to get her to a bed. The men slid free as she made a quiet sound of protest, but her head lifted, her eyes opening to focus on Gideon's face.

"Bet this was more of a session than you bargained for." Her voice was little more than a weak whisper. Reaching out, he tugged a lock of wet sable hair.

"I'll be sure and put in a complaint to management. Or send her a giant bouquet of roses."

"Men." She closed her eyes, her face so weary that Gideon's chest ached. "You think everything can be solved by rose petals and chocolate."

"Well, they never hurt."

"No. They don't hurt." Her lids tightened, her mouth becoming a hard line; then she opened her eyes and began to struggle to get up. "I need to get out. Dry my hair. Have a few minutes to myself. Then we'll decide what comes next."

"Of course, *cher*." Daegan's voice was neutral. Nodding at Gideon, they both helped her to her feet. Maneuvering her out of the tub, they brought her safely to her vanity with a couple towels wrapped around her. As they did, Gideon noted that, whereas she'd seemed so eager for their touch moments before, now her skin shuddered with every casual contact.

He took an extra pair of towels from the shelf and tossed one to Daegan, wrapping his own around his hips and tucking it in. Daegan held on to his, but, far less concerned with his modesty, knelt in front of her. He rested a hand on her knee, despite her attempt to pull it out of his reach.

"We will be just outside, *cher*. When you are ready to come out, call and we will help you."

She nodded. Daegan didn't move, however, even as she turned away from him toward the mirror. Gideon understood why when she made a startled noise in her throat. Reaching out, she touched the glass with trembling fingers. Seeing himself through her reflected image, her stricken face, his heart ached in his chest like a weight. Vampires couldn't be seen in a mirror's reflection, just as the lore said, but he hadn't known that a vampire in transition appeared as a ghost, a transparent image in the glass. He guessed it would keep fading, more and more, until it was gone. She'd never see her own image again after that, unless she had an old picture or someone painted her portrait.

Daegan reached out to close his hand over hers, but she drew it back to her, shook her head. "Please don't touch me right now."

Tucking her chin down, she let her hair slide forward to cover her face. "He wanted to see fear. I hope I didn't give it to him. I tried not to give them anything. I fought, Daegan. I *did* fight."

"I know you did. I saw their flesh under your fingernails." Daegan straightened behind her, and Gideon saw his powerful hands close, an obvious struggle not to touch her. When he spoke again, his voice had a harsh note. "You call, *cher*. If you need anything. I will respect your privacy, but I can hear you."

Her jaw tightened. "Afraid I might decide to end it?"

"No. I know you are too strong for that. Too strong. You don't call for help when you need it. They were here earlier tonight. James told me. You should have called me then. Could have done so instantly, if you'd ever . . ."

Anwyn jerked her gaze up to him, sparks in her eyes. The vampire stopped, his lips pressed together hard.

"Daegan." Gideon spoke quietly. "Whatever this is, it's not the time."

The other male's attention flickered to him dangerously, but after an apparent fierce internal battle, he inclined his head. Despite her stiff posture, he brushed a hand against Anwyn's shoulder. "Right outside, *cher.*"

She didn't acknowledge either of them further. Merely sat there, staring at her translucent image. Daegan looked as if he swallowed several creative oaths, and Gideon agreed entirely. But after they left the room and closed the door, Daegan jerked his head, indicating Gideon should follow him. He took him into the small TV and reading room off of the main sitting room, complete with two comfortable chairs and more shelves of books, as well as a portable furnace that emulated a flickering fire.

It wasn't overly made up with female things, Gideon noticed, an indication that perhaps she was used to sharing her space with a male, or that Anwyn just had sparse taste in her decorating, choosing only the essential comforts. There was a Waterhouse on the wall, though. *A Mermaid.* The vintage look of the female mermaid, sitting amid lily pads, stroking her own hair, was oddly reminiscent of Anwyn, her unfathomable expression and yet intriguing, lush feminine appeal. Since he didn't see Anwyn as especially narcissistic, he assumed Daegan had bought it, for exactly that reason.

"You will stay here with her while I go obtain the sire's blood."

Gideon turned from the painting. If he'd had his jeans and weapons on, he might have caught his thumbs in his belt loops and taken a hip-cocked aggressive stance that would tell Daegan Rei exactly how he responded to orders. Of course, wearing a towel made that a bit harder, but he still gave Daegan an eat-shit-and-die look. "Last time I checked, I don't answer to a bloodsucker."

As Daegan's expression hardened, Gideon raised a brow. "You can throw down with me if you want, but a lot nastier things than you have tried to make me afraid of them. Think that's what she wants right now, you and me tearing into each other?"

"You're not listening."

"No, you're not being straight with me. Maybe if you do that, instead of trying to order me around, which will happen when hell freezes over twice on your ass, then we can figure out our best game plan."

Daegan snarled. It was aggressive frustration, not an immediate threat, but it was still impressive. If Gideon gave enough of a shit to be scared of vamps anymore.

The vampire closed his eyes. "Put your clothes on. I feel like we're in a fucking Roman bathhouse."

Gideon shrugged, returning to the living area to retrieve the pile of clothes and weapons he'd left there when their remarkable interlude in the tub had begun. He waited to drop the towel until Daegan strode away from him, disappearing down one of the wide hallways. Since he heard a closet opening and closing, he assumed the vamp had gone to another bedroom. So she and Daegan didn't always share a room. Though the fact he had one here was uncomfortably significant.

Third wheel, anyone?

Gideon pushed the ugly, useless feeling away, and finished zipping and fastening his jeans, threading the belt through the loops. When Daegan returned, he was wearing a pair of dark jeans, dark rubber-soled shoes and a close-fitting long-sleeved shirt. He was going hunting, shrugging into another duster, under which Gideon was sure he would stash a variety of weapons.

Most vamps that emanated this type of power had a few centuries under their belt. In this section of the country, Gideon should have heard some whisper about him. The way Daegan handled himself, like some kind of supernatural Special Ops, Gideon knew he had to be dealing with a vamp who had a trained purpose. Would Lyssa know who he was? She was still privy to a lot of Council secrets.

His T-shirt and weapons were still on the chair. Before he could reach for either, Daegan picked up the shirt with two fingers, staying away from the firearms and knives. When he held it out to Gideon, he was close enough the cotton slid across his bare sternum. Gideon snatched it away.

"You were wearing that inside out when you came into the alley," Daegan observed.

"I was more concerned about getting here than offending your *GQ* fashion sense," Gideon responded. "You're not going after this guy without me. No matter what's crawled up your ass you don't want to share."

He refused to step back, even though Daegan had crossed his personal space barrier. Which, given how he felt about vampires, was somewhere in the next state. This one in particular made him feel boxed in.

Daegan eyed him critically, as if evaluating his ability to chew food and tie his shoes. Therefore, it surprised Gideon when the vampire at last gestured to return to the reading room. After pulling on his shirt and jacket, Gideon followed him in there. Daegan closed the door, putting another sound barrier between them and the bathroom.

"Before long, she will be able to hear conversations anywhere in these rooms, but for now this should be sufficient. Can you detach yourself enough to do what needs to be done, vampire hunter, even when it's something you cannot bear?"

"Believe me, when it comes to this piece of shit, I'll take him out singing 'Howdy Doody' and go to Chuck E. Cheese afterward to celebrate. What, is this bastard some kind of friend of yours? If you think—"

Damn it, it was the second time the asshole had gotten the jump on him. This time, though, Gideon was flat on his back on the floor, Daegan's rubber sole on his throat, before he even knew what hit him. He stared up into eyes that had gone bloodred. All right, this *was* the scariest vamp he'd ever seen. Perhaps even scarier than Lyssa in a temper, and that was saying a great deal.

"Shut up, human," Daegan said with quiet menace. "Or I swear by

all the Holy Relics I will rip out your tongue so it will cease annoying me."

Gideon grabbed the shoe, twisted hard enough that Daegan was
forced to pull back. When he rolled, reaching for his blade, Daegan
spun with his movement, picked him up by the scruff and knocked him
face forward into the chair. He held Gideon there, his body crowded up
hard behind him. Personal space barrier completely eliminated. Gideon
didn't care to feel any man's groin up against his own ass, particularly
when it had been naked not too long before, but Daegan's hiss of an-
noyance in his ear told him it wasn't his virtue in danger.

He was being an idiot. He'd been captured by vamps before. Once
they had you, you couldn't go toe-to-toe with them. You had to wait for
an opportunity. This was just a stupid, dumb-ass pissing contest, the
two of them venting their frustration about what they couldn't do for
the woman behind the door. Who was probably going to come out at
any moment and kick both their asses in that demeaning way that only
women could, with a disappointed look and a sharp tongue.

As if coming to the same conclusion, Daegan let him go with a
shove and a curse, and stepped back. "While I am gone, the whole
time I am gone, she will have to be restrained. Heavily restrained.
Chained."

Gideon rose to his feet, gazing at him warily. "Why?"

"You know why. You've been through this with your brother, as you
said." Daegan gave him a grim look. "When I took her blood in the
bathroom, I exercised the right of a sire. I gave her a locater mark,
vampire to vampire. If she gets away, I can track her, but that's just a
safety net. Under no circumstances can we allow that to happen. She
will kill during fits of bloodlust, and she won't care if it's a three-year-
old or a drug dealer."

Gideon did know that. Jacob's bloodlust had lasted a good several
months, but they'd learned to anticipate its cycles. Keeping him at Mason's estate during the worst of it, away from people, had allowed him
more freedom. They'd had to restrain him only periodically for the first
couple weeks.

But restraining her, after what she'd been through . . . Realization
dawned. *Something you cannot bear . . .*

Daegan nodded, seeing Gideon's comprehension. "It's going to be far harder on her than it was on your brother. Not only because of what happened tonight. I have a bad feeling about this transition. It feels different from others I've witnessed. I can't leave her alone during this. While you would not be my first choice, you are my only choice. Even that would not sway me, but she trusts you. Anwyn trusts no one lightly."

"You're giving me such a warm fuzzy feeling. Should we hug now?"

"Don't push it," Daegan warned. "One of us must go get the blood and one of us must stay. Someone must be here to reassure her. I'm best equipped to go get the blood."

Gideon gave him an incredulous look. "Yeah, look under 'nurturing' in the dictionary and you'll find my phone number."

Daegan blew out a breath through his nostrils that should have billowed steam. "You are successful because you take time to plan your attacks. I will track them, find them and get that blood. That's the extent of the plan, and it's one only a vampire can execute, particularly when the odds are one against three."

"Pretty confident, aren't you?"

Daegan shook his head. "These vampires are not old. They are depraved, vicious and likely unstable. That fledgling I killed was young and his Master's residual blood tasted weak. I can kill them as easily as you could decapitate three toddlers."

"Thanks. The day hasn't had enough disturbing images in it."

"Will you stay with her?" Daegan said impatiently.

Gideon studied him a long moment. "It's more than that. If something unexpected happens, I'm the only one who will know how to end her suffering the quickest way."

"Yes." Daegan held his gaze. "I also know, despite your feelings about my kind, you will make it as painless as possible. When you touch her, your hands are gentle, vampire hunter."

Gideon cleared his throat, looked down at the carpet. "Okay," he said at last.

"'Okay'? You will no longer argue with me on this?"

"Your logic's sound. You're not making up bullshit to keep me out of harm's way, the usual 'humans don't know how to fight vampires' crap."

"Believe me, I would not hesitate to put you in harm's way."

"Likewise." Gideon shrugged tense shoulders. "And though I couldn't care less about seeing you again, for her sake, come back. I don't want to make that choice."

"Nor do I. Though I almost prefer walking into a nest of vampires to what we are about to do." Daegan looked toward the closed door. "She'll agree to it to protect those she cares about, but few things are as sacred to her as her control. When we have to restrain her, the stress will certainly trigger another episode. A very bad one. We need to prepare."

~

When the door to the bathroom closed after them, some distant part of Anwyn was aware of it. In that area of her mind, she felt steadier, calmer. She'd made a reasonable request, and Gideon and Daegan had reasonably respected her wishes. No matter what had happened in that alley, she was still Anwyn. Mistress Naime.

She jumped as the shadows moved, and gripped the edge of the vanity. *No.* She wasn't seeing anything. There weren't dark creatures slithering around her, hovering at the corners of her eyes, snickering at her. *We saw you. You were nothing. A piece of meat to them, and they cut you up and ate you in little bites . . .*

She stared into the mirror, at that fading image. As far as symbolism went, it was an in-your-face, direct upper cut. A fist across the cheekbone.

Was Barnabus so diabolically intelligent to know that by turning her, he'd denied her the protective fog that severe physical injuries could provide? Somehow it was worse to have the memories of what happened in the alley in her head, and yet look at the half-healed scars and not feel their pain. When her fingers slid over the puncture at her neck, she forced herself to think of it as Daegan's bite. The pain had been unusually sharp, like biting into an infected area, but she'd reveled in it, because he was driving Barnabus's mark away.

Daegan said she needed the sire's blood to be okay, but she didn't think so. The wounds weren't fully closing, but they weren't gaping or running blood, either. Her hair was softer to the touch, as if she'd conditioned it, and her undamaged skin was almost glowing, as if she'd dropped ten years and returned to the unlined freshness of her teens.

She'd often kidded Daegan about his beauty, about the beauty of vampires in general. *The cost savings in hair and beauty products alone . . .* Goddess, the crazy thoughts she was having, when madness hovered so close she felt its heat on her nape. That heat boiled in her blood, a poison making her feel faintly nauseous. When it had seized control, such that she'd almost sunk her fangs into Gideon's neck, it had scared her to the marrow. But that had been hindsight. In that moment, all that had mattered was his blood.

"I can't do this, Daegan. I can't. I can't." She pressed her forehead against the mirror, looked at double images of herself. "I'm strong, I'm so strong, I'm the strongest goddamned woman in the universe. I can do anything; I can be anything . . ." A sob caught in her throat. "I won't let this beat me."

In the roiling fire in her blood, slowly building toward another eruption, she didn't sense any trace of what Daegan was. It was as if the creature she was becoming was something far more monstrous and out of control. Not a vampire at all, just a demon of blood and hunger. She couldn't survive being out of control like that.

So she wouldn't be. She straightened, turned her back on the mirror. She didn't need to see a transparent reflection to know who she was. Defying her trembling legs, her bilious gut, she moved through the bathroom exit that led into her bedroom. She closed that door before she could see the men waiting wherever it was they were waiting. Going to her closet, she began to select what she needed, ignoring the shadow creatures snickering and winding around her feet, or the endless, involuntary tears she had to keep brushing off her cheeks with trembling fingers.

∾

Gideon took a seat at one end of the sitting room, while Daegan stood at the mantel. Daegan had taken him into the appropriate room, shown him what they would need to do. There seemed to be little else to say, though Gideon's gut was tight with it. Guess if you had to restrain a vampire, there was no better place than a BDSM club owner's private dungeon, particularly one who might regularly entertain a vampire. Though somehow Daegan didn't strike him as the kind who'd let anyone tie him up. Gideon hadn't quite figured out the dynamic between Anwyn and her mysterious roommate. At times it seemed she submitted to his commands, and other times, it was as if they were conducting some elusive dance, hard for an outsider to fathom.

He didn't want to go there. But like Daegan, he was listening for movement in the bedroom and it was hard to keep his mind from wandering into weird areas. The bedroom door had swung shut a while ago, only a brief flash of Anwyn through the crack. A woman adept at not being seen when she didn't want to be.

"You're not an overlord, or a Region Master," he said slowly, his hands linked between his knees. "I know pretty much all of those in this area. I also don't get the feeling the Region Master or overlord of this territory knows you're here, which is pretty rude in the vampire world."

"Are you going to report me to them?" Daegan gave him an arch look.

"Next time we all go play nine holes together, maybe." Gideon returned a bland stare. "So who are you?"

"What amazes me, human, is that you think I owe you any explanations."

"You're trusting me to stay with her, though you already know who and what I am. I think that gives me some latitude."

"And if I tell you that you only need the information I deem appropriate?"

"Then I tell you I can shoot an arrow pretty damn fast. It might just hit your excessive vampire ego. Target's large enough."

Daegan straightened from the mantel. "Then do your parlor trick, vampire hunter, and see where it gets you."

"You'll just smash my face into a wall and try to get overly personal with my ass again."

"Not unless you plan to start bathing regularly." Daegan stepped forward and spread his arms, less than ten feet from him. "Shoot, Gideon. I will not move until you loose the arrow from your wrist gauntlet."

Apparently the two of them were getting pretty damn desperate for something to do, Gideon reflected, because he itched to do it. "You were the one who had to be all honorable and say we wouldn't come in until she was ready."

"She is fine, moving around and getting dressed, from the sound of it. Afraid I'll call your bluff? I will not touch you."

"Let me guess. This is one of those *Karate Kid* moments, like catching the fly in chopsticks. If I pin the vampire to the wall, I'll get my answers."

Daegan raised a brow. "Let me make this easier for you." He closed his eyes and turned his back on Gideon. The coat spread out like a bat's wings.

Son of a bitch. No freaking way. Still, why the hell not? Gideon brought his hand up, even took the time to steady his aim. He was accurate with it up to fifty feet, so ten feet was nothing, but maybe he was waiting for the other shoe to drop. Daegan merely held his position.

Fine. Gideon hit the trigger. At the last minute, he aimed at the lower back, in case the son of a bitch *was* too damn arrogant. He couldn't care less, but Anwyn didn't need any more stress today, and a chiropractic adjustment would be more palatable than a staked vampire.

He'd worked with this weapon until it could fly almost as fast as a vampire. But apparently not this vampire. Gideon blinked. Daegan was in the same place, same position. The folds of the duster fluttered, but that had to be due to the currents of the recycled air in the underground environment. He cocked his dark head, glancing over his shoulder. "Did you fire, vampire hunter?"

"You know I did." Gideon rose, circled in front of him. There was no arrow, not in the wall and not sticking out of Daegan, as far as he could tell. "And you accuse me of parlor tricks?"

"Parlor tricks can be deadly." Gideon abruptly found the point of the arrow notched under the soft tissue of his throat, Daegan's other hand on the back of his neck, holding him steady against it. The dark eyes glittered, the firm mouth too close. "You have some good ones, vampire hunter, but not good enough to beat me."

"Every vampire can be beaten, Daegan." Gideon forced himself not to struggle, holding that mesmerizing gaze. "Because every one of you has a weak, undefended moment. If you know enough about me, you know I'm damn good at finding it. If I hang around long enough, I'll find yours."

"Hmm." Daegan pursed his lips, then shoved Gideon back, tossing the arrow in the air.

Gideon caught it, gave him a narrow look as he reloaded and jerked his sleeve back down. "You moved that fast, didn't you? Moved out of the way and then grabbed it. Or spun around and grabbed it. That's why your coat was still moving."

"A trick's no fun if you know the secret." Daegan returned to the mantel, though Gideon noticed his attention flickered across the closed bedroom door. He wasn't the only one feeling the bite of impatience.

"No vampire could avoid that weapon at that distance, standing still the way you did. I adjusted the firing mechanism and the force behind it to make sure of it."

That got a response. Daegan looked surprised, and then keenly interested. "How did you manage that? The fastest weapon of that style and size is still twenty percent slower than a mature vampire's speed."

"A trick's no fun if you know the secret."

Daegan snorted. "Show me the weapon."

Gideon stripped off his jacket and unclipped the wrist gauntlet, passing it to him. What the hell. The guy could outrun it, so it didn't make it hugely effective against him. But Daegan sat down on the ottoman, his knees splayed, studying it with peculiar intensity. "How did you do this?"

Gideon went to a squat and explained the engineering of it, indicating the relevant points on the weapon. Daegan's rapid-fire questions surprised him as well. The vampire showed a keen grasp of the mechanics, a scientist's fascination with his experimentation. Though he could be faking it, it felt like the interest of one warrior in another's techniques, not one enemy trying to find an advantage over another.

It had been a while since he'd talked with someone as . . . well, *intelligent* as himself wasn't the right word. Okay, maybe it was. Most vampire hunters had a different mentality. They liked a weapon, but once you showed them how it worked, they didn't really care about the design, except as it related to keeping it in firing condition. Then again, he hadn't really talked with anyone much at all since he'd made sure Jacob was adapted to his fanged lifestyle and gone back to hunting mostly on his own.

"Ingenious," Daegan murmured. At an involuntary surge of pride, Gideon was disgusted with himself. What was he, twelve? Looking for a big brother's approval? It wasn't like that, though. It was . . . camaraderie, an alien word to him these past long months.

Gideon groped for an acid reply, something along the lines of "If you're so impressed, don't avoid the shot next time." But before he could fire the volley, the bedroom door opened.

～

Not really certain what to expect, he was surprised to see Anwyn step out of the room with her hair arranged in a twist on her head, wearing tailored slacks and a silk blue-green blouse that matched her eyes. Her ears and throat were decorated with silver jewelry. While the shirt and waistband of the slacks had to be uncomfortable on those unclosed scars, she didn't move as if her skin was being irritated. Despite the light application of makeup, he could still see that turning bite on her throat, which Daegan had re-punctured at her request.

"So let's discuss this," she said, as if they'd just stepped into her quarters to address a club-related matter, rather than having just shared an intense experience in her garden tub. At first look, and he took a hard, thorough one, Gideon didn't see any trace of nerves. No shaking in her hands, no desperate look in her eyes. What he did notice was that she gave them both wide berth, skirting the couch and love seat to sit in the wing-backed chair, which only allowed one person occupancy. She perched on the end like a bird ready to take flight, looking up at them expectantly.

He did register a vibrating intensity around her. Part of it could be the transition she was experiencing, but it could be concentrated force of will, perhaps as formidable as a vampire-turning. She was maintaining a veneer, likely at a high cost to her emotional and physical energy. The question was, how long could she hold the line?

He saw Daegan recognize it as he did, but the vampire obviously realized that it was best to reward the impressive accomplishment without comment. For the moment. He took the love seat, which positioned him directly across from her. Gideon stood between the love seat and chair, which gave him the ability to study the profile of each. He wasn't much for sitting.

"Tell me what I must expect, Daegan." That velvet voice was even and smooth, like the purr of a late-night female DJ. As much as he loved her voice, the careful modulation he sensed was unsettling. It was as if he were watching a robotic or cardboard Anwyn, not the real thing.

The vampire met her gaze. "I can tell you how a transition normally works, but I expect this one may be a bit different. I will know more when I seek out your . . . the sire."

A muscle twitched in her cheek, but she nodded. "So tell me how it normally works."

"You're already experiencing the transition cycles of adrenaline and lethargy, mixed with the occasional spurt of bloodlust or pain. As you progress over the next seventy-two hours, that cycle will get tighter and tighter. The bloodlust will happen more frequently. You'll think it's never going to end. When I get his blood, it should get easier. If it goes as it should, you'll be able to learn control, anticipate the rise and fall of the cycles. Since you already have a good grasp of what control is all about, I expect you'll handle yourself better than most."

Daegan leaned forward, his hands clasped loosely between his spread knees, the duster pulling across his broad shoulders. While Anwyn didn't move, a shimmer of reaction went over her skin, something close to a quiver. Gideon's eyes narrowed, but she didn't move. She just gave the impression she wanted to move, badly. From the keen focus of Daegan's eyes, Gideon expected the vamp could see it as well, but he didn't back off. Instead, he stared into her shuttered gaze.

"This isn't going to be easy, Anwyn. It's going to be the hardest thing in your life you've ever faced, because you're going to have to completely trust the two of us. You're going to lose control of everything for a while. Your body, your mind. Those reactions are entirely chemical, beyond your ability to suppress them."

"What happens if I don't take his blood?"

"That's not an issue." His words took on an edge of steel Gideon could appreciate. "What I need you to focus on, Anwyn, is not giving up." He reached out a hand.

She jerked her hands back before he made contact, an involuntary reaction that seemed to startle her, for she stared at her fingers as if they weren't a part of her. Daegan extended his hand farther, turned it so his knuckles were on her knee, his palm faceup. "Put your hand in mine, Anwyn," he said quietly.

Gideon's attention sharpened. While the words weren't unkind, there was a firm note underlying them that made it clear Daegan Rei expected to be obeyed. Anwyn closed her eyes, her hand balling into a fist. The veneer was cracking, and it was painful to watch. "No. I can't. I don't want to be touched."

"Yes, you do. You're just afraid of what's going on inside of you, and you think if you put on the right clothes, the right makeup, and exert that iron will of yours, you'll stop it from happening any other way than you want it to happen." Daegan slid his hand up her knee, hooked the smallest finger of her clenched fist with his forefinger, tugged it loose and brought the rest of her hand into his clasp, leaving their joined hands resting high on her thigh.

Whatever their relationship, it was clear the vampire knew her to the core, and was refusing to let her withdraw from him. While Gideon would still be pleased to stake him, he couldn't deny the unwelcome relief to have him here now, using his knowledge of her personality to help keep her safe with them.

"As beautiful as you look, *cher*, I'd suggest you change into something you won't mind throwing away later. You're going to vomit on it, shred it, bleed on it." With his other hand, Daegan touched her face, drawing her eyes to him. "Perhaps one of my shirts would be most comfortable to start. But don't be surprised that, as your temperature rises, you might resist having anything against your skin."

Jacob had avoided being entirely naked for the bloodlust cycle, though he'd been down to loose boxers when all was said and done. Even those had been plastered to him from the sweat his body produced.

She nodded. Her jaw was going to crack in a moment, she was holding it so rigidly. Daegan caressed it with a light finger. "This next is going to be hard for me to say to you, *cher*. But hear me out."

He shifted, glanced toward Gideon, then back at her pale, strained face. "Until we can get the sire's blood into you, and see how it does, we are going to need to restrain you, to keep you from harming yourself or others."

Her reaction to that was immediate and decisive. "No." She shook her head. "I won't. You'll be here. You can stop me."

"I have to go retrieve the blood you need," he reminded her. "You wouldn't want to hurt Gideon, would you? Or force him to put a stake through that beautiful breast of yours, right?"

Her lashes had swept down, but now they flicked back up, red swirling in the iris like a shark's fin cutting the water. "Why don't you just force me? That's what you want anyway, what gets you hard."

Wrapped in the nastiness of the accusation was a hissing note that didn't belong to the face of the woman who said it. It gave Gideon a chill up his spine. A shudder went through her, and she was up and out of the chair, moving away from Daegan. "No. I'm not going to become this. I'm not."

"Anwyn." Gideon put a hand out as she passed him. "He knows—"

He'd forgotten how quick even a new vampire could react. One moment his fingertips were grazing her upper arm, the next he was airborne, those deceptively small hands having latched onto him, yanked him forward and thrown him so that he arced over the sofa like a highwire athlete. In that split second, he knew he and the coffee table were going to collide. It was a solid oak, so it would cheerfully crack a couple of his ribs.

Instead, he rolled over a pair of very strong arms that changed his trajectory. He landed with a bounce on the love seat. The impact knocked it over and sent him tumbling unscathed to the carpet on the other side. He rolled to his feet in one complete move, instinct pushing him to a fast recovery.

Shock gripped her features. She stared at her hands, then her gaze snapped up. "Gideon. I'm so sorry." She looked as if she wanted to go to him, but instead, an intense quiver went through her limbs. "Oh my God."

Daegan took a step toward her, drawing her attention. "You walk around freely, *cher*, trying to pretend this is not going to happen, and it will not be one of us you will hurt. It will be Madelyn, or James, or one of the others. Until you have this under control, you'd tear into your alley cats like they were an afternoon dessert prepared by your chef."

His words were ruthless, though he spoke in a moderate tone. When he stepped to her, put his hands on her arms, she flinched, but didn't pull away. "You are a strong, intelligent woman, probably the smartest and strongest I know. If you truly want to take control, prove that nothing rules Anwyn Naime except Anwyn Naime. Until this has passed, *choose* to give us control, to protect you and others. Do that, and I swear to you, upon all that I am, all that I feel for you, that when you get through this, you will reclaim your life and take joy in it again."

Gideon's feelings were mixed as he saw her stare up into Daegan's eyes. Whether she realized it or not, her fingers were clutched on his forearms now as he cradled her elbows. His reassurance was absolute, his authority filling the room like the warmth of a security blanket, a nothing's-going-to-get-past-me-to-hurt-you blanket. Except something had.

Anwyn closed her eyes. Despite himself, Gideon drew even closer. Even telling himself he was the outsider didn't keep him from putting his hand on her hair as Daegan continued to hold her arms. She opened her eyes, looked at Gideon. "I'm sorry."

"As he said earlier, you don't have to apologize for anything to us. And some little girly toss over a couch isn't going to do much to my hard head."

"Girly toss?" She summoned a weak smile. "You were headed straight for that table before Daegan caught you in his manly arms." Before he could fashion a suitably gentle retort to that, she'd closed her eyes again.

The broken sound of her voice was a wrenching contrast to her straight posture, the way her head remained high on her regal neck.

"I'm going to try very hard to let you do what you need to do, but this thing inside of me, and who I am . . . I'm pretty sure I won't be able to let you do it without a fight. I want you to gag me, Daegan, so I won't say terrible things to you both."

"No, *cher*." Daegan shook his head. "Whatever you need to say, we will bear it. I won't deny you any more than I have to. And," he added when she would have argued, "as I said, you will be throwing up. While you can no longer die from choking, it's not very pleasant to strangle on your own vomit."

"All right." She looked toward the wall. "Then I guess the easiest thing is to start with one of your old shirts. Something you don't mind losing. The playroom can be hosed down and"—she swallowed—"so can I, when you need to do it. Though I'd appreciate warm water and low pressure when it has to be done."

The visual of hosing her down like a prison inmate was unacceptable to both of them. Daegan didn't even have to say it, because Gideon did it first. "I think we can figure out a better way than that."

"Go to my room, *cher*." Daegan tilted her chin up to him, giving her cheek a quick stroke, though she vibrated under his grasp as if she held back a vicious beast on a chain. "Pick out whatever you would like to wear. You are the only thing in my life I would mind losing."

"The only possession?" Before Daegan could reply to the painful, caustic comment, she'd wrenched away and disappeared down that corridor.

Gideon let out a breath. Emotions had gathered around her as swiftly as an impending nuclear meltdown. Daegan was right. This was going to suck. Maybe the vampire was prepared for it, but Gideon didn't think he could be so damn evenhanded about it.

Then Daegan glanced at Gideon. "Go with her," he murmured. "Stay at a careful distance, but I think you will be fine. I will be listening, just in case."

"Why me?" He was more than happy to be the one to stay close to her, but it was the first time Daegan had relinquished that honor, and Gideon didn't trust a vampire's generosity.

"Because you submitted to her last night. In her mind, that makes you less of a threat. Less of a threat is less likely to trigger what is moving through her blood."

"I didn't submit to anyone. I chose to do everything I did with her. But I don't think that's the real problem here. You've wanted her to submit to you before and she never has. Now you're in the perfect position to take that upper hand you've always wanted with her. And she knows it."

Daegan's gaze snapped to him. In those depths Gideon saw something that made him wish he already had a crossbow pointed at the vamp, no matter how fast he was. But the vampire did not move, merely gathered that eerie stillness around him that seemed to reflect a desire for violence or other extreme emotion.

"If you understood anything about true submission, Gideon Green, you would know that this is the furthest possible thing from that. You also would not be lying to yourself." His voice softened further, the dangerous growl of a lion. "Your ignorance has saved you this time. Don't speak of it again."

Gideon had a few choice words on that score, but he held them. Surprisingly, Anwyn was back in the doorway. She'd chosen one of Daegan's black T-shirts, the hem falling well past midthigh, the wider neck showing an expanse of delicate collarbone and slim neck. Jewelry was gone and even makeup. She must have been testing her vampire speed, for she'd been gone only minutes.

She didn't speak, her face pale, her lips pressed hard together. She'd tightened the wrap on her hair, added pins so it gave her face an even more strained look. Gideon was moving toward her before he even thought about it. She was barefoot, and he remembered how the stilettos had put her within a few inches of his height, rather than letting him tower over her. While it should have felt awkward, dropping to one knee before her didn't. He took her hand, looking up at her conflicted expression.

"I like this look better," he said. Though he knew she might not appreciate his meaning, he hoped she did. It took guts to let vulnerability show as she faced her deepest fears. Even more guts than putting on the façade.

Her fingers tightened on his, and her lips curved, a humorless smile. Then her gaze shifted up to Daegan. "The dungeon?" she asked, her voice breaking slightly.

At his nod, she tightened her jaw. Sweeping her glance over them both, she moved away from them, toward that hallway. With a look toward Gideon, Daegan moved after her. It felt as though they were escorting a queen to the gallows.

11

THE chains in the wall were like those she'd used on him last night. They'd been bolted and run through a St. Andrew's cross, which in turn was permanently embedded into the concrete wall. On top of that, the cross was inside a cell that could be securely locked. Gideon didn't really want to think about what kind of person would want to be caged *and* bound. Or the men Anwyn had tormented in her private apartments. However, there was no denying the cell would come in handy now.

While they'd been waiting on her earlier, they'd moved in a small love seat and some bedding, a few of her books and a side table, so she could find comfort when needed. Daegan had adjusted the chains to give her free movement to these things, but shown Gideon where the controls on the outside of the cell could be used to draw up the slack. With the touch of a button, the manacled person would be yanked back to the cross, with no freedom of movement at all. Fortunately, there was a dial to control the rate of retraction, so it wouldn't have to be so violent except in an emergency.

"Bring her back to this wall every time you enter her cell," Daegan had said, "no matter how lucid she seems. She can change in a blink, and you will be dead. She'll wrap the chains around your neck, break it, and then feed on you to her heart's content. I'll find a drained husk on the floor."

Looking at Anwyn's delicate limbs, the curve of her back and set of her shoulders, made Gideon feel even more averse to putting those heavy, ugly things on her than she was. And she was pretty much against the whole thing already.

She did well, though, until she actually saw where they intended to put her. Then her steps slowed. Daegan slid a hand under her elbow. "Let's go, *cher*. It will be all right."

She shook her head, but made it a couple more steps. Then all hell broke loose.

She tried to break free, a snarl of protest tearing from her throat. Daegan didn't waste time on any preliminaries. He seized her about the waist and throat, holding her against his taller body as he carried her into the cell. Her knuckles hit the bars of the doorframe with what normally would have been a bone-breaking thud. Grabbing onto them, she tried to get her foot and ankle hooked as well. She was shrieking, kicking. What made it worse was there was no trace of red in her gaze. Anwyn, not her vampire self, was fighting them with everything she was, fighting like a wild, panicked animal at the threat of being bound and caged.

"No, Daegan, don't. Stop it." Her screaming protests were agonized.

"Gideon," Daegan snapped. "Free her hands so I don't break her fingers."

Trying to silence his ears to her wails, Gideon grimly moved in, prying her fingers loose while she shouted terrible things at him. They were no better than the ones who'd fucked her in the alley. Held her down and bit her, gagging her with her own torn and blood-soaked underwear to keep her from crying for help. Men were all beasts who only wanted to hurt women, beasts who deserved Hell.

Since Daegan couldn't see as well with her limbs thrashing before his line of sight, once he had her fingers free, Gideon put pressure on his back. Guiding the vampire, he turned him so her foot and ankle slid free of the bars as well and he could move into the cell without further encumbrance.

Though kicks and punches flew, they got her into the manacles.

Anwyn wasn't a trained fighter, but her bursts of vampire strength gave her the ability to hit with the force of a wildly swinging baseball bat. If he could have bruised, Daegan would likely show as many dark smudges as Gideon himself was going to have in short order.

He'd handle twice as many blows if he could block out the tears running down her face, her struggles. It was the things she said that weren't anger that tore into his gut the worst.

"Please, don't. Not again. Don't hurt me. I can't stand this . . . Please don't do this to me . . ."

Then he heard Daegan's warning shout, saw the lunge in the corner of his eye. Gideon wasn't quick enough. She'd broken free of Daegan's attempt to manacle her left hand and the right one wasn't yet retracted. There was enough chain to let her leap forward and land on top of Gideon, knocking him face forward into the floor. Her fangs sank into the back of his neck, perilously close to his spine, her arms locked hard around his throat. Daegan wouldn't be able to free her without breaking his neck.

Gideon's skills as a fighter, and her lack of them, saved him. Reacting as he would to any vampire attack, Gideon flipped them. Yanking the knife out of his belt, he jammed it into the soft tissue beneath him as his vision blackened.

Her grip loosened and he rolled free. Daegan hit the control and the chains retracted into the wall, yanking her up and back, holding her fast. He seized her other wrist and, despite her cry of pain, forced it back into the other cuff and locked it down. He did both of her ankles as well.

In that brief blink of time, Gideon had made it to his feet. He whirled, rage taking over. Ten years' worth of life-and-death struggles with vampires determined to kill him, torment him, mock his pain with their laughter, their fucking self-righteousness about their strength and superiority, obliterated his rational awareness of her plight. Sheer, harsh survival instinct took over.

"Vampire hunter." Daegan's voice was soft, but resonated with that unmistakable command that captured attention, no matter how resistant or reluctant.

Coming to himself, Gideon realized he was standing with the point of his fist pressed into the tender flesh of Anwyn's breast, his thumb within a hairbreadth of the trigger that would send a wooden arrow spearing into her heart. He still held his knife in the other fist, and it was running with blood. Blood that matched what was leaking out of her side beneath her rib cage.

Her fangs embedded in his neck, her hot breath, had become the fangs and hot breath of so many others, their bloodlust trying to overpower him, take from him as they always took from him . . .

"Oh Christ." He stumbled back, registered that Anwyn was breathing hard, his blood staining her mouth. The T-shirt had gotten raked up in the struggle, caught against the wall behind her, and she was naked beneath it. Her careful hair pinning had been destroyed so she looked like a feral creature, her breath throttled in her growling throat. Rolling her head back against the stone wall, she made a keening wail, a hiss mixed up in the sound. Her chest heaved with exertion. As he watched, though, the red in her eyes shifted back to blue-green, the ebbing of bloodlust.

He wished she could stay in the grips of the madness, because as her awareness returned, so, too, did her awareness of what had just happened. Her eyes filled with horror and fear of herself, her lips pressing together against the apology she already knew was useless. She seemed oblivious to the knife wound in her side, still leaking blood.

Daegan went to her, examining the stab point, and then knelt, placing his mouth on it. With methodical precision, he licked the edges, then across the tear in her flesh, aiding her slowly developing healing ability with the clotting agents in his tongue. His large hands rested on her waist, nearly meeting. Her trembling lips pressed together as if the sensation was unexpectedly soothing, and perhaps something more, but it didn't dispel the anguish in her face

As for Gideon, he'd made it to the far corner of the cell. Putting his hands on his knees, he bent down to take a shuddering breath. When he saw Daegan's feet approach at last, he would have knocked him away, but his gut was cramping so hard he couldn't straighten.

"Don't," he said hoarsely as Daegan's touch whispered over the open wound on his neck. "Don't touch me."

Surprisingly Daegan stepped back. Since he didn't seem the type that took orders from anyone, it meant he was being considerate, giving Gideon space. That annoyed him more.

Still, Daegan's irritating implacability, his close presence, was a clear command to Gideon to pull his shit together. Or maybe he was about to tell him to get the hell out, because he couldn't be trusted. He'd fought vampires too long, too hard. In the end, he wouldn't be able to tell the difference between her and any of the others he'd killed.

Yes. He. Would. With a vicious oath, he stripped off his jacket, unbuckled the harnesses, yanked out all the knives and guns, ignoring the fact he was showing Daegan every place he hid his weapons. Since that was stupid enough, thrusting them all at Daegan to divest him of any defenses against her, or him, was just more of the same idiocy. "Put them in the study, where they're out of reach, goddamn it."

"Gideon." Anwyn's soft voice was a stripe of fire through his mind. "Look at me."

He wasn't a coward, damn it. He straightened, determined he was not going to hurl his last meal, whatever and whenever that was. For one thing, he knew he'd be the one cleaning it up. Daegan was giving him that peculiar look, but he inclined his head, leaving the cell to take the weapons away. Gideon forced himself to look at Anwyn.

The blue-green eyes were vivid like a tropical sea again, his blood still on her lips. Her hair tumbled over her breasts, but he could see the firm, round shape of them against the T-shirt in her restrained position, the hint of the nipples. With the cotton hiked up, she was all long, creamy thighs and shaven sex. The wound was no longer bleeding, getting the same fused but not completely healed look of the other wounds. Despite that, chained, helpless, she was so . . . tempting, that savage sensuality swirling around her like an irresistible perfume.

He closed his eyes. *God, to even have such a thought right now.* Maybe she was right. Maybe one male wasn't any better than another. But only some of them were evil enough to act on such vile ideas. He wasn't one of them.

"Gideon. Come to me."

"Not a good idea, *cher*." Daegan had come back. While his gaze toward her was compassionate, his voice was firm. "Not while he's bleeding. You won't be able to stop yourself. And he obviously does not have any desire to be a donor. I will arrange for that when it is time."

"I just want . . . I don't want him blaming himself. He should defend himself, however he needs to do it." Anwyn drew a deep breath, closing her eyes. For a long moment she stayed that way. Gideon could see her forcing her body to relax, muscle by resisting muscle, despite the quivers and jerks she couldn't control. The frustrated whimpers that vibrated in her throat speared his gut. It took a while, though, and he forced himself to emulate Daegan, both remaining still so as not to distract her.

When at last she spoke, her voice was calm, oddly detached, as if the past few moments hadn't occurred. "Funny. When you bind a submissive like this, the body decides its own movement. Writhing, arched. Begging for a Mistress's attention, or a Master's."

She opened her eyes, looked toward Daegan. "But like this, unwilling, the mind is in control. So you have to make decisions. If your feet are free, do you cross them at the ankle, spread them out to relieve pressure on the lower back? Clasp the manacles with your fingers, or let them hang loose? I guess however's comfortable, right?"

Tossing her head to get hair out of her eyes, she hit the back of her head on the stone with another wincing thud, though she didn't seem to notice. Her lip curled. "And of course your face is going to itch, right?"

Damning Daegan's warning, Gideon moved toward her. Even though the red was gone, he recognized that instantaneous flick of attention from her gaze. The predator was already growing in her blood, making her hypercognizant of any movement around her. So he approached slowly, easily, pushing down his unreasoning anger at her, his justified guilt at himself. Pushing away thought at all.

He readjusted the T-shirt, sliding it back down over her hips. As he did, his fingers made contact with the silk of her thighs. He wanted to linger there, but he didn't. He pushed her hair carefully from her face. "If you want, I'll braid it. That might hold up better."

She licked her lips, discovered the blood was causing the itch there. She swallowed, made a visible effort not to keep licking at it. Unsure what was guiding him, and though Daegan made a warning noise, he took her chin, used his thumb to collect his blood off her lip, put it on her tongue. Anwyn watched him, her eyes so preternaturally focused. He could sense the combustible heat below the surface of her skin, the strength and violence churning like a whirlpool.

"You're hungry and I'm giving you the blood," he said softly. "There's no reason to take. Willing submission, right? That's what you crave. It's so much sweeter than force."

He heard Daegan's indrawn whisper of breath, a reaction to his rash act, but Daegan himself had planted the seed, hadn't he? *You will be less of a threat. You submitted to her . . .*

He'd never willingly allowed anyone, even Jacob, to feed directly from him. The two vampires that had captured him had done it to taunt him, and he'd felt as though his blood was poisoned by their saliva. The desire to scour himself internally had persisted for days.

Yet this was different. She hadn't volunteered for this. She needed him. Plus, he found he didn't like the idea of Daegan providing her another donor. Maybe from a bag was okay, but for some reason he couldn't bring himself to accept the idea of watching her feed off someone else. Vampires preferred their donors to be those who suited their sexual orientation, so a straight female vampire would prefer males.

It was ludicrous, since he'd known her for a couple days, and her vampire lover stood behind him. Nevertheless, he was getting possessive. *Yeah, I'm an idiot.*

"I want to lick your neck. It's bleeding, too." Anwyn swallowed. She kept her eyes on Gideon's, though, not shifting to the wound her flared nostrils detected so keenly.

"All right." Putting his arm against the stone wall and sliding his other behind her back to steady himself, he bent one knee, pressing it to the outside of her hip so he could drop down a few inches, bring the shoulder within comfortable range of her mouth. Her bound arm stretched before him like a supplicant reaching toward Heaven, so he reached out to the end of it, linked his fingers with hers.

This was madness. She was going to rip into him like a wolf devouring a sheep's stomach. Daegan had said it was chemical, that there was no way she could control herself. But he'd never been as smart as he should be. He just followed his gut most days, and dumb luck so far had helped him survive his missteps.

Today, he had help from more than luck. Without invitation, Daegan had stepped close, his hands sliding under Gideon's arms to rest on his rib cage. Though he thought about telling him to back off, it was logical. Daegan was ready to pull Gideon away if needed. Functional, but also a strange reassurance to it, a steadying force behind the touch.

His gut aside, he'd been pissed by Daegan's comment that he would refuse to be a donor. He'd donated blood for his brother when it was needed, albeit not straight from the vein. But he wasn't so much of a bastard that he couldn't look past his own squeamishness. With this sensual gesture of trust, he could tell her that he believed things were going to work out for her. God knew, he'd been in situations where everything had gone to hell in a handbasket. The right word at the right time was the only thing that told him the world wasn't ending, even if it had come close to being the end of *his* world.

Tightening his grip on her hand, he encouraged her to get started before he changed his mind. Anwyn's head dipped, her hair brushing Gideon's cheek, her mouth touching his neck where it met his shoulder. His shirt was in the way, even though she'd ripped it in the back when she bit him there. Daegan slid the fabric to the right to expose the bite area, his fingers grazing bare skin. The brief, startling brush of the man's mouth flashed through Gideon's mind, discomfiting him. Hell, he'd never let a vamp touch him this much, but it was necessary. Whatever else the creature was, Gideon didn't doubt his devotion to Anwyn.

He couldn't help tensing a little, though, when Anwyn fastened her mouth over the bite, but she didn't use her fangs. Just her tongue, licking at the wound, tasting him and stimulating new blood flow. His mind had been focusing only on a way to soothe her, but now he was reminded of other side effects that came from a woman, particularly this one, putting her mouth on his flesh. The thin T-shirt didn't disguise the pressure of breasts against his chest, the nipples a noticeable difference in the soft give of her flesh. Her bare thigh brushed the inside of his. Glancing down to distract himself, he saw she even had pretty knees, smooth oblong curves of bone beneath her pale skin.

Her motion brought him the scent of Daegan's shirt. Daegan had known, like many women, she could draw reassurance and comfort from her lover's smell. Gideon used all his senses to the nth degree in his line of work, and knew he practically had a German shepherd's olfactory skills. Right now, it wasn't an advantage, because the unique male smell, mixed with the scent of Anwyn's skin, wasn't as unaffecting as it should have been.

Daegan had registered the spike in his tension when she'd put her mouth over the wound. His thumb began to rub Gideon's hard shoulder muscle. While he used enough pressure to ease the knot growing there, and maybe he was doing it to keep Gideon calm for Anwyn's benefit, Gideon didn't like it. He twitched, an unspoken message to the vampire to cut it out. The erotic heat of Anwyn's mouth so close to that massaging touch gave both of them more of a sensual flavor, and he was not going to let his cock get hard over Daegan Rei's touch, even if it was just incidental to hers.

Anwyn made a sound in her throat. Her mouth was cruising up the side of his neck, where the artery pulsed even harder. Daegan paused. Gideon wondered if he should pull back, but from the heat coming off Anwyn's body, he thought that might be interpreted by her newly minted vampire senses as prey trying to run. So he stayed where he was as her breath teased the flesh directly beneath his ear. Then she was moving along his jaw, the tip of her tongue tracing that bone, her lips dragging along his skin.

Damn it, his cock *was* getting hard, and the fact her nipples were tightening even further wasn't helping. Yeah, she was getting aroused. No surprise there, because vamps stayed horny about 120 percent of the time with that never-ending fountain of pheromones.

He didn't like the sound of that crude word in his head, though, not applied to Anwyn. Maybe he'd done it to distance himself. *Too late for that*, he observed ruefully, considering he was positioned between a fledgling vampire who could tear out his throat and a vampire who could dice him with his own switchblade and be sitting on the couch, paring his nails with the blade, before the last piece hit the floor.

When she found his mouth, he turned into the kiss, letting himself go with it. She had his blood on her tongue, but she opened wide, encouraged him to plunge deep, another sexy sound coming from the back of her throat. Pressing into her, he let her feel his arousal against her thigh. He moved his hand around her back, cinched her tighter to him, and she moaned full-out into his mouth, the need vibrating through his own vocal cords.

Daegan's hand tightened on his shoulder. The vampire drew him away, slow and easy, as if he didn't want to antagonize the beast, but Gideon wasn't sure which beast was being soothed. He resented being pulled back from the heat of that kiss, but before he could accuse the vampire of jealousy, he saw what Daegan had. Her head fell back against the stone, her red eyes fixated on him, fangs long enough to slide over her bottom lip.

"Hungry," she rasped. "More."

"Soon," Daegan said. "Just a mouthful is enough for now. I need to go, *cher*. I'll be back as soon as I can."

Her attention went to him then, and some of the red receded, Anwyn struggling to the forefront. "Daegan . . ."

"I know." When he moved in closer, Gideon stepped back, but not far enough to miss the softening of Daegan's austere features, the look in his eyes as he cupped her face and brushed his lips gently over hers. Her body quivered, a revulsion toward her restraints, even though it was obvious she was making a concerted effort to focus on him, not them. "I would give anything not to leave you right now," he added, sliding his hands down to her tense shoulders, his thumbs teasing her collarbone. "But you will need the sire's blood."

She shook her head. "I won't take it, Daegan. You might as well not bother."

"You will take it, because it will keep you alive. I won't let you die. Even though"—a slight smile touched his lips, but not his eyes, which were fixed on her face—"you have been insufferably strong-minded as a human. I expect you'll be even worse as a vampire female."

She swallowed. "Perhaps I'll finally have the strength and speed to punch you in your arrogant face when you need it . . . and run fast enough to get away with it."

Instead of humor, he responded by pressing his forehead to hers, cradling the sides of her face as she closed her eyes. "I'm so afraid," she whispered. "Daegan, I've never been so afraid."

Gideon was leaning against the wall, and he put his hand over hers. Daegan registered the gesture, and Gideon didn't sense disapproval.

"I know. Which is why it tears me apart to go. But I'm not leaving you alone. You trust Gideon, don't you?"

Her lashes fluttered up. "Yes," she said, surprising Gideon with the simple sincerity of her answer. "But how do you . . ."

"I know everything. I've told you that before." Daegan pressed a kiss to her forehead and then backed off, even as she summoned a half-serious look of irritation.

"There's that arrogance."

"I'll look forward to discussing it more when I return." He glanced at Gideon. "I'd like a word."

As they moved out of the cell, Daegan pressed the control, giving Anwyn slack on the manacles again as he closed the iron door. She took several unsteady steps under the men's watchful eyes, then sank down on the sofa, the chains at ankles and wrists clanking. As her head went to the pillow, her eyes closed.

"Good. A period of lethargy. Let's hope she can get some rest before the next episode."

Gideon noted that the chains did not give her enough slack to reach the door, but Daegan took no chances, locking it. He extended the key. "It's already past dawn, but I can use the alleyways and sewers to track them," he said, low. "He came asking for me, so he and the others should still be in the area. In the interim, human blood can help slow the madness. Give her a quarter cup every two hours. There are several bags in the refrigerator." At Gideon's questioning look, the vampire lifted a shoulder. "I have been injured, once or twice. Anwyn suggested I keep some here, ready, in case she could not fully supply my needs fresh. Her own human blood can feed her. Follow me."

Daegan moved past him then and back into the sitting room. As he moved out of Anwyn's sight, the unhurried calm the vampire had demonstrated until now disappeared, replaced by the mantle of a dangerous predator on the hunt. He lengthened his stride to a cabinet. While Gideon stayed in the corridor, so he could keep an ear to their charge, Daegan pulled the panel back with a rumble of the wood, revealing a silver safe. He keyed in a combination and the door released, showing a stockpile of gleaming weapons. Knives, both metal and wood, stakes, throwing spears and crossbows were there, as well as an array of swords, everything from a claymore to a katana.

Stripping off his coat, Daegan methodically began arming himself, much as Gideon did on a normal vampire-hunting workday. The duster had a place to hang the sword so it would be concealed but readily available. He chose the samurai blade, twirling it once expertly to test the balance before he fitted it into the straps.

"Remember, under no circumstances should you enter that cell when the chains are slack," Daegan said, as if there'd been no pause in their conversation. "Her moods will be mercurial. It will get painful, as you know." He threw a glance over his shoulder, holstering what looked like a sleek Walther nine-millimeter. "When the bloodlust takes over, she will be as bad as the most dangerous drug addict, willing to say or do anything to get you close enough to take a vein straight from the source. She will hate the refrigerated blood, but it and the sire's blood are all she can have until she learns control. If she gets hold of your throat, she will kill you." He gave Gideon an even look. "Your motivation of a few moments ago was not entirely misguided, but you will not repeat it by yourself."

"I already told you about giving me orders."

Daegan's gaze could have seared flesh. "If you wish to get your throat ripped out, vampire hunter, I do not object. Just do not do it when she still has need of you."

"Nice. Blow me. What I meant was, you could just say, 'Feeding her from your neck won't be a great idea unless someone's around to keep her from getting overenthusiastic.'"

"That's what I just said."

When Gideon snorted, Daegan pushed the safe door closed. "You are as dumb as you look, vampire hunter. Fear can sometimes be your ally."

"Being scared means you give a shit about your life. I don't." Gideon drew his six-inch wooden blade, flipped it over in his hand and extended it to Daegan, hilt first. "Know you don't need it with that arsenal you're carrying, but if you manage to sink it into the bastard, I'll feel like I was there by proxy. It's got a good balance to it. Best kind of throwing knife if you need to pin someone. I know I won't need it here." He met Daegan's eyes. "You'll be back, after all."

The vampire inclined his head, taking the knife. Briefly, his hand closed over Gideon's, then slid away. "While your childish rejection of authority is irritating, your faith is mildly gratifying."

Dickhead. "Fine."

Daegan had put Anwyn's razor tips in a small bowl on the coffee table, and now he collected them. "I'll use the smell of their flesh to track them," he explained. "Regardless of what you think of me, Gideon, take particular care with her. If she gets free, the casualties would be unimaginable, particularly if it's at night, when the club above is full. The sexual energy would incite her bloodlust further."

"Do you really give a rat's ass about them, or would that merely be an unnecessary complication to an already shitty situation?"

"Your hatred of my kind is blinding you," Daegan said, briefly showing fangs. "You've already seen that Anwyn has a deep-seated aversion to being out of control. Now imagine what would happen if such a loss of control resulted in her harming people she cares about, even killing them. She would not survive that, Gideon."

He met Gideon's gaze without blinking, that peculiar vampire stillness lending the look additional weight. "But to answer your question baldly, she is what matters most to me. Enough that I will do anything necessary to see her safe and well. So don't goad me. I am depending on you now, but your worth will decrease in direct proportion to how much you get on my nerves."

"I'll tremble in fear over that while you're gone."

"You do that." Daegan turned for the door.

Gideon cursed under his breath. *Shit.* "Rei." When the vampire tossed him a glance, already halfway through the frame, Gideon spoke gruffly. "Good hunting."

Another flash of fang, a feral smile, and the vampire was gone.

12

GIDEON came back into the dungeon room. On a thought, he brought in a couple vases of her flowers, set them on benches he supposed were normally used for flogging happily helpless male slaves, their bare asses sticking in the air. He flinched from the distasteful image.

He knew it was kind of hypocritical, but he didn't classify their session or how he'd responded to it the same way. Course, maybe he was just being an asshole because he didn't really want to be lumped in with those pathetic losers. He also didn't want to think about men who might have been something more than clients to her, brought down to this personal dungeon. Maybe there hadn't been a lot since she'd known Daegan. The vampire didn't seem the sharing type, not that way. *Yeah. That makes me feel better.*

Anwyn was still curled up on the couch, but at his appearance, she sat up, so obviously relieved to see him, he was sorry he'd stepped out of her sight for even a moment. However, she rearranged her expression immediately to appear as calm as possible, adjusting the dark T-shirt. Almost primly, she crossed her sexy long legs and folded her hands in her lap, a composed image somewhat ruined by the clank of the chains. "You promised to braid my hair. Of course, under the circumstances, I guess you could just give me a brush and I'll do it myself."

"No, I can do it." Gideon moved to the cell door, key already in hand, and then thought of Daegan's admonition. He had half a mind to ignore the supercilious son of a bitch, but unfortunately his gut and Daegan's logic were on the same wavelength. *If she kills you, she's got no one.* "If you don't mind me taking you back to the wall, that is."

She swallowed, that composure wavering in her pale face, and lifted a shoulder. "Maybe in a few minutes. I want to be able to move around right now."

"Okay." Gideon looked around, found a chair. He couldn't stand sitting at the door where she couldn't reach him, as if she were a wild beast he couldn't trust, no matter how close to the truth that might be. Seeking a good compromise, he moved the chair around to the couch side and straddled it. The sofa was pressed up to the bars, so if she wanted him to do so, he could put his hand through the bars to touch her. Since the chains were almost at full extension at that point, it was an acceptable risk.

Turning, she folded her legs under herself and laid her temple on the sofa back. It was natural to reach through, stroke her hair. Her eyes closed again.

"I'm sorry, Anwyn," he said quietly. "You don't know how much."

She didn't reply, but sat beneath his touch, not discouraging it. Her beautiful hair already felt like the tempting silk that all female vampires had. There was a spot of blood on her shoulder, his blood, but he decided not to remark upon it right now. "This reminds me of the time my parents took my brother and me on a cross-country trip," he ventured. "The first part of the trip, where we suddenly realized how many hours we'd be in the car, trying to figure out how we were going to pass the time."

Her hand slid up, curled in the cushions. He would have covered it, but instinct told him to wait, to let her make the request or demand. "What did you do?" she asked, though her voice didn't reflect much interest.

"Magnetic chess and checkers. Mad Libs. You remember those?

Short stories where different parts of the sentences were left blank. You'd tell the other person to give you a noun or verb, an adjective, et cetera. They'd give those to you, without knowing the story. When you read them back, with their words filled in, they'd make you laugh."

"If I laughed right now, I'd feel like I was laughing at a funeral."

"You didn't die, Anwyn. You're going to be okay."

Her jaw tightened, her head lifting. "You abhor what I've become. You want all vampires dead. So why would you lie to me?"

"Because it would make you feel better to believe it. And I want you to feel better."

She stared at him. "You're an honest man. I'm not sure if I appreciate or hate that."

"I've heard both opinions. Usually from the same people, so feel free to vacillate. You'll be in good company." Spearing his fingers into the hair at her temple, he gripped her there to draw her attention. "You didn't ask for this to happen."

"So that makes it different, because I'm an accident rather than someone who embraced this?"

"Yeah."

"Why does that make me think of someone who got AIDS through a blood transfusion instead of sex? I didn't ask for it, so . . ." Her voice drifted off, and a shudder went through her.

He knew where her mind had gone, to what had happened in the alley. Not to the turning, but the more insidious invasion of her person. Drawing away from his touch, she slid down the side of the couch to the floor and folded her arms over herself, bowing her head. "It's been a long time since I wanted to be dead," she said in a voice that could have come from the grave, running chills down his spine. "Maybe I should have you go ahead and do it. Maybe that was why Fate brought you here."

"Sorry; I've made my vampire kill this week. No new appointments until next week." He said it lightly, but her words had clamped like a vise on his gut. Her arms shifted, linking beneath her knees, keeping the T-shirt pulled up to her thighs to retain her modesty. But when her head lowered farther, he thought she was mainly trying to make herself as small as possible.

Damn it, he didn't care about Daegan's warning. He knew she wasn't normally a morbid person, so he wasn't going to let her sink into the clutches of such black thoughts. Getting up, he took the key and unlocked the cell. Her head lifted only when he squatted in front of her, his boots inches from her bare toes.

"This is stupid," she said. "I heard what Daegan said to you. And he's right. Gideon, I can feel it inside of me. It's like being seasick, feeling it coming and knowing you can't stop it."

"I don't think a Mistress should be on the floor," he said instead, giving her a steady look. "Why don't we get you back on the couch?"

"It's a sham, Gideon. It's all a stupid, stupid lie. Look at me." That tremor went through her hands again. He covered them with his own. Their coldness was frightening, but he remembered at times Jacob had been ice-cold as a corpse. Other times he'd burned like a denizen of hell. That might be his key. Keep a hand on her, and the body temperature would indicate when the bloodlust might be returning. Jacob's always came with heat.

"You're not a lie. You know I've been caught by vamps twice?"

She shook her head. "No. I didn't know that."

"You know the one thing they seemed most determined to do? They tortured me, yeah. Fire, whips, all the usual melodramatic movie props. But those were tools. They hurt and scared me. Big fucking deal. You'd have to be dead not to be scared of that. But what they most wanted to do was make me doubt what I was. They wanted to take that away."

Her face lifted to him then, and he met her gaze. "Those other ladies you sent, they were okay. Yeah, they were Dommes, but not down to the blood and bone. The minute you walked in, I felt what you are, all the way down to those fuck-me shoes you were wearing and wanted to grind into my ass. It was why you scared the shit out of me, because I knew you had the shovel. You were the one who could dig down into the rotting things I didn't want uncovered. That's not an act, Mistress. You can't fake who you are, what you become. No one can take that."

Before he could regret the raw admission, she tightened her chin. "They hurt me. I hated that. But worse than that, I hated that they *could* hurt me. I can't stop thinking about it."

"I know. That's always what rips you open the most." Sliding an arm around her back and under her knees, he lifted her onto the couch from a kneeling position, staying that way as he settled her, adjusting the chains leading from her arms and legs as best as he could. She pressed her fingers to her temples.

"If I'm not interested in Mad Libs, what else can we do to pass the time?" Her voice was soft, a vulnerable, tired woman needing distraction.

He cleared his throat. "Well, if you tell anyone, I *will* stake you, but I give a decent pedicure. Not that you really need one right now." His glance went to her perfect toes, a mockery of what else had been done to her.

Regardless, the comment startled a short, strangled chuckle out of her. Anwyn put her hands down, regarded him with amusement. "Daegan will be so disappointed if we don't tell him. He loves to have his toenails painted."

"Yeah, right." At the flash of worry that crossed her face, he grimaced. "He'll be fine, Anwyn. I wouldn't want to be the thing standing between him and that blood."

"I know." She blew out a breath. "Female thing, to worry, I guess. I'm sorry. I know you think you should be out doing that, rather than babysitting me."

"I'm where I need to be," he said, covering her hand and letting her see the truth of it in his face. Before she could worry about it further, he latched onto an idea.

"How about Twenty Questions? That's one that kept us going for hours. In hindsight, it was a sneaky way for our parents to find out things about us we wouldn't tell them otherwise."

"And hence a way to find out things about me that are none of your business?"

"Just finding a way to pass the time, Mistress." He gave her a guileless look. Settling back into a cross-legged position on the floor, he brought his shins within inches of her small feet. He laid a hand on one, keeping tabs on her temperature, and forced himself not to caress the elegant arches and slim heels.

"Well in that case, I'll play only if you play. Question for a question."

Her gaze glimmered with that insight she'd wielded so well earlier. "If you're going to pump me for information, it's going to be equal time."

"All right, but if you find out I sleep with a teddy bear, then we'll have to stop playing." He stopped. "Aw, fuck."

Her smile was almost genuine, and it warmed him. "You have a sense of humor, Gideon. That's unexpected. Rusty, but charming."

"Well, it's a muscle I don't work out much. You get first question."

She pursed her lips. "How does a fearsome vampire hunter know how to give a pedicure? And no lying or avoiding questions," she added. "A penalty for every lie, to be collected at a later time."

Heat shimmered under his hand. Taking a quick look at her face, he saw her focus had shifted internally, her hands closing into fists as perspiration collected on her lip. While Gideon felt a grim satisfaction at having his detection theory confirmed, it was short-lived.

"Hurts," she managed.

"Breathe through it," he said, moving carefully onto his heels. He knew he needed to get the hell out of range, but found himself unable to leave her when that panicked note was in her voice. "This is a transition seizure, different from the bloodlust. Right now, your internal organs are changing."

"Oh, is that all?" she gasped, giving him a narrow glance.

"Jacob, my brother, had his at pretty consistent intervals the first few hours. We time the first two and we might know when the next ones are coming. For a while."

"Like labor pains. And no, I've never had children." A deep breath shuddered through her. "Talk. Tell me . . . Answer my question."

"It was a hooker. She taught me."

∼

Anwyn tried to breathe through the pain as he suggested. It was an odd sensation, because breathing had become optional, requiring conscious thought. But the heat that licked at her insides wasn't anything she could stop. Like thunder, the pain was counting down toward the lightning strike, a place where madness would take her, those shadowy voices in her head getting stronger.

When they'd put her in here, she thought she was going to lose her mind in truth, break her sanity with the fear of being chained, caged. It was still there, a panicked animal hidden in the corner of her mind, whimpering, exacerbated by the betrayal of her own body, but he was here. He was with her. He was helping her not think about the horrifying reality of the other things she couldn't stop.

"Gideon. *Talk*."

He braced a hand on the couch by her knee in his squatted position. A position that made it clear he was ready to retreat if needed. She wished that didn't prod something savage inside her, something that wanted him to try to run.

"Most the time, these past few years, when I needed to fuck, it was with paid women." He put it out there quickly, maybe for his sake as well as hers, as if it embarrassed him to admit it. "I chose women in pretty good circumstances, maybe not the best, but not in the gutters, either. That night . . . She had an ex-boyfriend who was giving her a hard time, so for whatever reason, after we'd done our thing, she said she liked my company, and if I wanted to stay the night at her place, it would give her a night off from worrying. She said I looked like I might need a night off, too."

Remembering the jaded weariness in his more unguarded moments during their session, Anwyn could imagine what the prostitute had seen. A good man who could be trusted, who could use a bit of mothering in exchange for the protection of his presence.

"She made me soup," Gideon confirmed. It was crazy, that she could feel amusement while her internal organs were cooking and she was worried she'd tear into him like a rare steak. "Anyhow, she had to redo her toenails that night and asked if I'd mind doing the foot that's harder to do with her dominant hand. I told her I'd probably mess it up. She thought, with instruction, I'd be pretty precise."

He would indeed. Feeling a surprising lick of lust become part of the turbulent sea of responses within her, she let her gaze pass over him. "I thought the same thing when I first saw you. Next question— oh hell."

Laying her head back on the couch edge, she pressed hard, stretching out her neck, all of her body, spasms working their way through the muscle groups like electric shocks. Over his protests, she forced out her questions between gritted teeth.

"Why . . . did you come . . . here . . . last night?" She snapped out the last two words through a locked jaw. "What . . . were you . . . seeking?"

Had he known a game that involved uncovering personal truths would help? She could survive the pain, the pounding and white noise that made it seem as if a construction crew were frenetically working inside of her, if she could draw truth out of him. Never mind she was relying more on his compassion than her finesse as a Domme. She just prayed he would speak before her mind was sucked into a vortex of pain.

His blessedly cool hand touched her hot face. She latched onto it with both hands, rocking against the pain. "Easy," he murmured. He stayed on the floor where he could see her eyes. Probably anticipating that change that coated everything in her vision red. Still, she knew it could leap, not crawl, into her gaze. He *so* shouldn't be here, but she didn't have the courage to tell him to leave her.

"You were right," he said quietly. "Once, a long time ago . . . I spent the night with a woman like you. She was a vampire, and she flat out took the reins away from me, took every choice away. It took me a long time to admit it, but I was at peace that one night. It's dogged me ever since, no matter how I tried to push it away. No one—not until you—made me feel they could take me to that place, whether I wanted to go or not."

He stroked her brow, drifting down to her temple. The pain ebbed off, and that whirlpool settled down, slyly slinking back into the shadows. Anwyn took deep breaths, leaning into Gideon's touch. Her chains clanked when she moved, but she forced herself not to recoil. She put her fingers against his firm mouth.

"You can find peace there."

"It's still wrong." He shook his head. "I don't deserve that peace, and I shouldn't be wasting energy looking for it."

"Hmm." It struck a hard, resonating chord inside of her, but peace was something she thought Gideon had deserved for a long, long time.

Her fingers moved against his lips, the texture of them strumming through her nerve endings. When he instinctively parted them, her stomach fluttered, heat growing in her lower abdomen.

She knew what Daegan had said about chemical reactions, but a determined mind could do a lot of things that science said it couldn't, right? She followed his nose, an uneven line where it had once been broken, up to his forehead, then traced that slope back to his lips, which remained taut beneath her touch. If he parted them, tasted her, would they slacken, grow sensual in their teasing, the suckling of her slim fingers? He was on his knees to her already, had placed her on the couch above him. For comfort, yes, but was it more than that? An instinct?

Dangerous waters, for while the heat in her stomach expanded at the mere thought, so, too, did those violent whispers. Fire was washing over her anew. Lust was a craving she'd always trusted, but would she know the difference between female desire and a predator's urge to take?

Placing his hand over her wrist, below the manacle, he caressed her pulse, and her breath shortened. "My turn, one question for your two. When did you know you wanted to be a Dominatrix when you grew up?"

"Probably when I had Barbie torture my Ken doll." When she gave him a tight smile, she noticed how it felt, her lips stretching over the slick enamel of her fangs. She moistened them with her tongue. "It's always been in my blood, Gideon." *Red, rich blood.*

Those blue eyes didn't waver, and she suddenly realized, with a lurch that somersaulted her heart into her throat, that he knew. He could feel it coming, but he wouldn't leave her, wouldn't go until she said it was okay. Impossible, crazy man. Hers, in a way she'd never experienced before.

"Trust is . . . part of it. A sacred gift. I swore never . . . to abuse it. Which is why you need to leave, right now. *Go.*"

Thank Goddess, he obeyed instantly, in a way she was sure was a rarity for him. The flush she'd been experiencing was nothing next to the sudden spike of body temperature, a burning all over as if she'd been dipped in liquid fire. Unexpected nausea hit her stomach so hard it was as if she'd been punched there. It was a blessing, because the bloodlust that roared in over top of the transition convulsion, distinctly different from the pain spasm, would have propelled her after him much faster if she hadn't been doubled over from it.

As it was, she fell a few inches short. He made it to the cell door, slammed it after him. Snarling, she was jerked to the ground by the snap of the chains pulling tight. Madness closed over her, drowning her, and she went down into it fighting.

Gideon hit the control, dragging her slowly back to the wall. As she shrieked and writhed like a mythical animal, she bared long fangs, her body deeply flushed, her unhealed scars turning crimson and beginning to drip fresh blood down her skin. As Daegan had predicted, she threw up on herself. Blood started to come from her eyes and nose, alarming him, because he'd never seen that happen. Then he realized that, while the scars were leaking blood, her pores were oozing it, thin smears showing up across her limbs, her hands and feet, almost like stigmata.

Christ, sweetheart. He wasn't sure what he'd been trying to prove to her, but he hoped it had helped, letting her make the call. He knew he wouldn't be able to risk that again, for a couple reasons. When they'd been eye to eye and he'd felt it coming, it had crossed his mind, what dying at her hand would feel like, letting her have it all. Something in him had yearned for it.

I know many things about you, vampire hunter. Which is why I have my doubts about having you near her.

Daegan had meant his penchant for killing vampires, not self-destruction. This guy wasn't crawling around in his head, for Chrissakes.

She howled like a demented animal, jerking his attention back to her and away from Daegan's words. When her bloodred eyes focused on him, he saw no vestige of Anwyn, just a hungry creature who wanted to kill. An entirely different instinct kicked in, pushing away all those other twisted feelings. Though he'd divested himself of his weapons for this very reason, he hated that the compulsion to have one in hand returned instantly. Even more shameful were the other thoughts that flooded his mind.

When the transition was complete, she would be one of them. Whether she wanted to or not, she was going to have to take at least one life a year to survive. Would she want that? Worse, she would be allowed up to a dozen corpses a year. She was a made vampire, who, as opposed to born vampires, habitually had a much harder time with impulse and bloodlust control. She would also be part of an underground world with only a thin veneer over its feudal system of power and violence. They could take what she was, a female Dominant who thought trust was a sacred gift, and turn her into a fucking sadist in truth, one who took whatever she wanted.

He could end it for her before she ever had to face that, or those unbearable choices. He clenched his jaw, remembering Daegan's other words. *She is becoming what you kill, vampire hunter . . .* Desperate, he reached for thoughts of his brother. He'd seen Jacob come to grips with the human and vampire parts of himself, and while he had sacrificed some of the former to embrace the latter, he was still Jacob.

Just as Anwyn was still in there, damn it. Becoming something different and the same at once. While she screamed and thrashed, her expression monstrous, her upper body soaked in blood and vomit, his eyes clung to one small part of her. The straining tendons in her delicate wrists, a reminder of the resilient femininity and dedication he'd seen in her. How she'd made him feel.

He couldn't take the choice away from her, but not because of some nobility on his part. She needed him, and he couldn't resist that connection between them, pathetically temporary though it was. When she fully embraced being a vampire, and she would, he couldn't be with her. Just like he couldn't be around Jacob anymore. No matter what vestiges of his brother remained, there were certain things he just couldn't accept and handle about him being a vampire.

He knew all that, but he was here now. That was what mattered. What had she said before? Just this moment. Maybe he understood what she'd meant.

Forcing his mind to shut up, he found her human blood in the refrigerator, measured it out in a quarter cup. He hurried, because when he'd moved away from her cell, the convulsing of her body, her struggles against the manacles, grew twice as bad. Another indication that Anwyn was still in there, the woman who hated and feared being restrained.

When he returned, he steeled himself to do what needed to be done. Opening the cell, he moved quickly toward her. He made himself tune out the animal sounds, far too reminiscent of demon possession movies.

Keeping his arm well out of range of her fangs, he gripped her hair to still the movement of her head and forced the cup to her lips. The smell snapped her attention to it immediately, thank God. Vamps didn't like refrigerated blood, as Daegan had said, but in this state she would take it. She gulped it down, the excess running sloppily over her chin, but this time he didn't bring his fingers close enough to catch it for her. Her gaze was fastened on the artery in his throat, because he knew she could hear the pumping of blood through it. She snapped at him when he took the cup away and let go of her hair.

"Your wrist," she demanded in an eerie rasp. Shaking his head, he turned on his heel and left the cell, forced himself not to falter as her howls became hideous wails.

Daegan had been right. He would give anything not to be here. He was sure she felt the same way.

Going into her bathroom in the main living area, he found a basin and washcloth beneath the sink. As he let the water heat and filled up the basin in the sink, he noted the eye makeup she'd left out, the tube of lipstick. Female things, normal things. The blouse she'd been wearing was draped over the vanity chair. Lifting it to his nose, he smelled her sweet scent from the bath.

Returning to the cell, feeling a bit calmer, he double-checked that her arms and legs were still firmly secured to the wall. Now she was making low, plaintive growls, like a frightened lioness. Occasionally, she'd break off into harsh whispering to herself, her red gaze clocking around as if expecting a threat from any direction. That gaze had latched onto him as he reappeared. He didn't meet her eyes, and kept his movements calm, deliberate, as he brought the chair up close. Close enough that his knees were pressed inside her spread thighs when he sat back down. She made a strange noise and he responded with a quiet, soothing murmur.

The positioning of the manacles at the ankles was wide enough the T-shirt rode high on her thighs. Gently, he began to clean off the blood and vomit. She was fine while he worked on her legs, but she got agitated again when he worked on the shirt. He decided to pour the warm water over it to rinse out the blood. She was still sweating, so he knew it would feel good.

"You have no right to touch me, human," she snapped abruptly, spraying him with bloodied saliva from her split lip. "I am an untouchable. Chosen to lead other untouchables . . ."

Her diatribe descended into gibberish, interspersed with foul combinations of words he wasn't even sure Anwyn, for all her vast sexual experience, knew. Terrible, crude things a male might say. A sibilant lisp exactly like Barnabus's voice came through, gripping him with cold fingers. This was *not* normal.

She slammed her head back, so hard he let out an oath, hearing the stone crack and seeing her eyes glaze over as if she'd given herself a concussion. But when he tried to slide his fingers to the back of her skull, to feel for damage, she almost got his arm, and he yanked it back again. She laughed, those red eyes glinting.

"You fear me. I fear nothing."

He made himself focus not on those red eyes or unnaturally long teeth, but on the toned length of her legs. The nip of her waist beneath the shirt. The column of her throat and the delicate holes in her ears where she'd been wearing diamonds earlier. *Would those close up?* he wondered. Some older scars did, when a vampire turned. How about the place on her back where the stained glass had cut her?

As he cleaned her slim arms, he saw she'd rubbed her wrists raw against the manacles. While he knew they would heal as well, he had to fight the unwise desire to put his mouth on them, sooth the fragile pulse pounding beneath the skin. He studied her toenails again, each cuticle a translucent white and each nail embellished with one precise silver stroke over the polish.

The prostitute who'd made him soup had had scarlet nails, yet on one of the big toes, she'd had the tiny emblem of a teddy bear. For her kid. He didn't know if she did it to remember him when she had her feet locked around some john's shoulders, or to amuse the kid when they were together. Probably both.

A lot of shit happened to everyone in the world. The only thing that kept anyone going was knowing someone out there might need them. Someone who might give a shit what happened to them.

He gave a shit what happened to Anwyn, and hell, he'd already admitted he had a pathetic need for her. So he kept sitting there, cleaning her as best as he could, until she was back down to hissing and spitting. Holding on to the picture of the woman she'd been last night, her urgent desire in the tub, the game of Twenty Questions they'd begun, he set the basin and cloth aside.

When she was coherent again, he'd ask her about this playroom. Ask if she'd had a lot of guys here. Piss her off by going places she hadn't given him permission to go. Ruffle those beautiful feathers.

Slowly, deliberately, he placed his face against her abdomen, the damp shirt, his crown pressed to her breasts. Her heart beat fast, a rapid thunder. He ignored the smell of blood and stroked her sides with gentle fingers. He murmured to her, soothing, nonsensical things. To Anwyn, the woman inside this beast. And God help him, though she continued to hiss and mumble like something from an 80s horror flick, he felt . . . something. Something that was Anwyn, reaching out and holding on to him, using him as her anchor.

Yes, she was becoming what he killed, as Daegan had said. But in some ways, he wondered if they were even more alike now, because often the face he saw in his mirror had become what he most hated. He'd come to Atlantis because the reins had been close to snapping. Just like her manacles, if they gave way, he wasn't sure what destruction he'd commit, if he became that which he most feared.

"It's all right." He pressed his mouth to the slope of her sweet stomach. "I'm not going anywhere. I'm right here. You're safe."

The cycles were going to intensify, but the chains were strong. If she needed him to do it, he'd lock himself in the cell with her and toss out the key. She might drain him, but she wouldn't get anyone else. He just couldn't leave her in there alone if she begged him to stay, because he couldn't detach himself from the woman desperately fighting inside her own body. Just as it had been when she'd pressed the razor edge to his throat, his life was literally in her hands.

She would have had coffee with him; he knew it.

Daegan might call him a fool, but she could have thrown him back into the street, given him nothing when he was at the end of his rope. He wouldn't do the same to her.

13

HENRY Barnabus and his pair of made vampires weren't hard to find, though they were holed up much farther out of the city than Daegan had expected. The few times the trail got confusing, street people clinging to the shadows through which he could safely pass during daylight filled in the blanks. He suspected they saw something in his eyes that told them it wouldn't be wise to wheedle bribes out of him. Being left with their life and limbs intact was payment enough for the information.

As he retrieved his BMW with its specially treated windows from a private garage and headed for the outlying industrial town his quarry might have chosen as their falsely defensible position, he cursed fluently. Every minute was one minute too many.

To get authorization for a kill, he called it in to his Council contact before it happened. He discarded that idea now. He wasn't risking any delays. He was given a certain latitude for the more obvious violators of Council directives, after all. He'd get the sire's blood and exterminate the whole nest before they killed too carelessly and attracted more widespread human attention. Because of a recent uprising by made vampires, the Council, most of whom were born vampires, still had prejudicial attitudes against their manufactured brethren.

Unfortunately, he would have a different problem with the Council when this was done, which was another reason he wasn't going to notify them. Barnabus had walked right into Club Atlantis's front door and asked for him by name. No one had that information but the Vampire Council.

He had a good idea which Council members had been stupid enough to expose him. Even though the Council was currently harsher on the infractions of made vampires, they'd duplicitously attempted a more egalitarian approach, expanding their numbers to allow two made vampires to serve on the Council, with limited voting privileges.

Political correctness for vampires. It gave Daegan a throbbing pain behind his left eye. Vampires worked best as an aristocratic oligarchy based on power and control. Their fucking politics had destroyed a part of his life he'd foolishly believed was beyond the reach of what he did for them.

Hours ago, Anwyn had been in his arms, confident and sexy, his face buried in her thick hair, her body arched with sensual strength and will against his hands. He recalled the soft gasp as his cock pushed deep into her. Her eyes had said things she would never say with her mouth. It was the way of it, with vampires as well as humans. They never said what they should, when they should. Everything had changed for her, but maybe if he'd ever said straight-out how he felt about her, she'd have had one more thing to help her through this. Or it might have never happened at all, as Gideon had said, as ruthless as an arrow.

She'd never believed she could be completely vulnerable around him. She understood far too well the relationship between humans and vampires, ingrained in his blood. It seemed he knew everything about her, how she would react to every situation, and yet still her heart did not lie trusting in his hand. Even if he'd marked her three times so she could hide nothing from him, not her nightmares or dreams, he wasn't sure he would have had the essence of her. Taking knowledge was not the same as being given it.

He recalled her desperate emotional hunger, the need to have him and Gideon fill her, kiss her, wipe it all away. Gideon had been surprised that a woman would want that, but for some things, Anwyn thought more like a man. She needed to destroy Barnabus's hold on her flesh, do whatever was necessary to keep it from permanently branding her with fear. Above everything else, Anwyn couldn't abide being weak and afraid.

So he'd left her with a vampire hunter and gone to hunt her attackers. He hoped that his abrupt departure had sent her an unspoken message, that everything was going to be fine, because they were going to make it so. But it wasn't the only reason he'd left her with Gideon.

How could he fault her for guarding her secrets? She didn't know why he'd been as intrigued as she was when Gideon had first crossed their threshold. Fate had brought to Anwyn's door a vampire hunter whom Daegan had been monitoring across various parts of the country for months. However, as far as he could tell, an astounding coincidence was all it was.

He thought about when he'd handed Gideon back his knife. The man's hands had the rough skin of a man with no façade at all. Gideon had had admirable luck as a hunter, too admirable to be all luck. But like so many in this profession, he was carrying enough baggage to stock a 747. Though life had eaten away at him deeply, Gideon had swallowed depair, integrated it with the battle-ready toughness at his core. He was too stubborn or stupid to abandon the honor code that was destroying him. Ironically, for that and many other reasons, Daegan had known Gideon could handle being with Anwyn. He'd care for her even if it tore his soul to shreds, because he was used to that feeling.

Most important, Gideon hadn't been connected to what happened to her. In fact, he'd stood at her back, where Daegan should have been, when Barnabus had dared to set foot over the threshold of Atlantis. When James had sketched him the brief details, Daegan's blood had boiled, imagining her surrounded by the violent filth of those three. How could her trust in him, already limited, be anything but damaged beyond repair now? Gideon had surrendered to her, given her more of his soul in one night than Daegan had done in five years.

He shook off the weight of such thoughts. They wouldn't do Anwyn any good. Trust issues aside, the cruelties or kindnesses of the gods had given her two men who could provide her the different things she needed now. While it only added to the throbbing pain in his chest, being here, knowing what she was enduring, Gideon was the one who could give to her emotionally, though Daegan's lips twisted as he remembered the man's response to that.

Yeah, look under 'nurturing' in the dictionary and you'll find my phone number.

"You don't know the effect your surrender has on her heart, vampire hunter." Something Daegan couldn't give to her, because it wasn't in a vampire's nature. He was Dominant, through and through. He'd overwhelmed her soul and body, time and again, exulting in the way she gave herself to him, knowing that his desire to possess her overrode his feelings toward any other, but it hadn't been enough. Not as long as she was human.

Another reason that any chance they would ever have complete trust between them was gone.

Damn it, enough of this. He'd contacted James, had him relay to Gideon he was going to be gone at least until the following night. As much as he wanted to speak to Anwyn, she wasn't likely in any condition to speak to him. He needed to be ruthlessly calm for this, and hearing her in distress wouldn't help.

But soon he would find his target. Then he would vent his frustrations *and* get back to her side.

As he drove, he reviewed what he knew about his prey. While he hadn't come into contact with Henry Barnabus before, he already had profile information on him. The bastard had been the next assignment on Daegan's list. He'd hoped to take him out where he'd taken out his sire, but Barnabus had been here, not his normal hunting grounds. Daegan had dispatched his sire much farther west two weeks before.

Sydney Lawrence had made Barnabus a vampire without Council approval, one of the most serious Council violations, but he'd been made without authorization himself. Lawrence was a mental patient who escaped from his hospital after a Council fugitive, Elliot Bernard, had decided to turn him for amusement. Elliot had been part of the recent failed uprising against the Council, and he'd been sowing trouble here and there ever since. One might call that foolish, because it left a trail of bread crumbs to follow, but Elliot was impulse-driven and narcissistic, weaknesses that too many "made" vampires had. Which was perhaps why he'd chosen to turn vamps among the criminally insane.

Daegan had taken out Bernard in Rhode Island six months ago, and dispatched Lawrence when he was snacking on the still-warm blood of an eight-year-old, cradled in his arms like a doll. He'd been having his meal on a pier at two in the morning. From a distance, it had looked like a father tenderly holding a sleeping daughter.

Following the pyramid down to the bottom was standard procedure, so he'd taken out another of Elliot's older whelps last night, in the adjacent town. He'd been scheduled to go to New Orleans to take out another, but Daegan wished to God he'd bumped Barnabus and his two illegally made vampires up on the list. He would have tracked them and discovered them in the area sooner.

He'd been too damn busy this past year. Council rules worked only on vampires willing to follow them, or intimidated by the repercussions of not doing so. Lawrence had been gurgling on a hysterical laugh when Dagean staked him. The insane lived in a different world.

His fingers gripped the wheel, hard. Barnabus was a homeless schizophrenic, sired by a criminally insane male. Anwyn was the latest in a chain of made vamps characterized by weak blood, poor impulse control, and outright madness. Daegan couldn't avoid the significance of that, or the images they spawned, what could happen to her.

He'd seen a similar knowledge in Gideon's eyes, watching her initial transition struggles. The hunter knew that this might end badly. Would it be over before Daegan even returned? Would Gideon be forced to stake her, or choose to do it for her own good?

Typically, Daegan refused to give "forethought to grief," as the William Blake poem said. Life was long for a vampire, and yet he already knew certain things would always be too short. Like the last time he'd held Anwyn in bed, listening to her read that very poem. He'd been stroking her hair, her cheek pressed against his bare chest, the book propped on his abdomen as her thigh slid against his. Her lashes had fanned her soft skin, her mouth curved in a slight, romantic smile, her mind immersed in the words. When he imagined her reduced to violent madness, no innocent safe from her, facing the need to put her down like a rabid animal, he felt a howling rage curl inside him, the pain greater than any he'd felt in a long time.

It forced him to stop thinking for several moments, take the necessary deep breaths. He'd taught himself to modulate his temperament, to be far calmer in demeanor and deed than most vampires. With his special circumstances and abilities, it was mandatory.

Daegan's jaw hardened. Unlike the vampires he'd dispatched—or was about to dispatch—Anwyn had strength of character. Plus, she had him to help her. As well as Gideon. At least for the time being.

Daegan remembered the tender way Gideon had removed that one slipper. With her many dark, pleasurable skills, Anwyn might have been able to help heal him, but Gideon Green would never surrender to a vampire Mistress. Once he was certain Anwyn was adjusted, Daegan was sure the hunter would decide to leave, no matter his feelings.

What he didn't realize was that Anwyn's feelings would take precedence over his own. If Gideon decided he'd overstayed his welcome before she decided she no longer wanted him, Daegan would make sure Gideon Green's far-too-uptight ass stayed at her side. He was going to make sure she had everything she needed, no matter how much of a challenge her needs posed.

And though the difficult hunter didn't yet realize it, staying at her side would benefit him as much as it would her. Daegan knew Gideon wouldn't be surprised to find out why Daegan had been monitoring him. He *would* be surprised to know Anwyn was the only thing saving him from an execution order.

It was getting closer to noon, and even the protection of his car windows couldn't stave off his increasing discomfort. Muttering another oath, he pressed down on the gas, knowing he had to take temporary refuge from daylight.

~

At dusk, he was prowling through the industrial district, leaving his car in a public lot. The warehouse district had fewer street people and a wealth of places for a vampire to hole up. For a vampire who had left such an obvious come-and-get-me taunt, Barnabus had proved tediously difficult to track down, though nowhere near impossible, because he was erratic, not clever. If he had more time, Daegan knew he could make the vampire severely regret trying his patience. And that was the least of his crimes.

Henry had been a social loner even among the homeless, one who couldn't attract friends or anyone to stroke his ego. What was merely pathetic in a human could become dangerous in a vampire. As a vamp, he'd been able to create drinking buddies and a fan club all in one.

It was after midnight when Daegan finally caught their scent through the crack of a broken window. He slid into the shadows outside the warehouse, every other thought melting away, leaving room only for the hunt. Finding an open window, he moved inside and lithely swung up into the rafters. He could move silently there and get a bird's-eye view of the goings-on below. He wanted to sit for a while, see what he could find out from loose tongues, ones he wouldn't have to waste time loosening himself. He tuned everything out, becoming nothing but a spirit that drifted, connected to nothing and no one but this moment and what had to be done.

"Dark Ghost" or "Black Spirit" was the meaning of the name his mother had given him, and he lived up to it, most of the time. Yet in Anwyn's arms he'd always felt surprisingly real, solid. Alive.

Glancing left, he saw a rat, motionless on the beam, a scavenger hoping not to catch the attention of a pure predator. The harmless creature might be in luck tonight, but Barnabus's luck had run out.

～

He'd been up all through the daylight hours, but Henry Barnabus didn't like to sleep. It made it harder to sort out the voices in his dreams from the ones that were outside of them. All the time talking, driving him crazy.

He sat apart from the two vampires he'd made, as a leader should. Distinguishing himself. Just like one of those fat-cat types that rode the subway in their suits, pretending they were so important as they looked right through him. Ignored him and the voices that screamed for their blood, so loudly it made him shake, snigger with it and earn their mistrustful glances. He didn't have to beg from them anymore. Now they begged from him.

Sydney hadn't let him kill them all at once. He'd said to make them wait, draw it out, strike from the shadows so they never knew what hit them. But Syd was dead. He knew. He'd been told that it was someone's fault. A vampire named Daegan Rei who thought he could get away with that.

He scraped his nails over his cheek, felt the pocked marking. Childhood measles. Mother there with cool cloth, but she was long gone. Or was she close by? Sometimes she came and talked to him.

He pushed himself back and forth in a restless rock on the office chair. He liked this place. They put supplies in this warehouse, things to be shipped to those big office supply stores, so they'd taken chairs and a table out of the boxes, set themselves up their own temporary office tonight. But instead of reports and other stupid things on the tables, he had real treasure. Just like when he was a child and Mommy hid it in the house, let him go find it. But the voices sometimes hadn't let him find it, had spoken in whispers, told him he should hide instead.

He sorted through the shriveled ear, the long braid of red hair, and then closed his fingers on the panties stained with dried blood. She hadn't screamed as much as she should have. She'd screamed for help, not out of fear, so he'd gagged her with this until he'd gagged her with other things. She'd even tried to bite him, but they'd held her mouth open with their fingers shoved into the corners, ruthlessly stretching her pretty lips. The way they'd stretched her cunt.

He was twirling the undergarment on his finger, and then, sure that he'd caught his crew's attention, he snapped it like a rubber band at Casey. Casey looked sixteen, because that was how old he was. A boy prostitute that he'd turned, who liked being able to beat up on others the way he'd been beat up on. Henry understood that, even if he thought the skinny, fox-eyed boy was too much like those who whispered in his mind, telling him that no one could be trusted.

Casey caught the panties, tossed them back. "Why didn't we kill her, Henry? And where's Louie?"

Bastard. Casey's barely broken-into-adulthood voice grated. "He probably found other prey. Maybe he'll bring us some more body parts."

"Shouldn't we post a lookout or something, in case *he* comes?" This from Tim, who, despite the question, was rubbing the heel of his hand slowly over his dick, staring into space. Probably still thinking about her writhing helpless in that alley. It made Henry hard, too, but he didn't want them to see that.

"He went to New Orleans." He sneered, vaguely irritated his contact hadn't told him that before he went looking for the vampire. "He'll be back in a day or two. Maybe sooner, if he finds out about her, but not before tomorrow."

With a speculative look, he drew the panties back over, stroked the fabric. He decided not to be angry, because if he hadn't been given incorrect information, he never would have found *her*. "She'll be completely batshit by then. Maybe we'll go back and get her. Might do good to have a girl with us. I like that idea. We'll give her blood, make her our new pet, so we won't miss Lawrence so much. We miss Syd."

He heard his voice change, Henry the boy coming forward, gripping him with that sense of loss, no mommy to guide him anymore. Casey stared at him with that faint sneer on his mouth. Just like that snot-nosed kid Louie. He didn't care if Louie came back, anyway. He shouldn't turn teenagers.

With a snarl, Henry cleared the table, landing on the young vampire and tumbling them both to the ground. Tim watched with indifference as Henry pummeled the younger vampire. "Don't question me. You don't ever do that. I'm going to tell Mommy that you—" A childish wail wrenched from Henry's lips before he even finished the thought, and he tore at the young vamp's ears. "I'll take yours off, too. You never listen. No one ever listens to me."

Casey cried out for help, was ignored. Tim started making a sculpture out of a box of paper clips. Henry saw the dumb vacancy in his eyes, wondered if he was real, or if all of them were an illusion. When he disemboweled Casey, yanking out a handful of intestines, the boy screamed, so loud that it rang in his ears, but it still didn't sound *real*.

Then something did. A chain rattling.

Henry abruptly surged up off the young vamp and kicked him. Casey rolled over, cradling his stomach, trying to push everything back in. Henry focused on the dark aisles that went back into the bowels of the warehouse. A stray beam of a flashlight, accompanied by the sweet scent of human flesh. Maybe a security guard, coming to check on things.

The voices in his head calmed down, because they were always happy when it was time for this. He whistled low, like a master calling his hunting hounds. It brought Tim out of his absorption. "Kill," Henry commanded.

~

Daegan hadn't gone to New Orleans because he'd had an unsettled feeling. He'd attributed it to some concern about how Anwyn's session with Gideon Green would go, so he'd decided to check in with her before heading on to Louisiana.

He hadn't told the Council he was going to do that, because a short side trip back to his home base seemed hardly relevant to a Council status report. More evidence that his backstabber was in the Council ranks.

Daegan moved swiftly through the rafters and dropped down behind the overweight night guard. Before the older man could turn, Daegan had placed a gentle hand on his windpipe, held him steady until the man fainted. He listened to the two come toward him with the stealth of a herd of cattle. When they burst forth, he'd moved into the shadows, so their gaze fell on the prone security guard. "He's already lying down," Tim said stupidly. Casey stood with him, breathing hard, his hand on his bloody but already healing gut.

They were his last words. Daegan took both of their heads in two elegant sweeps of his blade, an effortless spiral of motion that brought the blade back to rest at his left hip, his arms bent at his sides. He'd put more effort into cutting fresh roses to give to Anwyn. With vamps so young, he normally would have felt regret, said a prayer for young souls who hadn't had a chance to be anything different, but Anwyn's pain and fear were too close to his mind right now for even reflective mercy.

The heads rolled down the aisle, almost tripping Henry where he was rushing up behind them. He stopped, looking around wildly.

"You're here, aren't you?" He clapped his hands abruptly, took a spin like a child at his first real birthday party. "I made you come to me. She was scared. She didn't want me to know, though. But when I took these off her"—he lifted the panties, balled up in his hand—"she knew what was going to happen. She knew she was mine."

He turned away from the bodies, looking through the shadows, and found himself face-to-face with a crimson-eyed demon, a shadow of darkness with the silver gleam of metal in his hands. Henry stuttered to a halt, his sense of victory draining away, the voices going completely silent for once.

"Monster in the closet, Mommy," he whimpered. "You told me it didn't exist."

"The Council will protect you," the demon whispered. "Who will you call?"

"The woman with Mommy's voice. She said Mommy and Daddy would protect me. She's right. Go away." He put on his best scary voice, the voice that kept all the other vampires afraid of him.

"No one will help you now," the demon said. "But you are going to help someone else, before I end your miserable existence." A fist shot out of that darkness and clipped his temple. There were stars, and blurriness, and then suddenly Henry was falling in the darkness of his closet, grabbing at Mommy's dresses to slow his fall, but it didn't help. He fell, those demon eyes falling with him into blackness.

Daegan glanced around. Two bodies, one prisoner and a passed-out security guard. He had a damn lot of cleanup to do before he could get back. Sighing, he drew his knife and bent down to get to it.

14

As he'd predicted, the attacks came closer together, each more vicious than the last. The only blessing was that Gideon discovered his precognitive sense got better at anticipating them, even before her body temperature changed. While it gave him a key few minutes' lead time, all that did was save his miserable skin, not any agony to her.

Several times she broke bones in her arms and legs, her human panic at being restrained combining with her bloodlust to drive her past any cognizance of what she was doing to her body, until she'd done it. The pain tore screams from her throat. While the bones knitted, they did so far too slowly. It was excruciating to watch her thrash about, see her bite through her tongue. He could do nothing to relieve her suffering until the powerful convulsions and mad bloodlust let go of her again.

Having to watch the process helplessly was the second-most horrible thing he'd ever endured. Considering the array of things he'd experienced, that was saying something.

Between one attack and the next, no matter how little time that was, she'd scrape herself back together. Though she lost the battle more than won it, she fought the tears and involuntary trembling of her limbs every time.

At least he could help with each aftermath. He washed her off every time. She'd destroyed the T-shirt quickly, so he brought in a stack of towels and wrapped one around her after each episode. He carried on one-way conversations with her when she was too exhausted to respond but still needed his voice. When it was possible, he'd stroke her head or lay his hand on her trembling thigh, reminding her that, though she was trapped by her bonds, he was there. He wasn't going anywhere. He cleaned up the floor so she wouldn't be ankle deep in filth, and firmly coaxed her human blood into her.

Now he was rebraiding her hair. She kept her face turned away toward the opposite wall while he did that, her breasts rising and falling rapidly, like a winded horse. "You shouldn't worry about the towel," she said. Her voice had become a hoarse rasp from all the screaming. "Kind of pointless, right? More work for you."

Gideon tugged on the finished braid lightly and picked up his washcloth again. "You're no work at all."

"Oh yeah." A snuffled sob, perhaps the raw attempt at a grim laugh. "Piece of cake."

"You got it, sweetheart. With frosting and sprinkles. If I didn't have this easy duty, I'd probably be out . . ."

"Hunting vampires." She finished, turning her face toward him. Her eyes were shards of blue-green glass. "You have one here, don't you?"

"That's different," he said. Tenderly, he wiped her face. He was concerned by how her eyes never stopped that restless shifting now, her limbs in a constant sickly tremor. Sometimes, even in the middle of a calmer moment like this, she'd say something strange and menacing, and then resume as if she didn't realize she'd said anything. Like vampire Tourette's, with a lisp. "I don't mind wrapping a towel around you. It makes you feel better."

"That's pretty relative, all in all."

"Yeah." He gave a serious half chuckle. She pulled off a smile, though it was so weighed down by weariness, he wanted to brush his lips over the corners of her mouth to give them additional strength. "Anyway, without the towel, I might get lustful ideas. You've been firing some pretty creative ones at me."

"I don't think 'fuck you' screamed at the top of my lungs is a come-on."

"Well, guys are pretty literal. Particularly about that subject."

"You're not." She locked gazes with him. "You'd never touch me unless I wanted you to. That's the kind of man you are. You don't take choices away from women. You give them."

He firmed his jaw. "When a murderous bastard gives you a hand in the trenches, it could be because he likes having the company. Doesn't mean he fits in a civilized, gentle world."

Her haggard face flickered with spirit. "Maybe I felt sorry for you and wanted to make you feel useful."

"Now, see, that, I believe." Still, he put his hand over hers, which was balled into a tight fist over the harsh steel of the manacle. "The first part is the worst. After forty-eight hours, it will become far more manageable."

If Daegan made it back with the blood, and if it was a normal transition, which, of course, it wasn't. Holy God, he hoped it would get better, though. He had an unwise desire to let her fingers lace with his, but he resisted and went back to running the cool cloth along her throat. If he tangled with her fingers, she might break his with a stray remnant of violence, tempted back to life by his proximity. She stared at his hand as he slid the damp washcloth down, patted the heated skin just above her terry-cloth-covered breasts.

"My aunt painted our trailer purple, when I was young," she said.

He grunted. "Royal purple, or a girly kind of a lavender?"

"Rock-star purple. She wanted to make me happy about something, do something to make me feel good for a few minutes. You, doing this, reminds me of that. Sad and incredibly generous at once. It hurts my chest and makes me want to cry, even as I want to thank you for trying to make the awful better with a little purple paint."

Damn it. His hand stilled on her. Even as her words touched him, he sensed another one coming. And she was too damn intuitive herself. Her face tightened in sudden, desperate denial.

"Gideon, I can't take anymore."

"You can." Setting aside the cloth, he swiftly reinforced the braid with another elastic hair band. He'd found them in a china teacup on top of her vanity, next to the silver-backed hairbrush he was using now. Ironic, considering he usually did his hair with a broken comb. Or his fingers. "You will, because you know you're too damn proud to do anything else. There's no other choice."

His voice was harsher than he intended, because he knew as well as she did that there *was* another choice. If she asked for it, if she begged him to kill her, it was going to tear him in half.

Shadows gripped her features, making him wonder if he'd taken her to that dark place with him. God knew, they were working so hard at this together, it was starting to feel as though they could reach each other's minds.

"There's always a choice. I almost wish there wasn't, because that's what makes this so hard, right? I made a choice I'll regret my entire life, going into that alley." Then the brittle pain in her gaze died away as she attempted one more smile, an unexpected, heart-wrenching expression. "The cats were hungry, though."

"You're a piece of work, sweetheart," he said with quiet fervor, daring a quick squeeze of her hand. "You hang in there. I know you can do this."

Her blue-green eyes pierced him to his scarred soul. "I won't ask you to take my life, Gideon. That's the one sure promise I can give you."

He nodded, his throat thick. "Hang on, then. Here it comes."

Once again, she slammed her head against the wall like a heavy-metal music groupie, lost in the harsh demand of pounding drums and chaotic dueling guitars. He'd tried to brace a pillow behind her earlier. She'd caught it with her teeth and ripped a huge hole in the foam stuffing before it tumbled to the floor amid the debris. Every time she surfaced, she seemed shocked to see the aftermath on her body, on the floor, as if she'd been deep in some mind-hell. He didn't know if that was a mercy, or twice the torment.

He'd taken the pillow from Daegan's room, of course. When she was in the midst of an attack, he didn't dare leave her, and when she was lucid, that just-below-the-surface terror of being chained up kept him almost as close. As a result, he hadn't had time to register anything about Daegan's room except it was sparse. A masculine-looking assortment of dark furniture, suitable for a guy over six feet, and a closet, the door cracked but the interior dark. A few books and personal items were scattered on the dresser, but nothing significant.

More vomiting, more bloody emissions from her pores. Nerve-splitting screams, raging shrieks. Agonized cries.

Often, the towel was so soaked with her fluids that the tuck loosened and it dropped to the ground with a wet splat during her struggles. After he cleaned her, he balled each one up, put it in the hamper he'd dragged to the cell from her bathroom. If she'd still lived, his mother would have fainted in shock, because she always claimed he didn't know what a hamper was for. But having his mom look at his dirty laundry wasn't the same as forcing an exhausted, chained woman to look at her blood- and vomit-soaked linens.

Now he slid another towel around her, working his way along the wood and stone behind her body so he could tuck the ends together over her trembling breasts.

It was probably the most dangerous thing he did, because his body was closest to her at this point, his throat briefly within range of her fangs. But he'd learned that the direct aftermath, when the attack had drained her completely, her eyes at their most brilliant natural color, was when the risk was most acceptable. Truth, there was a side benefit to it he needed as much as she seemed to. The physical contact. She laid her temple on his shoulder, her head turned away from his neck, but the fragile line of her skull pressed against it, the heavy weight of her braid sliding against his chest.

"You think about what's going to be on the other side of this," he murmured, risking it even further by sliding his arms around her, over the towel, letting her feel the pressure of his embrace. "You'll never age. You'll be able to pound a hundred guys like me into sand. You'll always be beautiful, just like you are now."

"You'll hate what I am. Be repelled by it."

"I'll never be anything but completely overwhelmed by you." Sliding back reluctantly, he saw she was staring into space.

"That wasn't a direct answer." She straightened, resting her head against the cross. He teased her cheek, made her lashes flicker toward him.

"Why would you care what a loser like me thinks, anyway? I've got two shirts to my name . . . Well, thanks to you, one. No social skills, no prospects."

"Not true. You have considerable social skills. The *anti-* kind."

"See, she still has a sense of humor." He couldn't smile, though. Despite his sponging, blood, vomit and sweat filled his nostrils. She smelled like something dying, and they both knew it.

"I was completely serious." But she closed her eyes. "I want you near, but I need to move, Gideon."

"I can stay close outside, like before." He pressed a hand to her bound arm but left the cell, cognizant of how she opened her eyes, instinctively tracking his movements with her heightening senses. After he closed the cell door, he adjusted the control so it paid her out enough chain that she could move to the sofa. But on the first step she staggered, falling to her knees, because her legs couldn't hold her weight right after her seizure.

"No." She barked it sharply, anticipating him. "Damn it, we've been through this. Daegan said no."

Instead, Gideon entered the cell, knelt at her side. Though she tensed, he slid an arm around her waist and helped her back to her feet, guiding her to the couch. "Daegan's not the boss of me."

"So if *I'd* told you no, you would have listened."

There was a disturbing flicker of truth to it, but he merely shrugged. "Of course. With you, I'm as obedient as a puppy."

"If you've had a puppy, you know there's nothing obedient about them."

He feathered a stray lock of her hair with his fingers in answer.

"Gideon . . ."

"I'm going." He didn't want her to be afraid of herself, so he withdrew. Though it ached like an open wound to do it.

When he straddled the seat outside the cell, beside the couch again, she slid down, curling her body in the sofa's embrace, facing inward. "You can feel them coming now, can't you?" she said softly. "You anticipated the last one before I did."

Her wrist was propped against the back cushion, the curl of her fingers the only thing visible, the rest of her hidden behind it. "Yeah," he said.

"Just like you knew about the alley. You came back. Gideon, you have—"

"Well-developed intuition." He hated to hear it called *psychic ability*, as if it was a gift. He and Jacob had both anticipated their parents' deaths, a few agonizing moments before it had happened. He remembered the way the two of them had stopped on the beach, eyes locking, whirling as one to see Mom and Dad out in the waves. They'd been playing the same way kids did, only in hindsight he remembered it was more flirtatious, Mom wrapped around Dad, as she tried to push him under . . .

They hadn't known which direction or how it would happen, just like the night Anwyn had been attacked. Not enough information, not soon enough.

But he could give her this. "I can sense them coming, and I'm not taking unnecessary risks, Anwyn. Be easy on that. I know the most important thing is that I be around to take care of you until he gets back."

Her fingers twitched. "I've lost count. Whose turn is it, on Twenty Questions?"

"If you can't remember, then it's my turn, of course." He heard her weak snort. Propping his chin on his folded arms, he rubbed a hand over the back of his neck, feeling tense steel cables. "Tell me about Daegan. I haven't crossed his path before. Since he has his own bedroom, it seems he's been hanging around here awhile."

Her chains clanked as she pulled herself up so she could rest her cheek on the back of the sofa, next to her manacled hand. Ragged tendrils of her hair caressed her cheek, and he was struck anew by the beauty of her eyes, no matter what she was going through. He was glad his appreciation was so obvious, because she noticed, and it made some of the tension in her face lessen. The vanity of a woman had its own healing balm. It almost made him smile a little, for real this time. "I don't know if I should tell you more about Daegan," she said, seeing it. "You are a vampire hunter, after all. You might stake him. Why don't you tell me *your* impression of him?"

She barely had enough slack to touch his hair, but she reached out to stroke the short lengths between her knuckles. It felt good for her to initiate touch, good for them both, he suspected. He stayed motionless, watching the curve of her cheek, the tender underside of her forearm. The tenuous grasp of the towel over the swell of her breasts. "He's faster than any vampire I've seen. There's something different about him, but I can't figure out what. He's like the difference between an Army Ranger and a guy who pumps iron to look like a badass. I don't think I could touch him, unless you're going to help me knock him unconscious."

"Hmm. He sleeps very, very lightly." She grazed his scalp, pressed down. "There's a scar here."

"Yeah. Vamp's servant got me pretty good with the sharp end of a shovel. It's the servants that are the trickiest. A hunter has to focus on the vamps, because they can outmaneuver you so fast. That means you sometimes lose sight of the servant, what he can do, if you're not paying attention."

"But when you kill his Master, you kill him. Two birds with one stone."

Gideon shifted, uncomfortable. "Vampire rules, such that they are, say the servant has to enter a vamp's service willingly. It does happen by force sometimes, but in those cases, the servant would beg for death, so it's a mercy. Otherwise . . ."

"Guilt by association." Cocking her head, she swept her gaze over him. She'd gotten blood and vomit on him, of course, so he'd stripped his shirt off a few seizures back. Her gaze coursed over his upper body, lingering on the flogging scars, and the pain he saw fill her eyes humbled and dismayed him. "Why doesn't your well-developed intuition keep you out of that kind of trouble?"

"It does. I'm alive." He tugged her hair.

"Did it bring you to our door?"

Gideon grunted, as always irritable trying to explain the inexplicable, even to this woman who needed his distraction. "I don't know. I just tend to follow my gut and things work out. That's the truth. My brother and I, we share that ability. Sometimes we're led by it. Of course, sometimes it takes us in stupid directions, but we don't seem capable of ignoring it. Hence, here I am and he's with a vampire queen."

Her brows lifted. "Your brother is a *servant*? While you're a vampire hunter?"

"I would have expected Daegan to tell you that. My brother's a vampire, as well as a servant. It's a long story." At her ironic expression, he grimaced. "Yeah, I know, we have time. But when you're ready to explain your relationship with Daegan, I'll give you the write-up on that one."

She gave him a saccharine look. "We're friends. Friends with benefits."

Gideon whistled. "Wow. You've got a pretty good poker face, but I can call that one a lie from a hundred feet."

"Do you really want to get into the lies we tell ourselves?" Before he could rally to that, she shook her head. "Never mind. I'll let you get away with that one, not because you're threatening me with quid pro quo, but seeing as you're trying to overcome your antisocial skills and talk to me."

"You're a generous Mistress, Mistress."

"Did you find the answers you were seeking, our night together?"

"Not sure." He gave her a wry smile. "We seem to have gotten derailed."

The glance she gave him this time passed over the lean muscle and scarring of his upper body, then followed the stretch of denim over his splayed thighs where they straddled the chair. "Delayed, not derailed," she said.

"Hmm." He told himself under no circumstances should he imagine that scenario between them again. No way in hell would he ever willingly allow a vampire to chain him up, even if he'd known her before. However, each time her eyes focused on him this way, or that tone crept into her voice, he sensed, remarkably, that current circumstances were only solidifying what had started the second he decided to cross the threshold of Atlantis. The answers were here, with this woman. It was just a hell of a situation, because she was no longer human.

"The silence is driving me crazy. Will you play some music for me?" Her fingers bit into his scalp, an urgent, unsteady note to her voice, though he didn't yet sense another attack. "Over in that cabinet. It's wired into the music system in the main room."

"Sure." He left her with a reassuring squeeze of her wrist and strode to the player. "Any preferences?"

"There should be something already keyed up."

As he depressed the play button, the room filled with a soothing mix of woodwinds and piano, a nature-oriented New Age sound.

She was watching him. "Do you like it?"

"Yeah. Yeah, actually, I do." It was calming and something else, something . . . He hesitated to use the word *hopeful*, because it wasn't his nature, but she filled in the blanks.

"It transports you to a different place. When I close my eyes, I'm in deep woods, an enchanted forest. There are fairies and unicorns, all a young girl's dreams."

"Like that old movie, *Legend*."

"Yes. Without Tom Cruise." She'd lain down on the couch again, her chains gathered against her, legs drawn up. Her lips curved in a mysterious, sad way. "I prefer my men less pretty."

"I'm your man, then, because pretty I'm definitely not."

"You're mine . . ." Her eyes narrowed to blue-green slits so the color was all he could see. Mesmerizing, like a Fey princess peering through the leaves. "I like the sound of that."

He cleared his throat. "Daegan would be crushed if he knew your opinion. He's been hosed down with pretty all over."

"Shhh . . ." Her eyes closed, as she obviously let the music relax her. Gideon watched her for several moments; then his grip tightened on the chair next to the player.

Shit. Another fucking one coming. It had been barely minutes since the last one, it seemed. But as she spoke again, he was loath to interrupt her, the drifting lilt of her honey-spun words.

"Listen to those notes. It's a magical place. You can see all of it, laid out inside your heart, in the place where this world hasn't intruded. If a hero is brave and strong enough, then all will be right again. Light will forever reign. And his heroine will love and be with him always. True to him forever."

"I like the sound of that," he said. "Anwyn, I need to take you back to the wall. Okay?"

Her brow creased, her lids squeezing tighter. "No," she said softly.

"I don't want the chains to drag you, honey. Just get up and walk over there—"

Her fingers dug into the couch; then the first shudders began.

Damn it. He moved swiftly to the controls, only this time he had to close his eyes when he depressed the dial. It was bad enough to hear her cry of protest; he couldn't bear to see her pulled off the couch while she tried to hold on to it, then was dragged step by resisting step to the wall. If she fought it with a vampire's berserk rage, he could take it, but she was fighting it with the panic of a strong woman who couldn't handle being made helpless.

"Can't breathe . . ." her voice rasped. Though he knew she no longer needed to breathe, the sense of suffocation was still no less real to her. He steeled himself against it, kept the chains retracting. Then the thud, the click of the control turning off, told him she was back against the wall.

When he opened his gaze, he saw one last second of that panicked anguish on her face an instant before red flooded her eyes like an injection of ink, spreading out and overflowing into bloody tears. Her mouth opened, the fangs glistening and frighteningly long. She uttered a hiss a dragon might have made in her magical world, before it opened its jaws and snapped up the hero in one less-than-heroic bite.

Beneath all that, Anwyn was fighting a battle for her mind and soul, far beyond where a hero, or even he or Daegan, could come to her aid.

Fuck, fuck, fuck. Gideon kicked a spanking bench, hit the bars with his fists and cursed profusely. If she was going to be taken from him by a fit of mindless rage, he was going to use some of the time to vent.

Concrete dust plumed from the wall around her left manacle, snapping him out of the moment. Shit, the anchor was loosening. He snatched up more chain that Daegan had left, just in case, and ran into the cell.

She was thrashing and struggling, her mouth wide-open, fangs spearing her, creating a fountain of blood over her full bottom lip. Shaking out the chain, he looped it around her arm, wrapping it snug around the limb and the solid arm of the St. Andrew's cross, glad there was some space between the wall and the beam. He bound the arm from wrist to armpit before she could put more pressure behind the loosened bolt. He stayed clear of the thrashing head except when he got close to her shoulder. Then she nailed him.

Neither he nor Daegan had wanted to bind her head, since the arms, legs and torso were almost more than she could handle. But he had second thoughts about that when her fangs sank into his forearm, a snarl emitting from her throat. Fortunately, she couldn't get a good grip, his blood sending her into a renewed seizure. He jerked out of range as her eyes rolled back in her head. She let out a sound that he'd never imagined could pass human lips.

Gideon used another titanium carbonari clip to secure the chain and then did the other arm the same way, not wanting to take any chances. Now she wouldn't be able to leave the cross at all. When she surfaced from this seizure, she'd likely freak as a result. Pushing that out of his mind, he went for more refrigerated blood, wrapping a dish towel around his bleeding arm.

Jesus, where the hell is Daegan? They needed the sire's blood. This stuff wasn't doing the trick anymore. Not only did she resist it more fiercely each time, but when he got some into her, she jerked like an animal in its death throes. The cries coming from her now, the wide, prickly fear in her eyes, beyond coherence, told him she was in excruciating pain when she was ingesting it.

"It's all right, baby. We're here. We're here. Hang in there. You can do this." He dashed away shameful, unmanly tears at her keening, glad she wouldn't remember them. He could get through it; she would get through it. *Never give yourself a choice, because if you gave yourself a choice . . .* Well, she'd said it herself. You'd regret it all your life. Best to react and pretend there were *no* choices.

He suspected there was more to that comment, something else in her past involving choices. Something that might haunt her even more than what happened in the alley. Another mystery to his beautiful Mistress.

It seemed to go on forever, but in hindsight, he suspected it was little longer than any of the previous ones, just more virulent. When she fell into lethargy again, hanging semiconscious in the chains, he collapsed onto the sofa, putting the blood container on the floor and his head in his hands, giving himself a second to regroup.

Vaguely, he realized he hadn't eaten or drunk anything. While nothing appealed to him, he guessed he should think about forcing something down, if he didn't want to pass out on her. And hell, she wasn't going to be finishing the food she had in her refrigerator. Jesus, even his hair hurt.

The music was still playing. It was good music. He gave a rueful snort at the thought, but noticed that she was registering it again as well, her weary head moving in a sway to the gentle beat of the woodwinds, mumbling as if she was humming along. It made it sound like a lullaby.

In between those tranquil notes, though, she murmured to herself, things he couldn't understand and probably didn't want to. As he cleaned her and the floor once more, he blessed the foresight that had put a drain in the stone floor, though he was sure he didn't want to think about all the uses for that in a BDSM dungeon. He tucked the last clean towel around her, wondering about his options after she destroyed that one. There had to be a washer or dryer down here, right? He'd just find one, or he'd cut Daegan's sheets into quarters. He was a vampire, after all. He could sleep hanging from the rafters.

When he snorted at that bit of vampire lore, she stirred. He was sitting on a chair in front of her again and put a hand on her leg, right below the hem of the towel. It was a calming signal he'd fallen into using when she surfaced, letting her know he was there still. Particularly since this time something had changed for the worse, her restraints considerably increased.

She focused on him from a far-distant place, but her gaze remained so intent on him it was as though she was trying not to notice or think of anything else. But then she winced.

"My tongue hurts."

"Yeah, you bit it pretty bad that time. I thought about getting one of the ball gags, but I didn't want to upset you more."

He saw a dark well of panic open in her eyes before she slammed a cover on it. Pretending he'd seen nothing amiss, he tugged the towel gently. "I wouldn't do it without your okay. You know that. It's already looking better. I think your refrigerated blood helped some, being directly on your tongue like that. Anwyn . . . I had to add the chains. You were pulling the one side loose."

She nodded after a moment, a more subdued response than he expected. Then he took a closer look. Though he'd never seen anyone who looked more exhausted than she did right now, in addition to that intent gaze that could bore holes into him, her pulse was rabbiting up and down. As if she was managing a silent panic attack. Her phobia about the restraints was getting worse, not better, and he'd had to increase them. *Goddamn it.* Her urgent request for music now made more sense.

"How can I make it easier, Anwyn? Tell me. Anything, short of taking the manacles off, I'll do."

Instead, her attention had latched onto his arm. "I hurt you."

The bleeding had stopped so he pulled the cloth away, showing her the two puncture wounds. "No worse than a shot," he lied. "Don't worry about it."

As if she forgot she couldn't touch him, she strained with her fingers, and Gideon met them, pressing pads to pads, tenting their fingers between them. "Take a break," she said softly instead. "I'm not going anywhere and you look like shit."

He blinked. "Once you get off that cross, you can try giving me orders. You don't know me if you think I'll let you deal with a minute of this alone. How about we go back to our car games? I'm thinking charades. Granted, I'll have the advantage, but you're not the kind of woman who whines about things being unfair."

Instead of laughing, something crumpled in her expression. He was out of the chair in an instant, bringing his much larger body close, cloaking her so she could only feel him, see the spread of his palms on either side of her face and not the chains. "I'm here, Anwyn. Hang in there. I'm not going anywhere. I'm okay."

"I know. It's so irrational."

"No, not irrational at all. I don't get all that thrilled about being tied up, either. In fact, you remember you had to use a gag to shut me up.

More than one vamp has threatened to cut out my tongue. Actually, I think my brother threatened once or twice as well. My third grade teacher—"

She pressed her forehead to the bridge of his nose and he slid his lips along her cheek. "A problem, even in third grade? You needed more spankings." The corner of her mouth quirked as he raised his head. "Or maybe that's what you were angling for."

"Not my thing. I'm not the 'I've been a bad, bad boy and why doesn't Mommy spank me' kind of guy."

"No, you're not. But you are the bad boy, Gideon. The kind that most every woman wants to experience. One that sweeps a woman off her feet." She laid her forehead on his shoulder again, breathing deep.

He stroked the back of her skull, followed the silky curves of her braided hair. "I don't know about that. But is that what you're looking for?"

"*I'm* not that kind of girl." Tilting her face into his right hand, she let it rest there, her eyes half-closed again. Her voice dropped to that alluring murmur, a whisper of breath on the syllables. "I'm the one who wants to take the bad boy and teach him how to be really bad, all at my command. I want to take away the pain that makes him so bad, give him a clean kind of pain, make him lose his mind so all he wants is to give his soul to me."

"Just so you aren't asking for a lot." Gideon's throat had thickened and she heard it, because her eyes opened, gazing at him with a speculative glint.

"Maybe you're not the put-me-over-Mommy's-knee type," she mused. "But you respond well to pain, administered the right way. The bite of my nails, the cut of a switch. Rawhide kissing your testicles with the right amount of sting so that you'd learn to say, 'Yes, Mistress,' when you kneel in front of me. Maybe we'll get the chance to see that happen."

The blue-green intensity of her gaze had ratcheted up enough that it was as if she had no chains on her at all, her focus all on him, his heat, his touch, his body. All hers. Gideon felt it as if she'd actually locked a collar around him with her words, her forthright stare that seemed to see nothing but him. For a brief, pleasurable moment, she'd found an avenue back to herself. As long as their gazes stayed locked, unblinking, she seemed able to stay in that spot. As for himself, he wasn't sure if he could have looked away if he'd wanted to do so.

"What else would you like to see happen . . . Mistress?" He told himself he was just keeping her going, distracting her, dispelling that panic attack. But it was doing something no less unsettling to him.

"I'd like to put your cock in a harness, watch it stay hard for me for hours, gag you with a metal bit when you mouthed off to me, as you'd be tempted to do. See you bend and kiss my foot for forgiveness, your beautiful bare ass rising high to the caress of my hand, knees spread wide so I could close my hand over your balls, squeeze them hard. You'd give me that, Gideon, because of what I could give you in return. Everything."

Leaving him staring at her, she laid her head back and softly hummed with the music. After a few unsettled moments where he realized he had no response for her, therefore making silence the wisest option, he straddled the wooden chair in front of her again. When he draped one arm over the back, he ran a light hand along her knee, the back of her calf, a reassurance. But for which of them, he didn't know.

"What does this song make you think about?" she asked abruptly.

He closed his eyes, listening. "Fish."

"Fish?"

"Yeah," he said, keeping up the stroke on her leg. "Reminds me of how they dart forward so fast, but then put on the brakes to drift, as if they have all the time in the world." The music changed to a staccato, and his lips curved. "That's them at the top, seeking food, making the water ripple up like when the wind passes over it. The slower, more tranquil part is when they all swim together."

When he saw her surprised look, he lifted a shoulder. "I've spent a couple days at an aquarium before. It was . . . quiet." It had been in one of the towns that had a large community aquarium. While he was between hunts, he sometimes ate a sandwich there, watched the fish, because in that place he didn't have to worry so much about guarding his back.

The music swelled to a crescendo. When she looked at him, obviously hoping for another visual, he shook his head. "I got nothing for that."

"It's a sudden rainstorm. The water is striking the surface in a thousand different places, so the fish are all floating on the bottom, listening to the drum of it, waiting for the storm to pass."

Gideon turned at the quiet words. Daegan stood in the doorway, watching them both.

15

DAEGAN had smelled the scent of blood and vomit throughout their ground-level apartment before he even stepped off the elevator. Fortunately, the strongest source of it appeared to be in a laundry basket set up just outside the dungeon area. When he'd slid silently into the apartment, he'd paused, listening to them talk. He'd wanted a moment, because though he'd known this was going to be a rough transition, he hadn't entirely expected the lingering vibrations in the apartment to be as violent as they were.

If that hadn't told him what the past day had been like, the haggard look on the vampire hunter's face, the stiff way he sat, as if only his will was keeping him vertical, would have. Then there was Anwyn herself, chained like a dangerous monster, though he could see where the anchor chain had been about to give way and knew Gideon had had no choice. Her hair was braided, but some of it had come loose and snarled around her face. He'd kept her cleaned off, but still there were smears of blood here and there, and of course she smelled like vomit and blood as well, her white face as strained as Gideon's was exhausted.

Still, from their quiet banter, it was obvious they were hanging in there. It gave him an unexpected sense of pride in both of them.

She saw him first, but Gideon was already turning, as if he'd sensed his approach. The raw need in Anwyn's face, never so naked and plain before, affected him with embarrassing sentiment, making him ignore any reservations he'd normally have in the hunter's presence. Dropping the black tote on the chair, he was with her within an instant. Daegan put his hands on her face, one under her nape, and kissed her hard, fierce.

As he did, he was vaguely aware of Gideon unsnapping the lock holding the additional chains on her arms and working them loose, using the manual control on the side of the cross to give her enough slack to put her arms around Daegan's shoulders. A bit of sensitivity he wouldn't have expected from the man, but he didn't question it.

Daegan brought Anwyn up against him, holding her shuddering body close. A tremor went through his own, feeling her fear and vulnerability, how much she had suffered these past many hours. Yet here she was, still Anwyn. Though he knew how strong she was, he was sure he owed a good deal of that to the male awkwardly standing on their periphery.

When Gideon started to ease back to give them the semblance of privacy, one of her hands fell away from Daegan and captured Gideon's fingers without even looking, keeping him there with them. Daegan could tell it surprised the vampire hunter, as well as when he himself gave the man's shoulder a bruising squeeze of welcome, registering the tense, weary muscles. Christ, did the man think they'd simply used him, and had no regard for him otherwise?

An issue for a later time. For now, it was a long moment before Daegan pulled back from Anwyn, but only far enough to put his forehead to hers.

"I'm so sorry, *cher*. Did I leave you in good hands, or do I need to rip his heart out of his chest?"

"You do that, word's going to get around and you won't be able to find a babysitter for her again." When Anwyn at last dropped his hand, Gideon backed up, but only to lean against the wall. "She's a real brat. She throws tantrums."

Anwyn smiled at them both through a sheen of tears. "He's been so generous, Daegan. Make him go rest now. I'm worried about him."

"I'm right here, and I'm not leaving," Gideon reiterated. "I'm going to help get that blood into you."

Daegan noted that the hunter had not doubted he would bring the blood with him. Of course, he would have done it or died trying, and maybe Gideon had understood that.

Anwyn spoke in an unexpectedly determined, cool voice. "I appreciate you doing that, Daegan, but as I said before you left, there was no need. I'm not going to take it."

It was as if she were politely refusing a dinner invitation because of other plans. Daegan exchanged glances with Gideon, but before he could draw the man away to get a better sense of what might be happening, Gideon straightened from the wall. There was a flicker to his expression that she apparently understood all too well, for the eyes she turned back to Daegan were a little wild, muscles tensing under his hands on her delicate face, slim neck.

"All I need is the two of you here. I feel balanced. The music is playing, and everything will be all right." His brow creased as her voice faltered. Red color blushed across her sternum and the base of her neck, obscenely like the rose tint of an impending climax.

"She's going again," Gideon warned in a low voice.

"No." She cried out as Daegan's hands tightened on her. "Don't give it to me, Daegan. It will be like . . ." A strangled sound ripped from her throat as she fought the convulsion.

"Don't fight it," Gideon urged her. "You know that makes it worse."

She ignored him, struggling to get the words out. "Taking his blood will be . . . like . . . raping me again . . ." The syllable became a long, low cry, and Gideon went for the wall control.

"No," Daegan said sharply. Turning her in his arms so her back was to him, the chains wrapped around his forearm, he went to a crouch on the floor. He folded her to the ground between his knees, his body sheltering her.

～

Gideon watched as the vampire held her fast against him, even as the convulsion swept over her full force. She struggled and snarled, whipped her head around and sank her fangs into his arm. Keeping his head bent over hers, his concentration completely upon her such that the energy around them was a heated, pulsing thing, Daegan let her drink, holding her with just his knees and the one arm around her upper body. With the other, he stroked her hair, watching her suckle off his arm like a vicious nursing cub, growling and hissing all along. Her nails stabbed into his flesh on either side of her embedded fangs. The chains clanked as she fought him, but he was far more powerful than a fledgling vampire. Even though that fledgling vampire could easily have thrown Gideon across the room.

Sure, he'd babysat her, held her hand for a day or so. This male could actually take care of her, keep her from all harm. Because he was a vampire, what Gideon was sworn to kill. Just like she was.

It was a red-alert flag, a reminder that this was all temporary. Soon, she wouldn't need him further. In fact, with Daegan back, he knew that was already the case, physically. A cold, hard insight that didn't seem to hold sway over his personal, selfish need. He wanted to stay. Even if she didn't need him any longer.

Evidently, she'd passed out, as she sometimes did right after the most violent ones. Daegan's gentler restraint had kept her from hurting herself, but she'd still oozed blood from her skin. He'd shifted her so the bloody vomit landed more on the tile than on either of them. Now he lifted her, maneuvering around the chains, and took her to the sofa. Laying her there, he caressed her face, arranged her limbs as comfortably as possible. Though his movements were smooth, tender, his face was back to that fixed mask. When he withdrew, he gestured to Gideon. The two left the cell, Gideon closing it. Daegan took them into the front room where Gideon assumed he'd keep a hypersensitive ear tuned to the dungeon area in case she woke.

"Has she been like this throughout?" Daegan said quietly.

"Yeah." Gideon glanced down at the blood smeared on his arm and Daegan followed his attention. "Each one leaves her more tired than the last; each one is more vicious than the last. Sometimes she talks like him . . . Barnabus. Short spurts. Nasty, crazy things. She doesn't seem aware of it."

Daegan digested that. Though his expression didn't change, Gideon wondered if he was thinking he didn't make Barnabus and his crew suffer enough. Whatever he'd done to them, Gideon agreed. "When she wakes, we are going to give her the sire's blood," the vampire said curtly. "I assume we don't have a disagreement on that."

"None at all."

Daegan pressed his lips together. "Her sire was a homeless schizo-phrenic turned by a fugitive from a facility for the criminally insane. Who was initially turned by a weak made vampire."

"Shit." Gideon rubbed a hand over his face. "Is his blood going to help or hurt?"

"It should help. Usually the amounts needed are very small, as you know. The timing for them is vital to help manage the bloodlust, and the violence of the bloodlust attacks are probably what are driving her deeper into his madness."

"Yeah. Probably." Gideon glanced toward their motionless charge. "Doesn't seem to cover all of it."

"Explain." Daegan's tone was that of a field colonel, demanding an answer or there would be hell to pay. But Gideon was more comfortable with that than circuitous chitchat.

"Whatever it is that makes her . . . what she is, is having a very hard time with this. For a while the bloodlust was covering it, but I caught it a little while ago. She's been having panic attacks all along, and those might be contributing to the increasing frequency of the seizures and bloodlust. Stress makes things worse. She's damn good at covering, too good."

"She always has been," Daegan grumbled. "It's very difficult to tell when she is truly upset, until it's too late."

"Particularly in this case," Gideon agreed somberly. "I think the lack of control is eating at her worse than anything. She can tell they're get-ting worse, and that an element of her mind is slipping away from her. If we don't give her back some true sense of control soon, something she can use as an anchor against all the rest, I think she'll break her own mind before the bad blood does it for her." He shifted. "The flip side is, if we give her that, I think she's strong enough to handle anything. I just don't know what'll do that for her."

Something clicked in Daegan's gaze, something that apparently startled him enough to disrupt his typically inscrutable expression. Gideon cocked his head. "I ring a bell?"

"Perhaps. Give me a few moments to consider it." The vampire sank to a squat on his heels, eschewing the furniture, his duster pooling around him. Gideon could almost hear the gears shifting; then he saw a humorless tug at Daegan's mouth, a flicker in his dark eyes.

"It is something I believe, oddly enough, you are best suited to provide, Gideon. So we will have to consider an alternative."

"What do you mean? I'll give her whatever she needs."

Daegan lifted a brow, tilting his head up. "Such heroic declarations are usually meaningless bullshit, vampire hunter. We all have our lines in the sand."

"The Kung Fu David Carradine Grasshopper crap hits the manure meter just as hard. Spit it out."

"Like most things, what could break her is also the key to what could save her. She is an incomparable Mistress, Gideon. Very focused. You said it yourself. If we give her something that is hers, something that can't be taken away from her, it may help."

"Christ, are you a woman? Would you just fucking say it?"

"Fine." Daegan rose. "Let her make you her servant. Let her into your head."

The words hit his brainpan, but they had to sizzle and burn before they penetrated. Gideon stared at him. "I didn't hear you right."

"You heard me well enough." Daegan gave him an even look. "A new vampire doesn't usually take a full servant for many years, because she must learn how to guard her thoughts, and not plumb the servant's mind too deeply. In Anwyn's case, because of the poison in her sire's blood, I believe she needs someone immediately. You already anticipate her attacks, and with a mind connection, you could help her with bouts of erratic behavior that may continue past the bloodlust transition."

"So you want me to be like some kind of dog for the disabled."

"If you like. She has many collars here. I suspect you like rhinestones."

"I suspect you can fuck off."

Daegan's look became steel, an expression suggesting Gideon was about to cross a line. *Good.* He liked to see it clearly when he stepped over it. "I'm not becoming any vampire's slave, not now, not ever," he said emphatically.

"As long as you see it that way, I believe you," Daegan agreed. "But I know you'd lay down your life for any woman in need. This is no different. A servant is not only functional. A third mark is a reserve of strength for a vampire. When something knocks a vampire off her axis, the servant can provide the strength to steady the boat."

Gideon knew that, damn it. Lyssa had drawn strength from Jacob when she most needed it. "You know, I'm getting sick of hearing the things you know about me, without explaining how you know them."

"Another topic, another time. We will stay focused on this."

"Then don't bullshit me. You're not the only one who knows things. She'll be a vampire," Gideon said shortly. "Doesn't matter what she was yesterday; I know what happens. How she'll change. And what being a servant means in your world."

He almost snarled at Daegan's fixed expression. "I'm the wrong choice for it. When and if she wants a servant, she'll choose someone else. Someone better. In a couple weeks, when she's well on her way through the worst of this"—he hoped—"you won't even need me. I'll head out."

"And go back to killing vampires like her." Daegan leaned against a support column. A small photograph of a peaceful beach had been hung there, some original signed print. A sunrise, lots of reds and golds and pinks. An early-morning beauty that would be a death sentence for Anwyn if she were caught out in it.

"No, not like her," Gideon spat. "More like that garbage you took out tonight."

"Fine." Daegan straightened. "As I told you, we all have our lines in the sand. Once you committed to it, there could be no doubts. She can't afford weak loyalty."

Gideon wanted to argue, but it was knee-jerk, irritation at the vampire's tone, not at the truth of it. "If you wish, you may go now," Daegan continued, turning away. "In fact, I think that's best, so her dependence upon you doesn't increase. I'll administer the sire's blood and care for her from here forward. We can achieve the balance she needs without your presence."

"If anyone's going to dismiss me like I'm some kind of bellboy, it's not going to be you. She can—"

Daegan spun back around. What Gideon had taken for an indifferent tone was revealed as something else altogether as he saw the tips of fangs and that deadly trace of crimson in the vampire's eyes.

"I will not allow you to work out your personal shit at her expense. She gave you a taste of something you were seeking, but, as you pointed out, she is a vampire now. You loathe everything she will have to become to survive. If you cannot set that aside, you are just prolonging a bond that will hurt her far worse when you hack it free with that dull-blade mentality of yours."

"It's not all or nothing. I don't have to become her servant to prove anything to her. And I sure as hell don't need to prove anything to you."

"No, you don't. But you have something to prove to yourself. That is what I will not tolerate, not here. I will not allow you to make this—make her—that battleground. Go back to your life, such that it is."

"Fuck you." Gideon spun on his heel, strode into the reading room. His intent was just to move away from the conversation before it got really nasty, but his gaze fell on his weapons. Daegan had left them in a chair hours ago, out of his reach as requested. Out of habit, a calming ritual, he began to strap them on, slide them into their proper places.

As he did, he imagined the day he *would* walk out of here and not look back. Headed to the next job, as Daegan had said. There was a vampire in Georgia, one that took his annual quota of twelve human lives, plus a few more. It would probably take a month to set it up, do the legwork, get the jump on him. If Lyssa and Jacob were back in Atlanta then, maybe he could visit them. And his new nephew, the one with tiny fangs and Jacob's laughing eyes.

He kept his gaze fixed on the easy chair as he put the weapons on. The more he thought about leaving, the worse the burning sensation in his chest got. The greater the desire grew to go back down the hall, steal a look at the woman curled on the couch in her cell, surrounded by a coil of chains. To see if she was waking. If she needed him.

Fate lets you run from nothing. Run as fast as you wish, and she'll throw a brick wall right in front of you, smash that pretty face. Lyssa had said that to him, on a recent phone call where he'd evaded an invitation to come spend Christmas with them.

If we don't give her back some sense of control soon, something she can use as an anchor against all the rest . . .

Hell, had he planted the seed himself? Because it seemed the damned thing was already sprouting in his brain, setting out runners. What scared the hell out of him was he'd known what Daegan was going to say almost before the words came out of his mouth. He recalled how Anwyn had asked what had drawn him to Atlantis.

What if it's this? A destiny that's been eating away at you ever since you shared your brother's Mistress.

Christ, next thing he'd be getting his palm read and reading Tarot cards. It was bullshit. She was a fucking vampire. But she was also a woman who needed him. No matter how capable Daegan was, Gideon possibly could provide her something that even he couldn't. Otherwise she would have let the vampire mark her a long time ago, right?

Oh yeah, ego stroking. His subconscious was working this angle hard. Freaking little internal hustler.

"Damn it, damn it, damn it." He rose with an abrupt jerk where he'd sunk down on a chair arm. His muscles screamed in protest, even his bones creaking. He was really beyond exhaustion, not a great time to be having an argument with himself. He wanted to go up above, breathe in the world and get some perspective.

The sudden, urgent thought brought him up short. No, he assured himself. He wasn't bolting. He'd come back. This wasn't good-bye, even though he'd donned all his weapons. It was just a quick run above for some fresh air. That was, unless Daegan wouldn't let him back in.

He strode back to the dungeon room. Over the music cabinet, Daegan had opened a panel that revealed a television screen. It figured Anwyn would have cable access in her dungeon room. Enjoy the latest *Dancing with the Stars* episode while she wrung some poor bastard out. She was still out on the sofa, her braided hair following the contour of her bosom, her hands curled under her cheek, giving her a deceptive, childlike appearance. She already had that peculiar propensity vampires had, not to breathe when they slept, the braid motionless.

Despite that, if Daegan hadn't been between him and the cell, he would have gone to her, stroked a hand over her head through the bars as he'd done countless times over the past few hours. "I need to go up top for a while and make a phone call," Gideon said brusquely. "What's the security code to get back in?"

"Twelve, seventeen, thirteen, ten." Daegan didn't even glance at him, and Gideon's eyes narrowed.

"Did you just make that up?"

Daegan held a disk up to the light to interpret some marker writing on it. "No need. I can change the code with a few keystrokes."

"Are you going to?"

"Are you coming back?" Now Daegan's gaze did alter, that lightning-quick movement that was so fucking creepy, because Gideon didn't even see the shift of his eyes. Or the shift of his body, because abruptly he was squared toward him.

"Yeah, I'm coming back."

"Soon?" With little effort, it felt as though the vampire's penetrating look could peel the layers of Gideon's outer shields like an apple skin, cycling around and around him until it dropped in an impressive, unbroken coil at his feet.

"Maybe, Dad. They're having karaoke night at Floyd's down the street. I've been itching to give them my rendition of 'Back in Black.'" He let his gaze course with deliberate insult over Daegan's opaque fashion ensemble.

Daegan's expression didn't change by one flicker. He would have made a hell of a Buckingham Palace guard. "AC/DC. Decent choice. If you choose not to come back, vampire hunter, do me the courtesy of calling the front desk so James can let me know."

Fuck it, he'd said he was coming back—

"If you are coming back, come back sooner than later. You look like hell. You need sleep and a shower. She'll be displeased if I haven't made sure you've taken care of yourself."

With that, Daegan returned his attention to the disk, an obvious dismissal. Gideon suppressed the desire to trigger the wrist gauntlet, even though it would have done his heart good to make him twitch, just a little.

He started toward the cell. He was going to touch her face, at least brush the sole of her foot, her curved toes peeping from the bottom of the blanket Daegan had laid over her.

"I wouldn't. She appears to be sleeping rather soundly right now, and she needs it as much as you do."

His jaw muscle might knot irrevocably if he kept clamping down on the emotions he wanted to translate into the appropriate invective, but Gideon swallowed it. Daegan was right. Again. Of course, was the bastard cagey enough to know that if he allowed Gideon anything he could rationalize into a good-bye kiss, it might increase his chances of bolting?

Damn it, he *was* coming back. Even if he wasn't going to go for the crazy servant shit, he wouldn't leave her until he knew she was okay. If Daegan knew anything about him like he claimed he did, he'd have known that.

Turning on his heel, Gideon moved out of the chamber and toward the elevator. It was harder than expected to take those steps farther and farther away from her, from the room where the only things that had existed for an intense day or so had been her need and his singular focus on keeping her safe. Everything else felt surreal, fuzzy at the edges and too bright in the middle. Yeah, he was a little tired.

He could handle that. It wasn't the first time he'd run on an empty tank. He took the lift up to the next floor, stepped out into that accounting office hallway. His internal time clock was off, but it had to be daylight, because some of those doors were open and he could hear the foreign sounds of office chatter—computer keys clicking, phones ringing, conversational voices.

Assuming his presence had been cleared, he strode past those open doors without stopping, but he registered a startled pause here or there as people caught a glimpse of him. He'd put on the T-shirt he'd washed out during one of Anwyn's unconscious spells. Since it was black, the dampness wasn't likely noticeable under his jacket, but he hadn't bothered to take a look at his face or hair. But then, he rarely did. He probably looked like a cross between a homeless person and an escapee from an action-movie set. One of the staggering victims of a car crash or fiery explosion. Fuck it. The most important part of his wardrobe were his weapons, and he had those. His steps quickened with purpose until he turned into the maintenance corridors.

He encountered only one person there, an older man rolling a set of chairs toward the service elevator. His back was fortunately to him. Though Gideon moved soundlessly, the clatter of the chairs would cover him. He made it to the exit door they'd used last night, not alarmed from the inside, so he escaped without incident into the alley and breathed deep of garbage and air. It was a sunny midmorning sky, moving toward noon. He wondered how Daegan had gotten back safely, and remembered he'd said he could use sewer tunnels. It suited the overgrown fanged rat.

The alley was shadowed, but filled with enough light he wasn't barraged by the memory of finding Anwyn there. He left it behind quickly, though, moving toward the street but stopping shy of the sidewalk, propping his back against the brick wall of Atlantis and sliding down to rest his forearms on his knees and take stock.

Not a lot of movement on the street right now. Like a lot of adult establishments, Atlantis was relegated to an industrial district, even though with its high-class clientele it probably had more stringent codes of behavior inside its doors than a lot of bars and nightclubs catering to the scantily clad, hormone-infested clubbing set. The industries didn't generate a lot of foot traffic, too many street people and criminal elements drifting around.

Gideon stared out at the street, watching the movement of cars, an elderly man rolling a shopping cart of beer and soda cans along. He had a small wire-haired dog trotting along with him. A rustle of paper snapped his attention back to the alley, and a black cat froze at his regard, only a foot away from him. Gideon lifted a brow as she resumed her approach and rubbed her face against his calf, sniffing him. She smelled Anwyn, obviously. But she still shouldn't have trusted him so easily. Hell, the monsters that attacked her would have smelled like Anwyn, afterward.

He closed his mind to that punishing thought and gave the cat a stare. "Not a cat lover, sweetheart. You have the wrong person."

Though he'd probably let James know that somebody should come out here and feed Anwyn's charges. It would be one less worry on her mind. He tugged the cat's tail, an absent offering of camaraderie for how the world sucked as he removed his cell phone from his pocket.

He stared at the face, then punched the only programmed number he called these days, and that one not very often.

He had enough time to regret it, but not to cut it off, before his brother picked up.

"Which jail are you in? Or are you ice-skating in Hell?"

"Nice. Fuckface. How's my nephew?"

"He has your stubbornness. I should've had it surgically removed during the circumcision, because I think it's located in the same area." But then, because Jacob knew his brother too well, he added, "What's happening, Gid?"

"I don't know." Gideon gave a half laugh, which he was sure probably alarmed Jacob more. "Don't start heading out the door in full panic mode. I'm okay. Not in jail. I wanted to ask you something."

"Anything, bro. What do you need?"

Gideon took a few seconds, tried to figure out how to word it, and gave it up. "You tried to tell me, a couple times, why you became Lyssa's servant. I didn't really listen."

"You tried to put my face through a diner wall."

"You've always been too pretty. I was just helping you out." Gideon rolled his head around on his suddenly far-too-tense neck. "I thought you were an idiot. Still do, by the way," he added for good form, but then continued, "I'm listening now. Can you tell me why you did it? Did you just follow our famous gut down Hell's paved road of good intentions, or was it something she did? Or you figured out?"

And please God, don't ask me why I'm asking. I'll have to hang up, and I won't get an answer.

If Jacob had been a sister, or anyone of the female persuasion, an interrogation would have been a foregone conclusion. Gideon never would have made the call. However, as had happened often enough in their life that he sometimes wondered why it still impressed him, his brother picked up on exactly what he needed.

"At first, I tried to tell myself that it was because of what she was facing. Danger, enemies, et cetera. You know how it is. I was sure I was meant to be the person at her back. But as time went on, I knew, whatever she faced, I wanted to be with her, be whatever she needed me to be. It's like deciding to be married. You know your lives are meant to be bound together forever so you want something to make that permanent. There's no other possible in-between choice."

Something in his voice told Gideon his brother was looking right at her then. Lyssa was probably gazing back with those mesmerizing jade eyes. There'd be the slight softening to her mouth that only Jacob seemed to bring out in her. Even that night the three of them had been together, she'd used Jacob to make it work. She'd made it obvious, no matter how Gideon had wanted to deny it, that somehow she and his brother were already linked; blood, bone and heart.

"Hell, even that's probably just the excuse I used to stay with her when I couldn't explain it to myself." Jacob gave a half chuckle. "I needed to be with her. Breathing, life—everything that mattered—wasn't going to be possible without her. It wasn't the teenage crush kind of craziness where you can't think with anything but your hormones. It was stronger, deeper, far more intense than that. Didn't matter where she was going; I needed, wanted, to be there.

"I don't think it works that way for everyone," he added thoughtfully. "Sometimes it's a slow-moving creek that builds into a river, making a permanent groove for the two of you over the years, and I bet that's nice, too. But this was . . . this was what it was."

He stopped. Gideon wondered what Lyssa felt, hearing his brother's words. He knew how it made him feel. That yearning was back, the clamp on his gut that had drawn him here in the beginning, that had eased when Anwyn first walked into the room. He'd barely touched her, talked to her. Hell, he didn't even know what side of the bed she liked. Or if it mattered, because, being a Mistress, she might prefer her bed partners to sleep on a dog pallet on the floor. That was definitely not his kind of thing. But he'd sleep in front of her door to protect her from anything that came through it, so maybe that was the same thing.

Even if she wasn't that kind of Mistress, he knew about vampires. He was no one's pet, no one's slave, as he'd told Daegan. He didn't bend over and let himself get fucked just because someone snapped their fingers and told him to do it. Didn't matter that the first thing he'd wanted to do when he saw her was to drop to his knees and hope for her touch.

She did need some form of stability. But maybe it didn't have to be the whole enchilada. There were three marks. Just one might help her, that one blood connection, and the only advantage she'd have over him would be knowing his geographical whereabouts. No way was he letting anyone into his head, the advantage of the second mark.

Fuck, what was he doing? Here he was, contemplating something there was no way he'd ever consider if he was in his right mind. This was jumping into a murky pond with no clue to the kind of monster beneath the water's surface. Or, worse, he did have a clue, but he was considering it, anyway. For a lot of the reasons that Jacob had uncomfortably just outlined. Of course, Jacob had claimed he'd dreamed of Lyssa years before he'd met her, some kind of past-life bullshit. Gideon hadn't even had a clear picture of Anwyn before he walked into her place. It couldn't be the same.

Sometimes it's a slow-moving creek that builds into a river . . . But did you dive headfirst in that shallow creek, hoping it would become a river before your fool head cracked open?

"Gid, are you about to get yourself into the kind of trouble you can't get out of?"

"Maybe. I'll call you later. Give Lyssa a slap on the ass for me and tell her to bring you a beer."

"Yeah, I'll get right on that. Gideon—"

"Be easy, little brother. It's all right. It's a different kind of trouble, not the life-or-death kind." *Maybe.* "Hey, do you or Lyssa know anything about a vamp named Daegan Rei?"

Jacob and Lyssa were of course telekinetically connected, so Jacob must have offered the question in his mind. Lyssa was suddenly on the line, her sensual voice frosted with ice he could feel, even long distance. "Gideon, what's your involvement with Daegan Rei?"

"It's a long story. I just wondered—"

"I don't care how tough you are, you do *not* go after him."

"I'm—"

"I am not prepared to attend your funeral, even if there were enough pieces of you left to have one. I don't have a suitably demure black dress, and it will make me exceedingly angry to have to buy one."

"Wear red lace, then. We're—"

He had only a blink of warning, a sense of impending heat. Electricity jolted through his hand, enough to spasm through his fingers so that the phone clattered to the cement. He swore, shaking the tingling appendage. Holy Christ, how had she done that? He knew Lyssa's Fey abilities were growing, thanks to her exploration of her father's side of the family, but that was damned unsettling. He retrieved the phone gingerly, surprised it was still functioning. "How did you do that?"

"That's also complicated." Jacob again. "You've really ticked her off. But I got the gist of it. You're not going after this guy, are you? If you are, I'm coming to you."

"No. What I was trying to say before she went all Electron Woman on me was that . . . we're sort of working together."

Because that brought on a sudden shocked silence, he pressed the advantage to get the full message out. "I don't really want to go into it right now, but I need to know what she knows about him. I'm fully aware he's a badass, and my intention isn't to tangle with that side of him. We're helping someone . . . someone turned by force. She means something to him . . . and to me, too. Maybe. I mean, I just met her, but there's something . . . She needs me. Don't start spouting damsel-in-distress-syndrome crap, or I'll hang up."

"Hold on," Jacob said absently. Gideon waited, getting a vague sense of conversation, though no one was speaking.

"Lyssa doesn't want to say a lot, but I told her you could be trusted with this. You can't repeat it, okay? Not even to Daegan, because no one outside of the Council is supposed to know. It's important."

"Yeah, got it. Like, who am I going to tell?"

Gideon cursed to himself, but of course his brother had already jumped on it. "You're completely solo now, aren't you? You're taking them out on your own. You stupid, arrogant—"

"You going to tell me about Daegan Rei, or you going to waste your breath on bullshit?"

"I swear to God, if I could reach you, I'd break your fucking neck." Jacob sighed. "Fine. Brace yourself for the irony. Daegan Rei is the Council's private assassin. He's a vampire hunter."

16

DEATH Bringer. Grim Reaper. All the clichés, of course, wrapped up in the name he went by, a mix of the East and West. Daegan for black or dark, Rei for spirit or ghost. Black Spirit, Dark Ghost, or just Ghost. Lyssa knew his origins, the story behind how he'd gotten to be the Council's private killer, but she wasn't willing to share any of that. Apparently, no one but the Council knew who the guy was. He existed outside even the strict vampire hierarchy of overlords and Region Masters, somehow moving under their radar like a ghost in truth.

It stood to reason, because though the vampire world worked through power and control, they had an illusion of diplomacy to maintain as well. Because of the nature of the species, a vampire disappearing from sight for indefinite stretches of time rarely caused comment. Therefore, the Council at times found it more expedient to have the more embarrassing vampires in violation of Council directives erased quietly, rather than hauling them up in front of the Council for a public execution. Translation: Daegan was handling population control of the made vampires, like Barnabus, who'd gone off the map and could expose the vampire world to humans in a big, violent way. Less red tape and politics.

But something didn't figure, if only the Council knew about him. Barnabus had asked for Daegan by name. Did someone on the Council no longer appreciate his services? Or were they trying to test him in some way? He wondered if the realization that he'd been sold out had enhanced Daegan's fury, an additional undercurrent to his intense reaction to Anwyn's attack.

Gideon was even more cynical than Lyssa—and being more cynical than a woman who'd been around more than a thousand years was an accomplishment—and he could see rampant possibilities for abuse of that killing power. But what he'd seen of Daegan so far didn't gel with that. Cool control, clear-eyed and objective.

His lip curled. Freaking politics. There were vampire hunters, few though their number were, who'd tried to band together into conglomerates, and Gideon had shied away from them for that very reason. One of the few times he'd made the mistake of being a joiner outside his own personally organized cells had resulted in the complete snafu at the last Vampire Gathering. They'd been used as pawns of made vampires, and a lot of them had been killed. There'd been too many egos and players involved. No one listened, so no one realized they were walking into what ultimately could have been a death trap for all of them.

The rattling passage of the old man and his cart coming back stirred him. After his phone call, he'd remained against the brick wall of Atlantis, staring into space, lost in thought. The black cat was curled between his boots, sleeping, her purr a soft motor at the back of his thoughts. He didn't know how long he'd been sitting there, but at length, he rose, dislodging the cat. Sighing, he stopped at the kitchen door, rapped with his knuckles and met the gaze of the startled kid who popped open the door, obviously expecting a delivery. Gideon gestured to the black cat.

"You have a customer. Anw—Miss Naime would want you all to be feeding them while she's unavailable, right?"

The kid glanced at the cat, then up at Gideon, his gaze wary. "I gave the whole lot of them a tray of chicken scraps a little while ago."

"Hmmph." Gideon glanced down at the cat. "Faker." He kept going toward the maintenance door, leaving the boy staring after him.

When he reached the elevator entrance and punched in the code, he thought about those eight numbers. Twelve, seventeen, thirteen, ten. If a code was random numbers, people usually spelled it out. One-two-one-seven, et cetera. But what if it meant December seventeenth, year

1310? Could vampires be as predictable as people, using their birth-dates for access codes? That would make Daegan about seven hundred years old. A hell of a long time for him to be around and nobody to know anything about him. The Council had been around for way less time than that, and Lyssa had indicated he'd served them for only the most recent decades. So where had he been before then?

Gideon was surprised to find that Daegan had moved Anwyn out of the cell in the dungeon room to the couch in the sitting room. She was draped in a satin robe now, the blanket tucked around her. It seemed she hadn't yet stirred, or if she had, it had been brief and then she'd gone under again. It was the longest time she'd subsided, and he didn't know if that was a good or bad sign. Maybe she'd dived deep into unconsciousness, knowing she'd have to take that hated blood when she woke.

The robe's neckline was loose, exposing the curves of her breasts, the column of her throat. With one hand above her head and another across her abdomen, she made an erotic picture even with her still healing scars. Her expression was at rest, her lips full, inviting touch, lashes fanning her cheeks. But as he watched, pain flitted across her face, discomfort, and she shuddered. She turned, curling into a fetal ball.

Moving forward, Gideon adjusted the blanket over her. Her skin was ice-cold. He picked up an additional throw from the nearby chair, unfolded and spread it over her, smoothing his hands over the curve of waist and hip, resting briefly on her thigh. When he went to a squat beside her, so close to her face, he remembered how she'd looked earlier, when she'd spoken so plain. *I feel better when you're both here . . .*

She didn't even know him. It was just Nightingale syndrome, or whatever the hell they called it. As strong as she seemed, this was about as rough as anyone could imagine things getting. He'd shown up with Daegan in the alley. Her fixation had to do with his falsely heroic timing. That was all.

The sound of the television in the reading room told him where Daegan was. It figured he'd be close enough to keep an eye on her. Since he was more than capable of controlling her during an attack, he could take the risk, give her the comfort of these surroundings instead of the cell. Maybe that was the other reason she was finally at rest, the weight of the chains off of her for the time being. Her body was taking the ease her fear had denied it these past long hours.

Rising, he moved toward the sitting room. With a shock, he recognized the voices on the television. It was the security tape from his session with Anwyn. He stepped in just as he broke loose on the screen, grabbed her and slammed her into the alcove where the stained glass had been. Jesus Christ. He looked like some rabid animal, no better than what had attacked her. And worse, he could now clearly see where the glass had sliced into her back. While that had later become one gash among all those others, he was no less culpable for it.

His attention jerked to the chair. Daegan's long legs were stretched out, hands lying with deceptive ease on the chair's armrests. His dark gaze flickered up toward Gideon. "You were fortunate I wasn't here tonight."

"She wasn't. If you had been, we probably wouldn't all be here. She handled it, though. Didn't even bat an eye, and I could have killed her in a heartbeat."

"She's always had a warrior's courage and a fool's sense of when to make use of it." As Daegan hit the mute button but forwarded the tape, Gideon scowled.

"You just get off on seeing me naked?"

The vampire ignored the barb, kept his attention trained on the screen. "Anwyn has watched you since you first came here. I was surprised it took her as long as it did to take over your sessions." Daegan shifted, draped one leg over the chair arm, like a sprawling panther. "But it has been a long time since she's participated directly."

"Maybe she was just feeling charitable."

Daegan snorted. "Anwyn is the last woman who would take on a session because she was feeling charitable. I cannot tell what it is between you, but it is there, radiating off the screen." Then his gaze snapped back to the monitor, sharpening like the edge of a sword.

He hit the play button, leaning forward. Gideon followed his direction. When he saw the bathing area of the Queen's Chamber, his brow creased, remembering she'd signaled all the cameras to be turned off. Apparently, at least one of them hadn't been. His jaw set. *James.* While he'd likely obeyed the intention of her order, being the only one monitoring or having access to the footage, her head of security hadn't been willing to take it on faith that she'd be okay.

As much as it made him wince to see his bare ass at this angle, as his recorded self took Anwyn to the floor, putting her beneath him, Gideon had renewed respect for James Watts. In his shoes, he wouldn't have agreed with leaving her completely defenseless, either. Of course, the tape was in Daegan's hands, suggesting James might have acted out of self-preservation.

When Daegan hit the pause button, Gideon suppressed the desire to squirm. While the actual moment had been something he'd like to experience again, he didn't particularly care to revisit it with another man.

But Daegan's head whipped around, his expression giving Gideon a more immediate concern. "She has never let a man do what you are doing there. Never trusted one to lie upon her like that. Never wanted that." His lip curled. "No human male, that is."

Gideon recalled the peculiar stillness of that moment, when everything they both were had melted away. It was as if they were staring at each other, soul to soul, no ground or sky, just floating. Up or down, above or under, didn't really seem relevant. The jab at his testosterone was enough to get his ire up, though. "Feeling threatened, vampire?"

Daegan smiled then, chilling enough to freeze blood. "I've had no more sleep than you, vampire hunter. Don't aggravate me. Why did you come back?"

"I told you I would." Gideon pointed at Anwyn's sleeping form, kept his voice low with effort. "Just because I'm not ready to commit my entire life to being on a vampire's leash doesn't mean that I don't want to help her. No matter how invincible you think you are, I know it's still going to take two of us to get her through this. She should be waking soon. Maybe we should try to give Barnabus's blood to her when she's groggy."

"Vampires are rarely groggy when we wake." With another of those thorough looks Gideon was beginning to detest, Daegan rose, thankfully clicking off the television. As he reached the doorway, he stopped, considering Gideon.

"I was perhaps wrong to push you so hard at a decision that is a lifelong commitment, so far from what you've known and been," the vampire observed. "But it doesn't mean I'm completely wrong. I believe you know it as well, no matter how much it panics you. She needs you. I think what worries you most is how much you might need her."

"We don't even know each other, not really. Hell, we haven't even had a real date."

"I knew Anwyn Naime from the moment I met her. It's like that with certain people in our lives. We know our fates will be interwoven. It may not be the way we expect or wish, but it will happen." Daegan took another step forward, closing the distance between them. With effort, Gideon held his ground. He refused to give the bastard the satisfaction of a retreat.

The vampire's unrelenting onyx eyes showed a flicker of sardonic amusement, acknowledging his obstinance with mere inches between them. The dark hair he kept cropped so short gleamed blue-black as he cocked his head, studying Gideon's face closely. "You've been a vampire hunter for many years, Gideon. It's showing. Before long, somebody *will* be faster. That, and many other things, may be telling you it is time to do something else, something as worthwhile. Perhaps more so. This situation may only be one simple story in a world full of stories, but it may be the story that you are destined to become part of."

Damn how it looked, Gideon stepped sideways, moved back into the sitting room. As he did, his gaze fell on Anwyn once again, the pale skin, the fragile grace of her hand resting above her head. The sable hair drifting across her face, her tense mouth.

"I won't walk away from her as long as she needs me," he said gruffly. "But you and I both know it will happen eventually, because of what she's becoming. I can't go with her on that journey, not past a certain point." When Daegan said nothing, Gideon added, "You shouldn't have been watching the damn tape."

"What I saw in the tape merely confirmed things I already knew about you."

"If you don't stop saying things like that without fucking telling me what you mean—"

The vampire made a warning noise in his throat. Gideon followed his gaze to see Anwyn beginning to stir. Their charge was waking up.

At least the next step of what they needed to do was clear, even if nothing else was.

~

Anwyn felt as though something had died in her mouth. Her blood was boiling, while her skin was arctic to the touch. That vividness, as if she'd stepped into a television screen where the brightness and contrast were on their highest settings, hadn't abated. Though she couldn't see it, she knew it was later in the morning, because her body was weighed down by daylight. It was unnerving, because she wasn't sure if she had the strength to rise off the couch. The shadows in her mind had returned full force. Whispering and shifting restlessly, the tiny gremlins with red eyes told her things. Insidious, terrible things about what she would do, what she wanted to do, who she was.

She jumped when Daegan sat down next to her. As he settled his hip on the couch, she tried to focus on him, but it was when she shifted to Gideon, standing to Daegan's right, that she was able to balance, take a deep, calming breath. Daegan had closed one of his hands on hers, and Gideon took the other when she reached out to him. Daegan's touch was long-fingered, smooth and firm. Cool. Gideon's was callused, broad in palm, warm with human heat.

The shadows mocked her temporary dependence on the two males. Daegan could never be more than what Daegan was and, right now, despite his willingness to help her, all those latent issues of trust and power had bubbled to the surface, so she vacillated between despicable dependence and bitter resentment. She knew he could detect both, but was refusing to back away from her. It both angered and relieved her, which she wryly recognized as typically female.

Then there was Gideon, stepping into her life for a brief moment, likely to step out of it as quickly. He was probably already rationalizing his departure. No matter how powerful the connections she'd made to them, Fate decided if they would be permanent or temporary, and she knew all too well that Fate was addicted to change.

Go to hell, she told the gremlins succinctly, and led with the most normal question she could. "Did everything go all right with the club last night?"

While it might not seem a high priority to them, it had been her whole life for the past few years as it grew into a success far beyond her initial dreams. It was a stable force, and that alone made it something worth her focus.

Daegan considered her with his dark eyes. "James told me that they had a very good night, no problems. He and Madelyn have it all covered. He e-mailed the night's receipts and deposit records to your computer."

She nodded, but as he continued to regard her intently, with the weight of expectancy, she remembered what they wanted to do.

"No," she said emphatically, drawing her hands away. "I told you, Daegan. I can take your blood. I'll use it and my human blood, and I'll be fine."

"For a transition, you have to have your sire's blood," Gideon said. His voice wasn't unkind, but it was implacable. They were in concert on this. The feeling of being trapped returned, even though her restraints were gone. The shadow voices began to clamor, pure gibberish, but the din was so loud, a tremor shuddered through her limbs.

"Anwyn." Daegan covered her hand again, despite her attempt to evade him. "You know I respect your free will, to a point. But this isn't a choice. Don't make me force it upon you. If you refuse, I will." His thumb stroked her palm, a balm on his harsh words. "I will do whatever is necessary to make you well, even if it makes you hate me."

"I've hated you before," she retorted. A grim smile touched those sensual lips.

"So you've told me."

She swallowed, looked down at their joined hands. "I can't do it. It's not . . . Maybe in a few days." She hated to beg, so she firmed her voice, but kept her eyes on their hands. "When I don't feel like he's still on top of me. When I don't still smell him." *When he and his monsters aren't in my dreams, laughing.*

Daegan's hand tightened on hers, but it was Gideon who drew her attention as he circled around to sit at the lower end of the couch. Her cold toes were outside the blanket's edge, and he tucked them under his thigh, his fingers caressing her ankle. "There are cultures that eat their enemy's flesh," he said conversationally. "Drink their blood. It's to ingest their power, to take it from them."

I consumed you . . . That mantra she told herself, every time she chose to drink a glass of the hated brandy. She met his direct blue eyes. He had such a strong face, handsome bones that formed that determined chin.

"Don't suggest it to the reality TV crews," she responded. "They'll decide it's the next big *Survivor* challenge."

He gave her a tight smile with those firm lips that were perfect for . . . everything. She could imagine a lot of things under the category of everything, but it startled her that she thought of them right now. Of course, she wasn't like most women. When under stress, sex was the first thing she thought of to resolve her tension, rather than the last. Added to that, Daegan had told her—hell, proved to her—vampires were very carnal, no matter how stressful or conflicted the current situation was.

It was actually nice to have something else to think about. Except for the unexpectedly whimsical distractions Gideon had provided her with his "car games," her mind had been trapped with the agony and fear of those seizures, then vacillated to worries about the club. Which in turn had been bombarded with intrusive flashes of what had happened to her in the alley. Then there was the ever-present fallback subject, the knowledge her life was being altered, drastically. She didn't even know how to start thinking about that.

Unfortunately, that brought her back to what they wanted her to do.

After Barnabus had bitten her, given her that turning serum, he'd forced his blood into her mouth to complete it. He'd sliced a knife over his wrist, then dripped the generous flow of blood onto the tip of his naked cock, jutting from his open trousers. The other two had wrenched her mouth open with hard hands, held it while he pushed the broad head onto her tongue, rubbed it obscenely there. With their fingers in her mouth, she hadn't been able to snap down as she wanted to do. She'd had to lie in that terrible, subservient position . . . swallow. *You wanted it. You reveled in it.*

"*Shut up.*"

Her hoarse shout echoed in the room, but it drove back the insidious whispers for a brief second. Gideon's sure touch was on her legs, Daegan's on her face.

"Anwyn, come back to us."

"No." She pushed her palms against her temples, trying to compress the image, make it go away. Heat swept through her, and she almost welcomed the oblivious anguish of an impending seizure. "No. I can't do it."

"Anwyn, he wants you to die or go mad." Daegan pulled her hands from her face, despite her hiss. She didn't want him touching her, but he refused to let her go. His jaw tightened. "Gideon is right. He wants to know that, by taking your blood, he took your power. That he took you."

She closed her eyes, nauseous with it. "He did. I feel . . . so empty."

"But what was taken from you is still here. He didn't take it. You protected it." Daegan's commanding voice made the voices cower back. Though they continued to writhe like a hive of maggots in her brainpan, she was able to open her eyes, look into Daegan's intense expression.

"You are still here, *cher.*" His voice was less harsh, but no less inexorable. "In the air of this room, of Atlantis, of all you created. The silver brush on your dresser, the sea pictures you picked out at that gallery we visited last fall. Your essence is being safeguarded by every single piece of yourself, everything that belongs to you. When you are ready, you will call it back into yourself, integrate it with the vampire in you and be ever stronger, because that is who *you* are."

She looked toward Gideon, seeing his agreement in his fierce blue gaze. "Everything I care about. Everything that belongs to me. Guarding me."

"Yes, *cher.* Including us."

"Especially us," Gideon added.

Two tall, broad-shouldered men trying to perch on the edge of her lady's couch, their legs so long that Gideon's boot was braced between Daegan's shoes, their calves brushing in wary accord. Like a butterfly, her hand drifted back down, coming to rest on Gideon's on her calf. His fingers turned, laced with hers, held.

The misinformed thought being a Dominatrix was about quid pro quo, an abused woman getting the chance to subjugate and humiliate men. For her it had always been about pushing a man into his own soul, guiding him through the complex tangle of strength and vulnerability and letting him see both for what they were.

Some girls had wanted to be an equestrian in the Olympics; others had wanted to be teachers or doctors. She simply craved to be along for that journey, because when she was immersed in a man's soul, that was where she wanted to be. When he reached that subspace peace, his body quivering with pain or near climax, his glistening muscles were knotted as if he were Atlas, holding up the world for her. But he reveled in it, because all was as it should be; all was acceptance.

With Gideon, she'd been as much a part of his journey as he was, somehow their strength and vulnerabilities tangling so when he lay down upon her, his face so close, it had not been uncomfortable, no childhood fears resurrected. Instead, she'd felt how she expected Eve had felt in Eden, the first time Adam lay upon her and the two of them had known they were connected in an undeniable way.

And Daegan . . . Her gaze drifted to him. Daegan was the one who'd taught her the pleasure of being in the shoes, so to speak, of the men she'd Dominated. The one who'd taken her into the complexity of *her* soul and shown her parts of it she'd sealed off or overlooked, opening those doors with something far more than seductive magic . . . something that had terrified and overwhelmed her at once, his unexpected power over her, giving to her.

She'd accepted it, because the laws of nature said one dominant animal bent to the will of one that was more so, when it was unavoidable . . . or desired.

"Do I . . . Can I have it in something else? You know, like taking terrible medicine in juice?"

"That, we can do," Daegan said. "What would you like?"

It was new to her, this craving, so though she wasn't typically shy, she couldn't bring herself to ask. Fortunately, he understood a fledgling's needs.

"How do you want my blood? From the vein or a cup?"

Daegan's casual comment was augmented by the knowledge in his dark eyes. He'd known her immediate craving would be for human blood, Gideon's, not his. But he'd also known she wouldn't force that on Gideon again. Daegan's blood would be rich, and it would certainly overwhelm the foul taste of that thing that she would never call "her sire," no matter how merely functional a term it was.

"A cup, so we can mix it. I'd rather not use your blood as a chaser," she said.

"All right." Giving Gideon a glance, Daegan rose and moved away to the kitchen. Through the pass-through, she could see him taking what he needed from the refrigerator. He kept his back to her as he measured the dosage, like a nurse hiding the syringe from the patient. She'd done that as an ER nurse, when the patient didn't like sharp objects. Just like them, her gaze turned away, focusing on something more pleasant. Her subject was frowning, though.

"I would have been fine with you taking my blood," Gideon said.

"I know you'd give me anything you thought I needed. I didn't want to take from you what I don't need to take. I don't want this to be harder for you."

"You shouldn't be worrying about me at all. You need to focus on yourself." His gaze shifted to her knees. "I'd like to hold both your hands. May I?"

For a man who believed in himself so little, he understood so much. Since they'd been holding her hands off and on these past few minutes, she knew he chose his words deliberately now, recognizing that it would help to coax the Mistress forth in her while she faced something this difficult.

Even more charming, his request had a touch of awkwardness to it. It was still new to him, knowing how she wanted this, what was proper. She met his gaze, keeping her expression neutral. "You may."

It was peculiar, getting well and truly aroused even with her emotions as topsy-turvy as an amusement park ride. Closing his hands on hers, he laced their fingers, his gaze on the differences between her slim fingers and his rough, strong ones. "We've been talking about the idea of you having a servant," he said conversationally.

There was a clatter of glass in the kitchen. She glanced back. Nothing appeared amiss, but then, as fast as Daegan could move, he'd never let a glass hit the floor. He'd turned toward them, his eyes riveted on Gideon with a speculative look.

"Daegan thinks this is going to be a rough road," Gideon was continuing. "That this asshole's blood is going to mess with your head for some time. If you had a servant's energy to balance yours—"

"No. Oh my God, no." She yanked her hands back, drawing back against the sofa, but it was toward Daegan that she leveled her accusation. "Tell me you didn't put this burden on him."

Daegan's expression remained cool. He returned to mixing the contents of the glass tumbler. "I made the suggestion. He's a grown man, Anwyn. He can make his own decisions. You should let him finish."

"Anwyn—"

But she rode right over Gideon's attempt to reclaim her attention. "Don't you dare tell me what to do. He's a grown man who has spent his life trying to make up for not saving the one woman he was supposed to protect. You fed into that, to trap him into something that's the antithesis of everything he is. You bastard."

Despite her weakness, she kicked off the covers, stumbled to her feet, holding on to the couch arm when she swayed. Daegan's face hardened, and she knew she was pushing it, but she could now, right? She wasn't some inferior human in his vampire world. Even though she was newly made, she wasn't going to stand for this kind of crap in this new world any more than she would in the old. Her resentment and fury with him, a vague mass of betrayal and mistrust, laced with fear and uncertainty because she didn't know how much she could truly rely on him, surged forth, almost as strong as one of her violent seizures. She opened her mouth to cut his legs right out from under him.

"*Anwyn.*"

Apparently Daegan wasn't the only one who could command attention when the occasion called for it. Gideon's tone was razor sharp, bringing her eyes back to him. He'd stood up as well. His eyes, when intensified with emotion, were like midnight blue slivers of sparkling sky, beautiful and almost as mesmerizing as Daegan's. "I'm not that gullible. Whatever his motives, I've been with you, and I can see it for myself. The transition process for humans turning to vampires is nearly identical. Yours isn't. I think it would be a hell of a lot easier if you had help staying in control. I can help you do that."

"What kind of woman would I be if I accepted your help?" Anwyn shook her head. "You would *never* leave a woman in distress if there was any sacrifice you could make to save her. That's not a decision, not a choice of your free will. Whoever she was, this woman for whom you're trying to make amends, I am *not* her."

Gideon's jaw clenched. "You don't like being second-guessed. Neither do I. Don't go there. I'm the one making this decision, and I'm making it for *you*. And it's not that fucking dramatic. I'm not talking about the full marking."

"Don't curse at me, Gideon Green," she said, low.

"Don't go off the handle before I've told you what I have in mind, then."

She narrowed her eyes. Returning to the sofa with precise movements, she sat, perched on the end, her back stiff, and folded her hands with deceptive calm on her knees. "Fine. Tell me, then, since you two have this all worked out."

She refused to look toward Daegan. The vampire hunter gave her an even look, but came back to the sofa. Interestingly, she noted he dropped to one knee beside her, rather than sitting next to her. He braced the points of a white-knuckled hand on the sofa, and his back was even straighter than hers, his jaw set. She wondered if he realized how she registered every nuance of his body language, looking for what that meant even more than his words. "I could let you give me one mark. It might not help as much as a full marking, but it might give you more stability, leave us both a little breathing room."

A shift in the kitchen made him look back at Daegan. The vampire leaned on the pass-through, watching them both like a still raptor. "One mark would have minimal impact. But two *would* help, because that's a bond between your minds."

As Gideon digested that, Anwyn's teeth ground together at the conflict evident in his gaze. Then it shuttered over. He nodded. "That makes sense."

"It's a chain between us," she said sharply. "Gideon, I'd be in your head. For always."

"Yes and no." He lifted a shoulder. "The range isn't limitless. When you stabilize enough to choose a real servant, all I'd have to do is travel out of that range, though I expect you'd learn how to shut it down. Lyssa was able to do that with Jacob at one point. She still had the ability to activate it, but she didn't have to do so. And look at it this way. While a second-marked servant can still be killed in all the normal ways, they're more resilient to injury and heal faster. During the transition, you can have more freedom when it's just me around."

"You would trust me that much? A vampire, the thing you hate most in the world?"

"I don't hate you."

"You hate what I've become." She fisted her fingers in his shirt collar, registered his tensing with a sharp nod. "See? You mistrust my movements, are prepared to fight me."

"That's just good sense."

"I told you I wouldn't tolerate you lying to me. Ever."

"We're not in the Queen's Chamber. You also said the lies we tell ourselves outside of your dungeon doors help us be what we need to be." Leaning forward, he met her eye to flashing eye. "If you don't want me as your servant, that's one thing. Hell, I wouldn't wish that on any woman. But the good news is I'm about as much servant material as he is"—he jerked his head at Daegan—"so it'll be easy to get rid of me when it's time."

She straightened her fingers, one at a time, so the nails dug into the tender flesh at the base of his throat, probably the only soft spot on him. She stared at the flush of blood beneath the skin that gathered around those sharp edges. "This is jumping the gun. It makes no sense to make this commitment now."

"Yeah, it does. If the madness grows, even with the sire's blood, the sooner you can use me to help corral it, the better." Gideon sighed, reached up to grip her wrist.

Instead, her other hand closed on his, stilling the movement so he couldn't alter where her fingers were. She let him feel the strength in her hand, which she already knew was growing to the point she occasionally could match him. Soon she would consistently surpass him. Lifting her gaze to his, she held the blue eyes. "Gideon, it won't work."

His fingers flexed slightly under hers, telling her he didn't care for the grip, but his voice remained calm. Too calm. A cauldron of emotion boiled beneath the surface. If she did as he suggested, she would know every thought, every emotion, going through him, a temptation that had the shadow voices in her head practically frothing at the mouth. *He would be hers . . . unable to hide anything from her.*

"No." She surged up from the couch, removing herself from him. "Gideon, you've already said it. I heard you. You know what vampires are, what I'll become. What do you think will happen, if you make yourself that vulnerable to me?"

"I expect that depends on how he views being vulnerable to you. And how sure he is of the small amount of trust that has already grown between you."

She snapped her attention to Daegan, still standing in that damned statuelike pose in the opening to the kitchen. "A tidbit of trust is nothing more than bait for a trap."

A muscle flexed in Daegan's jaw. Vampires didn't tolerate defiance for long from anyone lower on the feeding chain, even someone with whom they had a strong emotional bond. Gideon expected Anwyn knew that, though. Or was upset enough that she didn't care anymore, which might explain Daegan's restraint.

He rose. "Before you two go crazy with the passive-aggressive innuendoes about your own relationship, can we get back on point here?"

He might have been grimly amused by the matching dangerous expressions that swung his way, if not for his own feelings about the topic.

"There are plenty of things in my life that I wanted more time to consider," he said, meeting Anwyn's gaze. "But my gut tells me if we give this more time, I'm just delaying the inevitable. And my gut's always right."

The forbidding countenance slipped, and he saw the woman beneath, the one afraid to take what he was offering, for as many reasons as his own brain could check off.

Ironically, it made his mind up. As he stepped up to her, he noted Daegan was cutting his wrist vein with a switchblade, mixing his blood with Barnabus's. Her nostrils flared, detecting it, even as her eyes never left Gideon's face. He stopped with a foot between them, a barrier he'd let her decide whether or not to cross. "Let me do this, Anwyn. I want to take care of you. I think that's why I was brought here, though I can't explain my feelings beyond that. We're just going to have to muddle through."

She studied him a long moment; then she reached up, touched his mouth. "Be still," she said, when he would have reached for her wrist, or moved his lips against her. He capitulated as she traced his lips, passed her thumb over his jaw.

"You want to take care of me," she said slowly, "but do you want to belong to me? Because that's what this is about. I know it from watching him." She nodded at Daegan. "From what he asks and demands of me. I also feel it growing inside of me. Maybe because of what I already am, it's growing faster, or maybe it immediately happens, like the craving for blood."

She dropped her hand. "Gideon, what's in my head now . . . It's not the usual thing; I'm sure of it. I am afraid of being out of control. But the way my mind reacts to your willingness to be marked . . ." She swallowed. "It's the way a pedophile feels when he sees a child walking alone. Evil, dirty and unable to resist."

He heard it in her voice, a confident woman being destroyed by terror of herself. It wrenched his heart out of his chest. He was cognizant of Daegan drawing near, the vampire also responding to her distress. She was holding the reins on it so tightly they could practically hear the blood pumping desperately under her constricted soul.

Reaching out, Gideon closed his hand on hers. "Your fear only confirms I'm doing the right thing. If you lose your grip on your conscience during all this, the second mark will connect us. I can hold on to it for you until you've got a good grasp on it again."

"What if I refuse to let you go, after I mark you?"

"You'll let me go." His eyes shadowed. "Because we both know I'm not the right person for this. I'm just the best person right now."

Daegan stepped forward then. "Perhaps it would be best if you go ahead and drink this, *cher.* If the sire's blood stabilizes you more than we expect, it is a decision you might not have to make right away."

Gideon tilted his head toward the couch. "Why don't we go sit down there? The first time will be the worst, right?"

She pressed her lips together. "I want to go to my room. I'll drink it there, alone."

Daegan shook his head. "You'll do it here, *cher*. Where we can watch."

"Like some kind of drug addict you can't trust. You're right. I do hate you." She said it in a monotone and Daegan didn't react, other than to place the tumbler in her hand, curling her fingers around it with a look that said she would strongly regret throwing it at him, as her expression suggested she might be considering.

As they waited her out, watching her stare down into that cup, Gideon wondered how long Daegan would wait before he would in fact force it down her throat. She was likely due for another seizure soon, and having the sire's blood in her before then would give them an early indication of how much it would help. Curling his fingers in a lock of her hair, loose at her brow, he tugged lightly.

"Maybe you don't really want it in a cup. Maybe it'd be better to take it from my mouth."

Her attention shifted to him, and as it did, he began backing up, keeping that light, nonrestraining pressure on her fingers, just the tips. She followed him, one step, two steps, until he skirted the coffee table to reach the sofa. Daegan moved behind them, and Gideon sensed his gaze on his face, but he made his whole focus Anwyn and her intense blue-green eyes, filled with so much he couldn't tell what emotion was holding the upper hand.

He waited until she was seated next to him, and then he carefully took the tumbler from her hand. "Ready?" he asked. "Remember, you're consuming your enemy. That's what this is."

Her jaw firmed in promising resolve. Daegan had taken a seat in the chair across from them, fingers steepled and damnable Sphinx expression firmly in place. Gideon wasn't fooled by it, though. He didn't care if the male was vampire or human; none of them fared well against a female cold shoulder. But he gave the guy reluctant credit—he wasn't letting that detract a bit from what he knew needed to be done. He wasn't sure he could have refused Anwyn the right to drink the foul stuff in the privacy of her rooms, but he knew Daegan was right. Her brain was just too unpredictable. She might run it down the sink.

Lifting the tumbler to his lips, he let the blood fill his mouth. Though he tried not to inhale, it was hard not to get the scent once he'd brought it onto his taste buds. It was curious . . . There was a sour, fetid odor, the odor he expected for blood. But there was something else. He didn't want to say it was a pleasant smell, but there was an appealing element to it . . . something additional that almost made him want to swallow, for reasons he couldn't explain.

Fortunately, she didn't keep him waiting. Threading her fingers under his hair at his nape, she slid her other hand up his thigh, bracing herself. Stretching her slim neck, she brought her mouth to his.

He'd done it like this, thinking someone of her sensual nature might find it more appealing. Totally selfless, thinking only of her. That wry thought was lost as the tip of her tongue eased into the seam of his mouth, still closed against her open one, and delicately tasted what he had to offer. With a slow curl, she gathered more of the fluid onto her tongue as he carefully parted his lips, letting the blood begin to slip in a controlled way into her mouth. He felt the motion as she swallowed for the first time, and relaxed somewhat. Of course, other parts of him became far less relaxed as the heel of her hand inched up, her fingers stroking high on his thigh. She tilted her head, pressing closer into the kiss, letting more of the blood slide from his mouth into hers. He put his arm around her waist, bringing her closer, so she slid onto the knee closest to her, the hand on his thigh coming up to his shoulder to hold on.

He wondered what Daegan thought, watching the two of them, and then decided that was something he didn't want to know. But considering he'd put the tumbler down on the coffee table and had to pick it up again to do the next swallow, he was going to have to look toward the male. Instead, he felt the tumbler pressed into his hand by male fingers, and two hands guiding his arm into a bend up toward his face, so he didn't have to break the kiss until the last moment.

Daegan had moved to sit on the coffee table, his knees spread to accommodate Gideon's, the vampire's own knee pressed into Anwyn's hip where she sat on Gideon's thigh. Gideon turned his head while Anwyn moved to his cheekbone, over to his ear and the vein that pulsed beneath it. It leaped under her mouth, much like his cock did as her hand lowered, stroking him through denim, though for once his mind stayed with her mouth rather than migrating to his cock. If she actually marked him, would she bite him there? How would it feel? If the sire's blood worked better than they expected, would they even have to do it? And why did that give him a small, absurd feeling of disappointment?

It was because he was fucked-up. The only successful relationship he'd seen close-up these past couple of years was his brother's, with a fucking vampire queen. But, Christ, Anwyn's mouth tasted so good, blood or no blood. He gave her another mouthful, now experiencing three textures: that sour, repulsive one, the curiously pleasurable one, and the undeniable feast that was Anwyn's tongue and lips. Thanks to Daegan's steady hand, he didn't have to let go of her, his hands spanning the nip of her slender waist, thumbs on her rib cage, close to the curve of her breasts, fingers splayed out to feel the hint of womanly hips. He brought his mouth back to hers and the provocative dance started over again, her tongue coming in to tease his mouth open slowly, letting him offer her the nourishment.

This was the way so many animals fed each other, mouth to mouth. It took him back to that night with Jacob and Lyssa. He'd fallen asleep in the bed next to them, but woken to see Lyssa feeding on her servant. Jacob had still been human then. Through half-closed eyes, Gideon had seen her fangs go in, and his brother's arms curl protectively around her, even as his body tightened in desire and need, demonstrating pleasure at nourishing the woman he loved.

How could he look at it that way, when he'd seen vampires crouched over bodies they'd drained, lives they'd taken? But how could he look at it in that brutal, terrible way, when Anwyn was in his arms, needing what he had to offer, totally dependent on him, at least for this brief, precious second?

One last swallow, Daegan's fingers making a disturbing overlap with Anwyn's at his nape to hold him steady for it, and then that touch went away, and it was all Anwyn, though Gideon was conscious of Daegan still sitting on the coffee table, flanking the both of them. She threaded both hands into his hair to hold his skull, now increasing the ardor of her kiss, cleaning all the blood from his mouth with erotic sweeps along his teeth, the insides of his cheeks, against his tongue. She shifted so she straddled him, a lithe move that required little help from him, though he slid his hands down lower on her hips, feeling the silk of her robe. She wore nothing under it, and he dug into a soft buttock, groaning into her mouth as she rubbed herself against his cock, still imprisoned in his jeans.

Releasing his lips, she brushed her temple against his, an unexpected, tender sweep of her hair over his face. Opening his eyes, he saw Daegan set aside the rubber bands that had held it, his long fingers completing the task of pulling it free of the braid, letting it sweep over her shoulders. Gideon caught a thick handful as it fell forward, brushing it against his mouth, the strands slipping through his fingers as she tilted back, letting him see the tantalizing loose neckline of her robe. Curves of flesh displayed, and lower, her thighs bare almost to her hips by the fall of the satin. He could smell her arousal, and wanted her to take him inside, ride him to her release, find pleasure in using his body in the way they hadn't been able to experience in Atlantis.

Then he got that tickling foreboding on the back of his neck. *No. She just had the blood. Give her a break . . . Just a few more minutes . . . Give her something that'll prove the sire's blood will keep the madness at bay.*

But he couldn't fool her or himself. He put his hands on either side of her throat, capturing her attention. She was leaning back, braced against Daegan's shoulder, because the angle at which he was sitting on the coffee table made it possible to cant against him that way without making eye contact. From her posture, it was obvious she was still holding herself from him, but Gideon thought it had moved into the hurt feelings as opposed to the anger mode, because he could feel her yearning to accept both of them.

"Another one's coming," he murmured regretfully.

17

IT wasn't another one. It was another three that came within minutes of one another, and were so violent, they thrust wooden utensils from the kitchen into her mouth to keep her from slicing her tongue and lips repeatedly with her fangs.

Daegan had restrained her during all three, but during the second and third, they took her into the cell, so he could hold on to her in an enclosed space where there was less danger to herself or others if she broke away from him. He didn't use the chains on her at all, Gideon was glad to see. After the third one, when she was curled up on the floor, Gideon passed Daegan a blanket to tuck around her until she stopped shaking. Then he squatted outside the cell and Daegan on the inside, waiting to see if she would pull out of it or go to another. As they regarded each other silently, Gideon broke the silence first.

"So the blood hurt, rather than helped?"

"Yes and no." Daegan shook his head. "She obviously has a bad reaction to it, and may react this way every time it's administered, but the properties of a sire's blood are unquestionably the only thing that staves off permanent madness."

"Unless he already gave her a case of the perpetual crazies." Gideon sighed. "So it's like chemo—it will make her terribly sick, but it's going to do its job."

A muscle flexed in Daegan's jaw, but he nodded. He passed a hand over her hair, now plastered back to her skull with sweat and blood. "Are you sure, Gideon?"

Gideon glanced at him. The tone of the voice told him the subject had changed. And he knew exactly what they were talking about, since it was clear that she wasn't going to do better on the sire's blood. "I'm sure," he said quietly.

Daegan raised his gaze, studied him. "No, you're not. But you've decided to do it."

"Isn't that what I just said?"

"Wisdom is a product of the heart, not the mind. Which is why it so often leads to unavoidable regret."

"You could put that on a greeting card. Seriously. The new slit-your-wrists-today Hallmark line."

Daegan's rueful expression surprised Gideon, a departure from the pretty constant poker face the vampire had adopted until now. Bending over, the male stroked Anwyn's hair from her cheek, sliding his fingers beneath her head to raise her up into his arms with tender care. Despite her animosity toward him in her lucid moments, there was no doubt of her feelings when she was physically depleted, because her arms curled around his body, burrowing into him, her torso still shuddering as he stroked her, moved her around into a cradle so he could lift her slim frame. "You've done so well, *cher*," he murmured. "But you're not going to have to be alone in there anymore. Gideon is coming."

Gideon nodded, mostly to himself, and when the vampire looked toward him, he took a deep breath. "No time like the present, right?"

"Yes."

"It will make her better."

"We both know it will help her. If you are sure, come into the cell now."

Yeah, he was. After seeing the convulsions nearly tear her newly immortal body to pieces, he wasn't going to fuck around about it anymore. If she'd been human, the violence of the convulsions would have stopped her heart, killed her outright. It didn't make it any less painful or traumatic for her. Rising, Gideon opened the lock and entered the cell. He spread a blanket out on the couch as Daegan lowered her, pulling it around her. Her hands slid away from him, her eyes half-closed. "Filthy," she murmured.

"No, just a little mussed." Gideon knelt at her head, took the place of Daegan's hand with his own, stroking her hair back. Her eyes still had a hint of red, but they'd been solid crimson for half an hour, as the three attacks had come right on top of one another. Her physical body was exhausted, he could tell. Course, they were all tired as hell. After this, it was going to be naptime, no cookies or juice boxes required. "You need to give me those two marks, okay?"

She opened her drooping eyes, studied his face. "This is wrong, Gideon. You know it is. I don't have the strength to refuse."

"You don't refuse a gift," he returned, keeping his voice low and gentle. "Especially when it's from a guy who doesn't give them out often."

"Gideon . . ." She shook her head, looked toward Daegan. "Tell him not to do this."

"He doesn't take orders from me, *cher*. He has made that quite clear."

"Damn straight." Gideon quirked a brow, but his heart twisted at the anguish in her eyes. "I'm going to make you a promise, okay? This is going to be all right. It's going to be the right thing to do, because it's going to help you get back on your feet, and because I'm not going to regret it. You're worth this, you know? Let me do something I haven't in a long, long while. Let me save someone. I'm begging you. And you know you can't resist that."

She licked her lips, moistening them, and pushed herself up, the blanket falling to her hip. Daegan had taken the robe off of her to save the satin, so she was naked and blood streaked beneath it, her hair falling loose to her hips so she looked like a wild and savage creature of the forest, unashamed of her nakedness. Gideon was reminded of his earlier arousal, how much he'd wanted her.

Down, boy. Definitely not the time.

"You think you know so much about a Mistress." She traced a nail down his jugular with unsettling accuracy, barely glancing at it. "I won't do anything I don't want to do."

"I know that. It's why I begged." Energy was gathering between them. She was going to do it. He was going to let her. And everything was going to change. Daegan was a palpable force to the right of them, probably in case she seized again and went for his throat, but as she reached out, Gideon leaned in, let her snag his shirt collar and draw him closer.

"Let your instinct guide you, *cher*," Daegan murmured. "You can smell his pulse, the blood pounding through it. Your fangs will lengthen, make it easier to penetrate."

A few things went through Gideon's mind. His conversation with Jacob, the way his life had gone for the past ten plus years. How the hell that path had brought him here. Why he wouldn't countenance any other vampire touching him, let alone biting him, but he was encouraging her to do it.

He wanted to take care of her.

Her blue-green eyes were close now. He wanted to touch her face. When he lifted his hand, her lips parted. "Stay still," she said, her voice that sinful purr, anticipating pleasure. He touched her temple anyway, feathering his fingers through her hair, all those shades of dark brown. When she turned her face into his palm he wasn't surprised to feel her teeth capture the pad of his thumb, the base of the finger, and tighten there, letting him feel the sharp prick of reproof. The churning in his lower belly became a more organized storm, a hurricane of feeling forming and rising into his chest, even as his cock started hardening.

She nuzzled him where she'd bitten his flesh, slanted a glance up at him through her thick lashes. "These feelings inside of me, Gideon. Not Barnabus. The vampire blood. It tells me if I do this, I'll consider you mine."

He nodded, one small movement. "I'll be here as long as you need me." Reaching deep inside for the calm he used before setting an ambush or facing odds not in his favor, he drew a deep breath and turned his head away from her, baring his throat inches away from those tempting lips, the hint of fangs that began to be more pronounced beneath them.

Averting his eyes meant he was looking right at Daegan. The vampire kept his attention on Anwyn, but he spoke. "Have you ever given blood directly from the throat, Gideon?"

"Not given it. No."

"Your blood was taken when you were captured by Mitchell or Sorensen?"

"Yes." He didn't want to cross those memories with this one, though. Anwyn leaned in, putting her lips to his jaw, caressing and teasing with the tip of her tongue. Her hand cupped the opposite side, increasing the pressure, the sense of sensual urgency. He shouldn't have been surprised that she knew the right thing to say to bring him out of those dark memories before he could even step through the door.

"This won't be like that," she whispered against his skin. "I can hear it, Gideon. Just like he said. It's not just your blood. I'm hearing the life flowing through your veins, the strength. It's as if all your energy is centering toward me, ready to give me what I need. It's the most erotic thing I've ever felt. Stay still; just let it flow over you. Goddess, I could have stopped a moment ago. I don't think I can stop now."

"I don't want you to."

He let himself get lost in the feeling, trying to focus on that and not what she was doing, not a vampire marking a servant, but a woman reaching out and connecting to him in a way that, while it lasted, would be a unique bond between them. He wanted to feel the touch of her mouth and hands forever, put his hands to her waist, turn her beneath him on the soft couch and sink into her, deep as he could go, as she drew blood from him, twined around them, binding them close. But he stayed still.

"The three serums are secreted up behind your fangs, small glands. Use your tongue to express the one farthest back first." Daegan's voice, barely a rumble of sound. "You don't want to do them at the same time, because mixing them creates an acid reaction. It will cause great pain to a servant."

Unsettling though it was, Gideon couldn't deny that velvet timbre was as sensuous an input into this as all the rest.

When her fangs sank into Gideon's throat, there was no hesitation, no painful puncture as might happen if she'd jumped the gun through nervousness or uncertainty. She sank into his flesh as naturally as though she'd done it all her life. But then, how often had she done blood-play or flogged a slave? She knew how flesh reacted, and she knew how to follow her instincts. It was still Anwyn.

A tingling came with it, a frisson of champagnelike reaction in the blood around the bite area that spread into his chest, drifting out to his fingertips, then turned around and came back through his blood as she slid her hand over his chest, splayed her fingers out wide over his heart, connecting to the beat there. She shifted upward, moving closer, and it was easy to slide his arm around her waist, help her move from a reclining position to a straddle of his hips. She came in close, so she rubbed against his cock, the denim the only thing separating them.

"Pull back, *cher*," Daegan said quietly. "Occupy yourself for a few minutes while the first mark circulates. Then you can do the second one. You have coagulating agents in your tongue. Use them to control his blood flow."

Slowly, she retracted, and Gideon felt his cock jump against her at the sexual overtones of something hard and unyielding pulling out of willing, moist flesh. Her hand cupped the side of his throat, keeping his head tilted as she licked him, taking her time with it.

His eyes lifted, not intentionally, but the pause made him want to take stock of his surroundings. Daegan met his gaze, his mouth a line, his eyes that distant and yet intensely present combination that was so unsettling. His focus shifted back to the woman on Gideon's lap, coursing down the curtain of her hair, trailing down her pale, slim back, to her bare buttocks around which Gideon's arm was securely cinched, keeping her steady, though it was the last thing he himself was feeling.

Was the vampire disturbed by this? It might give Gideon some sense of gratification to think so, but the way Daegan was directing her suggested something else. Gideon was becoming a human servant. Her possession, as she implied, and the way Daegan was leading her, teaching her . . . It implied that Gideon's submission was a given, a human servant obediently allowing an older vampire to help a younger one learn on him, because that was what servants did. They served their vampires, no matter what was asked.

Where he could handle Anwyn experiencing such possessive feelings, because they seemed wrapped up in her personality as a Mistress, not spawned solely by vampire blood, Gideon didn't like the idea of Daegan making similar assumptions. And that was how it suddenly felt.

He pulled back, drawing her away from him abruptly enough he could have unbalanced her, but she was already cultivating those catlike sensibilities. She straightened her arm, her hand still against his chest, registering his elevated heartbeat. He didn't want to be away from her, but he didn't want Daegan so close. In her confused gaze, he saw she thought he'd changed his mind. The vampire instinct to take wrestled visibly with her desire to respect his wishes, while fighting the roaring need to finish what she'd started. He understood it well enough. For an unsettling moment, he'd felt it just as strongly. He also saw some relief, telling him she was afraid of the consequences of this act, what it would mean about herself, what it would do to him.

"I don't want you here." He turned his attention to Daegan. "I can't do this with you hovering over us. She understands how the rest works. Let her finish it alone."

"No." Daegan met his gaze. "If bloodlust takes over, she could injure you enough to kill you. Until the second mark takes effect, your resilience will be no greater than usual."

"Then move back to the kitchen at least. Give me some fucking breathing room."

Daegan lifted a brow. Instead of complying, he leaned forward, bringing his face within a few inches of Gideon's. "Can't keep your dick hard with me close, vampire hunter? Or worried that having me close is just making it harder?"

Everything in Gideon stilled into one red pinpoint of anger. It burned in the center of his chest like a cigarette, goading dark, fearsome things in him. "I think that bloodsucker's need you have to mark your territory is greater than any feelings you have for anyone or anything else. You want this done? You want her to have me to help her? Then go piss on some trees in the kitchen until this is done."

The world froze. Menace emanated from the vampire, the transition from cold dispassion to near-death experience so swift Gideon almost reached for the knife sheathed at his back. Self-preservation and the fact Anwyn was on his lap stopped him, because he knew if he'd done it, it would have been over. The hellfire flickering in Daegan's eyes told Gideon he was a breath away from being dead.

Even Anwyn felt it, her hand clutching over his heart, her breath drawing in. Her thighs tightened on the outsides of his hips as if she could protect him, but he wouldn't let her do that, no matter how much stronger physically she might be at this point. This was between him and one seriously pissed-off vampire. Which was pretty much how he'd always known it was going to end. He just had a bizarre, fleeting regret at not knowing what that second mark might have felt like, connecting him so closely to her. Feeling so close to anyone.

A blink, and Daegan wasn't there. He was across the coffee table, standing in front of the wing-backed chair positioned there. With elegant and precise movements, he lowered himself into the chair, propped his ankle on the opposing knee and templed his fingers again, his eyes still fixed with deadly intent on Gideon's face.

"This is as far as I go, vampire hunter. Now, let her get on with it, or change your mind."

Damn. The vamp did care about her, more than his ego or excessively dominant vampire nature. Either that, or he figured he'd rip Gideon's head off when Anwyn was done with him.

Fair enough. With an infinitesimal nod of acknowledgment, Gideon turned his attention back to Anwyn. Unfortunately, he had a new problem there.

～

Anwyn slid off him, stood. She had no problem being cloaked in just her hair, but wished she wasn't still marked with blood from her last seizure. However, it was because her flesh felt cold that she picked up the blanket and wrapped it around her body, staring between them. "This is wrong," she said, even more sure of it now than she had been before. She could already feel the impact of that first mark inside of her. It was if there were a silken cord between her and Gideon. She could have closed her eyes and known exactly where he was in the room, without the use of any other senses.

When he'd pulled back from her, in that first instance she'd been so bereft, deprived of something that every cell in her had been screaming to have, she hadn't even been able to rally herself to interfere in whatever was happening between Gideon and Daegan. Just as well. It was never a good idea to get into a testosterone match between two highly physical males, though the undercurrents of it had disturbed her greatly. Gideon was doing this to help her, to keep her safe. Not because he truly wanted to be a human servant.

He'd been clear about that, but it was the undercurrent that bothered her. Even during their first session, she'd sensed his nebulous yet overwhelming desire to serve a specific woman with all he had to offer. As such, it wasn't going to be so easy for him to walk away from this, despite his soul-deep antipathy to being part of a vampire world. She knew what was expected of vampires and their servants, things she'd learned from Daegan's stories. Gideon's soul couldn't survive that.

Whether Gideon thought it applied only in the Queen's Chamber or not, she was his Mistress. She had a responsibility to protect him. She'd had submissives who couldn't be trusted to use their safe words when they were physically or emotionally in jeopardy, because they got so deep into their needs and yearnings they couldn't make that call anymore. That was why she had to be wholly focused, vigilant during a session. Gideon didn't even know the concept of a safe word. He'd follow his gut to his death.

While she knew her own feelings were secondary to protecting him, she also knew there was that component as well. What if she did make him hers with this second mark? What if it tangled their souls and hearts together, such that she couldn't let him go, or force him to do it, when it was time?

"We can't do this," she said. "We'll figure out something else."

Gideon rose, his brow creasing and his jaw getting that stubborn look. "I already said I'd do it."

"Yes. You're honorable. You're trying to do the right thing. But I don't want your sense of honor. Not for this. What if I become just like those you've killed, Gideon? If I'm second-marked, and you decide you have to hunt and kill me, it will be near impossible for you to do it with me in your head, anticipating your moves. Right?"

"It's not going to come to that."

"You don't know that."

"Yes, he does."

Both of them looked toward Daegan then, still in the chair. His onyx gaze went to Anwyn. "I need you to think like a Mistress, *cher*. Can you do that?"

"I am," she responded, her jaw tight.

He made a neutral movement, shifted his glance to Gideon. "He will never hunt you. Never cause you harm. And not just because he would never get close enough to touch a hair on your head." That ripple of cold menace again, telling her that whatever had transpired between them before was still simmering.

"It won't happen because he's never killed a female vampire, except in self-defense. He's killed eleven vampires in the past eighteen months, an extraordinary count for a human hunter." Daegan quirked a brow. "Every single one of them has been male. And their servants, when they had them, were also male. I might deduce you are anti-homosexual"— Daegan's tone was faintly mocking—"but it's not that. You can't bring yourself to kill a female, except in cases where a female vampire, or a male with a female servant, has attacked you directly and there was no other choice. In those instances with a female servant, if there was a way to do so, you had her buried."

Gideon's jaw hardened in irritated response. "I'm glad you're so well-informed. Anwyn told me the only things I need to know about you. That you have a really small dick and tend to fart in bed louder than you snore."

"Since you've been in close proximity to it, I expect you know the size of my cock as well as she does. If yours was anywhere as formidable as your defensiveness, you might have half a chance of competing with it."

Anwyn made a noise between her teeth, the precursor to a scream of frustration. Gideon bit back whatever he'd been about to say and

Daegan inclined his head, a faint apology that was courteous enough to help her take a breath. "*Cher,* you are both taking a risk. His aversion to vampires is as strong as his fear of not being there when another woman needs him. Only time will tell which one will win out."

"Have you turned any of that on yourself, Dr. Phil?" Gideon's arms were akimbo, his eyes snapping sparks. "Commitment isn't your big thing, either."

"Stop it. Goddess, tripping over your own dicks, the both of you. And it's a tie—you're both fucked-up. *Men.*" Anwyn stomped away from them, turning at the limits of the room, the blanket twisting around her bare legs. "Damn it, damn it, damn it."

"Anwyn—"

"No." She shook her head at Gideon, as he moved a step toward her, regret in his gaze. "Don't you understand, Gideon? I want to give you that second mark so badly. It's the most important, most vital thing I've ever felt, worse than a drug craving. I'm all about control, denial, to heighten pleasure. This is boiling lava, an eruption I can't stop. You can't keep offering, because I won't resist it."

"You don't have to." When he took another step forward, she held up a quelling hand.

"Think, Gideon. For one quiet, damn minute, stand there and think about what it will mean, what can happen. Forget about me, and Daegan, and all of it. Just think, damn you."

Gideon stared at her flushed cheeks. The anger was gone, leaving desperation. What she didn't understand was, as strong as she felt that pull, he felt it, too. And he wasn't a vampire, dealing with a transition or unexpected cravings.

"I have thought about it," he said. "You'll be in my head. I won't be able to keep you out. Daegan's already given you the vampire version of the locator mark. If he gives you more than that, he could probably get into my head, too, because he's a lot stronger than you right now."

He felt the weight of the vampire's gaze. Ruefully, he reflected that the man already had too many avenues into his head as it was. "But for all that, we both know by the time you get to territories and vampire social gatherings, you'll have another servant. Those things will be his problem, whoever the bastard is."

Because she sure as hell wouldn't choose a woman. She'd choose someone whose cock she could have at her command, rub against like she'd rubbed against his, those slow strokes, with her lips suckling at his throat. It would make his hands tighten on her hips, make him whisper her name against her hair, drifting over his lips.

He thrust that away. "But I meant what I said earlier. I'll know when it's time for me to go. Or you will. But that won't happen until you don't need me any longer. I promise. I need you to trust me, the way I'm going to trust you. Give me that. Okay? Let's stop going over the same ground and do this."

He took another several steps forward when he saw her gaze drift down to his throat, linger there with a hunger that tightened his groin anew. *Hell, I've made decisions based on my gut all my life, not taking time to think any of it through. Why should this be any different?*

Wisely, he chose not to share that with her, though he expected if she'd been looking at his face, she'd have been intuitive enough to figure it out. But he did trust his gut. It told him to do what he did now. He closed the distance between them.

"I'm going to pick you up, all right?" His voice was thick, emotions closing in on him like a fog, making her his only focus. At last she gave him a nod, her gaze fastening on his. Her lips pressed together, her face getting that resolute look that told him she was making the decision to go forward, accepting the responsibility for it, even though fear lingered in her eyes. For him. For what it would mean to them both. He wouldn't let her worry. He'd take the consequences of all of it.

Slowly, he closed his hands over hers, loosened her fingers so the blanket slipped off her shoulders like a queen's cape, pooled around her ankles. "You're so beautiful," he murmured. It didn't matter that her flesh was bloodstained or her hair snarled. No man would see her as anything other than a goddess. He bent then, slid his arm under her back and knees, lifted her in his arms. She curled hers around his shoulders, and when her mouth brushed his throat, he shuddered, swallowing beneath the press of her lips.

He got her to the sofa before the rush of blood from his head to his cock could make him stumble, but it was a near thing, his body going back into overdrive as if resuming right where they'd left off. He kept her in his embrace, his arm crooked over her thighs, but she turned to straddle him again, pushing him back against the couch so she could run her fingers down his chest and abdomen, pull the shirt back up and mark him with her nails, leaving red streaks that arched him up into her touch. At the look in her eyes, the intensifying color, he dropped his head back, staring up at the ceiling, giving it all to her. He didn't want to look for Daegan, see what he was doing. He wanted only this, the feel of her body on his, the slow press of her breasts to his chest as she leaned in, the heated touch of her breath against his throat.

Do it, sweetheart. Just do it. Whatever it will mean.

He closed his eyes as her fangs pressed into that same mark, bringing a rich pain. He heard a quiet male voice and then the pain was gone. Daegan had instructed her to do what all vampires could do. Erase pain with a release of pheromones, also secreted in their mouth. It would rush through the blood, take an already straining arousal to a bursting ache.

Here it came. He hadn't needed that, wanted it, but his body was helpless not to respond. A low moan escaped his lips and his body went tight all along hers. He forced himself to stillness such that the energy quickly became explosive, building as she moved against him, not releasing him from the agonizing constriction of his jeans, cruel Mistress that she was, her hard nipples pressed against his chest. She caught both of his arms, pressed them to the couch cushions on either side of his hips, her small hands curved into the crook of his elbows to hold him there. His fingers dug into the pillows.

Then the power of that second-mark serum activated in his veins, grabbing control of his muscles in a different way, constricting them, making his body jerk against hers. Her mind moved forward into his, and there was nothing he could do to stop it. It was as if his brain were a murky, churning pool, and she was a mermaid in truth, plunging into those waters, an inexorable force that belonged there. Though he knew what a second mark was, irrational panic shot through him.

I'm here, Gideon. Don't fight me. I know it's instinct, but you don't have to fight this.

She was talking, with a voice like velvet and feathers, equal parts unconscious seduction and soothing comfort. No, she wasn't talking. She was talking in his head, clear as if she were talking outright. His awareness of her went beyond the proximity of her body or that tempting touch. She was inside him, around him.

His mind was wide-open, like a revolving door that couldn't slow, bringing in and sending out information with no control, a wild buzzing. He could handle that, but there was something else, a sense of menace. It curled at the edges of his awareness. As she continued to press deeper into his mind, it took more form. Darkness and shadows, laughing shadows that weren't funny. Their red eyes promised madness and pain, fear and loss of control beyond anything she'd ever endured before, that would be more than she could endure, so that she would lose everything, lose it all . . .

She. Not him. She. This was her mind. Anwyn's. He was in her mind, one foot in hers and one foot in his, and he couldn't withdraw from either, as if manacled there. He struggled up, vaguely aware of her moving off his lap as he confirmed he still had control over something, even if it was just his physical body. The shadow creatures laughed, and behind them he sensed her fear as he pulled away and left her alone with them.

Realizing his mistake, he tried to mentally lunge forward, to grab hold of that corner of fear and follow it to her, to Anwyn's helpless mind. Instead, he was yanked forward and pulled down, a sickening falling sensation. As he flailed, his mind burned with pain, eyes blinded by blood, all of him sucked into a quagmire of hellish screaming voices and suffocating anguish.

~

Fuck, his jaw was broken. Gideon rolled over to his side and spat blood, then realized he'd just spit onto the carpet. Pushing up to one arm, he found he was trembling like a baby. Insects were buzzing near his ears—no, inside his ears. He shook his head, but it was impossible to dislodge something coming from inside his brainpan. His neck was aching, his jaw hurt and he couldn't seem to get up. At least he hadn't soiled himself, as far as he could tell.

When hands closed on his shoulders, he jerked forward, trying to grope for a knife, but he was disoriented as hell, and could grab hold of only an arm, the same arm holding him.

"Easy, Gideon." The male voice spoke through the buzzing. Familiar, with the right touch of annoying I-know-it-all arrogance. Daegan. "Take it slow. You're all right."

"Anwyn . . ." He nearly groaned at the searing pain through his jaw.

"She's all right. She's back in the cell for the moment. But she needs you."

"What the hell . . . happened?" Gideon gave in to the mortifying need to be helped back onto the couch, and blinked until he brought Daegan into focus. The vampire's gaze had gone almost full black, no sign of the white sclera. It was a disconcerting effect he'd never seen on a vampire. Though their eyes were known to go completely red in bloodlust, the pupils remained the same. They didn't expand to cover the whole eye.

"She had one of her seizures. She completed the marking, though. As you can probably tell." Daegan studied him closely. "Can you hear her?"

"I hear . . . buzzing. Jesus, like being in a football stadium. What happened to my jaw?"

"I hit you." Daegan glanced left, drawing Gideon's attention to books scattered on the floor from the upended coffee table. A broken pottery piece lay beneath it. The chair was knocked over and the sofa was at an odd angle. "When she went into her seizure, you were trying to fight off whatever was in her mind. I was pulling her off of you, because she'd lost control. You wouldn't let go of her, and she was getting more and more violent. I knew you couldn't yet grasp what was happening, so I knocked you unconscious."

"Half the force would have been sufficient." Gideon wiggled his jaw.

"You underestimate how hard your head is," Daegan returned. "Stop whining. You're second-marked now. Your jaw should stop hurting shortly."

Gideon would have bared his teeth at him if it wouldn't have hurt like hell. Talking was bad enough. "I guess none of it was payback for how I pissed you off earlier."

"Oh, there was definitely that," Daegan said, unruffled. "But my main purpose was to protect you from her." His mouth thinned. "She's out now as well. When she wakes, you'll know because her mind will open to you."

"It's open," Gideon said softly. Now that he could get a breath, he was taking the time to investigate that buzzing, push past it to see the new rooms in his mind he realized were actually hers. No real images or thoughts, her mind drifting in an uncertain haze, but he could actually sense her turning toward consciousness. Cool.

What hadn't been so cool was that descent into Hell right before he'd passed out. If that was what was happening to her during every seizure, he couldn't imagine how she was pulling it together every time, on top of facing her fear of being trapped, restrained.

He tried to rise, couldn't quite get there yet. "She'll be fully awake soon. I need to go to her. She's . . . anxious."

"Take a few moments to steady yourself first. She'll be all right until then."

"I didn't think vampires opened their minds like this to their servants."

"They don't," Daegan said, a grim note to his voice. "It will take effort and training for her to learn to close the door between your minds, and make it one-way or shut it down completely when she has no desire to be in yours. That's why most vampires don't take a full servant, or even a second-marked one, until they've been around a few decades. She won't have much energy to spare to hold that screen between you, not with the seizures and bloodlust. However, that openness will help you anticipate her needs."

And Daegan trusted him not to abuse the privilege. It was a curious revelation. Gideon's brow creased. "You knew it would be this way."

"I didn't know she'd have a seizure during your marking, but yes, I knew that your minds would be open to one another, far more than most vampires and their servants. That's key to what will help her. Are you regretting your decision already?"

No, he was wondering how the hell he'd made this kind of impression on Daegan Rei. And why it felt oddly gratifying to have his vote of confidence, conditional though it was.

Gideon made another attempt, shrugged off Daegan's hand as he straightened. "Piss off. I'm fine. I want to be with her."

Why would you want that?

Those words in his mind brought him up short. While she sounded tired, her words were as welcome as the stroke of her hand. Daegan, watching his face, nodded. "She's speaking to you now?"

"Yeah. She wants me to go to her."

Liar.

Not a lie, Gideon responded. *You do want me to come to you. I can feel it. If you're looking into my head, you know I want to be with you.*

"Of course she does." Daegan gestured toward the hallway. "I left the cell door open for her. I'd recommend you help her clean up, if she'd like that, and then you both get some much-needed rest."

"You're leaving the two of us alone?" Gideon's brow creased.

Daegan quirked a brow. "Yes. That was one of the points of doing this, wasn't it? You'll find you are somewhat faster and stronger, though not as much as you'd be with a third mark. Being in her mind, you will be able to anticipate her seizures all the better. That, and your considerable defensive skills, should help buy you time if a seizure happens unexpectedly."

"Was that a compliment?"

"Unless I've experienced a head injury I don't know about, no. If she has a seizure, call out to me for help, and I'll hear you." He gave Gideon a hard look. "Don't hesitate to do so. I'll be in my rooms. I don't require as much daylight sleep as most vampires, so I should be back up soon."

Turning on his heel, he left Gideon standing there, wondering what he'd just missed. The vampire was distancing himself. It made Gideon feel twitchy and out of sorts, because there was a dangerous predictability to vampires. While the shit could always hit the fan when they were around, if they were acting unpredictable, it was far more difficult to see from which direction the shit would fly, or when to duck. Daegan was already more unpredictable than most.

Maybe he'd just decided to give them space to deal with this new second-mark thing. Maybe he was tired as hell and wanted to go to bed. Maybe he was grumpy because he hadn't had any fresh blood.

Gideon was swamped by a swirl of thoughts and images from the woman two rooms away. Part confusion, part worry. Part marveling, as he was, at their new connection and the need to sort through whose thoughts were whose. With all that in his head, he set his concerns about Daegan's attitude aside. He had to figure this out first. Daegan had made the most important thing clear enough. He was as accessible as ever to come to Anwyn's aid. Hell, not that Gideon cared, but the vamp might even deign to cover his back.

If it involved Anwyn, of course.

18

SHE was on the floor of the cell, her knees drawn up to her chest as she rocked. Daegan had given her another shirt. She was sitting on a pillow, the chains back on her arms and legs. With them, she looked like a prisoner awaiting beheading. That faint hint of whispering, coming from her mind on top of a jumble of mismatched thoughts, increased to a sibilant growling at his appearance, but he realized that it was a constant cacophony, not an indication that she was still in seizure mode. Christ, had this been in her head all along? He wondered she hadn't succumbed to more seizures than she had.

God, he hated those chains. He ignored the clutch in his gut that asked, *What if we can never completely put them away? What if she has to go back to them forever or hurt someone?* Had Daegan asked himself the same question?

When she lifted her gaze, he realized he was an idiot. Servants' minds were open to their vampires. But how the hell could he stop thinking?

"If you figure it out, let me know," Anwyn said, her voice muffled in her knees.

He realized he still had the manual key to her restraints in his jeans pocket. Kneeling, he unlocked the ones on her legs, then on her wrists.

She started to pull back when she realized what he was doing, but he reached up, pushed back her hair so he could see her face.

"That was just while I was unconscious," he said quietly, holding her gaze. "You're a Mistress, and now you have a servant. If you can hold a man on his knees with just a look, you aren't going to let this son of a bitch's blood control you. You're going to use me to help steady yourself. Granted, my head's not the best one you could get, but it's what you got. One thing I do know is how to keep my shit together in a crisis. You use my mind, my blood, whatever it is your instincts tell you that you need to get a grip on this. You're going to be okay, because Daegan, you and me aren't accepting anything else. Right?"

She stared at him, and swallowed. "I don't want to be around him right now."

So that was it. He should have known. Daegan's involvement in making sure his second mark happened would have tripped her off again, her not entirely unjustified anger at him handling her for her own good. The bitch of it was, he wasn't sure he wouldn't have done the same thing, if he'd been in Daegan's shoes.

She gave him a vaguely hostile look, and he lifted his hands, a truce. "While I did kind of get a thrill hearing you don't want him around, you know you're going to have to work this shit out eventually. He's just a convenient target. You need somebody to be pissed off at that you know won't give up on you."

"How do you know that?" She wiped at her nose with the back of her arm, an indication of just how crappy she felt. The woman he'd seen walk into the Queen's Chamber would never be that graceless.

"Because I'm more vicious to my brother than to anyone else. How about another shower? We'll get you into some nice clothes."

"I'll just ruin them again."

"You may throw up on them a few times, or tear them up, but they're just clothes. They can be washed. Don't know about you, but I'm also done with treating you like a rabid dog." He kicked at the chains, sending them rolling another foot away with a harsh clanking.

"What if I try to hurt someone?" He could hear her mind wondering about Daegan's absence as well, despite her claim to not want him around.

"He's close enough to come help us. We're underground, and you can't enter the security code to get out if you're in bloodlust or seizure mode. Daegan may have a key to override it, but he's probably put that up his ass. I know it's safe from me up there, and I don't think he'll let you get to it."

Her lips curved, just a tiny bit, but it was enough. When she reached out, he leaned into her touch, let her stroke his brow. He'd liked her touch before, but now, with her so closely connected, it felt like contact between a hand and a musical instrument, a resulting vibration resonating between them.

"I can hear your mind, Gideon. All the thoughts going through it. You can probably hear a lot of mine."

"Yeah." Right now, it was like listening to static on a radio station with occasional voices coming through, the channel not yet fully tuned in. It was amazing and disorienting at once. And painful, because there were flashes of terrible things, pictures that made him want to smash faces and cause great pain to those who'd made her suffer. Then there were those shadows.

"They don't belong to me," she said. "I don't know . . . Maybe they were his? Part of his schizophrenia? They seem to have picked up on my fears quickly enough. Demonic possession has a whole new meaning to me."

He gripped her hand, hard, and she returned it, the two of them bound in a moment of silence, though the things going between their heads would have made the New York Stock Exchange sound like a temple of monastic silence. She gave a half chuckle, half sob. "My God, Gideon, I can't believe this is happening. It's just too much to think about."

"Yet you're handling it. If it was me, I'd be alternating between crying like a little girl and trying to smash my head into a wall to make it shut up."

"I believe the smashing. The little-girl thing is just to make me feel better." She ran her thumb over his lips, down to his throat and settled there, her fingers stroking those two marks. Gideon tilted his head, giving her access, holding her gaze.

"It's crazy, but that feels good."

"I know. Your body got all still and focused, your mind, zeroing in on my touch . . ." She moistened her lips, drew her hand away. "This isn't the most horrible thing that's ever happened to me, Gideon. If I'm handling this better than you expected, it's because I realized a long time ago the world doesn't stop, no matter what terrible thing happens. At first that horrifies you; then you realize it's a relief. You can step back into the stream and let the current pull you back in. It will help you pretend that things are okay again. You can watch TV and eat at McDonald's with everyone else. Until one day you're not pretending anymore, and it's really okay again."

But he saw deep clouds around those terrible things, things more recent and things past. It would take her a great deal more effort to step into that current. This room, surrounded by all the things she knew, he and Daegan, they were her insulation, but she actually wasn't sure if she could leave this room again. Wasn't sure how she'd handle that.

When she lifted her blue-green eyes to him, he gave her the answer, though he realized she could read it from his mind. "Because we'll step out that door together. I'll be at your back. I swear I won't let anything else happen to you."

They both knew that he couldn't make such a promise, but Gideon knew that wasn't why he said it, or why she'd needed to hear it out loud. She turned her hand beneath his, entangling their fingers, stroking his knuckles. "As far as the crying-like-a-girl thing, you've been out for a little bit. So I've pretty much handled my hysteria."

He saw flashes of it in her head, saw how Daegan had held her while she screamed and bit, cursing him in ways that explained some of the strain in the male vampire's face. This time Gideon had compounded it, her anger at the suffering she'd caused him during the marking.

"Yes, I was hard on him." Anwyn's jaw tightened, her eyes flashing. "Part of it is the gremlins in my brain, but you said it yourself, Gideon. They came here looking for him. You got dragged into this, and here we are, both part of this world neither of us wanted."

Gideon sighed. "It would be really easy to let you believe that, sweetheart, but it's a little more complicated." He wondered how much she wanted him to talk aloud versus give her thoughts, but if he was having initial difficulties tuning in, perhaps she was as well. "I don't owe him any favors, but I'm going to tell you something, okay? I don't know how much of his world you know about, but my very reliable source tells me that absolutely no one other than the Vampire Council knew who he was or where he could be found. Which means someone sold him out. At the Council level, that's not only serious; it's extremely rare."

Watching her digest that, Gideon gave her the truth, though he told himself he'd have been happy to have her blame the bastard. "He had every reason to think you'd be safe, Anwyn. He may be many things, but it's pretty clear he'd do anything to protect you. I'm willing to bet if he'd *ever* thought you would be in danger from having him around, you never would have met him. Bust his balls for being an arrogant SOB, but not for caring about you. Even I can't fault him for that.

"As for me, I make my own decisions." He lifted a shoulder when her expression became reflective. "No, I didn't want to be second-marked by a vampire." He couldn't bring himself to call it being a servant, though he knew that was what it was. "But you called it right. I'm on a one-way path to self-destruction, and tickled fucking pink to be going that way. Daegan said I'm only waiting for somebody faster to end it, and maybe he was right."

Putting her hand on his cheek, she forced his face up to meet her eyes. "I would have been very displeased by that."

He was conscious of the heat of her palm, the flicker inside her brain that showed him her own awareness of the texture of his skin, how close his lips were to her thumb. As if her small moment of protective possessiveness had kindled another form of marking, of taking possession. Feeling that heat grow between them, he held still, held her gaze.

"When Jacob and I were younger, when our parents were still around, one of their friends killed himself. When I asked our mother about it, she told me that while she didn't believe that suicides go to Hell, because God was merciful, she thought the reason the Bible and everything else made it such a terrible sin was because God has a plan for us, and if we kill ourselves, we fuck that up. We gotta trust He knows what He's doing."

"And you believe that?"

"Hell, no." He gave her a grim smile. "I gave up believing He was even paying attention years ago, but you've reminded me that sometimes there are important reasons we need to go on. Reasons that make life worth living."

Daring, he leaned forward, put his lips on hers. By the way she stiffened, he thought she might not be used to being kissed without someone asking permission first. Or maybe she was afraid of her own reaction in her current circumstances, but for that reason he did it oh-so-lightly, a brush of the top lip, the bottom, a light nip to taste her mouth. The static increased, but then he received a message, loud and clear, her voice that cocktease purr in his mind.

Gideon, stop.

He did, but he stayed where he was, so close their foreheads nearly touched, hair brushing. She put her fingers on his cheek, close to his lips, teasing that corner. All he saw was her blue-green gaze, a sea of emotions upon which his own mind sailed. It was all open to him, the turbulence of fears, hopes and weariness all wound together. Amid that fractious sea, she spoke, her voice resonating in his head as if he were underwater.

"Remember earlier, when we were talking about what belonging to me would mean? Do you understand it?"

He struggled to respond to her through that fracas, but then he saw her recognize his trouble, both from the inside of his mind and from his expression, an odd dual sensation. Her grip tightened, and he saw her do the same thing he was doing, look inward and bear down. Daegan must have given her some beginner's instruction, because slowly she brought a very thin curtain back between their minds. The effort made her hand shake in his, but once it was there, she was able to relax a little. Though he could still hear everything, it was like listening to muted conversations instead of competing with them.

"Better?"

He nodded. "I've seen the relationship between a vampire and a servant, Anwyn. Between two of them who love each other. In the vampire world, you're never supposed to say that, but since the two of them basically told the vampire world to fuck off and made their own rules,

I'm going to say it for them. Watching them, I'm not so sure that kind of ownership, the Dominance and submission, isn't a fluid thing that goes both ways over time."

"Maybe you're telling yourself that to help you accept it. I don't think you can rely on that one situation to typify ours."

"Well, that's how I'm doing it. Your real servant will probably do it the right way."

She put a hand on his chest, exerted enough pressure to get him to lean back and away from her. He kept up enough resistance to have her gaze sparking, both the Mistress and vampire recognizing the challenge.

"I want to be cleaned up," she said. "We'll get into the shower, and you'll wash me, according to my direction."

No Queen's Chamber. No appointment. She was making it clear she wanted to take the reins, exercise them as a Mistress, and her mind waited, myriad thoughts tumbling, with an undercurrent of sexual intent and emotional need that he couldn't deny.

"My pleasure. Mistress."

She rose. "I like the water at 102 degrees. There's a thermostat in there. Run the water for me."

"Is there a vampire health plan for scalded skin? More important, do servants heal from it?"

She raised a brow, giving him an imperious look that gave him some perverse pleasure to see, compared to how beaten down she'd looked moments ago. "Daegan told me servants heal from almost everything, as long as the Master or Mistress's blood is available to them."

As she moved forward, he was ready to steady her, but she seemed to be moving far more gracefully now. Check that. She was starting to have that sensual glide that female vampires did so well, a mix between a cheetah's movements and Grace Kelly's. He followed her out of the cell, across the main living quarters and back to the opulent bathroom. Daegan's door was still closed, and he hoped the male was taking some time to rest, then wondered why he cared.

The bathroom had looked much better the first time they were in it. Now it had stacks of dirty towels, discarded basins. But the tub and vanity area were still clear, and she sank down in her chair there, her back to him. She didn't look at the mirror, but he saw the ghostlike image was gone. Now there was no reflection at all.

He began to run the water, but when he looked up, saw her studying him, he felt a tangle of emotions running through her. "I'm sorry I scared you," he said. "With the seizure and all."

She gave him an incredulous look. "I tried to rip your throat out. I don't think you need to apologize."

"Maybe. But isn't it a servant's job to make his Mistress feel better?"

"Perhaps." She cocked her head. Her hair, as in need of a wash as it was, still caught his attention when it shone dark bronze from the vanity lights. "Once I learn how to do this better, Gideon, I'm going to try not to read your mind without your permission. Only do it when we're talking to one another directly, if it's appropriate. I don't want to strip you of your private thoughts. No one deserves that."

"Until you master that curtain thing, I'll try not to listen in on yours, either," he offered. "But if you start having fantasies about me, or girl-on-girl action, I can't promise anything. It's biological. Not my fault."

That little quirk again. "I understand it's quite permissible to beat one's servant. I'm having a few fantasies about that."

"Past attempts to crack my skull have proven it really doesn't do any good." At her mental cringe, he winced. "I was joking. I didn't mean—"

"I know," she said quickly. Rising, she folded her arms around herself. Her back straightened as if she were wearing royal purple, instead of a cotton tee. "Is my bath ready?"

Though he was in a unique position to realize how thin her veneer was, there was something about her that made it real, solid. Dignity and class. He'd seen them exercised across the full spectrum of wealth, race and gender barriers when facing fear or death, and knew it had more to do with character than anything else. He bet Lyssa would really like this woman.

In the meantime, the man in him acknowledged both, the fragile woman and the strong Mistress. "Yes." When he stretched out a hand, she placed hers in it, stepping over the shower wall. She shrugged off the stained garment, handed it to him.

"Throw that away."

"Yes, ma'am," he said, balling it up and doing a basketball toss toward the trash can, scoring a direct hit. When she turned to give him a narrow glance, he gave her an unrepentant arch of his eyebrow.

"Sit there." She indicated the commode. "I'm going to wash myself, and you're going to watch. But take off your shirt. I want to enjoy looking at you."

Okay, she was *really* getting back into the swing of things. She turned on the spray then stepped in, letting it run over her hair. As she sleeked it down on her skull and made it cling to her pale curves, that energy of a second-mark servant made itself known in a very obvious way.

It had been pretty awkward the first time, stripping down with her and Daegan, but she'd been caught up in her emotions then and it had been one of those react-don't-think moments, self-consciousness quickly discarded. This was like a demand issued in her Queen's Chamber. Still, he found himself pulling the T-shirt up and over, and tossing it to the side as well. Trying to be casual about it, even though he felt her eyes coursing up from his abdomen like the trail of her sharp nails.

"Why did you have those? The razor nails."

"I like cutting," she said. "I like the way certain types of men react to it."

Though it hadn't done squat for her against three vampires. He didn't have to fill that one in, because it hung in the air, another gargoyle hovering. Breaking eye contact with him, she pumped fragrant soap into her hands, massaging it between her palms until lather started to accumulate between them. She started at her neck. The water combined with the lather to send cascades of cream sliding down her breasts. Taking up a washcloth, she began to clean herself thoroughly.

Her intent might have been to take them out of the troublesome waters of their respective thoughts. If so, she was damn successful. She spent time on every inch of skin he'd like to touch, and lingered on the places he'd linger on. Lifting her breasts, tossing her hair back so it was a shiny cascade, a sable waterfall, she soaped the generous curves, pinched her nipples, and then arrowed her hands down over her abdomen, taking away blood, sputum, everything except beautiful woman. Down, down, until she reached her pussy, and began to soap herself there, slow, massaging circles that had her leaning up against the side of the shower, her legs parting to give her better access.

"Don't move." Gideon froze. He'd intended to shift, adjust himself because his jeans were getting uncomfortable. She hadn't even looked at him, as far as he knew. While her mind could have anticipated him, from what he'd seen of her skills in this area, it was entirely possible the Mistress had anticipated him. "I want that handsome cock of yours kinked up, aching for freedom. You remember the bathing chamber where I had you chained?" At his short nod, her gaze glinted. "I've brought deserving slaves in there before, bound them, washed them myself, inside and out, then made them watch as you are watching. One of them couldn't contain himself. He came while watching me, because of the vibrating probe I'd put in his ass. Because he got his semen on my skin, I put him in a cock-and-ball harness with prongs and made him come that way, an excruciating mixture of pleasure and pain. He never forgot it."

"But you haven't brought them down here."

She met his gaze. "Why would I have a dungeon down here if I didn't intend to bring my favorites to it, keep them as my prisoner as long as I wish?"

The answers to it, the truth, were already in her mind, amid a teasing whorl of heat. He'd said he wouldn't look if he could help it, but it was easier said than done, not to look at a landscape directly in front of his mind's gaze. Never. She'd never had a submissive down here. She'd been too busy getting the business running to have time for personal relationships, and then she'd met Daegan.

She held his gaze. Though he saw mild reproof in her expression, she'd apparently realized this was a game of quid pro quo. "When you saw me walk into the Queen's Chamber, what did you want from me, Gideon?"

He couldn't have said it to her now or before, but his mind did, without hesitation. *Surrender, pain. Release. Acceptance.*

19

"Every mind has shields, *cher*. As the serum goes in, your mind will open his. Do it firmly, don't stop, but move forward slow. Give his shields time to lie down before you, rather than ramming through them. It's a seduction, not a rape. He will still likely convulse, as if he is about to seize, but that is just the physical reaction, one he cannot control. Just keep going, and then speak to him. Calm him from within his mind."

During the second marking, Daegan had spoken to her, walked her through it. She could tell Gideon had tuned out everything but the action, so she wasn't sure he'd heard the dialogue. When he'd reacted with such startled resistance, she'd known he hadn't.

Still fighting her reservations about what they'd done to him, she'd promised herself she wouldn't read his mind if she could help it. Hell, a few seconds ago, she'd made the same promise to him. Now the pleasure of being a Mistress, of plumbing the depths of a submissive's needs, had opened up to a new level for her, in this one particularly fascinating male. His rapid laundry list softened her, made her hold out the shampoo. "Do my hair."

He rose. She hadn't said to get undressed, so he didn't. He stepped into the shower in his jeans and boots, an automatic obedience she liked. Leaning back into him, she let him support her weight as he poured the shampoo into her scalp, set the bottle aside. His hands were strong and massaging, caring and needing at once.

He'd taken off her chains, looked her in the eye and told her she would stay in control. She knew it was an illusion, but he surrounded her with something, a sense of stability. He belonged to her. And he'd been willing to belong to her, never mind how it had actually occurred or when he would eventually change his mind. Despite the strange, awful things happening to her, this wasn't a bad moment, particularly when he smoothed his palm over her forehead so she laid her head back on his shoulder. When he dropped a kiss on her skin, she absorbed the texture of his mouth, the hint of moist heat. His strong, hard body supporting her, not a soft spot anywhere.

She couldn't begin to itemize the ways her body felt changed, let alone her mind, her instincts . . . everything. Even her automatic reactions as a Mistress had a new, additional quality to them. Something more feral and demanding, something frighteningly indifferent to limitations, boundaries. She was able to do anything she wished, to anyone weaker than herself. That was the way of the beast.

No. That was Barnabus's way, the way of a creature that had been twisted into a sociopath. Even wild animals did not prey on the weak maliciously. It alarmed her, to think that those shadow creatures might be clever enough to cloak themselves in her own thoughts and instincts.

"You may want to close your eyes while I rinse your hair." His voice was a steadying rumble behind her ear. "Vampire invincibility or not, I expect shampoo still stings if it gets in your eyes."

Anwyn turned in his arms, closing her eyes so he could do that. As he did, she threaded her fingers in his chest hair, moving close enough that she could press herself against wet denim. She registered the integration of bone and muscle, his hot, sweet blood beneath firm skin. The indentations of old scars, proof of his battles.

Battles with what she now was. She didn't let that thought snag her, though, because he was here now.

"I want to dance," she murmured.

"Here?" He was vaguely amused and very aroused, and she savored both. As he rinsed her, her hair was so long he couldn't help but follow the curve of her back to the rise of her buttocks. When wet, the locks caressed her hips. He was trying hard, in a touchingly chivalrous manner, not to take advantage, but she saw all the wonderful things in his mind he'd like to do. It goaded her own desires.

"No. After we finish. I know the song I want. It's slow and beautiful, and talks about how wonderful and terrible love is."

"You're going to make me dance with you, aren't you?"

Marveling at how much she wanted his closeness, she laid her head on his chest in an uncharacteristic move, letting his arms come around her. There was someone else she wanted close as well, but she pushed that away.

She knew Daegan cared for her, considered her his territory in that overbearing yet appealing way of the extreme alpha male. But would he have done as Gideon had done, gone against everything he was, sacrificed for her well-being? They were thoughts she couldn't shake, even as she despised herself for such pettiness and possible hypocrisy. Was she capable of denying her Dominant instincts any more than Daegan?

Daegan *had* denied himself for five years, she reminded herself. Refused to make her his servant when it was something he'd obviously desired. It increased her self-loathing, recalling what she'd done earlier when Gideon was still unconscious.

In the aftermath of her seizure, as she'd slowly drifted toward unconsciousness, Daegan had briefly left her to check on Gideon. When he returned, before his hand touched her, she'd flinched away from him. Rather than pressing the issue, there'd been a weighted silence. Her eyes had been closed, her arms curved protectively over her body, a tension in her shoulders that didn't ease, not even when she realized he'd withdrawn, gone back to her new servant.

She'd realized the horrible truth. What had made her flinch was his scent. Not his unique smell, but the species itself. Vampire. Whereas she didn't fear Gideon, didn't find any monsters in him, Daegan was connected with her fear and apprehension of what she was now. The part she felt he'd played in it.

Being intuitive, he'd felt her revulsion, and she knew that was why he'd withdrawn. He wouldn't have if it was just the festering issues between them. He'd given her Gideon to help her where he couldn't. It made her heart and head hurt.

While Gideon had been amazed at how well she had handled herself so far, she knew there was a whole cauldron of post-traumatic breakdown waiting for her once she got a handle on all of it. But she couldn't summon the energy for any of it. Not right now. She had all she could handle. She'd deal with it soon. No matter how shameful it made her feel, she knew Daegan could take it. She needed something else right this minute, and she was going to take it.

What was it about a hard-muscled man, with battle scars and a 100 percent trouble, devil-glint in his eye, that she found so irresistible? He was rubbing soap on her back now, his hands practically screaming their desire to mold over her ass. It wasn't natural to him to wait for permission, but he was trying. Probably not because of any desire to win the Sub-of-the-Month award, but because he was in her mind now. He knew how close to boiling that cauldron was, and he wouldn't want to take anything from her she didn't want to give.

Even so, he wasn't the type to beg for the right to kiss the sole of her shoe. He was the quivering mastiff at her knee, fangs ready, waiting for the command to leap forward with a powerful ripple of muscle. Only she was in the mood for a different type of attack.

If she wanted rough sex, she'd have it, and enjoy the hell out of it, would refuse to let it be dragged down to the level of what happened in the alley. *My first official command, Gideon. Take me as you want. Ignore everything that may or may not have happened these past few hours. Do it, now.*

To underscore it, taking advantage of the shock that coursed over his expression, she went up on her toes and seized his mouth. Cupping her hands around his skull and biting down on his bottom lip, hard, she caused him to growl.

I know it's not natural to you, to wait and ask, fawn and grovel. Be the man I know you are. Sweep me away. Fuck me so I can barely walk.

She heard that leash break, knowing hunger, lust and need were all leaping against those self-imposed restraints. Catching her under the arms, he put her against the wall, but his eyes burned into hers. "I don't want to hurt you."

"Speak in my mind."

I don't want to hurt you. The sensual impact of it, his voice inside her, was incredible.

You'll hurt me only by holding back. In the swirl of their emotions and tumbling thoughts, each of them struggling to hear the uppermost thought in the other's mind, she made sure that one was clear. *You said I have the control to beat this. I do. That I shouldn't be treated like a rabid animal. I don't want to be treated like a victim. I want your cock. I demand it.*

He fisted his hand in her hair, plundered her mouth. There was the lingering flavor of blood, where Daegan had to strike him and he'd bitten his lip. Lust was a glorious sensation, but she'd never felt it like this. Was this why Daegan was always so ready to take her, even within minutes of having pushed them both over a peak? She wanted to draw it out forever, make Gideon suffer with lust until he was a brutal, mindless male animal. She wanted him to come inside of her now, hear his lust release in a long, helpless groan as he clutched her with his callused hands, speared her with his thick cock and sank deep, so deep she'd feel impaled and never want the pain of having the weapon pulled free of her aching flesh.

He had another surprise for her. Putting her on her feet, he turned her, pressing her against the shower wall and himself against her, his palms over her hands, pushing them flat against the tile, fingers curving into the spaces. He ground himself against her buttocks and she lifted for him, gasping, stepping on the toes of the boots he still wore. Bringing his knee up, he lifted her on his thigh, his other hand circling her waist and holding her in place to let her rub there, have the glorious feel of his thigh muscle rubbing against her clit as he opened his jeans.

"Yes," she muttered. "Do it. Fuck me."

Water was pounding against them. Even so, she clearly felt the tender brush of his lips on her nape as he worked her hard against his body, his strength able to keep her there if she didn't use vampire strength against him. If he hadn't had the second mark, his lack of sleep, of nourishment other than what he'd been able to scavenge from her kitchen between seizures, would have defeated him, but that energy sustained him as their need for each other only increased.

So did madness, with angry, slashing claws. Her fingers dug into the tile beneath his. *No. Not yet.*

"Gideon." Panic gripped her. "Another one . . . another." Would it ever end? Would it be as bad as the last one, or could he truly help, now that he was in her mind and halfway oriented?

I'm here. I see it, feel it. We'll ride it out together. You won't hurt me. You're in control, Anwyn. Mistress.

As the seizure invaded, so did he, ripping open his jeans to drive himself into her to the root. He held her hands tightly, not to restrain her, but to tell her he was there as the pain of the transition ripped at her internal organs, made her cry out. She clung to the pleasure of him thrusting into her, to the way he filled her inside, how he pressed her against the shower wall so her clit made contact with it.

But that madness continued to build, the voices growing louder, the crimson haze covering her eyes. A renewed flood of panic was quickly swallowed by greed, the bloodlust using the sexual energy as fuel for its own purposes.

Breaking free, she whipped around and drove him up against the opposite wall, climbing his body to take control, slamming herself back down on him. With the thick breadth of his cock rubbing her slick tissues inside, her muscles milked him with ruthless craving. Her fingers fisted in his hair hard enough to hold his head back, his throat arched out to her. *Mine.* He was hers, to do with as she wished. That flimsy curtain she'd attempted was torn away, her mind invading his so he could hide nothing from her. Daegan had said the third mark was even deeper, soul deep. If she'd given him that last mark, she could clutch it in her hands, shred it if she wanted to do so.

They are never to be trusted. Kill him, now. He can still be killed. Blood is so much sweeter, easier, and a dying man's blood goes down so well. Do it when he's pumping his seed in you, let him die in the throes of orgasm, where you hold and take everything from him.

The gremlins screamed like a crowd of rabid fans at a rock concert. And threaded through it all, that voice, the sibilant lisp that had become a part of who she was, a part she was trying to deny. They all stroked her need for power and control, taking her places in her mind she hadn't known existed. Her fangs grew longer, the crimson tide bathing everything around her in blood, turning the water running over them into a shower of it. She heard Gideon's voice in her head, a distant, weak thing, attempting to bring her back to that pathetic creature she'd been a moment before. He would fail.

She snarled in protest, an angry, aroused cat, when an arm circled her neck from behind. A strong body pressed her harder onto Gideon's, creating a storm of sensation as her head was jerked to the side and a pair of fangs sank into her throat.

No, no, no . . . Gideon's surge of anger joined her own, but they were both helpless against the power of the creature holding them joined against the shower wall. Though she fought it, need grew heavy and hot again, for as Daegan drank, desire doubled and tripled in her blood. It spun around her, rousing every nerve ending. She began to rise and fall on Gideon, her fingers digging into his shoulders, nerve endings singing at the clutch of his fingers low on her hips, the way they convulsed to make the stroke of his cock, every velvet steel inch, the friction of the broad head, even more pleasurable. Though he appeared resistant because of their company, he couldn't resist the lust any more than she could.

Fuck me, the wildness in her screamed. *Do it, or I'll tear your heart out of your chest.*

No, you will not. Daegan's voice in her head was a startling and new experience. Gideon registered it as well, for it came right through her open mind to his. *He is your servant. You care for him, and he cares for you. His desire is all for you, Mistress Anwyn. Accept it, use it. Make him yours by winning his heart, not his fear. That is your way. His mind may be yours, but it is a gift. His surrender is a gift. Win the gift, Anwyn. Don't take it.*

Words she'd lived by all her life. She felt the heat of the man inside of her, the one behind her. Saw Gideon's desire and felt the fragile pounding of his heart at once.

A gift . . .

Whatever had changed in her face had altered something for Gideon, for he decisively cupped her throat, the opposite side from Daegan. Leaning forward, he brought his lips to that sensitive juncture. He worked his way down her sternum, dragging his open mouth over the top of her breast, and she arched up into Daegan as he took the nipple in his mouth, suckled deep, causing that luscious low pull in her belly, in her pussy.

The wracking pain, the throb of bloodlust, was still there, but it had a counter now. She knew how to work pain and pleasure together. That experience, working with two opposites, made her work around the chaotic storm, the division of her own mind between herself and the unstable vampire she was becoming. She reached for the voices of the two men she wanted inside her.

Daegan intuited her every thought so often, so hearing his voice, now actually there, wasn't as disruptive as she'd expected. Though she knew she should be really pissed off at whatever he'd just done, she had nothing to spare for that right now. Not with Gideon's mouth working on her so deftly, teasing the nipple, his teeth squeezing down on it just right, that slow build of pressure. Years ago, she'd been told by a favored cop client how to handle a gun. Squeeze, don't pull. It apparently worked in myriad, volatile ways.

Daegan was braced behind her, and she registered that he still wore the dark jeans but no shirt, water rolling down his fine muscles, pressed against her back and the outside of her arms. She had her head on his shoulder and now she looked up at him through a film of mist to find crimson lights flickering in the depths of his dark eyes, his bloodlust obviously roused by this, and by the blood he'd taken from her.

With a trembling set of fingers, she reached up, traced his wet lips, watched him stay still beneath her touch, his breath hot and moist on her. Whatever else they couldn't resolve, she could never deny him her body. And he knew it.

Drawing in a breath, she couldn't look away as Gideon pulled out, slowly surging back in. He took over the pace, his gaze flaming further at her reaction. As he fucked her this way, while simply holding her, there were a million things in his eyes. Moaning at the next thrust, she arched upward, found Daegan's mouth and dug her fingers into the side of his neck to hold herself there. He didn't disappoint her, taking instant command of the kiss, capturing her head to prolong the erotic duel of tongues and lips as Gideon worked his way back up to her throat. Cinching his arm in between her back and Daegan's body, he began to ram into her in earnest, reading what she wanted. That hard rutting that overwhelmed the new attack, like a tidal wave swallowing high-tide surf, mixing together in one violent event.

Gideon . . . She gloried in the small victory of issuing a command during such a storm. *Do not come until I say so.*

She felt his acknowledgment, his frustration because he was so close, but too mindless to question why he submitted to her desire.

Her own climax was fast approaching, and she devoured Daegan's mouth, scraping his fangs with her own and earning a growl that made her lips stretch back in a feral response. It was so good to taste him like this, no thought, not having to deal with the minefield between them, all that swept away for the moment by the easy, familiar, never-ending desire for each other. Then the orgasm took her, shuddering up from the joining point between her and Gideon.

Do not come, Gideon. Not until I say. It was a breathless wail of sound in her mind that escalated into a long cry that echoed off the tile.

She needed so much, stripped so bare in this second, and yet never had she felt more powerful. As she came, the cry became a scream at the strength and pleasure of it, strangled by that savage bloodlust. She wrapped her fingers in Gideon's hair and turned his head into her shoulder, biting down into the meat of his. Though she held him there, he wasn't fighting her, even as his body was coiled-spring tension, his cock so hard and pulsing inside of her. Because his mind had become a red haze of pure lust, his control was astounding.

Daegan reacted to the blood scent, his nostrils flaring. Gideon recognized it, because tension rippled through him. It dampened his arousal, helped him hold on a little longer, but not by much.

Let him have a lick, Gideon. One long stroke of his tongue along your beautiful shoulder to clean up the mess I made. Then I will let you come.

The words weren't entirely her, and yet they were, a vampire's sensual cruelty mixed with her own Mistress inclinations. She had him. He was trembling with the effort not to release. If she tightened her muscles at all, the battle was lost. If he hadn't been so close to this pinnacle, he would shove away from her, tell her, *Hell, no,* but she'd driven him too hard. His body needed that orgasm like it needed air.

She was walking that edge, the one Madelyn had mentioned, a mere life-altering day or so before, and she exulted in it. *Tell me, "Yes, Mistress."*

In his mind, she saw the fleeting thought that, just like a man who'd soiled his hands with one murder, it made the next step toward Hell that much easier. That took her aback, something cold and unpleasant tightening in her belly as he likened his submission to her marking as a crime. However, he'd made his decision.

He pressed his forehead into her shoulder. *I can't. I'll do what you ask, but I can't say it. I don't . . . Jesus, please just get it over with. I want to come inside you so much.*

Daegan gave her a measured look as she turned her head, their faces so close. She'd never order him to do anything, but when he lowered his head, she had a feeling he was doing more than indulging her. As his lips touched Gideon's shoulder, the man made a strangled noise of protest, his fingers tightening on Anwyn's hips. A glint came to Daegan's eyes that Anwyn knew, that made both apprehension and pleasure unfurl in her belly. Daegan dragged his mouth over the punctured area, his tongue doing a slow, methodical cleansing of it. The hair on his forehead brushed Gideon's nape, the line of his shoulder. Gideon's cock jerked inside of her, unable to resist the stimulation of that clever mouth.

She fully savored her orgasm's aftershocks as she indulged the pleasure of holding one man in her arms, watching another taste his flesh in this bold, precise way.

Daegan's hands covered hers, and together they slid them down Gideon's broad back, following the shallow valley to the rise of his buttocks. Gideon had pushed his jeans halfway off his hips, and the vampire's hands were inside that cloth barrier, overlapping hers. Anwyn's hands gripped Gideon's flesh hard as Daegan provided the pressure on the outside of them. They pushed Gideon in deep, then pulled him out. In, out, with excruciating slowness, controlling the motion so he had to follow their rhythm.

Now, Gideon. It was both of their voices, she realized, offering the release to him in her mind. And though he tried to resist, he couldn't. He began coming almost before the command completed, but Daegan was as diabolical as she was, controlling that rhythm, so it continued as a slow thrust and retreat. Gideon tried to increase the pace, jerking against them, his strangled grunts building into a shout of release that echoed in the shower, and kept echoing, as their rhythm made sure his seed was shooting in thick, continuous spurts inside of her. With a surge of primal satisfaction, she knew it went on far longer than he usually experienced with his hundred-dollar, fifteen-minute hookers.

Those women weren't in his mind now, and she hoped never to see them there. They'd been a receptacle for his release, not what he needed. Not her.

When he finished, Gideon was leaning into her, and Daegan was the solid support for both of them. Her servant's mind was fogged with the power of that climax. Bemused by how easy it was to think of him that way—her servant—Anwyn took advantage of that lull to separate her hands from Daegan's. They chose different paths up Gideon's back, hers up the center, Daegan's fanning out from the buttocks, following the rib cage back up to the shoulder blades. They came to rest on the back of Gideon's head, where her own hands rejoined his. Both tangled in his hair, indulging in easy, soothing affection.

Anwyn closed her eyes, feeling relief. The seizure had passed and, just as Gideon said, she hadn't hurt anyone.

"Because I was here. You're an idiot." Daegan gripped a hank of Gideon's hair and jerked it, not ungently, and the other man grunted. "I told you to call me when you felt it coming. You thought you could handle it."

"You were here, right? With your supersonic hearing. Did we pull you away from *Oprah* or something?"

"I think your first instincts were right, *cher*. You should have ripped his heart out."

Anwyn couldn't summon a smile. As Gideon pulled his head away, his shoulder was twitching under Daegan's forearm. He averted his eyes from hers, but he couldn't avert his mind. She knew enough to read a man's body language, but hearing the thoughts made it a sharper underscore.

Sex was a powerful distraction, but reality always had to return. The aftermath could make the guilt or betrayal all the sharper. Gideon was already reliving Daegan putting his mouth on his shoulder. How it became part of the arousal, both of them stimulating him, what that meant. And—faintly accusing—why had she done that to him, knowing how he felt about being touched by a male? More important, a vampire.

I'm a vampire.

Startled, his gaze flickered up. *I wasn't really talking to you, you know.* His tone wasn't resentful, but it was a near thing, rippling along her raw nerves. *You know you're different.*

Am I? Or have you pulled that moral yardstick out of your ass and decided I've taken another tick closer toward becoming as bad as he is?

From the way Daegan's hands stilled on her back, she knew he'd heard that. Good, because she had an even deeper level of anger stirring for him. Her reality was returning with Gideon's. When she slid down their bodies, her feet finding the tile, they both steadied her as she swayed. But she pushed away from them, standing apart and leaning back against the side of the shower. Folding her hands behind her, she propped her hips on them, and met Daegan's gaze. "You promised you'd never do that to me. Mark me like a servant so you could read my mind. Speak inside of it."

"You're not a servant; you're a vampire. I did it because it's clear you're going to need my ability to reach you in your head. And so is Gideon. It's only temporary. With practice, you'll be able to keep me out, where a human servant can't."

"Oh well. What am I complaining about? As long as you know what's best."

~

Daegan didn't add that, with their age difference, it would be almost impossible for her to keep one of his strength and maturity out of her mind when he was determined to find out what she was thinking or to speak to her. It was his hope he never had to do that, but she needed the stability a servant *and* a vampire sire could bring to her. He'd been wrestling with it ever since giving her the locator mark, but this had cinched it. Gideon was handling things well, all things considering, but he wasn't objective enough when it came to her.

Pressing his lips together, Daegan pulled a towel off the rack, went to her despite her forbidding look and spread it over her shoulders, using that tether to pull her slightly toward him and slide the rest of the towel between her and the wall. She remained wooden, her condemning gaze on him. He didn't linger, but he didn't let her refuse him, either, spreading her hair over her shoulders before stepping away to get a towel for himself. Gideon already had one.

She glanced toward the human, who'd tugged up his wet jeans with difficulty and refastened them. Despite their barbed exchange, there was a softening to her expression, some regret, when she looked at him. Probably because she knew she'd pushed him to accept Daegan's caress.

But it hadn't been because of a sadistic vampire urge. Daegan wondered if she realized it had been purely her instinct as a Mistress, knowing how to push a sub toward the surrender he needed, to help his soul as well as give pleasure to them both. He wondered how long it would take Gideon to figure that out.

Something else twisted in his gut at that soft look, but it wasn't jealousy, not exactly. It was knowing he wasn't forgiven, and knowing there was nothing he could do about it. Correction: that he was willing to do about it. While it was past time to confront her anger and disrespect head-on, the truth was that an inferno of emotions about what had happened to her was barely banked within him. Because of those events, events he should have been able to prevent, he was having to take even more of her choices away. Even if it was to protect her, he knew he was systematically destroying what fragile trust they'd had between them. He honestly couldn't trust his own emotions if he let them slip in any way.

None of that mattered. He would do whatever was necessary to make sure she survived this.

The dark clouds she turned toward him now made it clear her anger against him was only compounding, as the pleasure of the climax was washing away. Of the three of them, she'd had the most sleep, though it had mainly been due to unconsciousness after her seizure. It made him take a firmer grip on his self-control, bracing himself for her next words.

"Once I get in some semblance of a routine again, with control of who and what I am, I intend to make some decisions about my life."

Daegan met Gideon's dark blue gaze, then shifted back to her face. "You will have latitude to do that eventually, *cher*. But it's not that straightforward for us. Vampires are not like humans. Our society is not as free. There are too few of us, and we live in the shadows."

"So you're saying yet another person or persons is going to be trying to control my life?"

"We will speak of this later. Not right after something like this."

He didn't need Gideon's visible wince to know a command had been a poor choice.

"So that's your decision, hmm?" Her voice, velvet and breathless moments ago, was now brittle, acerbic. "When to tell me something, when not to? When to decide that I need a servant, when I need you in my fucking mind, without asking me? For five years, you tried to get me to believe you respected my independence. But it was never that, was it? You always thought you owned me. I only saw the pretty, sparkling collar, not the leash attached to it."

His face went completely expressionless. He knew it, because Anwyn registered it in her mind. She recalled it from times in the past when she'd pushed too hard for something he wouldn't give her. Couldn't give her. In her mind, he saw her remind herself that was why she'd sworn to herself, years ago, that she would never beg him for anything, never let him see that she couldn't stand on her own, away from him. Never give him her heart fully.

Only now he could get into her head, see the truth. Her head jerked up, eyes meeting his as she recognized that everything in her mind could be read like a book, and was being read, right now. He told himself to pull out, to shut that wall between them, but it was too late. Her next thoughts were shots right in the gut.

What makes you so different from Barnabus? How is this different?

He took a step back from her, might have even backed over the tub wall if he'd gone any farther, the first time in centuries he'd been in danger of tripping. The understandings of the past few moments, when sensuality and need were all that mattered, were gone.

"Anwyn . . ." Gideon began.

"You don't need to defend him for my well-being, Gideon. You don't even like him." Her voice was low, strained, as her gaze met Daegan's head-on. "Last week, my life was entirely different. I don't know whether to wish I'd never met you, or that Barnabus had just killed me in that alley. I'm too tired, too numb, to decide. Please don't disturb me until I come out of my room. I don't want to be or think of anything.

"And before either of you says it," she added, "if I go into a seizure, my mind twists open like a bubble gum wrapper. To you both now, I guess." She shot Daegan a hard look. "So I'm sure you'll know if I need help. Until then, fuck off. "

Turning on her heel, she left the two of them standing there.

20

GIDEON caught the brief flash of pain in the vampire's eyes, an anguish so strong, it was as if she'd taken out a poisoned stake and stabbed him in the chest with it. Then it was gone. No matter how much he wanted to hate the guy, Gideon couldn't help the sympathetic pang that bound all males together in the face of female scorn.

He'd been unbalanced himself by what had just happened here. Hell, all of them were dealing with too much shit. He, being her servant and throwing in his lot, however temporarily, with two vampires. She, being raped and becoming a vampire. And Daegan, having to ride herd on both of them, and deal with the pain she was suffering, even as she kept him at a straight-arm distance, blaming him for myriad aspects of all of it. Maybe he wouldn't have seen that if it hadn't been for Mason, working with him and Jacob over those several months, having to deal with a lot of the same kind of shit.

He didn't know what to say, even if he'd been inclined to do so, but he was saved from the effort. With an impassive nod, the vampire left him there.

Great. With a lack of other options, Gideon threw his towel in the hamper and straightened up. For him, cleaning up a room meant checking out and not leaving a noticeable amount of blood on the floor.

But once, a long time ago, he'd had a civilized home with his aunt and uncle, and he did know some things.

Going back to the cell, he straightened that area up. After some consideration, he moved the sofa and other furniture out of it. It looked as though she wouldn't have to go back in there again unless it was unavoidable. Progress, though of course those last few moments in the bathroom had felt like anything but.

Though she had a right to be pissed off about all of it, he already knew when she came down from those attacks, she was typically attacked by feelings of despair, a sort of postpartum baby-vampire-blues thing. Though this time she'd had the pleasure of an orgasm tangled with the seizure, and the episode itself hadn't been one of her worst ones, that aftermath may have remained the same.

He wanted to comfort her, but knew she probably needed some space. And he didn't want to be in the personally uncomfortable position of finding himself apologizing for the guy. Particularly after he'd put his fucking mouth on him.

He did touch her mind periodically. She'd come back into the bathroom after they left and did those things that women did—powders, lotions, brushing, et cetera. Then she'd slid on a summer dress and lain on her bed. As she'd said, she was incredibly, painfully numb, and almost as tired as he was. Hell, he should probably sack out somewhere until she needed him again. But it was hard not to reach out, to say something that wouldn't infringe on her need for solitude. Before he could decide one way or another, she drifted off into a dark, whispering sleep.

As he sank down on the couch in the sitting room, he sat quietly in her mind, oblivious to his immediate surroundings, just getting the lay of the land. He wanted to stroke her in some way. Fortunately, he found a way to be useful.

Those hateful shadow things were there, slithering around like street predators in the alleyways of her brain, waiting for the reappearance of her awareness to prey on her again. He examined them more closely, was disturbed by how formless and yet integrated they seemed to be in those passageways, suggesting any treatment for them would have to be a muting strategy, nothing that could be extracted. It made him wonder if someone like Lord Brian, the vampire scientist who had worked with Jacob after his unexpected acquisition of Lyssa's powers during his turning, might have something useful to help her. He wondered if Daegan had ever interacted with the vamp geek, and made a note to mention it to him.

In the meantime, in the anonymity of her dream world, he decided to send things through that might keep those gremlins down to a dull roar. He recalled songs in his head, a way to sing lullabies to her without offending her ears. Though he hoped Daegan wasn't squatting at the fringes of her unconscious, listening, he also sent images he remembered as a kid, short home movies to go with the songs. A trip to the Grand Canyon was coupled with "Sand and Water," a song his mother had sung to Jacob when he was younger. After she died, Gideon had continued to sing it to him, though the meaning of it had often caused a hitch in his throat. Now the notes drifted like wind currents over the wide expanses of red rock.

Then he moved onward to the California redwood forests with the strains of the Goo Goo Dolls; "Better Days" spiraled around and around that awesome girth, all the way toward the heavens.

After that it was the beach, with the smell of salt and sand, the sun reflecting off the waves, so bright and sparkling. He had no song for that one, because he always got lost in the music the wind and waves made together. With deep satisfaction, he saw the shadows melt into those corridors, stilling so that her mind could slip deeper into dreams, far beyond their reach, and the reach of her worries and fears. It amazed him to be there, to be inside her mind as if he'd walked hand in hand with her somnolent mind and escorted it to Sandland himself.

The vampire connection aside, it was one of the most awesomely magical things he thought he'd ever experienced. It gave him the fleeting, disturbing thought of how he'd ever do without such a connection once he'd had it. It also made him wonder at what he'd heard from Jacob, how the third mark was an even more profound bond.

Surprisingly unable to give himself to dreams, he rose and examined the music selection at the entertainment center. He wondered whose music was whose, as well as the movies. In light of all the things that had happened, it was bizarre to see the mundane details of their life together. Or perhaps this was all Anwyn's.

He mused on the two of them having separate rooms. They were certainly having sex, but perhaps one or both didn't encourage the intimacy of sleeping together. Only sex and companionship when needed. Friends with benefits, she'd said.

Yeah, right. The relief and sense of balance he'd felt from her every time Daegan joined them suggested something way beyond friendship. While Daegan also didn't show much of what he was feeling, it was obvious, at least to Gideon, that what he was holding back had the force of a category-five hurricane. He remembered what Daegan had said. *A warrior's courage and the fool's sense of when to use it.* When it came to pushing the vampire, he thought his Mistress might be wise to ease off a bit.

Maybe that was why, when Daegan touched her, Gideon didn't feel the same sense of possessiveness he'd experienced at the thought of another male servant, or even an imaginary blood donor. He'd occasionally felt like a third wheel, but he'd never questioned Daegan's right to share her, except for the wisdom of being tangled with a vampire. Gideon wasn't sure he even wanted to explore why deeper than that, though. Maybe it was the circumstances.

She'd wanted to dance. He'd have to see if he could remind her of that later, make her smile. Sighing, he ran a hand along the back of his neck. In truth, he felt at a loss here. When he had spare time, he worked on his weapons, went out and wandered the street, watched people as his television. Their lives were far removed from his, but their stories held his fascination regardless. All those small dramas and happinesses, things like car payments and Sunday dinner with the parents, squabbles over whether the kid was going to get a PlayStation, or Xbox, or whatever the hell it was kids wanted now.

He could think about the good things that had happened in the shower, the way her body had felt, the wetness of her mouth and clutch of her hands, but there were some disturbing things about the sex, too. Specifically, the number of participants and how his body had responded to that. So he pushed it away for now.

But weapons . . . He found he'd shifted to the cabinet holding Daegan's cache. Opening the wooden door and examining the safe's combination lock, he spun it, wondering. Twelve. Seventeen. Thirteen. Ten.

As the lock made that whoosh noise, Gideon shook his head. Daegan really needed to work on his password security. Course, in all fairness, the code he'd given to Gideon had apparently never been given to anyone before. Which suggested again that Daegan had given Gideon a level of trust he hadn't granted to anyone else, like the uncontrolled access to Anwyn's mind. Another mystery.

Nonplussed by that, but suffering no guilt at breaking into the safe, Gideon opened the door. Holy mother lode. Crossbows with beautifully engineered draws and balanced arrows. Guns, of quite a few types and sizes. But of even greater interest was Daegan's ammunition. Gideon lifted one of the capsules to the light, looking at the dark movement of liquid inside. There were knives, of every possible description, weight and curve. He picked up a misericord, examining it. Hanging behind the knives, on another backboard, was the collection of swords. He expected he was looking at weapons that might have belonged to warriors of old. Of course, if Daegan was born in 1310, they could be his—

Gideon dropped and rolled a second before the vampire reached him, his precog sense alone helping him avoid that snatch and grab. He was able to get the sofa between them, made a well-aimed jab with the misericord that almost snagged Daegan's shirt, but that was as far as he got. Daegan had him against the wall, another weapon against Gideon's throat. A nice six-inch wooden blade that could punch right through the neck.

"It's good manners to ask a man before you handle his weapon."

Before Gideon could think of a suitable retort to that, Daegan backed off and tossed him the knife. When Gideon caught it, he realized it was his own wooden knife. "It served the purpose you wished," the vampire said briefly. "I took Barnabus's blood with it, though I am keeping him alive in a holding facility until we are certain we no longer need him."

"Good." Gideon hadn't expected him to honor his request, but Daegan had taken it seriously, warrior to warrior. While he couldn't bring himself to say thanks, Daegan seemed indifferent to his response. The vampire had changed clothes, now wearing faded blue jeans, the cuffs worn and frayed with age, and a white muscle shirt. His feet were bare. The casual, contemporary look might make him seem as approachable as a Gap commercial, except for that stalking-game walk and his closed expression.

"You've got an impressive amount of hardware here," Gideon observed, returning Daegan's daggers to the safe. "What's in the bullets?"

"Acid." Daegan moved to join him. "They explode in the vampire, eat away flesh. It won't kill him, but it hurts. Works for a distraction, slows enemy response time."

"Hmm." Gideon grunted. "And these?" He reached out, touched a small metal capsule.

He yanked his arm back as it became a whirling dervish at the pressure of his fingers, catapulting out of the box with a pinwheel of lethal blades. Daegan caught the ball in a move too fast for Gideon to follow. Whatever he did retracted the blades and saved his fingers, though he noted a stripe of blood across three of Daegan's knuckles.

"A version of a throwing star. It handles somewhat like a boomerang, and you release the trigger as you throw."

"Can it decapitate?"

"Nearly. It's more effective for removing limbs. It's difficult for a vampire who has suffered an amputation to fight back immediately. As you know, several seconds are usually the only advantage you need, if you're doing it right."

Gideon looked at the array of weapons again. *Fucking awesome.* He cleared his throat, shrugged his shoulders. "Pretty good arsenal."

"Mmm." Daegan replaced the capsule and slid his hands into his pockets, heedless of the blood spatter he might put on the denim. He stared down at the weapons. "With these, with my hands, with my body, I can kill anything. But I have no ability to turn back time or to heal her body, her mind."

There it was, the thing that had Gideon wandering, and had brought Daegan back out again, both of them acutely aware of the woman in the other room, the many things she might be suffering, and how she'd shut them out.

"You think she really wanted us not to be around her, or was that the female way of saying, 'I want you to insist'?"

Daegan arched a brow at Gideon. "Anwyn is not like normal women. She says exactly what she wants, when she wants it. The games she plays are clear challenges, as straightforward as a knight throwing down a gauntlet. As wonderful as that sounds"—his gaze returned to the weapons—"it means that she does mean what she says. She doesn't want us near her."

"Son of a bitch."

Daegan made a grunt of acknowledgment. Then he glanced at Gideon again. This time his look was penetrating and far more personal, reminding Gideon of earlier, when Daegan's mouth had been on his shoulder, only Anwyn's hands between Daegan's and his ass. He'd tried not to think about that much, because it didn't bear thinking about. It had been what they did for her; that was all.

"Becoming her servant was very noble. She may think I planted the decision, influenced you unfairly, but even she knows that's wrong. You despise my kind. Only a true belief that it was the right thing to do would have moved you. That, and your feelings for her. I hope you don't regret it, because regardless of my motives, she needs a man like you as her servant."

Gideon shifted, not wanting to get into that. "You've been watching us both like you're waiting for another shoe to drop."

Daegan lifted a shoulder. "You know a lot about our world, Gideon. I may have to take her before the Council to have her validated as a made vampire. Either way, they will have a hand in deciding how she will be integrated into the vampire world. She can't exist in a territory as a loner. You know this."

"Shit. Yeah, I know." But he hadn't thought that Daegan would broach it so soon. "If she has to appear before the Council, I'm going with her."

"That would be the height of folly."

"Yeah. I'm going. If the seizures keep happening, she'll need me. We both know it."

"We will speak of it soon. Not now, though." When Daegan continued to stare into space, Gideon felt that unwilling twinge of male empathy. *Fuck.*

"You know, she's not going to be pissed at you forever."

"With a woman, a moment can feel like forever." Daegan gave a rueful smile, making Gideon feel less like a fool for offering woman advice to a vamp who was obviously . . .

"How old *are* you?"

"Older." Daegan cocked a brow at him. "Much older. Tonight, I don't feel those years have given me any wisdom. For all of this, I've only found one consistent truth. No matter how strong and fast I am, being too late makes everything else irrelevant. And there will always be times I am too late."

Gideon understood that feeling, so powerfully that he had a horrifying impulse to reach out to the other man, grip his shoulder in silent empathy. Fortunately, he didn't have to cut off his arm to curb the impulse, because Daegan spoke again.

"I would just . . ." He shook his head, closed his eyes. "I almost wish as she did. That I'd never met her, never brought her into my life. I'd rather have spent my whole life with no one, than have given her a moment of pain."

Gideon's brow creased. Surely he didn't mean . . . Daegan had never let *anyone* get as close as Anwyn? That was unusual in itself, but it was even more unusual for a vampire to say something like that straight-out, especially about a human. It confirmed his suspicion, that there seemed to be quite a few things about Daegan Rei that didn't fit vampire etiquette.

"So if you love her, why *didn't* you ever mark her?"

"You heard why. I agreed not to do so. She didn't wish to be my servant."

He hadn't denied his love for her, a human. But he'd never told her outright, obviously. Christ. No wonder things were so twisted up between them. Gideon gave him an exasperated look. "I'm not saying you're like that scum that attacked her, but I know the dynamic. You're not the kind that asks. You overwhelm until you get what you want."

Daegan shook his head. "Yes, but the victory is not true when it's won that way. Regardless of how my nature compels me to take Anwyn over, before I cross that line, she has to make the vital decision to invite me over it. As you did, when you met her."

"I never said—"

"Very often, it's not spoken." Daegan reached out, slid his fingers down the blade of the misericord. "A good Master or Mistress knows how to read every flicker of the gaze, shift of the body. Very often a submissive needs to fight before surrender occurs. He must prove that Master or Mistress is the one who has the essential arsenal to defeat his defenses, deserve his surrender.

"She's a Mistress, Gideon. A very strong one. Though my nature makes me stronger, such that she has submitted to me under certain circumstances, I never intended to force her acceptance of a life that is against her true nature. It would dishonor the very reason she drew me to her in the first place." He suppressed a sigh. "And yet, now, she is part of a world where Dominance and submission often walk the line of tyranny and brutality. She will see things in my world that will be a sacrilege to someone like her."

Gideon knew there was no arguing with that, and they stood in silence for several more minutes, staring at that cache of weapons. At least crossbows and guns were something he could understand, though he often employed them against an incomprehensible world. He wondered if Daegan ever felt that way. He was definitely getting that feeling, which gave him more of that unwelcome sense of bonding. He moved slightly away from the other male, but Daegan didn't appear to notice. Gideon cleared his throat.

"You met her here?"

"Yes. Five years ago." He lifted his gaze back to Gideon. "She's a sorceress, one who weaves a very dark and tempting web around herself. Only certain people can get to the center of that web. Before this happened, I was as close to that center as our relationship permitted, but now it seems she is doing her best to restructure that web so I cannot get back to her heart."

"Not that I'm relishing the chance to throw the Grasshopper stuff right back at you, but that one's pretty obvious. You represent what her world is going to become, a world she didn't ask for. She's working through it. She'll figure it out."

When she did, the gift of trust she'd invested in Gideon so unexpectedly would likely be irrelevant. That erratic third-wheel feeling he kept having would become a constant tread, not just the occasional bump in the road. Good thing he wasn't planning on doing this forever, right?

Before he could slice his gut any deeper with that knife, he shifted his thoughts to something more productive. "In the meantime, if she doesn't want us around her, why don't we coax her into wanting to be around us?"

"Coax?" Daegan lifted that patrician brow again. For some reason, Gideon was oddly reminded of the stained glass angel. He expected that was what had attracted Anwyn to it.

"Yeah." Gideon snorted. "For most of us poor bastards, coaxing women is a fact of life."

"Based on what I know of your personality, you must have tremendous experience."

"Nope. Rarely get that far. But my gut usually helps me out. She said something about wanting to dance to a song about the terrible and wonderful parts of love. One of her favorites. You know it?"

Daegan nodded. He moved toward the music cabinet, but spoke over his shoulder. "I think she will surprise us both in the end, Gideon. As I think you will surprise yourself. You have already surprised me, and that is not an easy thing to do."

Gideon grunted at that, but as Daegan scrolled through the selection, the vampire took *him* off guard. "So, when you spoke to your brother, what did Lyssa decide you could know about me?"

"You know everything. Why don't you tell me?"

Daegan tossed him a humorless look. "You and your brother are very close. He trusts you, and Lyssa trusts him. So I expect she told you that I am a Council assassin."

"Yeah. She knows I have no friends and am likely to get myself killed anytime now, so she figures your secret's pretty safe."

"Lady Lyssa is usually a very good judge of character." Daegan gave an absent half chuckle. "But I know you will keep her confidence. Because you love your brother, not for any love you bear me."

"Given." Gideon took a seat on the couch arm, watching him. "So, in essence, you're a vampire hunter, like me."

"I am a vampire hunter. Not like you."

Gideon watched the male's shoulders flex as he twisted, the denim tightening over lean flanks as he squatted to look at a lower rack. He blinked at himself. Jesus, the pheromone-soaked environment was really affecting him if he was checking out the guy's ass.

"What does that mean, not like you? You aiming for a pissing contest on numbers?"

"No." Daegan's tone sharpened, a mild warning and reassurance at once. "I understand your anger about your fiancé, Gideon. But that kind of anger has to do with your own self, your fear of her pain and your own shortcomings. She is beyond her pain, and you loved her. You would have done anything to keep her safe, and she is where she knows that. So forgive yourself, and move on. While killing makes the gods weep, justice is their Will. Vengeance, death out of mindless impulse and violence, fear and insecurity, are not."

Alarmed to feel his throat thickening, Gideon set his jaw. "You don't talk about her. And all that's just more Grasshopper crap."

"You need to listen, and hear it." Daegan held his gaze. "Vampires are not the only ones I am dispatched to kill, Gideon Green. Your name has been on my list for some time. It was your brother who saved your life."

Gideon stopped in midretort. "Jacob never said—"

"No, he and I have never spoken. You were taking out vampires indiscriminately, vampires like Trey as well as Barnabus." Daegan's focus was unwavering now. "You were on the Council's list, after the Gathering. I began tracking you, collecting data on whether or not your execution was warranted."

"I thought a vampire like you barely had to think twice to kill a human."

"I plan and think about every assignment I'm given, thoroughly. Now be silent for a moment. Listen with something other than your anger." Daegan rose, faced him, as Gideon bit down on an uncharitable response. The male was going to tell him how he knew so damn much about him. He could always stake him after that. Or throw some serious insults his way.

"Your kill pattern changed around that time. I realized Jacob was giving you the names of vampires that fell squarely in line with those I am given to dispatch, because of their numerous Council violations.

I have not shared that with the Council, because the truce toward your brother and the lady Lyssa is still very fragile.

"I reported instead that your target acquisition was changing, and you were handling the lesser vampires that would have made my list anyway, thereby saving the Council the trouble of being connected to those deaths. If you were killed, which they agreed was inevitable, two birds would be gotten with one stone. We agreed that I would monitor you and, if your kill pattern changed again, our strategy would change as well."

Daegan's dark eyes held Gideon's blue ones, and the space between them seemed much smaller. "If things had not happened as they have, you would have been on that list again after the other night. Because of Trey."

Son of a bitch. Gideon repeated it in his mind, too flummoxed to speak it aloud, though tension made every muscle rigid. Bastard had been tracking him, had an execution order, but decided not to carry it out because Gideon had become Jacob's lackey . . .

The vampire turned back to the music. "I found the song. Do you wish to pursue this now, or do I need to unkink the knot I've put in your dick?"

"I'm half tempted to put one in yours."

Daegan gave him a sanguine smile then, the sharp ends of his teeth glistening. "If you want to touch my cock, vampire hunter, you need only beg to do so."

Before Gideon could answer that, and follow it up with a sucker punch, Daegan added, "Why don't you call her in your mind? See if she'll come join us."

"Just put the song in. Crank it up. Let's see if she nibbles at the bait."

As Daegan complied and the first strains of the song cut through the air, he commented, "Perhaps she's already heard our conversation."

"She said she'd try not to pry without permission, once she gets a handle on it."

Daegan's expression closed down. "Sometimes a made vampire attempts to hold on to her or his humanity, the rules of morality that apply to that species. But in time they discover our world is different, and every advantage and resource must be utilized. The relationship between servant and vampire is key to survival, the surrender of the servant to the vampire's needs. Your understanding, and acceptance of that, will help her."

"Sorry. Neither of us thought to take Becoming an Immortal Vampire 101 before Barnabus came looking for you."

A muscle twitched in Daegan's jaw. For a moment, Gideon thought they'd have a go at a far more physical sparring match, but then Anwyn opened her bedroom door.

21

Daegan knew the song, of course, but Gideon had to have been the one who suggested it. Anwyn stepped out of her room to see the two of them squared off. There were a few feet between them, but the combustible energy suggested they were about to become a lot closer, and not in a good way. She wanted to be angry with them both, but she knew how males dealt with worry. Daegan's temper was hard to rouse, but once it was provoked, it took a while for it to settle. She remembered one night she'd deliberately goaded him, purely for the repercussions. He'd made her pay for it in a variety of dark and delicious ways that had lasted well past dawn, until even her pleasure-sated body was weeping in exhaustion. And then, he'd taken her once more, to underscore the point, a serious message beneath the sensual play.

She'd pricked at him a lot worse than that these past couple days, but he kept holding back. Perversely, she wanted to push him over the edge, give him a reason to unleash toward her, scald them both in a response that would take them past everything. But it wouldn't. They'd just proven that, hadn't they? Though of course he'd been far from losing his damnable control or command of the situation.

There was blood on his white shirt, but her new senses picked up the scent, told her it was his own, an inconsequential cut. More of the games that boys played, of course. The music curled around her. Rufus

Wainwright's version of "Hallelujah." The whimsical piano introduction provided the lead-in to the rough, emotion-laden voice, telling her what love was and wasn't. Pulling everything from a lover, taking his strength and making him grateful for the privilege of having it taken. Love, a broken cry on a rainy day, not an unbridled shout of joy in the sunshine. The erotic and spiritual come together in one poignant yearning, joy and bitter pain mixed.

She realized then she was still standing in her doorway, only now her eyes were closed, her body swaying to it. Her senses detected him before he reached her, so she was already willing, moving into his grasp as Gideon's arms slid around her waist. She did like a man who didn't hesitate when she needed his decisiveness. And she had two of those in abundance. "I think you said something about dancing?" His voice was a murmur, as riveting as Rufus's.

No need to talk about what had happened in those last uncomfortable moments in the shower. Not now. Not until she was ready. They would give her that, and she might choose to continue to avoid the issues that seemed insurmountable.

Instead, she put her hands on his chest, stepping forward in a slow two-step, following the music. She kept her eyes closed, letting him lead. He knew the two-step. Small miracles. Wasn't there another song about those? She supposed there was a song about everything that had ever bloomed in the heart or bludgeoned it.

Moving one of her hands from Gideon's chest to his waiting palm, she made it a dance position so that they could execute a turn around the room. His left leading, her right following. Then Daegan's hand settled on her waist from behind, his other coming up over theirs to clasp both as he fell into step, his jaw against her temple briefly, his heat closing the circle around her.

She leaned back into him, but brought Gideon in closer as well, so they had to go to a simple sway or get their feet tangled. Her lips curved at the thought, and Gideon's mouth brushed hers. Daegan's teased her ear. Not sexual, though with two such men, there was always the simmering possibility. Just . . . present.

Her other hand still lay on Gideon's chest, and she stroked his pectoral muscle through the cotton, then decided to shift and lay her head there. Daegan kissed her nape, making her shiver. Soon there'd be another seizure to deal with, the whispers escalating to frightening, screeching voices in her head, the immersion in blood and pain. She'd pass the time this way, rather than fight.

Letting the fragile bond between them rebuild itself as it wished, she drifted in Gideon's mind. Daegan had told her to practice drawing the curtain, but right now she didn't have the mental strength. She was glad she didn't. He was thinking about that night, the one he'd told her about. *Once, a long time ago . . . I spent the night with a woman like you. She was a vampire, and she flat took the reins away from me, took every choice away . . .*

She was startled when she saw the vision in his clouds of memory and realized that the vampire in question was his brother's Mistress, Lady Lyssa. Though she'd not met that lady, the other male in the threesome was quite obviously his brother, as handsome and appealing as Gideon, in a different way. Seeing them with her, the beautiful ebony-haired vampire with jade eyes, Anwyn was surprised by a prick of possessiveness, watching another strong woman claim Gideon, however transitory a moment it had been. But when she pushed that aside, went deeper in his thoughts, a forest she hadn't traveled before, no paths or light, she saw how time had stopped for him then, bringing his conflicted soul to a place of unexpected stillness.

Like whenever the three of them came together like this, no matter their differences or worries.

Was that her thought or his? She wasn't sure. Gideon was conscious of Daegan's hand folded over both of theirs, how the men's forearms crossed where they held her around the waist. He was ambivalent toward the heat of Daegan's skin, the press of his fingers.

As a Mistress, she'd seen plenty of men who weren't gay enjoy another man's body, because they'd learned what most girls learned at an early age, that it was arousing to play with another body, no matter the gender. After all, masturbation was done on oneself, a female arousing a female body, or a male arousing a male body. She'd also seen situations where two men loved, but never thought of themselves as gay. She liked that. Love shouldn't be stuck into a box with a label. She hated confined spaces, particularly in the mind.

Daegan had put the song on repeat, so she was able to keep rocking with that lullaby rhythm, swaying within their armspans. Now she dipped under their arms, turned so she was behind Gideon. Sliding her arms around his waist, she worked her fingers up his chest, teasing his nipples through the T-shirt as she pressed herself against his buttocks, rubbing herself against the denim separating them. She spread her fingers wide, went down to his lean waist. Deliberately avoiding what she could feel and see in his mind was hardening for her, she brought her hands around to his back, followed the channel of his spine up to the broad flare of shoulders.

He'd come to a stop, of course. Daegan remained where he was, eying her, likely wondering what she was doing. If he wanted to know, he could just look, right? Though he'd told her a vampire could push out another vampire, it wasn't something she could do right now. He'd forced her to trust him without earning that trust.

Of course, if he was honoring at least one promise to her, he wasn't in her mind. Earlier, when she'd lain in her bed, drifting to sleep amid a lovely composition of gruff, off-tune, gritty love songs from Gideon, Daegan's voice had entered the arena. She'd stiffened, but his presence had been brief, short statements.

You do not have to answer, cher, but I wanted you to know this. I will limit my time in your mind to whenever it is a necessity, or when we are physically intimate. I will respect your privacy as long as it does not compromise your safety.

She'd had something short and succinct to say to that. He'd withdrawn without further comment. Pushing aside any guilt at her behavior, she'd focused on Gideon's charming attempts to soothe her.

Regardless, they didn't need a mind-link for this. When she met Daegan's gaze, she could tell he picked up her intent quickly. She'd never shared a submissive with him, because of what he was. Even with her, he'd held back because of his strength, or how violent his nature could truly become. A whole part of who he was might now be open to her. In the glittering calculation in his gaze, the arousal and curiosity mixed, she realized it was. She was far more interested in diving into that than dealing with any more anger or resentments.

For the moment.

Tightening her hand in cotton, she turned Gideon around, following feeling and desire, letting go of thought. When she leaned into him, pushing up on her toes to reach his mouth, Daegan stepped up, his hands coming to Gideon's hips to steady him.

Gideon immediately stiffened. *I don't want him there.*

Yes, you do. She brought her gaze up to his wary expression. *It feels right, the three of us, doesn't it? That's what you find difficult to accept, not his hands on you. Nothing is going to happen. He's only going to help me bring you more pleasure. Bring me more pleasure.*

Anywn curled her arm around his neck, inched even closer so she could press her breasts, loose under her light dress, against the thin T-shirt. If he kept washing this one out, it would never dry, she mused, registering the dampness.

When Gideon would have put his arms around her, Daegan's grip slid down to his biceps, held him. Tension instantly radiated from her servant, but she murmured softly against his lips, "Shhh. Just let me kiss you. Give yourself to me." *Give yourself to us.*

Daegan's mind flickered like a hot flame. *He's not ready for what you want, Anwyn. Do not push him too far.*

Just a taste. To help him recognize a man or woman's need to fight before surrender. Wasn't that what you told him earlier? She couldn't tell if Gideon could hear Daegan's voice in her head, or if Daegan had the ability to block that, but Gideon wasn't thinking anything directly toward her. He remained wary, though his fingers were curled into loose fists.

You were eavesdropping. Daegan's thoughts held a mild amusement with the reproof. *He is going to bolt in a moment,* cher. *I will have to wrestle him to the ground for you.*

That brought a very tempting flash in her head, of the two men in such a contest of wills, neither one wearing much of anything. She'd often thought she needed to live during the time of Greek Olympics, when the contestants competed naked, watching a beautiful male body pushed to the limits of its endurance.

Now, thinking of that strength, she indulged herself. She knew it wasn't kind, because he'd already clearly told her his clothing options were limited, but she'd had a difficult couple of days. This was her version of indulging in a high-calorie dessert to soothe nerves, or stimulate them in an entirely different way.

She ripped the cloth like paper, tore it right down the front, greedy fingers seeking his skin.

It stimulated more than her nerves. Jerking forward against Daegan's hold, Gideon caught her mouth in a hot, demanding kiss. When she put her hands on top of Daegan's, the vampire's grip was iron. Gideon's biceps were bunched in a rippling display of strength that said it would take nothing less than a vampire to restrain him. Or her demands, she thought, remembering their brief session.

I wanted you to prove that you could belong to me, Gideon. Remember? It's not time to give me that answer, but give me yourself now. I'll make you come so hard you'll forget everything but my desires.

Leaning back, she held his gaze. She slipped the belt out of his jeans, tugged to bring it all the way off. As she rolled it around both hands, she enjoyed the feel of the worn strap. An item that had the pleasure of hugging the erotic area of the waist and hip, those muscles that moved in such a mesmerizing way when he walked. Despite her erratic mood at the time, she'd enjoyed them with avid hunger when he'd come out of the shower with her and Daegan. Wet jeans snug on his hips and water beading on his body. His hair slicked back, emphasizing those brilliant blue eyes, the hard jaw, the dark shadow that was always there.

"I want him to let me go."

His voice was rough, and she saw that dangerous edge that she knew rested at the core of Gideon's nature. *Not a psychopath, but too close to it . . .* She had no need to worry about that part of him anymore. She could handle it, could handle him.

"I know. Do you trust me, Gideon?"

"It depends on what you want." He cleared a clogged throat. "Trust isn't all or nothing."

"At some point, it has to be." Her gaze shifted then, holding Daegan's briefly. "Or you know you have nothing."

"Take it or leave it." Gideon's blue eyes met hers. "It's the best you're going to get right now."

She arched a brow, recognizing the challenge for what it was. "Daegan is holding you for me. Because I like to see how tense your muscles get while another male holds you back." Her voice softened, yet became more implacable at once. She wanted this, and she thought she wanted it enough that he wouldn't be able to deny her. "All you need to do is submit to me, for this. Your choice, until things get far enough along that it all becomes my choice." When she registered the tremor he couldn't stifle through those solid muscles, she moistened her lips. "Your body wants it; your soul wants it. Shut down your mind and give yourself over to me."

She was surprised to see in his mind how she gained his capitulation. It had nothing to do with her vampirism. Everything she was saying and being right now was the same as what Anwyn the human Mistress had been to him. The command in her voice, the direct look of her blue-green gaze, had his cock stiff and aching, screaming at him to give her what she wanted.

"If you're in my head," he said, low, "I guess you know what I want."

"I didn't read what you want from your mind," she whispered. *Gideon, I've been reading minds for a long time.* "Being able to actually do it is a little distracting. I get not only truths, but laundry lists and meanderings into places that make little sense, like indigestion dreams." A light smile touched her lips. "Snippets of commercials you've seen, a beer you want, a flash from childhood. Your reaction to my touch. I like that part, but the rest can be a little overwhelming."

"I like to revisit *Girls Gone Wild* videos in my head when I go to sleep. Like counting sheep, only I'm counting—"

She stepped back into him then, curled her hand into his waistband, her fingers stroking down. "Pay attention to me. Be still, and just feel what I can do to you."

She saw him struggle with it, his initial rejection of her command. Daegan's expression was unreadable, but his gaze did shift to Gideon, linger on the shoulders and throat, and she knew he wasn't uninterested in what was happening. She had enough of a ruthless edge to her that she might be willing to take advantage of the fact they were both willing to indulge her. That, too, had predated being a vampire. When a grim smile touched Daegan's mouth, she knew he had gotten that. The flicker in Gideon's eyes, more somber, suggested the same, only he of course had more reason to be apprehensive about it.

Her gaze drifted over Daegan's face, noted the paleness there. For the first time, she thought beyond her immediate situation, wondered when he last had fed, if he'd gotten some of her blood from the kitchen or left it for her. She thought about the way he'd licked the blood from Gideon's shoulder, and her upper body and thighs tightened, remembering the play of rippling muscles, the resistant tightening of Gideon's, the sensual stroke of Daegan's tongue along hard, male flesh.

No, cher. His gaze snapped to her instantly. *I do not want the blood of your servant. And he will not tolerate that. Do not let Barnabus's brutality do your thinking for you. This is likely more than he can bear as it is.*

Gideon had obviously not heard Daegan's side, so though he'd gotten tense at Anwyn's tentative thoughts, not sure where she was going with it, he hadn't reacted the way Daegan had. Or the way she herself did now.

It was an abrupt shock, like cold water. In a mere thought, she'd been about to move far off base, destroy the web she was spinning now. Of course, Gideon wouldn't have tolerated that. Those shadow creatures in her head had moved out of the shadows, planted their seeds of evil suggestion. Or had it been them? Gideon had said, baldly, that vampire blood eventually took over a turned human, making free will only the right of vampires, not of the humans they dominated.

It had shaken her, but Gideon had now picked up enough from her thoughts to discern what was happening. Rather than tearing away from them, putting as much distance between them as she'd expect, he stunned her.

His mind reached out to her where his hands couldn't. *You won't let the vampire take over the Mistress. I know it. Anwyn the Mistress is far scarier than any vampire blood or crazy voices.*

She met his gaze, mixed with serious intensity and grim humor both. Taking hold of his reassurance with both hands, she put her hand on Gideon's bare chest, cocked her head. "I'd like Daegan to release you for a moment. Open your jeans. Take your cock out and let me see how hard it is for me."

When Daegan's touch obligingly eased, Gideon kept his gaze fixed on her, as if by that unrelenting stare he could pretend the vampire wasn't in the room. Pulling the rest of the shirt away from him, he tugged it out of the waistband now that she'd unbuckled the belt. She kept her hand on him as he did that. Sliding the button free, he lowered the zipper, and reached under her arm to scoop out his heavy cock, cradling it and his testicles in one hand as he pushed the jeans down far enough that it could stretch forth for her appreciative gaze.

Daegan had backed off to straddle an arm of the couch. It eased Gideon's shoulders down a fraction. "Put your palms against your thighs," she said. "You'll keep them there while I tease and torment your cock until it's ready to spew at my command. But only my command. Do you understand? The proper reply is, 'Yes, Mistress.'"

"Yes. Mistress." There was a tumble of thoughts in his head. He was unwillingly aroused, resisting and yet not wanting to resist. It was remarkable, as she'd said, to see the processes she had always known were going on inside her submissives' minds actually scripted out in his mind. Except he wasn't one. This was something unique and dangerous she was playing with, a man who wanted to serve but not submit. Who would play her game, knowing it was far more than that, just to care for her.

She saw that knowledge in his eyes, the exchange of thoughts. She liked the intimacy of it, even as she knew she really needed to work on that curtain screen between them. Sliding her knuckles down his bare sternum, she drifted over each nipple in turn, the fine whorls of dark hair around them, then down the center line of hard-packed muscles to the open front of the jeans. His cock was suspended there by its own rigidity now, his taut arms at his sides. She brushed it with her forearm and it jumped. If she'd had the use of her staff above, she might have some sweet, shy submissive come and suck him to climax, knowing that would send him off in no time. But for today, she closed her hand on him and watched the quiver run through all those impressive muscles.

Picking up his hand, she guided it to take the place of hers, then backed away from him, one step, two steps. Sinking down in a wing-backed chair, she gracefully slid her skirt up until she revealed the fact she wore no underwear at all, and propped her feet on the chair edge, letting her knees fall together at the level of her breasts. It created an open triangle below where he could see the folds of her pussy, the crease of her ass. She didn't touch herself, but instead languorously draped her hands on the chair arms, leaning back.

"Stroke yourself, Gideon. Make my juices flow. The closer you get to coming, the hotter you'll make me. Look only at me."

"I'm not likely to be looking anywhere else." Gideon's jaw flexed in that attractive way, but he closed his fist tighter on himself, began to stroke upward.

Daegan rose then, moving on silent bare feet. The vampire hunter tensed, and Anwyn sharpened her voice.

"Stroke yourself, Gideon. Stare at my pussy as you do it. Only my pussy."

His jaw hardened into concrete, but his eyes went where she wanted them to go. He licked his lips instinctively, and that was enough to make her pussy contract. She felt the first drop of liquid honey gathering, and from the flare in his eyes, he saw it, too. With his powerful hand, he moved the satin skin along his hard steel shaft, stimulating pre-come from the flared head she would dearly love to feel inside her again. Not all men's cocks were attractive, but Gideon's inspired her to think she'd like to devote some quality time to stroking, teasing and making it respond to her touch only, like a favored pet.

Daegan moved a step closer. Though Gideon kept his eyes on her, it was obvious the vampire was agitating him. She wouldn't define Daegan's participation in this, though. Indulgent he might be, but he had no intention of being ordered around, by human or fledgling vampire.

Speak to him in his mind, cher. *He is a warrior, not used to keeping his back to his enemy. His tension is going to snap him.*

Gideon, he's merely testing your resolve to obey me. He won't drink from you. Or fuck you. I promise. Bring yourself to climax. I'm watching and everything is fine.

He didn't respond directly. However, while his shoulders didn't ease, she noted his pace picked up, his breath harshly rasping. Those stomach muscles rippled, the buttocks tightening, and she envied Daegan's view. While in truth she wasn't sure what Daegan's stand was on seducing men, she had a feeling she was about to find out.

~

Daegan watched the vampire hunter follow her direction. The line of his shoulders was rock solid, suggesting the conflict radiating from him. Like any male, visually he was focused on the bare pussy put before him, the tempting hint of ass her pose provided, but most of his other senses—intuition, hearing, scent—were focused on what Daegan was doing. She was right—the view from back here was worth seeing. The man was as combat fit as any soldier could be, the ass so firm a lover would have to take a solid, bruising grip when fucking it. The jeans that had molded that ass were now at his knees, and the thighs were flexing in time with his jerking off, a slow rock.

Daegan reached out, trailed his fingers down the center of Gideon's spine. The male flinched in response, briefly interrupting his rhythm. Daegan heard Anwyn's soothing thoughts, but he wondered how sure she was of his intentions. Yes, he was testing Gideon's resolve, and not just for Anwyn. Despite his stated intention not to become her full servant, Gideon might be around long enough to face a situation like this with other vampires. Daegan was intrigued to see how he'd handle himself.

Beyond that, there was a personal component to this he wouldn't deny. He didn't particularly care for sharing Anwyn with anyone. He'd initially expected to view Gideon as an intrusion, a competitor of sorts, but he hadn't, and he knew that had surprised Anwyn. However, the thought that crossed Daegan's mind was the most startling thing of all. He'd never had a servant, but now he was thinking what it would be like to have one. One he shared with Anwyn.

This one. The one who would rather be chopped up to feed Anwyn's cats, a sprig of parsley put on the side, than be a vampire's servant.

It took very little to trip a male vampire's carnal trigger. Usually a warm body displayed the right way was enough, but he'd been around long enough not to get derailed so easily. So the surge of desire and possession he experienced at Gideon's uncertain response to his bare touch also intrigued him. The hunter was uncertain because it wasn't repelling him as much as he'd expected. While he'd rationalize it away by telling himself it was incidental to Anwyn's stimulation, Daegan's heating blood told him something different.

Turning his knuckles over, he trailed them back up Gideon's nape, then across, teasing the hair there.

The vampire hunter growled, the warning of one male predator to another, but it only spurred Daegan further. Of course, he had no intention of doing more than what Anwyn had intimated, using his power and Gideon's apprehension to make the man's cock harder, his reaction more intense.

Anwyn parted her knees then, draping her legs over the arms in a flexible display that caught both males' attention. While they watched, she sucked on her fingers and trailed them down to the pink petals of her sex. Four of them disappeared into that wet opening, her thumb beginning a slow massage of her clit as her hips lifted. She bit her bottom lip, showing a bit of fangs, her breath easing out, slow and sensual.

"I'm imagining this is you, Gideon."

"I'm right here. All you have to do is ask." His muscles twitched under Daegan's hand.

"No." She shook her head, her voice catching. "I want to see your seed spurt out of you. Rub harder, stronger. Handle yourself like another male would. Like Daegan would."

His arm jerked in reaction to that. Daegan moved in, bringing his body up against his back, brushing the bare ass with his thigh. Gideon cursed, but Anwyn must have been saying something in his mind, bidding him to be still. While Daegan wasn't in her head right now, her face was concentrated, eyes locked with her servant's, holding him still.

Daegan put one hand on Gideon's shoulder, his other sliding under Gideon's arm, his palm traveling across the abdomen. His fingers teased the coarse hair above the impressively engorged cock.

"Stop," Gideon snarled, but there was a catch to his breath that kept Daegan pushing it. It was a precarious line, knowing they might be about to disrupt Anwyn's pleasure, if Gideon decided to turn around and throw a punch, even bare-assed with his jeans caught at his knees.

But Daegan obeyed his intuition and didn't stop, sliding his hand down so he covered Gideon's. He coiled his own long fingers around Gideon's fist, increased the pressure on the aroused organ.

He wasn't stroking Gideon's cock directly, but he was vicariously feeling the give of that velvet skin stretched on the steel shaft. The heat was as rich as blood. The hunter kept his gaze locked on his Mistress, as she'd ordered, but Daegan thought it might be almost impossible to look away. She had most of her right hand sliding in and out of her pussy, her knuckles glistening, and she was starting to quiver and gasp with the impending orgasm. Gideon's hard pumping increased, with Daegan's unsolicited assistance. Gideon's buttocks flexed beneath the pressure of his thigh, his cock jumping under their combined touch.

You are not as dedicated to one sex as you believe yourself to be, vampire hunter. He could send that over the bridge of Anwyn's mind, but he kept that knowledge to himself, dealing with his own unexpected arousal at the thought and at Gideon's response to him. The man was shaking, a fine tremor running through the broad shoulders, rippling over the biceps, his emotional turmoil manifesting itself physically. Daegan didn't have to be in his mind to know that the hunter was fighting three forces. His overwhelming instinct to serve Anwyn's will, his unexpected desire for Daegan's presence, and his own will, so confused that it was the sensitive time bomb that could detonate at any moment, ending this for all three of them.

In truth, he was impressed Gideon had made it this far. He wondered if Gideon realized he was proving that he might in fact have what it took to be a vampire's servant, to hold still at her command and submit to the games that vampires liked to play, all for her pleasure.

It was also proof of the kind of trust he had in Anwyn, and perhaps in some way in Daegan, remaining still only on their insistence that Daegan wouldn't drink from him. *Trust didn't have to be all or nothing, after all.* He put his mouth on Gideon's shoulder, using his tongue, a firm stroke along one of the scars there.

Gideon groaned, hand flexing beneath Daegan's. "Let go of me," he muttered. In answer, Daegan just tightened their grip, made it more of a slick glove, pushing Gideon to take it all the way back to the tip and back, faster.

"Jesus Christ."

"You don't come until I do, Gideon," Anwyn reminded him on a sharp gasp.

"Tell that . . . to your . . . damn boy here."

Daegan slid the other hand down, gripped one firm ass cheek as an anchor, a counterpoint for the stroking of Gideon's cock.

Anwyn arched up, a cry breaking from her throat. "N-now, Gideon . . ."

With a rough groan, torn from him like a battle flag of surrender, Gideon did. His cock spewed a fountain of white fluid that gushed over his hand and Daegan's, down to splatter on the stone floor. It was intense enough to convulse his body, and Daegan clamped his arm across the man's chest, giving him a wall to brace against as the orgasm pumped forth, draining him dry.

As he did, the slamming of his heart against his chest, the way he pressed his head down hard against Daegan's shoulder in the involuntary search for an anchor point, made Daegan want to bring him to his knees. He'd order him to put his head in his Mistress's lap, let her stroke his hair tenderly while Daegan rutted on his ass. He'd watch Gideon lick her pussy under her ministrations, drive her up to climax again. He'd command him to stop just in time, though, and Daegan would take her, fucking her to climax, making sure he'd depleted them both, taken them to fully satiated exhaustion.

By the Holy Relics, what am I thinking? Though his cock was about to explode, that wasn't why he sought the steadying admonishment. He considered himself bound to Anwyn in a way he'd never been to anyone, though there'd always been that barrier between them as human and vampire. Now, with her as vampire, and this man as her servant, a male who inexplicably fascinated each of them, Daegan felt a hint of something he'd never had. The fulfillment of a yearning, something within reach, an answer they didn't have singly, but they might have together, as a trinity.

Or, as Gideon would say, he was losing his fucking mind.

By the time he was done, Gideon was leaning full into his body again, gasping, his head turned away so Daegan couldn't see his face. It affected him oddly, the hunter in his embrace this way, shamed. Anwyn, in contrast, curled up on her hip, pulling her skirt back down, her gaze lingering on the two of them, obviously approving of the sight they made. But the moment was short-lived.

Gideon pushed away from him, and yanked his jeans back up with an awkward movement. Though his back was still expanding and contracting like a bellows, he kept his head down, his body turned away from them. "I can't do that again," he said. "This isn't who I am."

He was speaking to Anwyn, even though he was looking at neither of them. But she didn't hear him. "Gideon," Daegan said urgently. "Another time."

Gideon glanced up sharply. Daegan realized it revealed just how upset he was, because he hadn't anticipated the seizure this time. It had already gripped her with both hands, propelling her out of the chair with a snarl, her eyes red and fangs bared.

"Stay back." Daegan intercepted her before she could launch herself, taking her back down to the ground, pinioning arms and legs. "Get another vial of the sire's blood."

"Death!" she screamed. "We must die!"

"Everyone does, *cher*," he agreed, as Gideon bolted.

This attack had come on the heels of pleasure, stealing its memory. As her agony tore into his heart, Daegan wondered how they would convince her life was worth living if his worst fear came true. If she had to live with the seizures for the rest of her life. A vampire's immortal lifespan.

22

GIDEON strode through the streets. It was light, headed toward lunchtime. He felt decent, finally having a solid eight hours' sleep, because they'd all agreed that he and Daegan would take shifts with her. Everyone could stay on the top of their game that way. Since it limited his exposure to the other male, he didn't mind. But he'd told the vamp he'd relieve him at noon, so he needed to get back shortly.

Every time she was given her sire's blood, the seizures were more intense than at any other time. And she was getting that blood every few hours, far more often than a normal transition vampire. Daegan apparently had seen bad transitions before, and indicated that giving more of the sire's blood, more often, could sometimes help.

Daegan needed to go out for fresh blood tonight. Gideon knew Anwyn was prodding him to do just that. The vampire might be like some freakishly engineered supersoldier, even for a vamp, but he needed something more than sleep. He was pale.

Gideon had been braced for Anwyn to try to get him to donate, but she hadn't. It had surprised him enough to ask her about it, and she'd told him that Daegan flatly refused to consider it. Which prompted two sets of disturbing thoughts. One, that she had possibly offered him the option, even knowing how Gideon felt about it, and two, that for some inexplicable reason, he didn't want Gideon's blood.

Why the hell should he care? Because it was a puzzle that didn't have an answer, and Gideon wasn't fond of those. Not when it came to vampires. Unanswered questions tended to come back and smack you in the ass, and not in any kind of pleasurable way. Not that he would find being smacked in the ass pleasurable. He was just saying . . .

Christ. As he had for the past few days, when his thoughts tried to go back to that night, to the sight of a male hand wrapped around his cock, the feel of a hard, muscular body behind him while Anwyn's tempted him in front, he broke into a jog. Then a flat-out run. He called on as much speed as his heart could give him, tearing past the startled gazes of human denizens of the day, sent even the more aggressive shrinking back into the shadows with his cold stare. Despite his need to escape, he was aware that his feet directed him in ten-block laps, never going farther than that from Atlantis. Occasionally, he reached out, touched the open door to a sleeping woman's mind.

She wasn't having nightmares right now, thank God. As he slowed to a half jog, he received a drift of innocuous images, no real connection, like clouds in the sky. When one did form a coherent picture, it was an unsettling and yet compelling one. She dreamed of a black car, a shiny BMW, that had slowed to a stop in heavy traffic. Surrounded by tall buildings, people, acres of concrete, it was closed in and crowded. Even as an observer, he needed to draw a deeper breath than his exertion made possible.

Anwyn's slim arm emerged out of the car window as a butterfly floated by. The delicate creature chose to rest on her fingers, as if it knew there was nothing to fear. It had no concern or awareness of its alien environment, even though it should be fluttering over a meadow of sweet grass and yellow flowers. Drifting up into a blue sky punctured not by skyscrapers and smog, but by darting birds, dragonflies and sailing clouds.

As Anwyn turned her hand, the butterfly moved into her palm. Her fingers came up, slow, forming a bowl, and then closed over it, holding the creature within that gentle cage. The butterfly continued to rest, pumping its wings. Then her fingers opened and it flew away, wherever butterflies went.

The clouds closed back in, her mind again floating amid a guile-less sky.

Gideon leaned against the wall, breathing hard, gulping for oxygen. He realized he'd run the circuit five, maybe ten times, and only now had he run out of breath. Even two marks had increased his strength and endurance. His senses were razor sharp. His physical senses, at least. His head was stuffed with cotton, making it hard to separate one thought or feeling from another. Or Anwyn's.

When his phone vibrated, he thought about ignoring it. Anwyn would call with her mind. But then again, it could be Daegan, so he withdrew it. *Jacob.* Intuitive bastard. Gideon had thought about calling him, because there was no one else, but one, it was broad daylight in South America, where they were visiting Lord Mason at the moment. It was Jacob's bedtime. Two, there was no way he could have that conversation. So he'd quelled the urge, and yet here Jacob was, on the line. Being a night owl, or whatever the reverse was for a vampire. Fine. He deserved what he got.

He snapped it open. "Have you fucked guys for her?" he demanded.

He wanted to ask the entirely reverse question—*Have you let a guy fuck you?*—but he just couldn't go there. Had that night with Lyssa and Jacob done something to him? Fuck, no. He didn't . . . Not once had he wanted Jacob during that interlude with Lyssa, and the idea of it re-pulsed him, his own brother. But maybe he'd gotten even more twisted and perverse since then. Maybe they were right about the things that happened to your mind when you spent too much time alone. Too much time alone, and stalking and killing vampires. Hiring the occa-sional hooker. Yeah, he was the poster boy for deviance.

But on his run, he'd reviewed every guy he'd ever met. Fellow foot-ball players in high school, some of the vampire hunters he'd worked so closely with. Hell, stripping down for hunting missions, he'd seen plenty naked. Nothing. Not even a twinge. And yet his mind kept coming back to Daegan, in a lithe, loose squat by the music player, the shirt pulling over his broad shoulders. The way the man had studied his wrist gaunt-let, the crease in his brow when he asked questions about it.

He'd even had an involuntary half dream about him. Coming up behind him at that music player, curling his fingers in the shirt, drawing Daegan to his feet. But Anwyn was behind Gideon, turning him around, moving into his arms, pushing him back into Daegan's embrace, her scent surrounding them both. Her desire to command him took over everything as her fangs pierced him as delicately as the woman herself. And Daegan's hands slid just as possessively over hers on his ass, around to his hips, as his fangs sank into him on the other side . . . He'd woken, sweating and cursing, and hard as a rock, still experiencing erotic tremors from the things he couldn't face now.

Distantly, he was aware that Jacob had cleared his throat at his jarring greeting. "Hold on a minute." Background noises faded as if his brother had stepped into a room for privacy. "Mr. Ingram and his grandson were in the kitchen with us. I thought this might be a little inappropriate for a kid's ears. Would you like to repeat that now?"

Not likely. "You heard me well enough. Shit." Gideon went to a squat. A strolling pimp eyed him, but when Gideon flipped out his switchblade to pare his nails, the man broke into a brisk walk, eyes wisely turning away. "Damn it, Jacob."

"You've gotten yourself involved with a female vampire somehow, haven't you?"

"It's complicated, and I'm not in the mood to explain." *Or ready, for that matter, until I get it sorted out myself.* "If you laugh, I swear I will come up there just to beat the shit out of you." *And though you're still a big, badass vampire, I'm stronger now, too. I might get in a punch or two before you drill me through a wall.*

A long pause. "Believe me, laughter was not my first response. Gideon . . . did she . . . Are you marked?"

"I would expect that's why I called you earlier," Gideon said between gritted teeth.

The mixed stream of Gaelic and Anglo curses was impressive, not only for the creativity, but for the fact that Jacob didn't rile easily, despite their shared Irish blood. When he did, he riled up hard. It made Gideon feel better. Of course, he thrived on adversity, asshole that he was.

"Gideon, hell, I don't even know where to start. You know about

vampires, the way they fight, how to take one down. But do you understand what it's like to live with them? As part of their lives? It's not your
kind of life. Not even close."

"It's not permanent. It's only two marks, helping her out until she
gets a real servant. Would you stop being a mother hen and answer the
fucking question?"

"Yes. I have."

It was so direct, Gideon had to rewind. "Things like that are part of
being a servant," Jacob added.

"Like bringing her tea or doing her nails." Gideon stared at the
concrete ground. "How'd you feel about it? You hated it, but you did it
for her?"

"That would be the cowardly response." Jacob gave a half chuckle.
Envy gripped Gideon. His brother sounded so relaxed about fucking a
male, while his gut was churning over one guy putting his hands *over*
his hands on his dick, not even touching it directly.

"No, I didn't hate it. There were times, at the beginning, it was difficult, but . . . when you surrender everything you are to a vampire, it's
different. It's not about what you think you can do. It's learning that
there isn't anything you won't do to please her, and by pleasing her, you
please yourself. You leave behind the idea that you have boundaries.
She sets the boundaries. Everything she wants you to do is a way to
prove your love and devotion to her, and you trust her to never ask too
much. When you do that, you find out there's lots of things about sex
that become within those limits. Does that make sense?"

"Not at this point, no. But in a scary way, yeah. Shit, I'm so fucked-up,
Jacob."

"Who is she?"

"She's new. The one turned by force, Jacob, and pretty violently. They
did other things to her, too."

Jacob's snarl was impressively menacing, even over the phone.
"Where are they?"

On one thing he and Jacob had always seen eye to eye. Guys who
hurt women, kids or animals deserved to be tortured, killed, then
brought back to life to do it all over to them again. "Two of them dead,"

Gideon said with small satisfaction. "The sire's on ice somewhere, I think. Daegan handled them. Got the sire's blood for her. We've . . . ah, been helping her with her transition."

"Okay, the earlier phone call is making sense. But the rest . . ."

"Not ready to answer any more questions."

Another of those pauses, but this time Gideon felt his brother's compassion in his silence. "I know you don't want to leave her, but do you need to come home? We're headed back to Atlanta soon and you've always got a bed there. Or you could come here. Mason would love the chance to kick your ass at poker."

"He didn't lose enough last time?"

Home. Jacob said it so easily, but Gideon thought of it as Jacob's home. Would he ever feel he had a home? His mind drifted toward Anwyn and Daegan, and more half-baked yearnings that proved how close he was to complete madness. "Not now. Thanks, though. I gotta go."

"All right. But you better call again soon, or I'll come kick *your* ass."

"You can try. You still have a tendency to give away your uppercut before you punch, no matter how fast you make it." Never mind that the power behind it could remove Gideon's head from his shoulders.

"I'll just settle for the kick to the groin, then."

"A girl's trick. Pussy."

"Takes one to know one. Prick." While there was worry in Jacob's voice as Gideon cut the line, he knew his brother would deal with it. If Jacob hadn't learned to accept the uncertainty of Gideon's life, Jacob's far-too-pretty hair would have fallen out long ago.

It was time to go back, and not just to relieve Daegan. He was feeling a pull back there. Toward Anwyn, wanting to make sure she was okay. He ignored the fleeting concern about Daegan again. He couldn't deal with that right now, and wouldn't. But when he closed his eyes, he remembered the two of them in that dream, Anwyn's mouth on him, Daegan's hands, and how his mind settled into a curious place, disembodied and easy, drifting and lust-filled at once.

Everything she wants you to do is a way to prove your love and devotion to her. Was it that? He wanted to say it was, but there was something else bothering the hell out of him, something he could hardly say in his own mind, let alone ask Jacob. *Did you ever hunger for his touch like you do for hers?*

He was truly fucked-up. It didn't matter, though. Anwyn needed him. He could hear her now, awake and seeking him. Breaking into a jog, he headed for Atlantis.

~

Gideon. That simple call, followed by his brief acknowledgment, reassured and amazed her more than she'd expected.

Daegan was worrying her. She knew he needed fresh blood. He'd said he'd go out for it tonight. If he didn't, she and Gideon would badger him together, because she knew Gideon was concerned about it as well. Though he amused her by refusing to admit it, since she could clearly see it in his mind, the situation didn't amuse her at all. Because more than that was wrong with the male vampire.

By mutual unspoken agreement, she and Daegan hadn't really discussed anything of significance when they were together, during the shifts when Gideon was sleeping. He helped her practice drawing that mind curtain, instructed her in a variety of things she'd need to know as a vampire. He was affectionate, touching her on occasion, sensitive to the emotional roller coaster that attended her seizures. He tenderly cleaned her up, held her during them so she didn't have to use the chains. In all ways, the vampire was thoughtful, caring, and everything she could want.

His passion, his emotions, the heated sexuality he poured over her like hot oil sliding down curved, quivering flesh, was as noticeably absent as if the vampire himself were missing.

Sometimes, while she worked at her computer, she could sense him watching her, but when she looked up, he was reading or watching the television, scribbling in his report ledgers. If he was in the weapons room, practicing, he worked himself into a ferocious sweat, which was almost an impossibility for a vampire. It was as if he were fighting an invisible opponent. A decision he didn't want to make. That thought made her uneasy.

She could have asked at any time, but she wasn't sure she was up to whatever it was yet, and figured he'd tell her in time. After all, she was forcing down blood that incited multiple seizures and made her feel as though she were being crushed in the jaws of a hideous monster. As it ground her in the back of its fetid throat, those gremlins nearly broke her eardrums with their internal shrieking. Ironically, while the sire's blood was supposed to be staving off madness, those whispers and mutters were starting to be an almost constant presence in her head. There were days she thought about jamming one of Gideon's guns in her ear, not out of any real suicidal bent, but because she so desperately wanted to obliterate the noise, even if it turned her brainpan into soup.

In addition to that, she was having to run a major business from her computer and phone, no hands-on work or direct contact. The number of things James and the others really couldn't handle, that relied on her knowledge, were stacking up. She hadn't seen the outside, breathed fresh air, in five days. Daegan had said she could perhaps start having escorted excursions in the next day or so, because though the seizures were no less violent or frequent, they were starting to have a minimum occurrence range. She could rely on two to three good hours at least between each one. One day, she actually slept six hours without interruption.

As a fledgling, she should be sleeping from dawn to dusk. However, Daegan had explained that, while sunlight was far more destructive to fledglings, they tended to be like infants, sleeping in fits and starts at first. The transition made it even more erratic. So here she was, up just past noon. Daegan's mind was never open to her, but she could sense he was settling down in his room, probably staying alert until he was sure that Gideon was back.

Fortunately, that was now. She sensed him coming through the corridors of Atlantis, and smiled a little, imagining the rangy stride, the fuck-off-don't-talk-to-me look he leveled at her staff as he made his way to the lower levels. The band of tension around her chest loosened.

While she'd had other concerns in the past few days, Gideon amazingly had not contributed to any of them. He was as good as his word. He was devoted to her well-being, no longer even flinching when she slid onto his lap or curled around him in the bed to draw blood from him. In fact, though he'd asked her not to use the pheromones, it was beginning to arouse him, his mind taking him past the mechanics of vampire nourishment to the primal significance of providing sustenance for a cherished mate. She'd seen that thought flash through his mind, and had chosen to savor it, rather than discomfit him with her knowledge that she'd heard it.

Like most males, and enhanced by the second marking, he was also more than ready to meet her carnal needs. She'd restrained herself, no pun intended, for the past few days since that volatile episode with her and Daegan. She'd enjoyed riding astride Gideon, milking him to climax, reveling in the clever and single-minded dedication of his hands, lips, body and cock to giving her pleasure. But the craving to take him over in stronger ways was growing again, such that she knew she wouldn't be able to stave it off much longer.

She kept practicing that curtain between their minds, while he worked on his own version of staying out of her head, a kind of peripheral mind-vision where he looked past or over the thoughts that filtered into his brain. However, there were times she couldn't help herself. She found herself hip deep amid his yearnings, seeing flashes of things he wanted, craved from her again. In the formless, shadowy world of his subconscious, she also saw hints of things he wanted from Daegan. But she kept that knowledge to herself as well.

She lifted her head, anticipating. Her servant was here. In fact, he *knocked* on the door. Waited.

What are you doing? Come in.

She heard the keypad tones; then he slid in the door, bearing a large duffel bag. Laying it down with a clank, he grunted. "I wanted to be sure that things were okay in here. Didn't want to open the door, if . . ."

"If I'd gone all Tasmanian Devil again?" She arched a brow. "You can tell that by reading my mind. But that wasn't it. You didn't think you were welcome here. Have you been knocking every time you come back?"

Gideon shrugged, a dangerous man looking suddenly awkward and out of place, as if they were strangers. Which, in many senses, she knew they were. "This is your home, Anwyn. And Daegan's. I don't make assumptions."

"You don't make commitments," she responded, giving him a

shrewd look. "But as long as you choose to be part of this, you live here, Gideon. Case in point." She gestured with her pen. "You brought your belongings."

"I figured I would be staying pretty close for a while, so the rest of my stuff would be safer here than where I'd stashed them."

Not some of his belongings. In his mind, she saw this was all of them. Curious, she beckoned him closer and pushed away from her desk. "Show me what's in it. Other than weapons. You and Daegan can drool over those later."

He slanted her a glance, but came closer, went to a squat. The way he looked at her, that lingering expression, quickly hidden in the duck of his head, but not in the disguising of his thoughts, told her he'd come back hungry for something that wasn't food. His hands were curled in the duffel bag, holding tight to it as if to keep his hands off her. She held that curtain between them to disguise her own reaction. She was pleased to see it might be working somewhat, because the denial of that window built his anticipation higher.

"Sorry if the knocking offended you," he said gruffly.

"No apologies are necessary," she responded. Reaching out, she stroked a hand over his head, teased the hair between her knuckles, and wasn't surprised when he captured her wrist in his palm, squeezed a little harder than she knew he'd intended.

"Anwyn, I haven't let anyone get close to me, let alone depend on me, in a long, long time. I have no friends, and one remaining family member."

"Gideon, you're not going to fail me." She held his gaze. "I know it, even if you don't. Even if you walked out the door tomorrow and never came back, you won't have failed me. You understand?"

"No. And yeah." He shrugged. "You have Daegan. I know—"

"Don't." She snapped it out, bringing him up short. She'd found very quickly, and so had he, that she wouldn't tolerate him undermining his own worth. Temper sparked in his gaze, intriguing her as such things always did. Like Daegan, he didn't like to be pushed or crossed. Her vampire blood delighted in it. *Down, girl.*

She drew a breath. "Gideon, whatever brought you to my door, I haven't been so personally, intensely interested in a client, in a very long time. That hasn't changed. If anything, it's grown stronger. The moment I saw you in that room"—she allowed herself to slide her finger down his jaw, letting the nail scrape—"I knew you were mine."

There. That spark again, only something a bit different in nature. "Show me what's in the bag," she murmured.

He gave her a studied look, absorbing the command, but then he unzipped it. "Sure you don't want to see the weapons? They're really nifty."

She suppressed a smile. "No, thanks. I was in your head when you and Daegan were getting practically orgasmic over *his* weapons."

"Like women don't get the same way over shoes."

"Shoes make sense." When she lifted her hand to touch his head again, Gideon's hand whispered along her calf, where her foot was braced on the floor. A stolen touch, done without her permission, but he kept it there below her knee, tracing the skin beneath the loose hem of her skirt. Sinc he wasn't a submissive, he didn't automatically remember rules about touching versus not touching. However, he did have an innate awareness of it. Somehow he knew he could get away with touching her calf, but needed her invitation to do more, even as he inched higher, trying to seduce that invitation out of her.

She passed her fingers through his hair, sifted the strands. His hair was almost as dark as Daegan's, if he grew his out. There was some gray there, something he was too young to have. "Who cuts this?"

"I do, when I have time. And a mirror."

"Maybe you'd do better without the mirror." She tugged, brought his eyes up. "I can have one of my girls cut it for you. Chantal does great hair. Show me what's in the duffel."

He swallowed, a look of such need and confusion there that she had to quell the desire to assuage it. *Let it build. Let him work it out.*

Looking down, though, she felt her heartstrings pull anew. So little. Weapons, notebooks and a few files. About four days' worth of underwear and socks, a pair of jeans and dark-colored athletic shoes.

"These were the vamps I was tracking." He indicated the files. "I destroy the paperwork after I get them. I don't take a lot of notes, mostly statistics and things. Lots of it is in my head, in case a vamp gets to tracking me and wants to figure out who I'm going after next."

She nodded. "Do you have photos in your wallet?"

He reached back, pulled it out in that unconsciously male gesture that stretched his shirt over his shoulders, twisted his waist and tightened his jeans briefly over his thighs and groin. He'd picked up a new T-shirt from somewhere, probably a street vendor, a plain navy color. Featureless, which would make it easy for him to blend into the night. Though he'd be on hiatus indefinitely from his profession, he still thought and prepared like a vampire hunter.

As he flipped open the wallet, she saw he had no credit cards. Only a driver's license. When he pulled out the three photographs he had, she noted he hesitated before extracting the last one. From his mind, she knew who was in that one, even saw the picture in his head, so she focused on the other two and let him keep that one tucked behind the others.

Two young boys, leaning against each other with open smiles and a sunny background. Gideon and his brother, as children. In the younger boy, she saw the facial structure of the man she'd seen in Gideon's head. Jacob. The other photo was a couple, obviously his parents, probably at the age they were when the other photo was taken. She passed her fingers over the snapshot. "How did you lose them?"

Daegan hadn't told her they were dead. But if this man had parents left, he would have still been connected to them. In fact, she suspected he would have been a different person entirely. As a vampire hunter, she also doubted he'd carry a photo of any living family members, just in case. Since Jacob was already part of the vampire world, he was protected in a way a pair of vulnerable parents wouldn't be.

"Lightning strike. We were at the beach. We got 'em out of the water, did CPR I'd learned in a class at school. Jacob didn't know how, but I walked him through it with Mom while I worked on Dad, but it was too late for both of them. Are your . . . are your parents alive? Any family?"

The significance of the question wasn't lost on her. "No. I had a sister, who died young. My parents also. My mother died during a miscarriage, and my father had a heart defect that killed him on a jog in his early thirties. I lived with my uncle and aunt until they divorced, and then I lived with my aunt until I was eighteen. We're not close. Don't even exchange Christmas cards."

"There's more of a story there."

"Yes, there is. But I don't want to dwell on it today."

"Would you give me a piece of it?" He cocked his head, and she saw how he wanted to know more, everything about her being of intense interest to him. He was both a delight and a danger to her currently way-too-fragile ego.

She stroked her finger over the picture of his parents, thinking of her own. "It's a typical story, Gideon. My uncle liked good brandy and young girls. He thought an orphaned teenage niece was fair game. When his wife figured it out, she did the right thing. Divorced him, reported him, but she could never bring herself to forgive the thirteen-year-old for being what he wanted, instead of her."

She wasn't surprised to see and feel the violence on her behalf simmering within him. As she raised her gaze, she realized his eyes were not exactly like his parents'. There was Irish warrior in those intense depths. "It isn't why I'm a Domme, but it took me a while to figure out. When Barbie first started smacking Ken around"—she gave him a tight smile—"I thought it was because I was angry and wanted to punish someone. So when I was old enough to give a name to my Dominant nature, I thought it was destructive, connected to that time period, something I needed to deny myself. But then I realized that pain and punishment aren't always about vengeance. Sometimes they're a path to freedom. I wanted to offer others what I hadn't had; a moment of pure safety, of knowing you could surrender yourself into the hands of another and feel completely, truly safe and cherished. It's a rare thing."

"Yeah, it is." His eyes fell on the picture of the two boys, who were obviously at a beach, their arms around each other. When she withdrew her hands, he placed the photos carefully back in his wallet. Stroking a strand of hair from where it was teasing the corner of her mouth, he curved it back behind her ear, his eyes warming on her face, so close, his fingertips caressing that sensitive place.

"You should learn not to touch me without permission."

"I hear what you want in my mind, feel it. I don't think I've touched you without permission yet."

Her body rippled at the sensual heat in that male voice, the truth of the words. "Then I want you to learn to wait until I ask you directly, whether in my mind or with my lips."

She laid her hand on his throat, collaring it with her slim fingers, and earned another flicker from those mesmerizing eyes, a tightening of that sexy mouth. "My desire for dominance wasn't all about noble, charitable reasons. I learned I healed myself that way as well. By taking a man into that moment, I brought myself there as well, in a different way."

He stayed so still under her touch, making her thighs shift restlessly against each other, a yin and yang response. "And what moment are you in right now?" he asked, low.

"I want to go check on the club."

~

Everything she was feeling right now was pleasure. Pleasure in his responses, in her strength. In his new connection to her, his hard cock and pounding heart, the way his blue eyes were hungry and full of fire. For the first time in several days, she felt balanced. In control of herself. Maybe the sire's blood was helping, but she preferred to think it was the strength that her body was drawing from that connection to Gideon, just as Daegan had suggested it could. Knowing how time was ticking toward the next seizure, and that the shadow voices were at their most muted, she found she wanted to exult in this one moment, make the most of it.

However, his startled expression, followed by wariness, cast a pall on such optimism. "Anwyn, that's not a good idea."

"Didn't your brother have limited freedom during his transition?"

"Yes, but this isn't the same. You know it."

"I know that," she said calmly, though her pulse started to hammer, the precursor of temper. "Daegan said he thought I was about ready for some short, supervised excursions. The club's not open right now, just a handful of staff topside."

"Well, then, shouldn't we check with Daegan first? He might—"

"I can make this decision on my own," she snapped. At his look, she closed her eyes, her fingers into fists. "That was normal temper, Gideon. It pisses me off to beg for it. I've had to ask for permission like a child to do anything for the past few days. I'm never alone, not in my mind. If it's not Daegan, it's you, keeping tabs on me, and even if I didn't feel you there, those godawful voices would be. I know you need to be there—I'm glad," she added, "but I'm trying to make a point. Do you know how long it's been since I've had to ask permission for anything, let alone something as simple as a walk through my own club?"

She took a breath. "I understand why you're concerned. But, as you said, I've handled myself damn well for having every scrap of control taken away from me. You've chained me up, put me in a cage." At his slight flinch, she pressed the advantage, not ashamed to be ruthless. "Hell, I've put manacles on myself. I'm not being irrational. I just need thirty minutes to give myself a taste of my own life. It's an acceptable risk. You know it. I won't try to put the screen between us while we're up there. If you sense anything about to change, we come back here right away. I wouldn't risk my people, Gideon. You *know* that."

He grimaced. She could tell, and hear in his mind, that he was vacillating between his desire to give her what she wanted and erring on the side of caution. But for reasons she couldn't explain, she couldn't bear to bring Daegan's passionless logic into this. She gave Gideon an arch look. "Do *you* feel the need to check with Daddy first?"

Okay, she knew that was a nasty ego shot, but like a wild bird who'd been slapped into a cage before she'd even realized she was caught, she wanted one little taste of freedom. Strength was pumping through her. She felt better than she had in hours, and it wasn't the false adrenaline surge. She was sure of it.

She rose and he straightened at the same time, emphasizing the difference in their heights. At the moment it was a good thing, underscoring that he was powerful, a skilled warrior, and connected to her in a way that would help him protect her. Sidling closer, she ran a hand up his chest because she could, feeling the tempting terrain beneath. It was a woman's hunger heating her blood, not an uncontrolled monster's. She opened her mind fully, let it wash through him, the images in her mind. How she'd like it if he never wore a shirt, so she could stroke him, lick him, bite at his nipples and tease his throat with fangs and tongue. She knew he wasn't a man that could be led by his cock, but this wasn't about that. It was letting him see that she was in control of her own desires, her own wants. *Please, please don't make me beg, Gideon.*

She arched a brow, letting the emotional entreaty give way to sultry humor. "Unless you think you can defy me?"

23

OF course he could defy her. She was stronger now, yeah, but short of throwing him over her shoulder and carrying him up there, he didn't have to do what she said. Maybe she'd pushed his own buttons by implying he was checking in with Daegan, rather than believing her or having faith in his own abilities, but he wasn't that easy to manipulate. He did understand her need to take a short jaunt, and all other things being equal, it did seem like an acceptable risk.

At least that was the conclusion he came to, hoping he wasn't being guided by the fact he was so aching hard, he had to please her, even at the expense of personal humiliation. She'd been devastating to the senses even when she wasn't in his mind. With that flood of images, it was a shotgun double charge to his cock, seeing what she wanted, how she was feeling.

As she'd worked on screening her mind, he'd figured out how to manage the open access to her mind without taking advantage of it, like standing by a rapidly flowing river but keeping his focus on the trees on the opposite bank. He was aware of the sound of the river, what lay in its depths, but he could do that without looking closely at it or hearing the individual nuances of the sounds. Of course, right now she'd invited him to be there, to make sure this turned out okay. If she kept throwing erotic images at him like that, though, he was going to lose his mind. He'd never wanted a woman so much.

Yet he knew his inability to say no to her wasn't lust. It was something far harder to get under control. It was his understanding of how she felt, swept away by circumstances beyond her control. His empathy with the fact she was having to face everything she hated and feared.

She'd donned the slacks and tailored blouse of a business manager, along with a pair of stilettos that hinted at the smoldering sexuality of the woman beneath the clothes. Of course, the vivid eyes and lush mouth, beautiful hair twisted up and piled on her head, would do that if she wore sackcloth. Though the gremlins were still quiet, he sensed a new tension simmering in her muscles when she came out of her room. Now that she'd resolved to do it, she wasn't entirely sure she'd made the right decision.

Though he'd been prepared to test her with a few more objections, that knowledge made him change direction. He knew how formidable she could be, but he wondered if she realized that when he looked at her, he saw the delicacy of her wrists, the thin fragility of her skin, how her eyes held so much. She was a tough lady, but she'd been raped, violated down to her soul, her very identity threatened, and really hadn't been given any time to deal with that. She needed to believe in herself, in her own strength, to handle this. That small but powerful thought—*Please don't make me beg*—was the key to what could break her.

He rose from the couch. "You look beautiful."

It surprised a smile out of her. Her gaze passed over him, lingering indecently at his groin, passing over his thighs and then back up over his chest. "Stay close. I wouldn't want any of these ladies to get any ideas."

"I'll be right behind you. Keeping my eye on every round, soft inch of your ass."

When she narrowed her eyes at him in mock reproach, he attempted a sexy, reassuring smile. He wasn't much on flirtation, but it felt right, and the increased warmth he sensed in her manner told him it might have helped. She moved to the door, but he got there first, putting his hand on her wrist to stop her. "I think that's my job, right?"

As her blue-green eyes flickered up to his, he dared to slide his knuckles along the small of her back, just above her waistband. He indulged the male desire simmering through him, the compulsion to touch and reassure at once. "I'll stay close to your mind; don't worry. Just keep it open to me and everything will be fine, like you said."

She nodded, her glossy lips pressing together, making him think of all sorts of moist, heated places. She apparently received that thought, or maybe it matched her own generous reservoir of lust, because when she preceded him out the door, she let her hand drift across his groin, giving his tormented cock a cruel caress.

That was okay, though. He was beginning to understand what things helped steady her, even if it unbalanced him, made him have to work extra hard to sharpen his senses and be on guard for her the way he needed to be. If an attack threatened, he wouldn't be distracted.

Though it had been less than a week, it still seemed surreal, how things above had remained essentially unaffected. As she'd said, it was afternoon, so the club wasn't yet open. Gideon was impressed by the efficiency with which the starting shift worked, methodically checking and cleaning playrooms, inspecting and sterilizing equipment. Fresh flowers were being placed in the appropriate playrooms and in the small bud vases on every table in the public areas. The dance floor was being waxed. Despite the din from the waxing machine, the evening DJ was doing sound checks for his equipment. Bartenders checked their alcohol stores and kitchen staff took stock of limes and lemons, as well as prepared the gourmet appetizers and desserts they provided as part of the club's amenities.

James had done his job well. The club staff had been told Mistress Anwyn had taken a few days' leave to deal with some business, the unspoken message being it was nothing out of the ordinary. She was greeted and approached as if she'd never been gone.

However, Anwyn was intimately involved in her club, so Gideon quickly realized they weren't going to make it back downstairs in their agreed thirty minutes. Each area had questions and requests for her to wade through.

She handled it with easy grace, though, falling into a rhythm that seemed to soothe her mind. So, while he wouldn't say he relaxed, as he stayed close to her, inside and out, he hoped this brief eye of calm would help prove to her the storm was in fact moving, that it would eventually pass over her. He wanted to believe that as much as she did.

~

After an hour of talking to various staff members, Anwyn turned to locate Gideon. She'd touched him with her mind constantly, felt his responding mental caress, and been pleased with that intimate form of communication, no words, just a feeling passed across a bridge. But now she wanted to see him.

He was leaning a hip against the bar, his arms crossed over his chest, while she discussed a supplier issue with Carlyle, the first-shift bartender. It was an intriguing combination, to experience his tenderness, his sexy warmth toward her, all in her mind, while on the outside he looked unapproachable and tough, a walking bad attitude. If Madelyn or any of the other Dommes had arrived yet, their jaws would have dropped. No one had tried to talk to him.

It made her want to saunter over, break that exterior by putting her palm over what the denim outlined so well. Though the images she'd shown him downstairs had been a while ago, his cock had stayed decently interested, probably because the scoundrel was passing the time by watching the shift of her ass under her snug trousers, thinking about sliding a well-lubricated cock along the channel between them while she lifted her hips from the bed to facilitate the movements. He'd lingered on the curve of her throat, wanting to lick her there, take sharp nips, since he'd discovered that she was ultra sensitive in that area. And of course he'd indulged his obsession with her hair, imagining pulling the pins from it to bring it tumbling down, covering her bare breasts, but then sifting through the curtain of it to find her aroused nipples, plucking and squeezing them until she was arching and gasping, her thighs loosening to invite him in to give her a just-short-of-fainting orgasm.

She was going to take him downstairs, tie him to a spanking bench and blister his ass. Of course, he was hungry for her because she was hungry for him, one response feeding the other in a slow, pleasurable spiral. It was the one thing she definitely liked about being a vampire, how it enhanced and increased the stamina so no fantasy was out of reach. She imagined pushing him with pain and pleasure until those eyes became cobalt fire and he begged for her cunt in his rough voice, part plea and part insolent demand.

She gave him a severe glance. He almost made her laugh as he blinked those cobalt eyes in guileless innocence, when the bartender wasn't looking. The routine of the club had dispelled her initial nervousness about her defiant decision, and now she realized something remarkable. For the first time in days, she felt *good*. As though it was going to be all right.

This was *her* place, and she'd never felt it so keenly. Daegan had said vampires were very territorial, but she liked that feeling, this roll of slow power through her. She was strong, fast, so aware of everyone around her. She'd always been a sensual creature, but now she seemed to emanate pheromones that scattered like fairy dust over everyone she encountered. Her fingers drifted across Carlyle's forearm as they spoke. She'd touched the small of the waitress's back, encountering bare skin through the corset spacings, as they spoke about drink prices and the floor coverage for the evening. Now, as she moved out of the bar area and into the security office, she even slid a kiss across James's cheek that lingered near his mouth one tantalizing moment before she drew back and thanked him for his help.

He cleared his throat gruffly. "You're welcome, Miss Naime. You look . . . you look wonderful. I mean, like you're doing very well."

"I feel wonderful," she said, and gave a throaty laugh that she knew would go straight to his testicles. It was a rare thing to see James off balance, and she loved it.

~

She looked like sex in motion on those preferred stilettos, Gideon thought darkly, as she sauntered back out of James's office, leaving the man studying her with a slight flush on his usually stoic face. Every decision and word she offered was useful, productive, but as she continued through the club, the way she studied each employee was impossible not to notice. Like a fox sizing up each chicken in the henhouse.

He didn't for one second wish to be marked by Daegan Rei, but Gideon did have a sudden wish he could speak directly to him. Vampires were oversexed, yeah, and Anwyn was already chock-full of sensuality, but he was getting a strange vibe. He didn't sense one of her seizures coming, either bloodlust or transition, but something definitely wasn't right.

Of course, could he trust his own judgment in the absence of that key indicator? Her touching every guy in range but him was starting to piss him off. She knew damn well he was aching hard for her.

No, that wasn't it. This had all the earmarks of growing bloodlust, whether or not he was getting the signal for it. What would he do if she lost control and threw someone against the wall to suck their blood? He'd focused too much on the seizures, not on the impulse control that all young vamps had. Why in the hell had he let her come up here without letting Daegan know?

Because it was new to him, calling on someone else for help. Calling on Daegan particularly rankled his pride and those other issues he'd been wrestling with. However, he couldn't help but recall his words. *She will be as bad as the most dangerous drug addict, willing to say or do anything.*

Ah hell. He might have really screwed up. Another alarm went off, big-time. He realized he was hearing only *his* mind.

Are you all right, Anwyn? Gideon tried to reach out, and hit a rock-solid wall. Son of a bitch. She didn't have the strength to close the door between their minds yet. No way she'd learned to do it in one brief stroll through her club. What if that fucking psychotic legion in her mind had figured out how to slam the door shut, closing her off from him? Not only confusing the signals, but shutting her off from the strength and reassurance he could give her as a second mark.

Plus, he could only stabilize her mind. He wasn't connected down to her soul, to the level of her heart's blood, like a third-mark was. But they apparently had access to all of her right now, places he couldn't go.

So far the battle was only beneath the surface, though. As if all was well, she'd stopped to speak to one of the maintenance men. Pointing to a cage in need of repair by the dance floor, she drew him over to it. As Gideon watched, she put the broken manacle welded to the bars around the befuddled man's wrist. She circled his hand just above it, tapping the locking mechanism with her forefinger.

"It gets stuck and won't come loose easily." Her voice was that velvet fuck-me purr, rankling him like an alarmed, fuzzed-up cat. "In case there's an emergency, that trigger needs to release instantly. I expect one of our ladies put a very strong, determined male in there, and he was able to bend it." She gave him a dangerous, moist-lipped curve of her lips. "Though I'm sure the reason he was struggling *wasn't* to get free. You should be able to straighten this latch back out and then lubricate the mechanism so the pin will slide in and out, the same way you'd—"

"Mistress." Gideon cut in before the man started foaming at the mouth. Or his fellow crewman in the scaffolding, leaning out to hear what she was saying, fell to his death. "There's a matter over here requiring your attention."

The maintenance man withdrew, which was a good thing, because he didn't see the expression Anwyn snapped to Gideon. A trace of red in her gaze, the tips of her fangs showing.

Thank God for training. All thoughts of guilt and self-doubt vanished. Body and mind went into pure battle strategy. Deadly calm, centered. Drawing closer, Gideon leaned in, so his throat was close to that bared mouth. Brushing her ear with his lips, he murmured to her, "I can feel your hunger. Use me to appease it. I'm begging you, Mistress."

Carefully, he slid his arm around her waist, bringing her close to him as he nuzzled that ear, teased the soft neck beneath it. Despite his intent, his cock couldn't help swelling further as her hip brushed it, but that reaction helped. Her fingers closed on his upper arms.

A jerk told him that her self-awareness had kicked in, helping her realize she was in a red zone. "Easy," he whispered, feeling a flood of relief himself when that curtain between them dropped, though her panic flooded through it. Those bastard gremlins apparently couldn't hold the block indefinitely, not when she was focusing. "What's the closest private place?"

"There." He had to angle his head to see where she was looking, because her face was turned in toward his sternum. On the opposite side of the dance floor there was a small corridor.

"Okay. We'll move slow. Hold on to it."

"I can't, Gideon." Her body had started to shudder. "Oh God, what if I—"

"You won't." In one movement, he swept her off her feet, cradling her in his arms and moving swiftly toward that hallway. At the surprised look of the waitress he passed, he snapped, "She's fine," hoping that would do, then shouldered through a curtain of beads into the narrow hall. He saw there were a series of private rooms. Small like dressing rooms, they were probably a temporary place for people who needed a quick moment with one another or alone to relieve sexual tension.

In each space there was little but an elegant chair, a wide mirror and a table. The table held tissues and a pitcher and basin, like an old-fashioned bordello. And of course the fresh, exotic flowers that Anwyn favored.

He took the room farthest down the hall, shouldered in and slammed the door. When her hands clamped down on his shoulders, he heard that ominous hiss.

Sitting down on the chair abruptly, holding her on his lap, he caught the back of her neck and brought her mouth to his neck. "All yours." He gave her the urgent encouragement, even knowing she might rip out his throat. When she hesitated, he pulled his knife and made a shallow cut at his carotid, letting the smell of the blood fill her. She knocked the knife out of the way in a flash of response. Latching on like a viper, she went deep and hard enough that the pain nearly overcame him. Instead, forcing back the grunt of agony, he held her with one arm and yanked open her slacks.

Furrowing down into a silky scrap of panties, he found petals of damp flesh that gave way to full, slippery arousal. She growled against him, a sound of lust and need as he sank his fingers into her, working his thumb against her clit. Though his head was spinning, his heart thundering in fight-or-flight demand, he held fiercely to one directive. Expel her energy; focus the violence of that bloodlust. Selfishly, he wished she'd worn a skirt so he could have just thrust her down on his own aching cock, and thereby distracted himself from worrying about whether he was about to be sucked dry in a less pleasant way than a male might imagine, at the mercy of those luscious lips.

But even if she'd worn a skirt, he knew he wouldn't have done it. Something connected to this moment, what he was letting her do, what she'd done to him before they'd come up here, told him that he wouldn't do it. Hell, she'd made it clear he had to wait for that until she was ready for it, and it challenged him to obey her commands, indulge her desires.

He didn't want to think too much about the why of it, and fortunately he didn't have time to do so. She shifted her bite without withdrawing, tearing flesh. He closed his eyes tight as her hand squeezed his shoulder, and he heard the collarbone groan in protest. Another millimeter of pressure and . . .

He muffled his cry against her shoulder as it fractured, and her bloodlust rolled over him. *Fuck.* Here came the seizure right on the heels of it, but he wasn't in a position now to get her out of there. The shadow creatures screamed in triumphant frenzy as the red haze bathed the walls of her mind. He could almost see the essence of her mind in the middle of them, like the sacrifice at an insane bacchanalia, confused and unable to separate reality from insanity. She didn't even realize what she was doing to him.

Oh, Anwyn. Despite the physical pain he was feeling, seeing that twisted in his gut. She hadn't deserved this. It wasn't going to go away. Those damn shadow things, that blood, had gone beyond her brain, into her heart and soul, just as he thought. It was hard enough to fight the battle in her brain. How could she fight an enemy invading wherever she was vulnerable, where her deepest self resided?

He knew how. He could make it all right. Daegan had known it, still probably knew it, the bastard. The woman on his lap was becoming a bloodthirsty monster, fast moving beyond his grasp. Even with his help, she might go that way. She was a vampire. She was a fucking vampire.

And she was a woman who needed him. Who needed him more than she needed anything, not because she'd told him that, but because he could feel it.

Think through the pain and fear for her. She loses if you lose it.

Anwyn. He reached out to her in her mind, fought his way through those creatures. They weren't real; they weren't her. They didn't belong there. He saw her consciousness find him, see him, desperation swirling through her thoughts. *I'm here.* He set his jaw. *We're here. Give me the third mark. Do it.*

Fuck, he'd done it wrong. She was a Mistress, and you didn't command a Mistress to do anything. Not unless you were more Dominant than she was, and Daegan wasn't here. Those creatures rose up shrieking, filling her mind with such an overwhelming cacophony of anger and protest, he could barely hear himself think. She was completely covered up by them.

Anwyn seized his hair, yanked his head back, and punctured the other side, leaving the carotid flowing. He gave a hoarse cry at the excruciating pain to his collarbone, but fought through it to find the wound, put pressure on it. Then she was straddling him, rubbing herself against him like a cat in heat. Even weakening from blood loss, his body responded.

Anwyn, I'm yours. You don't need to hurt me. I'm yours.

It was how Daegan had centered her. But that brought another thought. He didn't have an avenue to Daegan, but Anwyn did, and Anwyn's mind was wide-open now.

Daegan. He called out to him, praying he'd respond. It was afternoon, and Daegan hadn't gone down until about lunchtime. Without fresh blood, he might be sleeping deep. Otherwise Gideon was sure he would have been here by now, sensing her distress. Hell, he probably would have known they'd headed upstairs an hour ago, but he'd gone under, trusting Gideon to use sound judgment. *Double fuck.*

It didn't matter. He had to try.

No. Her frenetic rage and lust swirled in a thick cloud around them, but he'd caught her attention. *You're betraying us. Trust no one.*

That's not you, Gideon returned fiercely. *That's Barnabus's blood talking. He's a virus, Anwyn; he's not you. He's a disease you fight.*

The fury almost shoved him out of her mind. *It was your kind that held me down, that took away everything, that made me lose everything.*

No, it wasn't. Look at me, Anwyn. Look at me. His vision was blurring and he realized unconsciousness was close. He had to reach her. "You don't talk . . . in melodramatic . . . movie clichés."

He'd used humor before to break her away from them, but in the aftermath of a seizure that had already spent itself. She was on the upward curve and she wasn't responding to him at all. He was no longer Gideon, or even a man. He was prey, food, an enemy to be destroyed. She pulled back from him without retracting, and he gave another painful grunt as she came away with more flesh. When she spat it to the side, her expression wasn't her own. He'd lost her.

She was up off the chair, her hands on his shirt. He tried to twist, to stop her, but she heaved him off his feet and threw him into the mirror. The glass shattered, the drywall giving way. But she hadn't let go. She drew back, knocked him back into it again. The mirror had been affixed to a support beam, a steel beam that he now felt make solid, bone-breaking contact with his body. His back, his skull, hammering into it as she shook him like a doll, screaming.

Anwyn.

It was faint, but Gideon realized it was faint only to him, because his brain cells were jittering like a crazed Jell-O mold. In contrast, she jerked as if she'd been slapped. Her eyes were glazed, but her hands spasmed, releasing him. Gideon gave a hoarse, feeble grunt as he fell limply to the ground. He couldn't make his legs move . . . his arms. There was something wet on his face. That spiral into darkness was becoming a spin, like one of those nauseating rides at the fair . . . What had they called it? The Oaken Bucket?

His body might be an odd mixture of pain and paralysis, but his mind could still see into hers, see her turn her mind toward this new looming shadow, a shadow darker and even more intimidating than any of the other shadows. This one didn't whisper. He'd thundered her name, so strong and abrupt it hit the surface of her mind like storm surf, reeling her back. It even rebounded off Gideon's dazed mind, spearing sharp pain through the back of his skull.

They are attacking your servant. He needs you. If you do not fight them, they will take him.

That last part did it. She might give up her own soul, but she wouldn't give up another's. Unable to do anything more than stand on the sidelines and watch, he saw her spirit straighten and snarl like a lioness awakened by the cry of her cub.

While under normal circumstances he might be offended by the image of himself as that cub, he was immersed in her transformation. He experienced firsthand the astounding, superhuman—hell, supervampire—effort it took for her to seize back control. If it had translated to a physical effort, tendons would have snapped; organs would have overloaded from the strain.

But she was doing it. Still, a second-mark could give a vampire some strength, though it wasn't the same as a third-mark. Hell, he was likely dying, so he might as well give her what he could. Instinctively, not sure how he knew what he was doing, he threw open the doorway to his mind and let that energy pour out to her. When she seized it inside of her head, it looked like tendrils of crimson light wrapping around a small, brain-sized icon of herself, fortifying her like a form of blood. Her shrinking form in the middle of the shadows became infused with light, a black and red fearsome priestess whose essence expanded, took control. Though she gave a terrible snarl of fury and desolation, hinting at the agony of effort it was taking, she shoved the monsters back into the shadows.

Had it taken minutes, or hours? He didn't know. All he knew was he was still on the ground. Anwyn's mouth was on those puncture wounds, urgently laving them so they would clot, putting pressure on the other ones. When she accidentally gripped his shoulder, he gave an involuntary grunt of pain, and her hand withdrew. Vaguely, he recognized she was shaking all over, and his face was wet with her tears.

Give him the mark, Anwyn. Daegan's insistent voice. *He has asked for it. He will heal more quickly that way.*

Daegan . . . you need to come help her. Gideon knew what dying looked like, felt like, because he'd seen it often enough. He'd be gone soon. It was Anwyn that concerned him. Her expression was stark pain, eyes hollow and haunted.

How could he have been so stupid? Her periods of strength, her amazing ability to survive such a terrible ordeal, had been cocooned in those underground rooms, cushioned against facing how her control had changed. Now, faced with it, the sheer enormity of what she'd lost was upon her, a worse enemy than any other she could face.

It's bad blood, awful blood. I don't . . . I can't.

"It's the only blood I want," Gideon said hoarsely, trying to hold her attention. He wanted to put a hand on her face, but he was too weak or his spine was snapped.

Instead she shoved herself to her feet, stumbled back. "No. I've . . . Great Goddess, look what I've done to him. I thought I was all right. I was sure of it . . . I'll never be in control again. I can't live like this. I'm sorry, Gideon . . . I can't—Daegan, come help him." Her fists clenched, her voice full of pain, face a distorted mask, even more horrible than when the shadow creatures had controlled her, because this was her turned inside out, all her raw, deepest emotions naked and trembling before Gideon's straining gaze. "I can't help anyone. You shouldn't have saved me. Neither of you."

Gideon tried his best to grab her, and found he had one weakly functioning arm. She was gone, the door open. *Daegan, she's running. Go after her.*

I will.

Then he remembered. It was still broad daylight.

❧ 24 ❧

S HE was headed for the alley, and thank all the gods she was too upset and too new to her powers to move at full vampire speed. Daegan held on to her mind as if he were a fish she'd hooked, the barbed edges of her thoughts puncturing him and dragging him through the chaos of her mind. As he burst from the underground rooms, he took the side hallways so quickly his presence was felt but not seen, a rush of cold air that shivered through the waitstaff, maintenance and security people he passed. He snatched a radio from one, earning a startled yelp, and barked into it. "James."

James came on immediately. "Yeah."

"Privacy room three. Gideon needs help, but do not call an ambulance. Do what you can for him. I'll be there as soon as I can."

Dropping the radio, he hit the side door and automatically shielded his eyes against the sunlight hitting the brick wall of the next building. She'd returned to a place she never would have wanted to see again. Traces of her blood or clothing probably still remained in this hated alley. Quickly evaluating the scene, he saw several cats grouped in the corner near the Dumpster.

The sun's angle seared his shoulder, but he dodged and moved along the shadows of this building. Despite the fact it wasn't direct sun, to a fledgling it would feel like a searing-hot wind, threatening to burn her flesh off her bones. He heard her cries. Rage and something deeper had him shoving the Dumpster away from the wall. She was curled in a fetal ball behind it in garbage, a kitten standing on her hip, meowing plaintively. When he caught her up in his arms, kitten and all, he ignored her painful scream as his arms tightened over her, rubbing her clothes over her sensitized skin. The kitten jumped free and in two blinks, Daegan was back inside the door, holding her against his heart, which was thundering in his chest.

He didn't trust himself to speak, but took her back to her rooms at the same speed, so their passage would not be noted. When he reached the apartment, he strode directly to the cell, put her down on the sofa. She curled into the couch, away from him.

Should have let me die.

He was on his way back out of the cell, but her broken, repeated whisper was too much. Everything he'd been feeling in the past few days, unable to accept or share with her, was too much. With a snarl, he spun back to the couch, caught her hair in his fist and yanked her head back, lifting her half off the couch so she had to face him.

She'd never feared him. He'd always been amazed and reassured by it at once, never sought to test or change it. But facing his full, unfettered wrath, he saw she finally understood why it was smart to be afraid of him. Anyone with sense would realize swords or guns were the least hazardous thing about him.

"If you ever, *ever* say anything like that again to me, Anwyn Inara Naime, I will chain you to that fucking cross and blister the skin from your back with a tawser, far past when you are begging me to stop. I may still do it. You are alive. You are loved. You *will* get through this. That's the end of it."

He gave her a quick once-over, knew she was in pain, but the skin was already knitting. "You stay right here. Remember that I can be here faster than anything you can do to yourself. If you try to hurt yourself again, you will truly know what suffering is."

He left her wide-eyed, like a terrified, chastised child in truth. Slamming the cell door shut, he locked it and the apartment and headed topside, ignoring the ache in his throat, in his chest. He made it to that privacy room in a matter of seconds, startling the hostess coming down the hallway when he suddenly appeared at her side. "James asked me to bring this," she faltered, handing out the first aid kit.

"Thank you," Daegan said. "I will take it to him. Go back to your work."

She fled, not questioning why this male she didn't know was giving her orders. But then, he expected nothing less. He shouldered into the room, which was too small with the three large men in it.

Holy Mother. He'd been focused on Anwyn, knowing Gideon was badly hurt, but now he saw the extent of it, understood why Gideon hadn't been concerned about himself. Not that the man had ever possessed much of a sense of self-preservation. His body was broken in too many places, and he lay in blood that seemed to be mainly from his ripped throat. The second mark and his own clumsy efforts had slowed the loss of arterial blood, but he was still in an astonishingly large pool of it. James had wisely not moved him, but seeing Gideon sprawled, his arm still stretched toward the door as if trying to stop her, made the whole scenario harder to swallow.

He squatted, nodded to James. "I'll take it from here."

The security man knew enough to be wary, but Daegan gave him credit for the balls to ask after his employer. "Is she all right?"

"Yes." *For now. Until I get my hands on her again.* But Daegan gave a short nod. "Thank you, James. You are a credit to her, and to this place. In a few minutes, send someone discreet to clean up the room. I'll call from downstairs if we need you."

The man left with visible reluctance, but some relief as well. Daegan ignored it. No one felt comfortable around him on a good day, and this one was far from that. Gideon grunted. He didn't move his head, and Daegan was fairly sure it was because he couldn't. "Don't be pissed off at her," he rasped. "It was my fault."

"No, it wasn't. It was mine." *All of it.*

"Bullshit." But Gideon obviously didn't have the energy to pursue it. "I'm going to be dead in a few minutes." His eyes closed. "Go help her. She needs you. Especially since I'm not going to be around to take up the slack for you."

Daegan ignored him, taking a quick assessment of his injuries. The back of his skull had a soft spot the size of his fist. His lips compressed.

The fact the hunter wasn't protesting being touched by him was an even greater indication of how wounded he was. He seemed uninterested in anything but the last thoughts stumbling through his mind.

"Do what you n-need to do with my body, but l-let my brother know I'm gone. Dress it up a little . . . 'kay? Make me sound . . . heroic. Like I rescued a busload of handicapped orphans . . . puppies. That way . . . won't think . . . should have been here. Save me from myself. Irish Catholic guilt . . ."

He coughed, and blood flecked his lips, breath rattling in his throat. His eyes were glazing in a way that Daegan was not going to tolerate.

"Gideon." He put as much command in his voice as he'd delivered when he'd roared in Anwyn's mind. While this was a lower decibel, it was no less emphatic. Gideon's eyes opened, swiveled to him.

"I'm going to take you to her, and she's going to take care of her servant, the way she's supposed to. She's going to give you that third mark, and you are going to live."

Gideon gave a weak half snort. "Too far gone. Better this way, anyhow. Third wheel . . ." His voice faded off, his attention oddly detached. "You can do a better job . . . You didn't let her come up here. Don't carry me."

"Shut up and save your strength." Daegan had slid his arms under the man's body but paused, mentally preparing himself for a very fast transport, plus a very rapid third-marking, even if he had to force Anwyn to it unwilling. It was possible moving Gideon would be enough to kill him, but even if it didn't, the man might be right. He might be too far gone. But it was the only possibility for saving his life.

As he lifted Gideon, the man's heartbeat began to stutter. Daegan took off, moving faster than the light sparking along the shards of the blood-soaked mirror they left behind.

⁓

Anwyn was still curled on the couch when he got there. He brought Gideon into the cell, laid him on the opposite end of the sofa, stretching out his legs so that they slid against her hip. She curled into a tighter ball, but Daegan closed his hand on one of her arms and yanked her loose from the tight coil.

She came off the couch in a flash of motion, her fangs bared, hands going for his face. Part of it was the monster in her blood; part of it was the woman, enraged by the way he'd pulled her back from the suicide she'd sought. She hadn't even really registered the body he'd laid next to her.

He fixed that quickly enough. Twisting her around, he knocked her to her knees beside the unconscious Gideon. She froze, her gaze riveted on the too-pale face. "He's dying."

"Not yet. Mark him."

She fought his hold. "No, you do it. I can't—"

He shook her, hard enough to snap her head back painfully, drawing her attention to him. "Your mark is the only thing that can save him."

"But you—"

"I'm not doing it. You are."

He forced her head down to Gideon's throat. The man was covered with blood, so it was easy enough to activate a young fledgling's hunger. Her fangs elongated. She was weeping, her hands shaking. "He didn't want this."

Daegan hardened his heart to her, to all of it. *He doesn't know what the hell he really wants. A vampire takes what she wants. You take him, make him all the way yours. And then you'll make him glad you did it.*

❧

As a human, she would have known only that he was badly hurt. The supernatural predator she was now knew the damage was mortal. She'd killed him. He was dying. She could smell it, the insidious voices in her head delighted with her.

Gideon had known it was a risk, but he'd cared more about her need to reclaim some sense of herself than his own well-being. He would have stood between her and anyone she might have hurt, taking them both down before anything happened. She knew that about him. But she'd thought only of herself.

"You're still doing that." Daegan was merciless, plundering her mind. *Mark him . . .*

The vampire in her craved to do what he said, the vicious predator Barnabus had put in her mind egging her on. But it was that commanding tone that blasted away the last remnant of protest, the tone that wouldn't be refused, even by a Mistress. He was a Master who would not be defied, not now or ever.

She sank her fangs into Gideon's throat, goaded past the part of herself that was beyond morality, deep in animal instinct. *He'll never escape you.* The shadow voices rejoiced.

"Keep drinking, but get the serum in there. Don't stop until I say so, no matter what he does."

She didn't know why that admonishment was necessary, because the primal part of her took over, eager to keep tasting the rich fluid, the mix of her binding agents in it. Then Gideon started convulsing.

$\sim$

The hunter's humanity was vital to her, but that strength had been a weakness. Daegan had forgotten how an honorable, decent human being would think in such a situation, respecting her free will in a way he wouldn't have, keeping her ass down here even if she swore an oath in blood never to forgive him.

Even to him, the vampire hunter who'd survived so much, killed so many, had seemed far more invincible. But humans were so fragile, too fragile. The compromise to his skull, the internal hemorrhaging, would kill him in a matter of minutes, unless Anwyn could win the race.

If there was time to do this right, she could have aroused him, minimized the seizurelike effect. At least she hadn't had to mark him with all three at once. He had told her that combining them like that was like shooting acid into the veins of the unfortunate human. It also inflicted a simultaneous paralysis on them so the agony didn't have the relief of movement or unconsciousness. Some more sadistic vampires did it that way for that very reason, but he wasn't one of them. Even now Daegan wished he could close his senses to the rigidity of Gideon's body, trapped in that straitjacket of pain and agonized transition, which reawakened deadened nerves. While it could be a good sign that she was pulling him back from the brink, he'd been very close to the other side. The trauma could still take him in the end.

Gideon's distress was reaching her, though. Several times she tried to pull back, but Daegan held her fast. The moment she'd taken enough of his blood, though, he yanked her up. Pulling her arm to his fangs, he punctured her wrist as she yelped, startled. Ignoring that, he put her arm in front of Gideon's mouth. The man was barely conscious, despite the convulsions, so Daegan had to open his jaw, let the blood drop in. Rub his throat until he'd swallowed the requisite number of times. Thank God it didn't take much of the vampire's blood to complete the marking, because Fate chose that moment to bring another seizure upon Anwyn. Given the stress of the past few minutes, he was surprised it hadn't come earlier.

Take him as yours. Feed on his blood. The shadow voices swelled in her mind, matching her own desires. *Rip out his beating heart, just to prove you can.* Hearing her thoughts, he was ready for her response.

"No. Let me go," she shrieked. She was being pulled down in the maelstrom. Howling at the haze coming over her vision only made the rush of bloodlust come in faster. Still, Daegan held her grimly in place until the blood was in Gideon, though her struggles became like those of a wild animal. Her awareness of Gideon's plight deserted her, her eyes rolling and fangs bared as she spouted the invective that came from her sire's broken mind. She even landed a few punches on Gideon's immobilized body before he restrained her, pushing her down to a crouch over her knees until the urge passed.

Daegan had been up to his elbows in blood, witnessed the stink of fear, the horror of dying an unexpected, violent death at his own hands. Yet every time he'd killed, it had been an assignment, the target someone who'd reaped the consequences of illegal actions. What he'd just forced her to do felt like destroying an innocent life. No matter that Gideon had tentatively made the decision himself, that didn't deceive Daegan. The man was nowhere near prepared or committed to being a vampire's full servant, and it was very likely he never would be. The repercussions of taking a servant who wasn't fully committed to belonging to a vampire were usually disastrous.

Gideon's face flashed through his mind, the cocky attitude and grim half smile, the wary eyes. The way he looked at Anwyn, as if everything he could ever want resided within her slim frame. The life dying out of his eyes as he told Daegan to leave him and go help Anwyn. As if he were an afterthought, his body just garbage to be discarded. Anywn's words: *He didn't want this . . .*

Damn it all to hell. Daegan shut it out, everything out but what had to be done right now.

She continued her berserker efforts to break free, her mind encapsulated in pure, raw rage. He was fine with responding in kind. Though she was in the midst of a violent seizure, he knew what would bring her back to them. Taking hold of the thin, feminine fabric of her slacks, he tore the seam down the back, ripping through the silky panties. She stilled in a moment of shock, but Daegan brought her back onto the couch and slid his fingers between her legs, reminding her of his touch, his claim on her, which had burned inside him without outlet for the past few chaste days. A lifetime. She was still slippery from her earlier lust and now she shuddered, a whimper breaking from her.

No.

Freeing himself from the jeans he'd so hastily pulled on, he slammed into her, hard enough to rock her into Gideon's body. Gideon's eyes flickered open, his expression dazed, her blood staining his lips, but he was barely conscious. Daegan kept his focus on her.

Anwyn the human woman had been brutally raped, but he wasn't worried about any comparison at this moment, because he was in her mind, immersed in her new but raging vampire instincts. He knew exactly how to respond to a vampire female in this state.

"If you truly wanted to deny me, your body wouldn't respond. But your cunt is wet, hot and welcoming, Anwyn." *You've told slaves that letting go of control is the greatest power they can embrace. You're a hypocrite. But hypocrites can learn the same way a slave can. By having a Master force the issue.* Rotating his hips, he stroked with deadly accuracy, and her body shuddered again. Sliding his fingers around front, he found her clit, his knuckles braced against Gideon's thigh. She cried out, part anger and part desire, as he started ruthlessly manipulating her.

Daegan caught her wrist, guided her hand across Gideon's waist and down to close over the man's cock, even trapped behind denim. He wanted to remind her of what also belonged to her, what was worth living for. Anwyn swallowed against his hold as he pulled her head up with a hand collared on her throat.

"I don't give a damn about who's in your head. You'll climax for me when I say. And you'll surrender everything to me, the same as you demand of Gideon. It's not only because it's what a vampire is; it's the only sure way to save a soul. You know it, but you don't believe it. It's time I make you believe it. You will climax *now*."

One final pinch, one rotation of his hips, and it tore out of her, the climax shuddering through her as she took his thrusts, crying out with the brutal strength of each one. Finding Gideon's mouth, she devoured it, kissing him mindlessly through the orgasm, breathing her whimpers into his mouth. Whether unconscious or not, the man was responding. It might be only in his dreams, but Gideon aroused to her in his darkness, his lips moving lethargically against hers. His biceps flexed under her tight grasp.

Even wounded, a third-mark's response time was as predictable as a rutting stag's—with the right stimulation, he could practically be ready to fuck on his deathbed. Daegan hoped to God that wasn't what was happening now.

She was half-draped on the couch between Gideon's now splayed thighs, one of his booted feet braced on the floor. Her soft ass pushing against Daegan, her pussy gripping him, was all it took. Daegan released then, spilling his seed inside of her, knocking her knees apart farther so she had to grip Gideon's arms harder.

He didn't spend time on a tender aftermath, even though he could tell he'd called her back from the savagery that had claimed her. Too much was swirling in the air between them, and he had a different purpose from tenderness. Biting her sharply on the neck, he left a mark. She responded with a mewl like an angry, exhausted kitten. "You don't shower until I tell you that you can. You keep his blood on your clothes, and my seed trickling down your legs, your pussy damp and musky, so you remember who you answer to."

He lifted her, took her to the cross. She was frothing at the mouth, her crimson eyes spewing hate and betrayal in equal measure. When she landed a lucky strike to his groin that made his vision gray, he took it as his due. But he got her back in the manacles, left them loose enough she could move around, then slid the couch out of the cell, taking Gideon out of harm's way in case she had another seizure.

As he closed the cell door, he made himself close his ears to the broken weeping that finally swept away the remnants of the savage attack. Closed his eyes to the way she fell limply to the floor at the base of the cross. He'd accomplished what he'd intended. The foundation that circumstances had laid in the past few days had come to fruition. Or maybe, he thought bleakly, it had been growing for far longer than that.

Her self-loathing, her sense of self-destruction, had been replaced by hatred for him.

He wanted to hold on to the combination of fury, frustration and soul-deep terror at how close she'd come to taking her own life. But even during the marking, as she struggled and screamed, fighting an enemy inside of her he couldn't touch, he'd had a dangerous need to make exactly the same mistake Gideon had. To hold her, touch her, give her whatever reassurance he could that she could still be what she'd always been, in the hopes that some of it might reach her embattled spirit, give her strength. If he turned around now, he'd do just that. And she'd never become what she needed to be.

Her growing impatience with her situation that had prompted this ill-advised outing wasn't going to abate, and now she'd faced the very real possibility that this wouldn't get any better. He'd always known her so well. At the center of Anwyn's soul, there was a tough, hard streak, one that understood the need for cruelty as well as mercy. She needed his cruelty to survive, Gideon's love to live. He intended to deliver both to her. So he slid Gideon out of the dungeon area and into the sitting room, where he could keep an eye on him but not be tempted to go to her aid. Anwyn would want him to sit by her new servant, watch over him, until she'd regained her composure. That much, he could do for her.

Gideon was still breathing, but mercifully had subsided into full unconsciousness. The energy required to knit bones and recover from his near brush with death, process the changes the mark would make within him, would keep him out for a while. That was probably for the best. With the marks in place, Anwyn could now be inside his heart, soul or mind, but wouldn't have any control of that connection during her seizures. If he was conscious, Gideon might think he'd died and gone to Hell, surrounded by the shrieking thoughts of some she-demon. Of course, the more sobering question was whether he would regain consciousness at all. As yet, Daegan saw no indication the wounds in his throat or his broken bones were knitting, though the brief span of convulsions might mean his spine was mending.

Now away from anyone's scrutiny but the disapproving gods, Daegan sank down in a chair next to the man, briefly rubbing a hand over his face, distantly recognizing a slight tremor in his fingers. *Holy Mother of Christ, bless His name.* He felt sick, a rare occurrence for a vampire.

Years ago, he'd seen a dog run down by an SUV. The driver hadn't stopped, and it had been late at night. Daegan had carried the poor creature out of the road, found a quiet hill to lay the dog down and sat by him. He'd known the wound was mortal, that the life would die out of his liquid brown eyes in a matter of moments. From the condition of the skinny, feral animal, he could tell he'd had few options in a cruel human world. Daegan had given him some of his blood, which the dog had lapped at for a few minutes and then subsided into semiconsciousness. He'd died with Daegan stroking his coat, his head.

What did it say about him, that he recalled that moment as one of the few times he'd felt truly connected to another? Until he met Anwyn. All those years alone, then he'd met her. And what were the chances that, remarkably, within the same five years, he'd started tracking a hunter who always hunted alone . . .

Gideon muttered, his voice tinged with a fear he'd never heard when the man was conscious. They all had their nightmares.

He could give Gideon what he couldn't give Anwyn right now. Laying a hand on Gideon's brow, he murmured to him. "Easy, vampire hunter. You're safe. And you're all hers. Go to a good dream now. A good memory."

It wasn't a bad idea. From the sounds he detected in the next room,

Anwyn's tears had mercifully given way to a menacing series of hisses and threatening mutters, another seizure coming on the heels of the earlier one. Moving to the sofa arm and bracing a leg up near Gideon's shoulder, his fingers still drifting across the man's feverish brow, he let himself visit one of the best memories of his life. One he desperately needed right now.

The night he'd met Anwyn.

VAMPIRES tended to like upscale BDSM clubs. They were open at night, and they catered to vampires' unique sexual tastes, though it was rare a vampire indulged in an actual session. Most clubs didn't allow bloodplay, and many vampires didn't have the control to maintain the human façade in such a stimulating environment. Daegan was one who did, but he'd gone in only for a drink, liking the environment and the quality vodka. He'd had an assignment in the area, but had finished it up early. The following day he'd head for New Zealand.

He needed to start making some time for other things. He was getting too grim, too tightfisted on his emotions, so that they were growing hard and dull inside his heart. It was too easy for an assassin to become a cold-blooded killer. Though of course, only an assassin probably knew the difference. It was also too easy for a vampire to lose touch with his emotions. When he did, he could succumb to the dangerous apathy of the Ennui.

What would he do with more time, though? He didn't consort with his own kind, and the human world had too many dangers. He could afford the occasional seductive evening with a pretty female he'd see only once, but in truth, he thought maybe he should return to Tibet for a while. Spend time in one of the monasteries. There they asked no questions, each man seeking his own answers and peace from the silence.

The fact he was here, though, suggested his carnal appetites were more urgent this evening than his meditative ones. He scanned the assortment of submissives available for play with a discerning eye, feeling like Goldilocks, not finding anything that was exactly right.

Then he saw her.

She was moving among the crowd of Friday night guests. She missed nothing, the aura of energy around her a silent but powerful force that drew every eye, yet warned even the Doms from speaking to her uninvited. The blue-green corset and tight black skirt with matching stilettos molded her figure, moving with the graceful sway of her body. Her hair had been piled on her head. Around her neck had been stenciled a complicated henna tattoo collar the color of old blood.

There might have been a hundred feet between them, filled with more than two hundred people in the crowded bar and dance floor area, yet she stopped, turned and met his gaze squarely, dead on target.

Things moved faster for vampires. He didn't need time to vacillate or contemplate. The minute she made that extraordinary connection, responding to his energy even through the crowd, he was on his feet and moving. People instinctively shifted out of his way. She watched him, every step, until he reached her.

When he stopped, his feet were planted so close they were practically on the outsides of her slender heels. His coat slid against her forearm as he stared into her eyes. He moved from them to the curve of her lips, the pale skin and bone structure of her face. He'd seen beauty before, countless versions of it, but this . . .

Less than an hour before, someone had begged him for her life. A female vampire. He'd closed his ears to it, because he had to do so, because her crimes required her death. Most begged for life at the end, because fear of the unknown, of saying good-bye to everything they'd ever known, was the greatest fear of all. Just as finding the place that felt truly like your own, your home, what you were bound and connected to, was the greatest need.

"I want you," he said.

No compulsion, nothing but the driving beat in his cock, his heart, his soul. When she reached up to touch his face, he closed his hand on her wrist, a warning that he was not to be touched without permission. But she pushed against his hold, her smile telling him she knew she couldn't battle his strength, but that she would have her way regardless. Remarkably, he let her win, let that delicate forearm he could snap slide through the closed circle of his fingers so she touched his hair, her silky skin grazing his temple. Then she drifted down his cheek, the line of his jaw.

A large man had stepped up behind her. This was her security, come to make sure she was in control of the situation. He had to block an absurd desire to bare his fangs and snarl, send him skittering back. Instead, she made a motion with her other hand, a subtle signal, and the man nodded, moving off, though he kept a wary eye on Daegan.

"I have a feeling that what you want may be more than I have to give," she murmured. "Can you accept that?"

"No." He bent and touched his lips to the tender underside of her forearm, grazing his fang over her wrist, letting her feel the sharp prick. A shudder ran through her.

"Well, just so we understand one another. Come with me."

She walked him back down a quiet hallway full of plush carpet and dim lighting, taking him into a private playroom that was all mirrors. Floor, ceiling and all four walls, and she wouldn't see his reflection in any of them. The only thing in the small room was a vase of red roses, sitting on a pedestal in the middle. A few petals had fallen, scattered on the mirrored floor like drops of blood.

He didn't wait. When the door closed, he turned and tore the side of that snug skirt, all the way up to her thigh. She wore nothing under it. Lifting her up, he pressed her back against the smooth surface of the closest mirror. Her arms and legs wound around him as he gripped her hair, pulled her head to the side and sank his fangs into her neck.

He'd planned none of it. Looking back, it had been an astounding series of events, because she hadn't known him, and he'd made no effort to prepare her in any way for what he was. He'd just seen her and known, from her lack of fear, from what she was and he was, that the moment could and would happen.

He'd never told her he loved her. He'd never told her he couldn't live without her in his world. She was human and he was something so odd, even to his own species, that he couldn't break that rule, make himself that vulnerable.

In return, she gave all herself to him, and yet nothing at once. It had always been that way. Though he desired her to be his servant with an urgency that bemused him, she had never been willing. She gave him everything else he demanded instead, responding to the inexplicable bond that had drawn them together from the first.

With every year he'd spent with her, he'd become more certain that, if ever he lost her, everything would end for him. He would walk into the sun and see if it could kill him, when nothing else seemed to do so.

∽

Even if the sun couldn't destroy him, her howls of pain and agony might. She went from the aftermath of the second seizure directly into another. As he'd suspected, the terrible stress of the past hour had unbalanced her. She needed more of the sire's blood and he gave it to her, steeling himself to be firmly brutal, rather than prolonging it with an attempt at gentleness. Her enraged cries vibrated off the walls, off every alert nerve and inside every cell of his heart.

If there was such a thing as Hell, he was sure this was it.

He knew she blamed him for all of it. In time, her logic and intelligence would reasonably accept that it had been unavoidable fate, that he'd not intended it. It wouldn't make the relationship any less over. Some things were never overcome, the feelings severed like a limb, blackened and withered by the fire of one significant event. How could he fight for her, fight against it, when he didn't think she was wrong? It *had* been his fault. He'd wanted her, needed her, had allowed her to be part of his life without giving her any protection. All because he'd capitulated to the human concept of free will, which had no place in his world.

What would have been best was leaving her alone from the beginning, letting her walk across the club and back out of his life without their eyes ever having met. Yet she'd turned toward him as if drawn . . .

It didn't matter. If she could do it over now, she probably would have blinded herself before making that turn, meeting his gaze in the crowd.

He couldn't do anything about that. So, as he had with that dog, he waited with Gideon. The vampire hunter muttered in his unconscious state, his brow furrowing in pain, stress deepening those lines from whatever haunted his dreams now. When Daegan reached out, he was startled to see his hand was trembling anew. Forcing it to still before he laid it on Gideon's brow, he grazed the hot skin with his knuckles. With bemusement he noted the hunter had some silver strands. By the Blessed Virgin, the man couldn't be more than thirty.

While he hadn't been certain if his touch would make the dreams worse or better, Gideon seemed to settle down, so Daegan kept stroking.

No matter what the future brought, no matter how she felt about him, Anwyn was his. Now that Gideon was hers, that made them both Daegan's. He would take care of them, no matter how much they despised him. He prayed for her attack to pass before her pain drove him mad, prayed like hell for Gideon to survive.

If he didn't, Daegan knew that disposing of the body and telling Anwyn he'd bolted after he healed wouldn't work. For one thing, Gideon wouldn't back away from a situation because he couldn't handle it. He'd rather it destroy than defeat him. And Anwyn, with that gift she had for seeing the truth, no matter how deeply it was buried inside a male, would know it. If Gideon died, Daegan couldn't protect her from the truth that she'd killed him.

That would destroy her soul in a way Barnabus hadn't been able to do. Or even Daegan.

~

Gideon woke with a hell of a headache. He wasn't entirely sure of his surroundings, so he played possum for a few minutes. Had he been taken captive by another vampire stupid enough to try and torture him, rather than kill him outright? It felt as if he was in a different place, almost a different dimension. Everything seemed . . . skewed, somehow.

His head was in someone's lap, though, and it wasn't a bad place to be. Female fingers were whispering over his face, tracing his lips, his brow, the broken line of his nose. Her knuckles slid down his neck, hesitated, and then kept on, but he'd felt the soreness there, the sense of a wound. When she passed over it again, he knew what it was. A bite wound.

It's all right. Don't be alarmed. I'm so sorry, Gideon. It's all right.

He shook his head like the confused, disoriented animal he was. He made it to his feet, seeking balance blindly. He stumbled into a wall. No, not a wall; another body. A man who turned him with firm but not ungentle hands. Now he was leaning back into him, a man who clasped his biceps.

"Let go of me."

"No. Reach for your third-mark energy, Gideon. Let it steady you. Let it focus the picture, help you get a handle on it."

Daegan. Daegan Rei. Whom Gideon should be shoving away because he was a vampire, and an arrogant asshole, besides. However, as Gideon reached out with his senses, he found it, a field of steadying energy, available because . . . third mark?

"Jesus Christ, tell me you didn't mark me."

"She did. At my insistence, to save your life."

Gideon's senses seemed to be on hyperdrive. He hadn't thought to open his eyes yet, not because of the headache, but because of all the input his other senses were handling. He could smell every distinct odor around him. Their clothes, the lingering scent of blood, the individual shampoo, soaps, fabrics and cleaners that attended a body and its home surroundings. There was an air conditioner running, a refrigerator. The faint hum of a computer somewhere. The air felt weighted with sound vibrations.

He tried to open his eyes and was refused. His brain had no spare energy for something basic like opening his eyes, not when it was processing all the rest. Jesus, he could hear their hearts beating, as well as his own. He wasn't sure, but he thought he even had some sense of the rush of blood through his veins and other internal organs.

But that wasn't the most significant difference. Those things were just an enhancement of the second mark. He had a sense of Anwyn so close, it was almost as though she was inside of him. Or he was inside of her. He could still hear the uneasy boiling of thoughts in her mind, the occasional sharp word or call from the shadow creatures, like shrill, menacing birds in a dark jungle. They were getting louder, responding to his awakening, apparently. But he was sinking, dropping to a deeper level than her thoughts, going down and down. Like quicksand, but it wasn't entirely unpleasant. He could discern her emotions, her state of being. Anger, fear, relief . . . a mind-numbing tiredness. Her emotions were spiraling inside of him.

The disconnection he'd felt from everyone for so long, the shielding that had exacerbated it and all his dysfunctionality, all that was still quite operable, but this was a wondrous sense of connection, of empathy, that made him aware of exactly how lonely he'd been.

It was unsettling, to say the least. He remembered Jacob saying it was hard to explain the third mark, how it differed from the second, just that it did, big-time. Maybe his experience was different because Anwyn couldn't yet completely shut the link between them, but right now . . . he felt as though he was walking in her soul, as connected to her as he would be connected to the earth, walking through soft grass barefoot. He wasn't normally a poetic man, but that was just the best way to describe it, no way around it. She was here, in every part of him.

"Anwyn, help him." Daegan's voice. "Try to draw the curtain closed. You must focus. Use my energy in your mind if you need it. He's getting mired inside of you."

No, really. It's okay. I'm fine with the miring. An unconscious, emotional reaction more than a spoken thought. Regardless of whether or not she'd heard it, a few minutes later, those shadow whispers became more muted, and the ground under his mental feet became more stable, taking him on a halting elevator ride back up to her mind. While he was aware of a background of white noise that must be her mind, held at a distance but not completely disconnected, Gideon was able to focus a little better. "What happened?"

Daegan's hold eased, but Gideon was mortified to find he couldn't quite straighten yet, leave the prop of his body behind. Daegan spoke. "Your skull was compromised and your back was broken. You were hemorrhaging internally."

Gideon digested that. "Why didn't you mark me yourself?"

"Because you were considering allowing her to do so, the closest thing I had to a consent. I don't force unwilling humans to become servants. And, under any circumstances, you wouldn't have willingly become my servant."

True enough. Gideon's eyes finally cracked open. Though he had to squint at the distinct colors, the excessively sharp details of his surroundings, he was able to orient himself. They were in Anwyn's cell. She was still on the sofa, her feet curled beneath her. Her hair was lank around her face, her eyes hollow and tired, her mouth tight from stress. "How long have I been out?"

"You've been unconscious for nearly a day. We thought at times we were going to lose you. Anwyn has fed you at proper intervals."

Which explained the faintly bitter, metallic taste on his otherwise furry tongue.

There was a pillow on Anwyn's sofa, and she'd gathered it into her body now. She was trembling, he realized, and perspiring, the way she did right after a seizure, so she must have recently come out of one. Though she'd been changed into a nightgown, it was filthy with dried blood, vomit stains. She was back in chains, but Daegan had let her have the slack, apparently having fixed the loosened bolt. The links and manacles firmly fastened to wrists and ankles had more of her bodily fluids crusted on them.

Gideon rallied enough to glare at Daegan. "Why is she chained? And why haven't you cleaned her up?"

"Because she preferred the manacles during her seizures. She has not allowed me to touch her."

Gideon blinked. Though Daegan's expression remained impassive, Gideon didn't need an inroad into the male's mind to know things here had been pretty volatile while he was out. Something in Daegan's tone told him the vampire might be remarkably close to a breaking point.

"Okay. Well." He cleared his throat. Things were coming back to him. He remembered he'd been pretty bloodstained himself, but he was in a pair of loose *gi* pants and thin T-shirt, probably both from Daegan's closet, because there was a lingering aroma of the man on them. Jesus, that was weird to notice, let alone receive a sense of reassurance from it. However, the headache was receding, and oddly, he was starting to feel pretty good. Better than pretty good. Realizing that was because he was third-marked gave him a sharp jolt in his gut. He had no idea how to feel about that. He vaguely remembered the sense of being in a vise clamp, his body wracked by convulsions, the horrifying pain of it. Jacob had never described it that way. But none of this had been the usual, had it?

"Um . . . Why don't you go take a break, and I'll help her clean up." He glanced at Anwyn. "If you're okay with that."

It was a long moment, but then Anwyn's head moved. One short nod. Her gaze touched Gideon's face, then moved away, not avoiding his gaze exactly, but more as if she wouldn't take the chance that she'd look toward Daegan, since he stood next to Gideon.

Daegan blinked once. "It would be best if I stayed close. Though she can no longer do you permanent damage, unless she finds a way to stake you with one of the metal bars, she will not have a great deal of control on the filters on her mind. You may have periods of great disorientation, where you cannot tell which thoughts are your own."

"I think he's telling you to fuck off, Daegan," Anwyn said. "Maybe give us a few minutes to ourselves, since you've taken every other choice we have."

Okay, correct that. The volatility wasn't past tense. Things were still pretty inflamed. Other than himself, armed with a crossbow and more guts than brains, Gideon had never heard anyone talk to a vampire like that, particularly not one as strong as Daegan. He found himself tensing slightly, not sure how the vampire would react, though he also wasn't sure what he could do about it if he reacted as Gideon expected, with a sharp put-down for the insolent behavior.

Instead, Daegan's jaw tightened, his eyes revealing a brief, dangerous flame before it was gone. "I will be near if you need me." He pivoted without clarifying to which person he was speaking, but Gideon assumed it wasn't really necessary.

As the vampire left, Gideon saw Anwyn's gaze at last flicker toward his retreating broad back. A maelstrom of emotions swirled in her expressive eyes. If Daegan could be in her mind, he had to know what Gideon could see, that she was really messed up right now. But maybe he'd been like Gideon, trying to give her privacy as much as possible, help her feel as if she had some self-determination. Of course, that was what had gotten them into this kind of trouble, wasn't it?

When she flinched, he cursed himself for forgetting. He could see some advantages to that curtain thing—with that faint buzzing noise that came with her presence in his mind, he'd have a better sense of when she was paying attention to his thoughts. "Hey," he said quietly. "I'll go get you some fresh clothes, all right?"

She wanted to touch him, wanted to assure herself he was alive. He could read it from her mind. She had forgotten that, too. But when he started toward her, she curled herself back into the couch, wrapping her arms around her legs and shaking her head.

"I could have killed you. I wanted to."

"No, you didn't. You were just hungry. It's hard to manage at first, for any vampire."

"I've spent my whole life staying in control of my emotions." The broken note to her voice alarmed him, even more than realizing she'd been about to go into full-blown bloodlust in a room full of easy victims. "I don't know how to rely on anyone but myself, and not feel like I've utterly failed."

"Ah, sweetheart." He sat down next to her on the couch, put his hand on her foot. She choked out a sob.

"Some all-powerful Mistress, hmm?"

He caught her face in gentle hands, brought it up to him. "'Nothing outside of you destroys who you are, what you want to be. If you're strong enough, you can put it back together, no matter who or what shatters you.' You remember saying that to me?"

She stilled, her gaze fixed on his face, and he nodded. "I don't know everything about being a Mistress or Master, but I know nothing prepares you for something like this. If anything, maybe that makes it harder for you, because you've been used to holding the reins, figuring things out for others. You haven't failed at all. It was like he said from the beginning. By choosing to let us help you, you stayed in control."

"When I overrode your common sense and insisted on going upstairs, I lost all of it."

"Hey." He dropped his hands, squeezed her foot, running his thumb over the painted nails. "I made my own choice, all right? It was the wrong one, but it was made for the right reasons. You'll get there. It's just going to take time."

"You make it sound like a twelve-step AA program," she said in a weary voice.

"Yeah. Maybe the principles are similar. Because in the vamp world, there are no small mistakes." He sighed. "In fact, most of the time they're brutal and violent mistakes. You can't hold on to it. You've got to get past it and just keep working toward that day when you'll be a hundred percent again. A hundred and twenty, since you'll be a vampire. And then you'll be the most formidable Mistress a man's ever seen."

"You didn't ask for that third mark. You didn't want that."

"You didn't want to be a vampire. Sounds like we're a good match, right?" He won a surprised look, followed by a small smile. "Why don't I get you to the shower?" He tugged on the chains. "And seriously, I'm going to throw these damn things out."

Instead, she reached out, traced his features. At the contact, her eyes closed, her face suffused with a sudden overwhelming flood of emotion that had him pulling her to him, impatiently unclasping those chains and throwing them to the ground with a decided clank. He enfolded her in his arms, bringing her onto his lap. She allowed it, clinging to him, trembling.

She was castigating herself in her mind again, for not holding on to her control, for not managing the situation. Getting a hand under her chin, he tipped it up.

"Anwyn, you've been turned to a vampire, raped, and you almost killed me." At her flinch, he shook his head impatiently. "I didn't tell you that to upset you, but to remind you that if you could keep it completely together through all that, I'd think you were a fucking cyborg. Crying and breaking down is how you get past this kind of stuff, find what you need to go on. I've had some wretched days as well, and you can't hold it all in."

"Do you cry?" Her lips trembled, her blue-green eyes focused on him. They were back to their rich color, but with his enhanced senses he could now see the permanent trace of red in the pupils.

"Of course not," he said. "I vandalize property. That's the male version of crying."

"I remember. You owe me a stained glass window." She pressed her lips together, took a hard swallow, and now her eyes intensified, clinging to his face. "I wouldn't have survived losing you, Gideon. You know that?"

He didn't know how to respond to that, the raw emotion in her expression, the flood of feeling that swamped him, but she saved him by continuing to whisper in that broken voice. "You balance me. Daegan was right about that. The moment you woke up, and our minds connected once again, I felt better. And horribly guilty for being so relieved about that, even more relieved than knowing you were alive."

"Until you get your feet back underneath you, you don't have to feel guilty about anything. You won't take anything I wouldn't give you willingly. Okay? You have to trust someone more than you trust yourself right now. He was right about that as well. Stupid, know-it-all vampire."

She didn't smile, the pain in her gaze now something different. Her hands closed around Gideon's forearm, her temple pressing against his jaw. Emotions trembled through her, something he sensed was too hard for her to feel, let alone say. Some things were too big. You had to go at them a different way.

"Hey," he murmured after a long moment. "Something's been bugging me."

"What?" she said, her voice muffled against him.

"Why does he call you '*cher*'? I mean, he's obviously not Cajun. Don't get me wrong, he manages it in a seriously sexy, suave way—big shocker—but I was curious."

"Seriously, sexy, suave . . ." She gave a half laugh, tinged with despair. "Say that three times fast."

"Seriously, sexy, sauve. Seriously, sexy—"

She placed her hand on his mouth, her head lifting to gaze at him from several inches away. But the amazing thing was, if she was in the next room, the next building, maybe even the next town, he'd feel this close to her. It was as if there was nothing that could separate him from her.

He wanted to tell himself not to lose his head, that this changed nothing. The vampire world she inhabited would separate them eventually. He still couldn't be part of that world. But despite all this shit happening, being here gave him this sense of . . . completion. Just like that sappy chick flick that was quoted every which way in the nineties, such that even he'd picked up the line. He couldn't imagine ever wanting to be without it.

"He took me to see *The Big Easy* at an outdoor movie showing in the park one night, soon after we met. Lying on a picnic blanket under the stars, I was quite . . . impressed by Dennis Quaid, how he said '*cher.*'" A light smile touched her lips, not quite so desolate. "It was a nice night. When Daegan teased me, calling me by that endearment, it stuck, for both of us."

"If he wasn't around . . ." Gideon said softly. She closed her eyes, but he cupped her face, rubbing his thumb over her cheek again. "This is another one of those car games. You have to finish the thought, the first thing that comes into your head. And remember, I already heard it, so you can't lie."

"I wouldn't feel as safe." Her voice broke. "But Gideon, we . . . Something is so . . . It's shattered, what was between us."

"He's here for you, Anwyn. I don't care how far you push him away, or how he holds himself behind that tight-ass façade of his, he'll never stop watching over you."

But I wanted more than that . . . She couldn't say it aloud, though. *And the chance is gone.*

He couldn't answer the sheer desolation in her mind, the grief. There was no answer to give when a wound was still free-flowing, hadn't even begun to heal. So he just folded his arms around her, held her close, rocked her through new tears, gave her the comfort he knew she'd lacked for the past few hours, sitting in her chains, refusing to take any from Daegan.

When she finally ran down, her hand slid down his neck, smoothed over his chest, resting on his heartbeat. She stroked him there, an absent, repetitive motion as she regained her composure; then her touch slowed, stilled. "Is this a scar? I don't remember it before."

"I have plenty of them. And unfortunately, a third mark doesn't get rid of the old ones. Just the new ones." Which was good, because his skull appeared to be as hard as ever, even though she'd pounded it like a grape, to his vague recollection. He placed his hand over hers, putting his fingers in the spaces. Then he frowned, realizing he didn't recognize the scar, either.

Seeing or hearing his confusion, he wasn't sure which, she lowered her hands to the hem of his T-shirt and tugged.

It was the unconscious, possessive way of a Mistress, and seeing her reclaim that did the usual odd things to him.

She gave him a glance, a faint trace of humor fighting its way into her gaze. But when she looked down, he blinked, bringing what was over his left pectoral into focus. At first, he thought it was a new scar because it was a burnished crimson color, like drying blood, but the edges were too precise. It was a trinity of teardrop-shaped scars, arranged in a rough circular arrangement to one another.

A vampire's third mark. He'd forgotten about the spontaneous, unique mark that would appear on a human when fully marked as a servant. A mark whose shape and symbolism were determined by some force outside the vampire or servant's control.

He could tell she knew what it was as well, and she reached out now. For a minute, he didn't want her to touch it, didn't want to feel solid proof that it was real. Almost as much as he did want her to touch it, for reasons he feared were the same.

As if she'd sensed his reluctance, her hand withdrew before the contact was made, fingers closing. Her gaze shifted from the mark to where she'd bitten his throat. *You have the mark, but some things haven't changed, have they?*

Before he could answer that, she pushed away and stood. "I'm going to go clean up now," she decided, her voice and face full of so much. "By myself. But thanks for the offer to help."

She moved away from him, a tired, filthy, beautiful woman, so messed up, and yet so strong at once. She turned at the cell door, looked back at him, her lips quirking.

Same goes, Gideon. Same goes.

~

He did follow her, made sure she had what she needed in the bathroom, and then gave in to her desire for privacy. It provided him a little time to absorb the way he felt, physically. It was unreal, because his body was healed, not even a residual soreness from being almost killed. It also gave him time to focus on other concerns, and he followed one of them to Daegan's room.

The door was cracked and the vampire was sitting on the edge of his bed, staring into space. He hadn't yet cleaned up, either. Gideon's newly enhanced olfactory senses caught another odor, though. "You . . . You threw up."

Daegan, obviously aware of his presence, pulled out of his thoughts to look toward him. "There hasn't been much time for hygiene, vampire hunter. It was yesterday. After she marked you."

Gideon had thrown up a couple times in his career as a vampire hunter. Usually after doing something truly terrible he knew needed doing, but it didn't make it any easier. Still, keeping it on a casual footing, he leaned in the doorway and eyed the vampire.

"Morning sickness? Or in your case, twilight sickness?"

Daegan gave him a gimlet eye. "The last time I threw up was after my first annual kill. Blood in a toilet looks obscene. But I expect you've had enough blows in the kidneys to know that." As he rose and began to turn away, obviously dismissing him, Gideon spoke again.

"I couldn't have done what you did. Making her mark me."

"You're not a vampire, Gideon. She would have ripped your head off. She just about did."

"I'm not a ruthless son of a bitch. That's why I couldn't have done it."

Despite the aggressive words, Daegan didn't seem to take issue with it. Maybe because he agreed with it, and that didn't sit as well in Gideon's gut as he would have expected.

"You shouldn't be on your feet yet. You're too pale," Daegan noted, without looking toward him. He was at his dresser, unbuttoning his shirt, apparently preparing for the shower. Or sending a less-than-subtle hint to Gideon to get lost.

"Pot calling the kettle black. Or white as my ass, in this case. I'm fine."

"Yes, you're ready to take on a vampire horde." The vampire's dryness was unsettling because it was reassuring, like an older brother's rough caress. But Gideon had never had an older brother. *He'd* been the older brother, the one who took care of everything.

The vampire shrugged out of the shirt, showing muscled, knotted shoulders. "I plan on beating you senseless for letting her go up there. It will not be as pleasurable if I feel like I'm kicking an injured puppy."

Asshole. "You know why I did it. She was feeling—"

Daegan brought a hand down on the dresser, hard enough that the wood cracked. It startled Gideon enough he reached for a weapon that wasn't there, but Daegan remained where he was. He leveled a cold eye on Gideon, reminding him that, brief moment of fraternal camaraderie or not, Daegan Rei did not view him as a family member. He viewed him as a human, and now as a servant. It struck a spark of defiance inside Gideon's chest. But the vampire didn't give him a chance to speak.

"Coddling her doesn't help. She's not some gentle, doe-eyed girl who wants to wear your varsity jacket. She is a Dominatrix who has become a vampire, who is going through a transition, who may never be able to have full control of her own life again. Accepting that, making the most of her life, is going to be the hardest thing she's ever done, but if you trust anything about me, trust that the only way we can get her to do that is to expect nothing less."

Because Gideon knew it was only the truth, his belligerence receded somewhat. He remained silent a few moments. "When *did* you last feed?"

"Unless you're offering me a meal, which, in your own words, will happen when hell freezes over twice on my ass, I expect that's my concern. What do you want, Gideon?" Daegan ran a hand over the back of his neck, tilting his head back to look at the ceiling rather than toward the doorway.

Gideon's jaw flexed. "It's going to take both of us to get her through this."

"All three of us, actually, because Anwyn's will is a very important component of it. This isn't going to be easy. Not today, or tomorrow. Not for months or even years."

"So we have to rely on one another. Trust one another."

"Well, let's not lose our heads." Something must have shown in Gideon's expression, because Daegan dropped the sarcasm. "What are you trying to say to me?"

"I've never been able to rely . . . on someone else. Not for a while. I don't have a lot of experience with it."

"That makes two of us." Daegan turned away, toward a wall mirror that showed nothing except Gideon in the doorway behind him, a tactical move where he didn't have to let Gideon see his face, but could keep tabs on his whereabouts. He stood for a moment in silence; then he spoke. "I'll be leaving in a few days."

For a moment, Gideon just blinked at him, not sure he'd heard him correctly. Then he led with his uppermost thought. "Have you lost your fucking mind? She's not even close to being in control."

Daegan turned, his freaking cyborg expression back in place. "A couple days ago you would have told me to fuck off if I offered you any help at all. Now you sound like a whiny child."

"Better than a bloodsucker who takes off because his girlfriend gives him the cold shoulder and he can't fucking handle it. Hell, you've been brooding for the past few days. Seems like the two of you are made for each other."

Gideon saw the male's hands clench, the shoulders knot further in impressive display. If it was possible, the vampire became more still.

"She could hate me with everything she is, vampire hunter. Curse me, spit on me, treat me like garbage, from now to the end of time. And if by her side was where she needed me to be, in order to protect and offer her the best chance at a meaningful life, then that is where I would stay. *Nothing* she could do would drive me from it."

The body might be still, the voice low and even, but the eyes were those pits of eternal damnation again. No matter how much he hated to admit it, Gideon couldn't move, could only hold that gaze. But because of that, he saw the darkness shift to something else.

"When I saw her in that alley, ready to burn herself to cinders, rage took over. I did what was necessary. I don't regret that, but you are very wrong, Gideon, if you think I haven't been tempted beyond endurance to allow her to mire herself in her fear and pain, cocooning her from the whole world, so she never has to stand on her own two feet again. But I can't even give her the luxury of time to grieve and heal. She's part of a world now that doesn't allow for that. We both know it."

Apparently the vampire was so motionless because the emotions he wouldn't show in his voice or body language, even now, were in danger of crushing him. But it was unmistakable, laden in every word. Daegan closed his eyes, and Gideon wondered if vampires counted to ten for patience. Because when Daegan opened them, that compressed energy around him seemed less explosive. Slightly.

"Every made vampire must be brought before the Council within thirty days of their making for a validation ritual. Did you know that?"

Gideon shook his head.

"Because of the Council's stance, often justified, on the dangerous weaknesses of made vampires, it is absolutely essential that Anwyn not appear unstable before them. She is obviously not ready for the ritual, and may not be for some weeks to come. Perhaps never."

Gideon studied the vampire's face. "So how do we handle that?"

"I am going to attend alone, convince them that her turning is a minor matter among other issues, and ask if they will give me temporary guardianship as her sire and overlord, rather than assigning her to a territory. I will also ask if they can accept her at the next Gathering, which is still several years away. The thirty days is usually mandatory, but there are some assignments they wish me to handle in Europe, closer to their home base. I can take care of those also, as a gesture of goodwill."

But given that someone on the Council had exposed his whereabouts, how far would that goodwill go? Would they view this as a minor issue or something they could use against him? He wanted to ask, but already knew Daegan wasn't likely inclined to discuss behind-the-scenes Council issues with him. So Gideon focused on the worst possible outcome. "What if they don't agree? What if she has to go now? Even if she goes in several years, what if the seizures aren't under control by then?"

"They'd treat her like an animal born mutated and deformed. They would order me to execute her."

Gideon straightened, his mind automatically cataloging the potential weapons in the room. "Not as long as I'm alive."

"Nor I." When Daegan held his gaze, that solidarity Gideon had felt one too many disturbing times with him locked in place, but now he was glad for it. "It doesn't matter if she speaks in tongues and gallops around Council chambers like a pony; they will not touch a hair on her head. I will not allow it. I will protect what's mine, even if I have to take every one of their heads to do it. My loyalty is to her. Not to the Council."

Gideon tightened his jaw. "You said that like you meant it."

"That's because I did." His face altered, becoming steel. "I have to act as her sire, first and foremost, if she's going to survive this. You are going to give her what I can no longer. What I should have given her all along."

The unyielding expression made the vampire appear bulletproof, but Gideon wasn't fooled. Course, he wasn't going to try to remove that armor, because if he started acting as if the guy had real feelings, he'd be tempted to shoot himself. Still, he owed him something, and he wasn't too proud to give it.

"Next time she wants to do something, and I'm not sure about it, I'll ask you. Not a permission thing, mind you. But it'd be stupid not to use the resources at hand. You know, to help her the best way possible."

Daegan moved. He didn't come forward fast, but there was a deliberateness to his steps that made Gideon wary. He stopped with a foot between them. Those intense dark eyes bored into Gideon's, and as usual, he had to steel himself not to step back . . . or quell the inexplicable desire to move forward. "You damn well better," the vampire said softly. But his tone was milder, and from what Gideon read in those usually so secretive eyes, he decided not to get riled about it.

"You know, your responsibilities as sire aside, if you took advantage of soap and toothpaste, she might be nicer to you. You know how women are."

Daegan showed fangs. "Sometimes I think nothing penetrates that rock head of yours."

"I know the difference between the things you believe and the things you feel." Hell, he was more practiced at it than most. Gideon could tell himself that guilt or a sense of honor was why he'd stayed throughout all of this. Why not? He'd been lying to himself so long, it had a comforting consistency to it. If he lied to himself, he wouldn't have to face the truth about anything. The same way that, by telling himself he needed to be her sire, Daegan could just switch off his feelings for Anwyn.

The vampire gave him a curious look, his focus apparently shifting. "You should bear me ill will for the third-marking, but you don't."

"No more ill will than usual." Gideon shrugged. "You rushed the decision we both knew I was going to make. Whether it's the stupidest thing I've ever done in my life, we'll know soon enough. But this way, if I regret it, I can blame you instead of myself, right? So a win-win, as far as I'm concerned."

Daegan's lips tugged. "What is she doing?" he asked quietly.

Gideon focused, and a muscle worked in his jaw. "Sitting on the edge of the tub, having a good cry. Giving herself hell for crying." He paused. "She's hurting, Daegan. She needs you."

"She despises me. That's for the best."

"No, she doesn't. And no, it isn't. You told me she's the bravest person you know. Trust her to use the intelligence that goes with it. She's beating herself up now, about you and me, and herself. She needs the other side of your sword now. The gentler side." Gideon spoke gruffly. "Hell, I wasn't completely unconscious during the marking. She couldn't see your face; I could. It tore your heart out to do what you did. Go see her, Daegan. I'll go hang out somewhere. She's in her room."

"Don't think you can order me around, vampire hunter." But Daegan gave him a light shove that took him back a step or two. "Go into my closet and get an extra shirt for when you ruin that one. That pungent T-shirt you were wearing earlier is mildewing. On your next outing, plan on buying a dozen of your $1.99 special tees."

Gideon gave him a sardonic look, flipped him off. "Still trying to do some of that ordering shit yourself. Piss off." But he went to the closet, because Daegan was right. This T-shirt was getting rank as well.

"Stay away from my dress shirts, though," Daegan called out. "They cost more than you're worth."

"Yeah, right." Out of sight in the walk-in, Gideon peered at the rows of mostly dark clothing, a function of the vampire's profession, he was sure, versus a macabre Goth vamp fashion sense. For just a moment, he imagined Daegan stepping in behind him while Gideon stood amid the masculine aroma of his clothes, amid the cool shadows. Anwyn would come in, and they'd surround him, none of them giving a damn who was in control, as long as they could touch and be touched . . .

Son of a bitch. He popped his neck painfully when he gave himself a sharp shake, and yanked the nearest tee off a rack. He stepped out, needing to get clear of that intimate territory of Daegan's clothes. But when he stripped off his current shirt and began to shrug on the new one, Daegan stepped forward, arresting Gideon's motion.

Before Gideon could draw away, he'd hooked his fingers in the neck of the T-shirt, pulled it down far enough to his left so that he could pass his fingers over the top of the scarlet teardrop mark.

"Interesting. It's always different."

His gaze flickered up to Gideon's face. For one, weighted moment, the touch Gideon was pretty sure Daegan had intended so casually felt intensely intimate. He froze, not sure what the hell to do with that, and wondered why he wasn't jerking away. Maybe because they'd dealt with so much these past few days, moving away from any touch that wasn't hostile seemed impossible, the way cockroaches and marsh grass looked appetizing if no other food was available.

Yeah, that explains it. In addition to the words that fell out of his mouth now, like the drool that came with severe brain damage.

"What you said, about your loyalty being to her before the Council. I believe you."

Daegan released him from the intense eye contact and withdrew his hand as well, giving him a short, brusque nod of acknowledgment. "Nothing is more important to me than her," he murmured, his tone suggesting it was meant more for himself than for Gideon's ears. "I should have done things, handled many things, better, but I will put nothing before her. If I'd done that before, this never would have happened."

When he gestured them to a nook in the corner that held two chairs and a table, Gideon took one of the seats, leaning forward. "You know that's different."

"A lot of things are different." A flash of bleak acceptance went through Daegan's eyes, the first real vulnerability Gideon had seen him reveal, but then it was gone, so quickly he doubted he'd seen it. "I'm not going to leave you without backup," the vampire continued, his quiet tone replaced by a purposeful one. "During one of her recuperations, you spoke of Lord Brian. His work is not unknown to me—his paper about difficult transitions was how I knew to administer the sire's blood more frequently. Though he works under the sponsorship of the Council, I believe he has a peculiar loyalty to Lady Lyssa that will ensure his discretion. Would you agree?"

At Gideon's curious nod, Daegan made a grunt of approval. "Then I have an idea I want to discuss with you."

"I'm all ears."

"Good. Because you need to know some other things. Things I'll tell Anwyn as well, but I need to be sure you're prepared for what I'm going to do before I bring her into it. And once we're done here, you will go to her, Gideon. Not me. You're who she needs. From here forward."

26

ANWYN sat at the desk in her bedroom, studying her computer screen with detached interest. She'd thought, once she'd dressed, this might help her focus a little better. But she'd quickly caught up on her e-mail requests, because the day she'd lost had been Sunday, the day Atlantis was closed.

She should be irritated by that, feeling useless, but she was discovering something about being a vampire. When nothing debilitating was occurring, like seizures or bloodlust, she could sense things she'd never been able to before. There was a cricket chirping somewhere in her apartments, and she could hear the movement of his legs, knew almost his exact location with her enhanced hearing and an intuitive, predatory sense.

Daegan was in his room, taking a shower. Gideon was headed toward her. She could have tuned in to both of their minds, but while Gideon was with Daegan, she'd had an admittedly petulant need not to listen in, not to hear what they were saying. So though she couldn't completely close that link, she'd put enough of a damper on it that their conversation was just a male rumbling of noise in the back of her mind.

Of course, she'd gotten impatient with their conversation and wanted Gideon back. Was it that vampires had a less-developed sense of conscience, or that their appetites were so unapologetic they over-rode everything else, including the fact she'd nearly killed him a day before? Or did she merely need the validation of the avenue she'd so often used before she became a vampire?

Daegan had told her so much about how vampires interacted, how they shared their servants. This compulsion of hers, so natural to her BDSM world, was an integral part of theirs. It was a startling revelation, but she was painfully aware Gideon had been part of neither. She remembered his charming offer to have coffee with him, take a different path. Now, if he wanted to keep being with her, he'd have no other choice but to be part of a BDSM world. Of course, he'd likely have less trouble with that than being part of a vampire one.

That wasn't something that would resolve itself today. She wanted Gideon with her now, wanted to do more than trace that trinity mark with her fingers. Despite reputed vampire healing abilities, the tender tissues between her legs still ached, and she didn't think it lingered from Daegan's sensual abuse. If anything, she was throbbing for far different reasons. Her mind wanted to reach for him. Wanted to reach for them both, but she'd settle for half her desires. When Gideon knocked lightly, the dangerous leap in response was enough to tighten her hands on the desk edge.

Come in. And come here.

He did, glancing immediately toward her, because of course he would know her whereabouts. They were linked permanently. Irrevocably.

"Come here," she repeated aloud.

She saw more in his face, an unspoken message, something he wanted her to know, something that didn't have to do with this moment. But right now she needed, wanted, only this moment, so she stayed out of his mind. And when he would have spoken, she shook her head.

"Be still," she murmured. "And quiet. Just obey me." *Take off the shirt.*

He arched a brow, but came to her, tossing the shirt to the side and moving with that warrior's stride that seemed somewhat hampered when he was inside. As if he needed enough space, like a weapons room or gymnasium, to exercise all the power he demonstrated in a simple walk. He and Daegan both had that. When he reached her, she indulged herself. Moving down his chest, she touched that trinity mark for the first time, a quiver of sweet possession coursing through her, and a hard shudder passing over him, their eyes locking for a brief, vulnerable moment. *Hers.*

She spread out from there, running her hands over the flat pectorals, the tight nipples, the hard abdomen, the broad shoulders. As she did, he closed his eyes, savoring her touch. Taking her hand down past his waistband, she covered his erection, the curve of his testicles that filled out that area of his jeans so well. She slipped the button, took the zipper down one tooth at a time, caressed him through the boxer briefs. He was hot and hard steel already. "Take it all off now."

He backed away so he wasn't looming over her, and pulled off his boots. Then the rest of it, so he stood tall and powerful, completely naked.

"Stay right there."

He did, but she could tell it made him self-conscious. He was a battle-scarred warrior with deep lines at the corners of his eyes and mouth, lines that only made him look more ruggedly handsome in that hateful way men had. They might be envious, but women enjoyed the benefit of looking. His cock was brushing his belly, a temptation all by itself.

"Turn," she commanded softly. "I want to see the back."

He swallowed, tensing a little, but he complied, shifting so he was standing in a half-cocked stance she could almost imagine as his standard pose, thumbs in the front pockets of his jeans. He'd be scowling. She suppressed a smile, but her chest was tight, looking at him.

She'd built a world around herself that was about consensual ownership, submission. There were couples at her club in a twenty-four/seven D/s relationship, the submissive completely contracted to the Dom in whatever arrangement suited their different needs best. She'd never found that, never found the man who made her crave that ownership.

Daegan was a different animal. Falling in love with him had been entirely unexpected, since he was as Dominant as Dominant could get and not be Attila the Hun reincarnated. He'd given her that sense of safety, as she'd told Gideon, each time she was with him. Something had challenged that safety and now everything was uncertain. But looking at Gideon, his trust in her, she wondered for the first time if it could be mended. If Daegan and she could find their way, not back to where they'd been, but someplace they'd never gone together.

"Step backward until you're between my knees." She adjusted her seated position so her knees were spread.

When he obeyed, she thought, if she had her way, she'd always keep him like this, where she could see that powerful interplay of muscles and sinew along his upper torso, the movement of his hips and lean thighs that said he was a very physical man, one who might have all sorts of debris going on in his head and heart, but who had no hesitation or qualms when it came to fighting or protecting what he considered his to protect.

His muscular ass, the lean thighs, were now right before her. She ran her hands up his thighs.

"Spread your legs out wider."

He did, and her fingers closed on his testicles, hanging heavy between his legs, earning a guttural sound from him. There was a mirrored wall across from her, so she could see him right here, saw the jump in his cock, the breath he held. It was still a shock not to see herself there, but she liked the fact he couldn't see what was going on in her face.

"Daegan tells me that a servant keeps his Mistress's hair styled just right, puts her makeup on perfectly. Given how you keep your hair, I expect I may need to hire a very discreet lady's maid."

"Jesus." He was having a bit of trouble speaking in a steady tone, and she loved it, the effect her touch had on him. "You don't need any makeup. You're beautiful the way you are now."

"Charmer." She squeezed his balls, and earned another exhalation of breath. She ran her other hand over the globe of one buttock, dragged her nails down it, then leaned forward and bit.

He jumped slightly, but she gave him credit for holding relatively still. She wasn't trying to drink blood, but she did lick the few drops that welled forth. She liked biting him, liked sinking into that muscular flesh.

"Turn around," she whispered.

He did, and there was his cock, stretched out long and tempting. "What would you do if I bit it the same way, sank my fangs into it?"

"I'd say there are other, better things you could do with it."

"Mmm. Maybe. You'd look very handsome with a ladder, Gideon. Barbells pierced all the way up the underside of your cock, perhaps a permanent steel collar latched around the base of the head and at the root. I could carry a key to it, so you'd always wear the symbol of my ownership."

"Kind of like going-steady rings?" He tried to sound flippant, but the moment he said it, she saw something dark cross his expression, a shadow he apparently hadn't meant to call forth. His expression was briefly seized with an old pain. She didn't pull back that curtain, willing to give him his memories unmolested.

"Something like that." She rose, pointed. "Lie down on my retiring couch, on your back. I'm going to ride you, Gideon." She arched a brow at his feeling of relief, desire. "But I'm not going to let you come. You need to know that. I'm going to leave you hard and suffering for a while, thinking of my wet pussy."

"What if I come anyway?" He met her gaze in challenge, and she raised a brow. Having him standing before her this way, hard, hot and hungry, so much bigger than she was, was a temptation that affected her all over, heating her blood.

"Then I'd say you're not a very smart man, because there are other ways I can make you suffer." But she lowered her voice, softened it. "Trust me, Gideon. Denying yourself for a Mistress's pleasure is worth the wait."

He nodded after a long moment, cleared his throat. "Guess I'm just used to the instant gratification, in case I'm dead an hour later, or tomorrow."

"I'll endeavor to make sure you come before our next brush with death." She said it lightly, though she found she didn't like the reminder of how often he'd been close to it. And not just from the danger she'd posed to him. While she'd never seen Daegan at work, so to speak, Daegan's supernatural abilities, his sheer command of every situation, mundane or otherwise, had been her comfort during his absences. But she'd still worried, knowing from his blood consumption when he returned that he'd been wounded in different skirmishes, even if the entry wound had healed by the time he'd returned. Had he gotten any blood, these past twenty-four hours? She remembered that she'd intended to have Gideon help her nag him into it . . . before.

"Gideon"—her gaze went to his face, demanding truth—"I assume, while you're with me, you're not going to be hunting vampires. Am I wrong to have that assumption?" As she asked, she closed her hand over his cock, started stroking it in a long, practiced pull, enjoying the weight and heat of it in her hand.

His voice was thick. "I think I'll be a little busy with you and Daegan for a while."

It was strange to have this growing sense of protectiveness . . . of forever, filling her when it came to him. She remembered how he'd said, *I know what she'll become.* He'd known this sense of ownership would grow inside of her, but did he understand what fiercely tender emotions attended that same problematic instinct? It reassured her, to feel that something she liked had been enhanced by her vampire transition, not twisted or destroyed by it.

"Lie down on the couch," she repeated. "Put your hands over your head, gripping the arm of the couch. You won't let go unless I tell you to do so."

One of her favorite things as a Mistress was watching the struggle of a strong man to submit, the expressions that would cross his face, the flash in his eyes. But Gideon eventually moved to obey, stretching his long, powerful body out, his arms lifting, the muscles rolling smoothly across his abdomen and chest, biceps curving up as he reached over his head and held on to the couch arm, opening himself to whatever she desired.

She put a knee on the couch and slid astride him. She wasn't wearing underwear under the skirt. While she'd finally washed, she knew that some residual seed from Daegan had to still be in there. What she was sliding over Gideon's cock might be a combination of hers and Daegan's fluids. It aroused her to think it, and she wondered if it had crossed Gideon's mind as well. He groaned, lifting his hips, but she tightened on him, digging her fingers into his chest.

"No. Don't move, not a muscle. See if you can obey that simple command."

She knew there was nothing simple about it. His eyes remained glued to her, his body getting progressively tighter as she impaled herself on him. All the way down, then a slow rise up, like a carousel when it first started turning. His hands gripped the couch with his need as she stroked him with her interior muscles. She devoured every expression, every muscle shifting beneath her, even as she gauged with a practiced eye how close he was to climaxing despite her command not to do so.

"If you come, you'll take whatever punishment I require. That's the price for you coming now." She gave him an additional squeeze and he growled, his blue eyes fastened on her face, the expanse of neck down to the swell of soft cleavage over the top of her V-neck shirt. Her skirt lay over his legs, so he couldn't see any part of her except what was clothed, could only feel her pussy sucking on him with each slow drag upward, and deep penetration downward.

"I want to touch you."

"Not this time. Your Mistress wants to pleasure herself on your cock, and that's all she wants from you. You're so goddamn sexy," she purred, stroking his chest, reaching back and cupping his balls beneath her once again, squeezing. "And your cock would satisfy any woman. But right now, it's all mine. Say, 'Yes, Mistress.'"

His eyes were definitely glazed, so he said it automatically, his voice strangled. "Yes, Mistress. Oh God, I can't—stop."

She stopped. "What's it going to be, Gideon? Do you want to come now, and take my punishment?"

He squeezed his eyes shut. "Shit, yes. Whatever. Let me . . ."

"Beg me, Gideon. Ask me to let you come."

He struggled with it, even where he was now, her strong alpha male, but the body wanted what it wanted, and it was the best way to overcome reservations. "Please, Mistress. Let me come."

"And you'll let me punish you, welcome that punishment?"

"Yes, fuck. Please. I want to come inside of you."

"All right. Remain utterly still while I come, and then you may come."

Two strokes, and the raging need that had been quivering in her voice gushed forth, her clit spasming against his pubic bone. His gaze followed the flush across her chest and up her throat, and she felt the heat of his regard when she threw her head back and cried out, her fingers digging into his chest. Then, when she called out breathlessly, "Now," his body shuddered, every muscle turning to gleaming rock. The ridges of his abdomen stood out with the strain, his face in a rictus of pleasure as his seed exploded within her, hot streams along her channel. He made a strangled groan, and she was overwhelmed by his control, the fact that while he quivered like a man with a fever, he didn't lift one limb, or even lift his hips off the couch. Just shuddered and came, in a way that had her body tightening anew.

It was over hard and fast, but she was going to teach him how long an orgasm could last, how intense it could become with denial. As he got his breath, she rose gracefully. With her toe, she opened the compartment beneath the sofa. "Roll over on your stomach, and take hold of the couch again."

He gave her a disoriented look, but he did it. Men got sluggish after climax, she knew, mellow. Which was exactly how she wanted him.

When he turned, she added, "Turn your face toward the sofa cushions. What I'm doing is none of your business. Not until I'm ready to tell you."

This was harder. She knew it wasn't in his nature to turn his back on anyone, so she stroked the line of his spine with light fingertips, a reassurance. When he complied, reluctantly, the uneven strands of his hair brushing his shoulder, she lifted the first item.

"Have you ever thought about spanking a woman, Gideon? Holding her over your knee, feeling her sexy little squirms as you give her enough pain, leaving a red handprint, marking yourself on her flesh?"

"Once or twice. Not really my thing."

"No, it's not. You found it difficult to watch the Masters with female slaves, the times you've come to my club. You know their cries when they're flogged, or their nipples are clamped, are pleasure as much as pain, but you can't see it done to a woman. You're all about protecting. At least that's what you tell yourself. Now, when you saw a male slave being flogged, you were very . . . attentive." Her fingertips glided along the curve of his buttock, watched the muscle shorten there and along the thigh in reaction.

"You like to watch," he said into the cushions. "That's what gets you off."

"Watching you made me wet. Every time, even when you were just sitting at the bar, staring at those rows of shiny bottles. I could feel it pulsing off of you, your desperate, angry need. Your desire for a Mistress to give you release. One particular Mistress. That's what made me hottest of all, because you didn't come just to jerk off. You came looking for me."

It was like watching a breeze ripple across a meadow of wheatgrass, the way his muscles were slowly tightening, his body already recognizing he was under attack. But he continued to hold on to the sofa. He let her do her worst, and stood open to it. It made her want to pull him into her body again, tumble them both off the couch, let him lie upon her as he did that night, so they would both find what they were seeking. But she knew that showing a slave his chains wasn't enough. He had to understand how he himself could strike them off.

"You're holding on to guilt about what happened upstairs, aren't you?"

His shoulders tensed. "I should have known better. I've been through this before and—"

"So that's a yes. And while I don't agree with the amount of responsibility you're shouldering for it, sometimes it helps to be punished. To let go of the guilt and move forward, let it go. Right?"

He hesitated, then gave a cautious nod.

"I'm holding a flat wooden paddle. It has holes in it, and when I use it, it will hurt. I don't expect that it will even occur to you to ask me to stop, but I'm going to give you ten strokes with it, to prepare you for the rest of your punishment. I'll do it in a steady rhythm, and I expect you to lift your ass up to the blows, to welcome them. To relax those gorgeous muscles, carrying all the heavy thoughts running through your mind. You must relax and accept the pain. This is important." She injected enough emphasis in her voice that she knew he heard her. "It's an important part of where I'm going to take you. Tell me you understand."

"I understand. Mistress."

It was said in a lower tone, as if it embarrassed him, the personal need to say it. She expected he was telling himself he'd said it because she had an implied command to do so. *Sweet man, lying to himself.*

"And . . ." He paused, his shoulder giving a twitch. "I'm not worried or anything, but remember you've got a vampire's strength now."

Holy crap, she had forgotten. Already aware of his thresholds, she'd intended to put her full strength behind the blows. She'd have to go a little easier.

"Relax every muscle. I want to see them all relax. Deep breath. Give yourself to me, Gideon. To my will. You can do it. You've already given me your soul, haven't you?"

Her mind had tentative fingers in his, unable to help herself. Emotion shuddered through his mind at that simple, unplanned statement, one that goaded her forward.

She brought the paddle down with a sharp, resounding smack against flesh that made him jump and left an immediate red imprint. She swept a hand over the area. "Keep relaxing. Every time you tense up, I start from the beginning."

She would have smiled at the muttered curse into the cushions, but that brief emotional lightning through his mind had struck her own heart.

"Lift your ass, Gideon," she said sharply, and he did on the next stroke. But he kept his shoulders relaxed, his grip on the sofa arm easy, and she got the result she wanted. He was starting to tremble.

His mind was a tumbling barrel, torn between a reluctant pleasure with the pain and humiliation that he was letting her paddle him like a child.

But it wasn't a child's punishment. On strike eight, his delicious ass was bright red, emanating a heat she could feel. She was fast learning to love her enhanced vampire senses, if nothing else. The paddle was building true, burning pain through his nerve endings, radiating down to his upper thighs and up his back. He was also getting hard again, particularly from the coital movement of lifting and lowering his ass to the strokes, his cock thrusting into the give of the sofa cushions, a rough substitute for the slippery silk of her wet pussy.

Daegan had said third-marks had faster healing powers, but until that kicked in, Gideon might find sitting a little uncomfortable. Nine and ten earned a strangled grunt from him. Setting the paddle aside, she stroked her knuckles over the burning flesh, dragged her nails back across it. Provoke and soothe the painful heat at once. "Raise your ass once more for me, Gideon, and hold it in the air."

When he did, she reached beneath, and found what she'd expected. His cock was raging hard. She teased him with her touch, and his cock surged in her hand like a horse out of a starting gate. She tightened her grip, holding him still.

"You liked that. No, don't say anything. Unless I ask you a question, you don't speak. You break that rule, I'll gag you. Now, hold still."

She picked up the harness, threaded the straps under his thighs, around his balls and to his waist. She kept them loose, let him feel the way they rubbed against him, like teaching a horse to take a bridle. She started humming a soft tune, alternating her careful adjustments of the straps with rubbing the abused flesh. Bending forward, she dropped kisses on the small of his back, giving him the tip of her tongue, tasting him. Then she tightened the primary strap, drawing the rest snug. It cinched in on his balls and the base of his cock, as well as around his thighs. He jumped a little again, but held still. She'd positioned the harness's back ring where she wanted it to be and now unsnapped the connector holding it into the rest of the harness to make way for what she wanted.

"You're going to feel pressure, Gideon. Deep breath and relax."

"No," he said. "Don't put anything—"

"This is my punishment. You agreed to it. Are you backing out?"

The next action and reaction were pure instinct to both of them. He attempted to shove himself up from the couch. With one powerful movement, she held him down, kept him on his stomach with a firm hand to the middle of his back, his head turned by clamping her other on the back of his neck and skull. He struggled, but she held him. As she did, it swept through her, the physical power of making him bend to her will, and his recognition of it.

Just like that, she was back to that moment she'd first walked into the Queen's Chamber. This she knew and understood, separate from anything that had happened to her. He needed so much of this. It was a drug she couldn't deny herself. Her own immediate, physical reaction had shaken her, though. It brought to mind the times she'd resisted Daegan, his immediate, almost instinctual reprisals to her sensual rebellions. She forced herself to repeat in a cool voice, "Are you backing out?"

He'd gone still, but now he set his jaw, shook his head. "Let me go. I'll accept it." His voice was beastlike, rough enough she knew it wasn't a command, but an entreaty.

"All right, deep breaths, then. Deep breath. This isn't large." She slowly removed her grip on him, her mind now inserting itself in his, another way of restraining him to her intent, because she could tell he felt her there. His thoughts wanted to escape her scrutiny, but they couldn't. They paced the cell of his mind, eyeing her warily, too keyed up to form coherent thought streams, just a rapid whitewater of rushing need.

Relax and accept, Gideon. You belong to me, and my will is what you serve. This was all her, not Barnabus, not those sullen shadows. She was sure of it, of herself, in a quiet way that differed from the desperate reassurance that had taken her upstairs. She wouldn't forget the difference again, or forget how the act of mastering a man could help center her. Of mastering Gideon.

She drew the relatively slim dildo out of the prepared jar of sensual, heated oil. When she guided it against his ass, she wasn't surprised to meet the hard resistance of tight sphincter muscles. It was a singular joy to break in a recent virgin to anal play who wasn't a virgin in any other way. Leaning forward, she blew a soft breath against the sensitive area. Goose bumps broke out on the curves of his buttocks. She used the dildo to paint the rim with the oil, let him feel that sweet slickness rub against the nerve-rich center. Then she leaned forward, parted the cheeks further, let her tongue dip and tease the rim herself.

"Jesus Christ." He started to lift up, but her command in his mind halted the movement.

Be still for me, Gideon. Take all the pleasure, let it build until you can think of nothing else.

That delicious trembling started again, this fearsome, powerful vampire hunter at her mercy as she used her tongue, oiled fingers and dildo to play at that rim, dip in and out. His buttocks were flexing, just minute amounts, an involuntary reaction, a need to fuck, telling her he was staying erect. Though Gideon didn't know it yet, he would be aching to come a long, long time after he wanted to do so. In that way she would teach him never to beg for a climax until it was his Mistress's desire.

This time the dildo made it through the first ring of muscles easily, and then she eased it past the second group, feeling that sudden descent. Like when the foot stepped into a soft, giving depression of sand in the ocean, now pulling in the phallic shape, rather than rejecting it. She'd threaded it through the harness ring as she took it in, so now she snapped the harness back in place and made one more adjustment so that he was well and truly yoked. The dildo would stay in, enough give when he walked to drive him crazy. The cock harness would hold him secure and tight, a reminder that the seed boiling in his balls and blood hardening his cock all belonged to her. She lifted off him. "Stand up for me now."

He pushed himself up on his hands, moving gingerly at the new sensations in his ass and around his genitals, and glanced down at himself. He swallowed repeatedly as his fists clenched, but she backed away, leaned against her desk and crossed her legs. "Walk across the room for me."

"Anwyn." If Daegan came in now, Gideon would die of embarrassment. She saw it clearly on his face as well as consuming his mind.

"Daegan would get hard just looking at you. Seeing your cock restrained like that, that dildo in your ass. I bet he'd imagine pulling it out, shoving you down over the couch arm and putting his cock there instead. As you know, he's substantially bigger and thicker than what's in there now. You could take him, though."

Seeing Gideon's shock and desire war across his face was a terrible and beautiful thing both, and she leaned forward. Her shirt had a low neckline, and his eyes immediately went to the generous breasts beneath, because of course now his mind was focused on any sexual stimulus. Even the cracks in the floor had likely become prurient. The pale curve of her desklamp globe was probably a gateway to all sorts of imaginings.

"I don't want him fucking me."

"Hmm. You're seeing your feelings in light of a world that judges a man who desires another man, tries to label him. Don't you realize the two of you are naturally attracted to each other? Two warriors, wanting to test each other, take each other down. Both connected to the same woman, who welcomes you both in her body." She went back around her desk and sat down, folding her hands on her knee. "Put on your clothes."

At his startled glance, she nodded, allowing a feline smile to curve over her face. "You'll keep that in until I say to take it out, or until it starts to hurt. You tell me immediately when that happens," she added, injecting a sharp tone. "That's not the kind of pain I want you to experience. If I have to hear it in your mind first, I won't be pleased."

He grunted, and she let that noncommittal answer go, because he'd already given her more than she expected at this point. She knew how to whip a man into a sexual frenzy, get him past the emotional hurdles that kept him from surrendering himself, but Gideon was a little different from that. He wasn't going to be the housebroken type. Though she was going to enjoy the pleasure of seeing how close she could get him to it.

He pulled on the jeans, working the zipper up with excruciatingly pleasurable caution, but came around the desk, resting tense knuckles on the wood, looking down at her. "So you took care of my punishment. What was yours?"

She looked away, feeling her cheeks warm. "Daegan took care of that one."

"Hmm. Did he hurt you?"

"Nothing I didn't deserve. Or that wasn't bearable."

He cocked his head, still looking at her; then he went to his knees. As she watched him, he cradled the ankle of her crossed leg, bent and brushed his mouth against the bones there. "Did he hurt you here? Or maybe it was higher?" His mouth moved upward, a few inches, and she felt the tip of his tongue.

"Gideon." She wanted to summon a chuckle, but there was a seriousness to his seduction that held her still. He moved up another few inches, just below her knee, and she quivered, her pussy getting wetter, making her want to shift and feel the slippery texture of movement. Getting him worked up had of course gotten her worked up, and he was keying into that. She should set him back on his ass.

Did he ram into you, punish you with his cock for coming so close to dying?

She swallowed, looking down at his head. "It wasn't like that. He was being a bastard."

His mouth moved up to her thigh, and it trembled as his hand slid under it. *If I thought I nearly hadn't gotten there, that you'd almost taken your life because I wasn't smart enough to figure out what you needed to know or hear in time, I'd take it out on your ass, too. Because it's hard to reach your own ass, you know. In the same way.*

A smile trembled on her lips, but then she sucked in a breath as he cruised higher with his clever mouth, nudging under the short skirt, his tongue flicking the seam between her thighs, coaxing entry into that pulsing heat. She hooked her fingers in his hair, tightened. "I didn't give you permission to do this."

"Your mind wants me to continue."

"I really need to get that shield working between us."

"You will. But not tonight." He lifted his face to her, his blue eyes vibrant. Lust poured off him in heady, heated waves, and she knew he was still hard as a rock, aching for her. Yet he didn't ask for that release. He asked for hers. "Let me pleasure you with my mouth, Mistress. He took. I can give. You need both."

She could have access to his mind and yet never anticipate such stunning insight, or how it would make her feel.

"Beg, Gideon. And I might just give you anything you want."

27

SHE'D fallen asleep in his arms, aware of him gazing at her, his hand stroking her hair, slow, easy, giving her pleasant dreams as well as a roll of languorous thoughts in his head, almost as conflicted as what she and Daegan had experienced earlier. Wanting her, but apprehensive of wanting her too much. Needing to care for the woman, but afraid of what the vampire would demand, particularly after what she'd demanded of him in his first few conscious hours as her full servant. She was vaguely aware when he left her, how he pulled the covers up over her shoulder, dropped a contemplative kiss there and left her to her dreams.

It sent her into some disturbing fits and starts of memory and prophecy at once. She remembered when Daegan had held Gideon's cock, and again, when he'd licked the blood from his shoulder. The time Gideon had turned away, the tension in those great shoulders, his quiet *I can't do that again.*

As good as she'd felt, bringing him to climax, letting him give her the same gift, the truth was she might be too messed up right now to be the kind of Mistress she wanted to be to him. So what did she say to him? That he needed to hang in there, doing things she had no right to ask of him, until she got it sorted out for herself? If she let him hang around too long, it was likely the vampire world would force him into such positions anyway.

It was about nine at night when she decided it was time to get up. Struggling to an upright position, she was surprised to find Daegan sitting in the corner. Her mind had been so caught in between dreams and thoughts of Gideon, she hadn't registered him there. Of course, he might be better than most vampires at blending, not being noticed. He was reading, a book in his lap. From the scent coming from the glass next to him, she knew he was drinking the last bit of blood she'd banked for him in the refrigerator.

"I really am going to lose my humanity in the end, aren't I?"

It was almost pitch-dark in the room, yet she could see through the darkness. She registered the serious set of his mouth, the brief flash of pain in his gaze at the unspoken implication that he didn't have any humanity. Then it was gone, that smooth, untouchable expression back in place. The brief flicker of hope she'd felt when she'd been with Gideon, that she and Daegan might find a connection again, faltered.

"You won't lose all of it, Anwyn," he said evenly. "But you will lose some, because otherwise you won't survive."

"When you made me mark him, I fought it, because my mind was saying, 'He's mine, I've marked him, and he'll do as I tell him to do.' That wasn't Barnabus's blood. That's what I'm becoming."

"You've trained for the role of Mistress all your life. It's not unexpected that, at first, when the bloodlust is harder to control—"

"No." She shook her head. "It's consensual, what goes on in the underground rooms. On the edge, yes—"

"For people who need that edge pushed, who want it to cut them. You know how to push them into that zone. You know when no means no, and when it means something entirely different. When it means, 'Make me face my fear, force me to let go.' You're just accustomed to having a firm grip on the reins, not having to run totally on instinct."

She stared at him. If he was determined to step back, be her mentor, her teacher in all this, trading what they had been for that, then she supposed she should take advantage of it. "I want to say I hate this, but I'm not sure what I feel. Nothing has changed, and yet everything has."

When he said nothing, just continued to look at her, as two-dimensional as that stained glass angel they'd broken, she changed her mind. Damn it, no. She wasn't going to play this game. Five years, and she'd seen things, felt things from him. She wasn't going to trade that. She wanted everything. Putting her legs over the side of the bed, she slid her arms into her robe. She'd been naked when Gideon left her, enjoying the feeling of his body along every exposed inch of hers. Daegan's eyes traveled over her throat, the curve of her bosom, the way she tied the robe around her waist, a barrier between them.

She swallowed. "If I say I hate becoming this, it would mean I hate what you are. And I don't." Her voice softened. "Though I know that's the way I've been acting."

When he merely looked down into his lifted glass, she set her jaw. "You liked the taste of my human blood. You'll miss it."

It was obvious, the way he cradled the cup in his hands. It made her think of other times, times when he'd taken that blood fresh from her throat, her thigh.

"Yes." He said it in a low voice. "I wanted you as my servant, Anwyn."

"More than you want me as a vampire?"

His silence speared her in the gut, so sharply she wasn't sure she could move, go to him as she suddenly, desperately wanted to do. He glanced up at her.

"Though you will never hear any vampire admit it, the reason many of us have human servants is because it keeps something inside of us, something ugly and savage, balanced. I've never regretted being what I am, Anwyn. But I do understand what I need to stay a vampire and not become a monster. You . . . Your humanity helped me. Nothing else ever has."

He said it in a quiet tone, no inflection that suggested he was trying to pull any sympathy away from her plight toward his loss in all this. Yet the power of it punched her hard under her heart, woke her up even further.

She'd always thought him too much of a mystery, the way he guarded his thoughts, but it suddenly occurred to her that maybe it had always been plain how he felt, what he needed. She, the one who gazed so hard at people, learning everything about them, every nuance of their expressions and body language, had overlooked those things in him, because he simply seemed invulnerable. Or perhaps she'd had the ability all along to read his mind, and that was why she kept him at arm's length. He owned too much of her soul already.

She rose then, though her legs were unsteady, and went to him. Letting her knees fold beneath her, she sank on the carpet between his splayed knees, put her hands on his thighs. When he laid his palm on her cheek, his long fingers resting on her throat, it made her want to shatter, because though he reached out to her in tenderness, some part of him was far away, beyond her reach.

"I want you no matter what you are," he said softly. "I always will. Never doubt it."

It was a good-bye. She could hear it in his voice, and now she knew what that message had been in Gideon's eyes, what he'd been prepared to tell her when he came into the room. Still, she wanted a few more minutes before Daegan spoke it, before it became a harsh reality.

"I've always wanted you so much I've never really sought to understand you," she confessed. "I guess that makes me a coward."

"No. You've learned to protect yourself, because no male has ever made you feel that you could rely on him to be there, no matter the circumstance." *Well, except James*, he added in her mind, with a faint smile.

She couldn't return it. There was a tentative pleasure to it, that he'd given her a touch of intimacy in the mind-to-mind communication. Yet she was still uncomfortable with it as well, that potential for invasion she hadn't accepted. Since she knew he felt both reactions, she pushed on before he could withdraw from her again.

"I know it's not your fault, Daegan." She stared up at him. "Gideon made it clear you had no reason to think I was in danger from Barnabus. Everything you've done since has been to protect me further. I have a choir of demons in my head." Her voice broke, then strengthened, refusing to be overwhelmed by it. "I've got to get over my own hang-ups and realize that having you and Gideon in there as well isn't a bad thing. It may be frightening to me, but I'm not stupid. I know I need all the help I can get."

Tightening her chin, she sat back on her heels, met his unfathomable gaze head-on. "So why the hell are you leaving me?"

She'd disrupted that blank expression this time. There was a brief hint of surprise, of a shocking weariness, and then he covered it once again. "The Council is holding session in Berlin right now, and I have to meet with them. And handle some tasks they wish me to perform in Europe. I'm not leaving you and Gideon alone, however. I've already contacted Lord Brian. He is a vampire, a brilliant scientist. He conducts his research on vampire weaknesses at the Council facility, but right now he is traveling the U.S., collecting data on sun sickness.

"Gideon has spoken to his brother," he continued. "Through Lady Lyssa's influence, Lord Brian is going to come here and stay with you. He'll figure out how to help you manage any lasting ill effects from your transition. He may in fact be far more help to you than I can be now."

"I don't know him." She didn't want to sound childlike, but it was an effort to firm her chin, not let it tremble. "This is our home."

Daegan passed his thumb over her chin, touched her lips. "I wouldn't leave you with anyone I do not trust, *cher*. Brian is one of the few I do, primarily because Lady Lyssa trusts him implicitly. And more important, so does Gideon."

"Gideon trusts a vampire?"

"He trusts his motives for helping you."

"I still need you."

Daegan let go of the glass, leaned forward so his face was closer to hers, though he linked his hands between his knees, brushing her forearm where her hand rested on his thigh to brace herself. "No, *cher*. You don't. Lord Brian will figure out how to bring the seizures under control and will provide the strength of an older vampire to help contain your bouts with it until you can manage it yourself. And Gideon . . ." That faint smile touched his lips again. "Your vampire hunter can do something neither of us can. He anticipates your attacks with that precognitive ability of his. Beyond that, for as short a time as he's been your servant, you are already reaching for his strength to steady you, keep the attacks at bay. Even help you to get through them. I've taken your blood; I can feel that. This last one was bad, but before the stress of Gideon's marking, you were improving exponentially. That's not all due to the sire's blood."

"I know." Anwyn rubbed her forehead. "But he needs things from me, too. And right now I'm going mad with voices in my head. Goddess, Daegan. I'm not prepared for this. I . . ." She grimaced, half laughed at herself, a note of despair in her voice. "You know, the first time he came here, I didn't even think about you being jealous. It's never been like that. I saw him . . ."

"And you knew he was yours." Daegan slid fingers down her throat, rested them intimately in the soft pocket of her collarbone, tracing the pulsing vein above it, the soft skin. "As I knew you were mine. As you knew we were connected. These things aren't mutually exclusive in our world, Anwyn. You know that. If I envied him anything, it was the intimacy and trust you offered him so quickly, but another part of me wondered if you'd inadvertently found a bridge between us in this stubborn male."

"You don't sound averse to the thought." She cocked her head, feeling that tiny flame of hope again. "You admire him. You . . . care for him."

"Once we resolve your transition issues, Gideon's future will concern me far more than yours. You are uniquely prepared to be a vampire." He held her gaze. "Trust me on that if nothing else. Everything you've been and done here has prepared you for it. The games of Dominance and submission you play, that we both know are far from being games, are what the world of vampires is. If you like, think of this as a training ground, and you have graduated. I think, in some respects, you will embrace that world in a way no forced vampire ever has, because it will call to something in your blood."

He gave a self-deprecating chuckle. "I wanted you as my servant, but in truth, perhaps what drew me to you was that you were a vampire in every other way but blood." He shook his head at her amazed look.

"But as far as Gideon goes, the armor is cracking, Anwyn. I believe part of it may be his brother's transition and service to Lady Lyssa. It was a catalyst that gave him a different view into the vampire world, and yet he has made his life's work the eradication of vampires. Since that started with a loss from which I don't think he's ever fully recovered, he is at a dangerous turning point."

"Yes," she murmured, thinking of how she'd seen it, felt it from him in their brief session.

"You've always sought a man who possesses a strong will to fight you, as well as a desire to serve you. You like that challenge. You were seeking the one who you could love and protect with all you are, the same gift he wishes to offer you, and the melding of the souls that can come from that. That is the true hope of the vampire-servant relationship. I saw the seed of that, the first time I saw you studying him, and I see the possibility for it in him as well, in the ashes he has made of his life."

She digested that, but lifted her gaze back to him. "What does that make you, Daegan? Why does it feel like Gideon is my heart, and you are my soul, and without either one of you I'm a shell?"

"It does my soul good to hear it, *cher*. As much as it pains me to say this. You must stop concerning yourself with his freedom." Daegan paused, then spoke again. "He either belongs to you, or it ends for him."

Alarm filled her at his tone, the brutal truth in his gaze. "What do you mean?"

Daegan shifted. "I was supposed to terminate him last year. Then he started choosing his targets differently. I convinced the Council as long as he was helping me do my job, no matter how inadvertently, that I would monitor him and it could help us all. Fortunately, Gideon's connection through his brother to Lady Lyssa, who has great influence in our world, made many of the Council members want to avoid the consequences of taking his life. But Gideon's solitude, his insistence on making everything in his life about killing vampires, turned him down the wrong road again, very recently. The night he came to you, he killed a vampire who did not deserve his brand of justice. It has been reported to the Council, and therefore would have been his death sentence. The final straw."

"No." She shook her head vehemently. "There must be something else—"

He placed fingers against her lips. "Because you have made him your servant, things are more complicated. As long as he stays your servant . . ."

"I'm his only hope of survival."

"You may be his only salvation, in more ways than one." Threading his hand in her hair, he massaged her scalp as she turned her head into the caress, seeking it like a worried cat. "I haven't told you this to put more pressure on you, Anwyn, but I know what kind of woman you are. If you will not fight for yourself, I know you will fight for another, with everything you have."

"You knew that about him, too, when you planted the seed about being a servant." She put her hand over his, her eyes searching his face in the semidarkness. Searching for truth from this complicated creature.

"I think you and he are well suited as vampire and servant, and I want what is best for you."

"Daegan, why are you leaving?"

He shifted, meeting her eyes with unflinching intensity. "The truth is, you need me to serve as your sire and champion now, more than you need me as a lover. While you claim to have accepted it wasn't my fault, you aren't certain you'll ever be able to fully trust or open your heart to me, because of how it happened. Because of what we were before it happened. And what we were not. Am I wrong?"

She wanted to deny it, but he could see in her mind, couldn't he? Of course, he'd said he wouldn't do that unless it was necessary. Either way, she couldn't deny it, though it made her throat ache, the inscrutable eyes that she sensed held so much of his own feelings about it. Five years . . . the deepest, most incredible relationship she'd ever had. Desperation gripped her, something slipping out of reach.

But then she focused on that smooth voice, and realized it was like a sealed Pandora's box, exploding with the pressure of so many secrets, but suspiciously well contained. Following her intuition, she really noticed the way his gaze dwelled on her face, how still the powerful body was. It was as if he had a leashed need that was quivering like a dog motionless at the end of a leash—while he put enough pressure on the collar to choke himself, straining for what he most wanted.

She thought again of the things they'd shared, small and large, like watching *The Big Easy* on a wide green park lawn under a star-filled sky. Their truth was in those small things. A few moments ago, he'd lightly touched her throat. When they slept together, he would do that, lay the pads of his fingers on her pulse, a constant provocative presence that followed her into dreams.

Yes, he was going to leave her. She could tell there was no way to change that right now. He did have the responsibility to the Council, but more than that, maybe he was right. Maybe she needed the space to think. But now she thought she knew what Gideon would have said to her, earlier, if she'd given him an opening.

Daegan might be leaving. But she damn sure needed to make sure it wasn't good-bye.

"So selfless." Standing slowly, watching the way his eyes followed her up, she trailed her fingers along his knee, a slow provocation that drew his gaze back down to her touch. "*A vampire takes what she wants.* That's what you told me when you made me mark Gideon. But you haven't done that. You've always wanted me willing, but when I thought I was ready, all those months ago, you changed your mind. Withdrew the offer. Never explained why."

Her fingers drifted across to the other thigh, narrowly missing the pleasurable curve of testicles that stretched the denim. "Trust isn't all or nothing, remember? It's a matter of degrees. I think I'm right. I think I do know more about you than I ever let myself realize, Daegan Rei. I don't think you'll ever let me go, no more than you let me go when you disappeared those six months."

She leaned forward, knowing the robe gaped open, revealed the deep cleft between her breasts. It also cleverly parted along the knee, showing a silky length of thigh.

His gaze covered all those areas, then rose to her face. "Come back down here."

Her lip curved, a sensual taunt whose impact she knew well. His gaze went even more opaque. "I'm yours, right? I expect you could make me do whatever you want."

He executed that quick movement she could never follow, like the part in a movie where the vampire came out of the shadows, up against his victim's back before she even knew he was there. So frightening on the screen, so thrilling when it was him. He'd stayed in the chair, but his arms were banded around her waist, pulling her forward into him so her knees pressed into the seat between his splayed thighs. He pulled her down low enough to clasp her hips and fasten his mouth on her collarbone, pricking her sharply. As she gasped, he nudged her head to the side, giving him better access. Her body tightened at the sensual caress, grew heavier as he sipped at her skin, with a restrained fervency that almost overwhelmed her, the controlled ferocity to it.

Her nipples tightened where they rubbed high on his chest. She wanted his mouth to move down her sternum, to suckle each of them. He loved suckling her nipples, nursing her to climax.

Soon, cher. You tease me, you pay the price.

Taking advantage of my mind now? And yet she saw the clear advantage of it, the way she'd so quickly discovered it with Gideon. She couldn't blame him for embracing the temptation of it.

He dropped his hands to grip her ass, kneading under the thin satin, the silky friction waking erogenous zones all through her sensitive buttocks. His touch was rough, impatient, as if he was afraid of slowing down and becoming tender. That was all right.

I feel you, Daegan. I know you're in there, deep inside. You can fuck me like a whore, and I'll still cherish every touch, every demand, knowing how much you want me. You'll come back to me, because you're as much a part of us as we are of you.

He cursed, pulled her forward, his hard thigh between her legs, and now she dropped lower, rubbing her pussy against the denim, giving herself relief despite his warning growl.

"What do you want, Daegan?" she whispered. "Tell me."

In the midst of such demand, his hesitation was unexpected. She tossed back her loose hair, and lifted his strong face to her. For once, he allowed her to see emotion in his gaze, and it took her breath, her heart.

"I don't want to take you back into that alley, *cher.* I would never want . . . If I could kill them all over again for you, I would."

"Stop," she said with desperation. "You could never be like them, no matter what I've thought in anger. Don't bring them into this."

His jaw flexed. "Then I want you on your knees. I want you to take me into your mouth. I need you to remember that you submit to me, even if you submit to no other. Because it will tell me that you trust me to keep you safe, no matter when or where. That you can obey me instantly, even when you might not understand why I tell you to do something. And that there will be no barriers between us. Not anymore. Whether I have your heart and soul or not, I am in your mind now, and I'm going to require that you trust me to be there, whenever I feel it necessary. Whenever I want to bring you to climax with the stroke of my voice in your head. Whenever I need to be as close to you as you wish to be to me."

The words rolled through her, erotic, powerful and heartfelt. *No barriers.*

The ruthless set to his mouth was as overwhelming to her as a lover's passionate declaration. Sliding off his thigh intentionally slowly, letting him feel the damp softness of her pussy there, she folded her legs and sank to the floor between his spread knees. His eyes were heat on her skin as she opened the jeans and freed him, sliding her hands with reverence up the impressive length and breadth of him. The beautiful broad head was already damp for her. Rising up onto her knees, she put her mouth on him. Her whole body shuddered as he wrapped his fingers in her hair and took control of her motion, taking her down upon him.

"Suck me," he demanded. And he didn't complicate it with the emotions they still had unresolved between them. His declaration that she belonged to him gave her no promises of his heart or soul, either; she knew that. But it meant she had his protection, his dedication to her well-being. They were so close to what they both might want, it was hard to give voice to it. But like that night so long ago when he'd come back to her after six months, he didn't let her pour out her heart now, wouldn't give her anything to regret.

"Give me your body, if you can give nothing else," he said, echoing her thoughts. "Give me everything you can, *cher*. I will take care of what you cannot give."

He only let her take him down to the root several times before he pulled her up, made her straddle his hips and brought her down on him again. She gasped at his power and size, overwhelmed by how quickly he could bring her to climax with him, how he took command of her senses, knew her body. Granting her wish at last, he leaned forward and captured her breast in his mouth, suckling her nipple to a straining peak, and then the other, as she pounded herself down on him, faster, harder, using all the strength she wished. He gave her more of his own strength as well, now knowing her body could handle more, even if her heart couldn't.

Oh, Daegan. She was his, in all ways, because she knew he was hers, even if the two of them went to their graves—or into the sun—without ever admitting it. She wanted to tell herself they had time, an immortal lifespan, to figure it out, but like he'd said, she was afraid that even time might not heal the damage that had been done in that alley, because they'd never put in place the foundation to weather something like that.

But they had this. And she would take it, because an immortal lifespan didn't make moments of pleasure or unspoken, yearning love any less fleeting.

~

When they'd both released, and were resting in the aftermath, Daegan was leaning back in the chair. She curled up still astride him, her robe draped over her body. Underneath it, his fingers drifted up and down the valley of her spine. They hadn't spoken for a while, but since her thoughts had wandered to Gideon, she wasn't surprised when Daegan's first spoken words were about him. "I watched the tape of your night together, you know."

She rubbed her cheek against him. "Why?" she murmured.

"You know why. I saw what you saw. Why he submitted to you. The other Mistresses didn't work, because he needed more than the domination. He was looking for the connection, the emotional switch that told him she was the right one. He was looking for his liege lady, the one he needed to serve, his savior, his tormenter. An impossible quest in a cynical world of Internet dating and smoky bars with lonely people. But he found her."

Daegan cocked his head, gazed down at her. "He found you. And that is Fate, *cher*. I would not argue with it. Not ever."

She didn't want him to leave. She wanted them both, even though she understood, in a painful way, why he was going. Why he had to go. His arm constricted around her back, and she lifted his hand from her ribs, pressed her face into it, kissing his palm, hard.

As if Fate had decided to speak at that moment, Daegan's gaze shifted. Anwyn followed it, though she'd already felt his approach. Gideon leaned in the doorway, his arms crossed, thumbs hooked in his armpits, that cocky, cynical posture that said he could handle anything. Anything she needed. The hungry way he gazed over the curve of her bare back, and Daegan's large hands pressing against her flesh, made her want him anew.

It almost made her smile, despite the ache in her throat.

If I'm yours, Daegan, then help me. Come back. Don't let me hurt him.

We will take care of him together, cher. *That much I promise you.*

For the conclusion of Gideon's story, look for

VAMPIRE TRINITY

coming September 2010 from Berkley Heat

Vampire hunter Gideon Green sure as hell never intended to become a vampire's servant. But when Anwyn Naime—a woman with whom he shared an unforgettable night—is turned by a vampire pack, they become bound by something far greater than either could have imagined. As a result, Gideon is forced into an uneasy alliance with one of the most terrifying vampires he's ever encountered: the mysterious Daegan Rei.

Daegan also has a vested interest in Anwyn. His history with the lovely nightclub owner is both intimate and intense. As Gideon and Daegan shepherd Anwyn through her dangerous validation with the Vampire Council, it's clear the trio must learn to trust each other. But as boundaries between them erode and vulnerabilities surface, Gideon realizes he is no longer the man he thought he was—changed by a strange and unexpected bond with the two new people in his life he can't survive without: *vampires*.